WAR
STORIES

New Military Science Fiction

WAR
STORIES

New Military Science Fiction

Edited By

Jaym Gates & Andrew Liptak

An Apex Publications Book
Lexington, Kentucky

This anthology is a work of fiction. All the characters and events portrayed in these stories are either fictitious or are used fictitiously.

War Stories: New Military Science Fiction
ISBN: 978-1-937009-26-7
Cover Art © 2014 by Galen Dara
Title Design © 2014 by Jaym Gates
Typography © 2014 by Maggie Slater

Published by Apex Publications, LLC
PO Box 24323
Lexington, K.Y. 40524

Visit us at www.apexbookcompany.com.

Table of Contents

Foreword

Gregory Drobny

TO SAY THAT WAR HAS had a large part in the evolution of mankind is not only a vast understatement, it is also, misleading. It implies that war is just one of many factors shaping our past—a piece of a historical puzzle.

That belies the reality, however. War is not simply a portion of historical study—it *is* what we are. The idea of combat—whether it is between two people, whole armies, or even a man with his own demons—shapes the fabric of humanity to its core. Struggle between ideologies and those who hold them, regardless of the scale, lies at the heart of all we do in this world.

Clausewitz famously stated that "War is nothing but a duel on an extensive scale," yet this is more profound than we would like to initially admit. The strategic sadly overshadows combat of the personal level. Those who partake in war are often engaged in that very duel with their own mind and body.

Within the minds of those who have experienced war first hand we learn about the battles of not just a physical landscape but of an emotional one, as well. It is the fighter's mind that gives us the deepest insight into human nature, because they have simultaneously seen both the best and worst mankind has to offer. It is the warrior's perspective that teaches far greater lessons than simply the taking of land or a victory of one style of government over another.

Yet it is also within the mind of the warrior that we can see the deepest scars and the clearest evidence of the pain inflicted by war. Writings from Homer's *Iliad* to Sledge's *With the Old Breed* do not transcend time because they explain strategic knowledge in a new light, but rather that they relate the war within one's self to those who fight their own battles on a daily basis.

Unfortunately, that comes with a cost. Some of those who have seen the most visceral examples of dueling on a larger scale often come away with scars that are not seen by x-ray machines or a CT scan; they are hidden deeper within the mind of those who have been in the teeth of conflict.

One of the biggest misconceptions about Veterans who suffer from mental trauma is that they are broken beyond repair and unable to function as a normal adult. The Veteran who has seen the worst of mankind is not a piece of glass, however. Though many shake their heads and claim to not feel that way, the sentiment is an underlying current in many of today's societal interactions.

This notion is patently false, but not necessarily for the obvious reasons. Namely, we were already warped and unable to function as "normal adults" long before we went to war.

Those of us who signed up, knowing full well what we were getting ourselves into, know all about not being normal. It's probably what compelled us to join in the first place. Our twisted senses of humor, which can make light of even the worst situations, would make the average citizen curious about the sanity of most of those who chose to join.

At Ranger Up and on *The Rhino Den*, we talk frequently of the ".45%." That is the percentage of American citizens who are currently serving or have served in the current conflicts in the Middle East. That number points specifically to the idea that, no, we are most certainly not normal. We are a very small minority of people who were willing to put ourselves through some pretty ridiculous things in order to wear the same clothes as everyone else and get yelled at a lot.

That's not normal.

It's not normal to go out drinking until the wee hours of the morning, only to wake up at 0500 hours, shave, and run five miles while singing songs about jumping out of planes into enemy territory.

It's not normal to find humor in things exploding. At least not when those things were supposed to be you.

It's not normal to walk 12 miles with 50 lbs. on your back and then go to work for the day.

And it's decidedly not normal to be willing to die for men whom you vehemently disagree with on nearly every major topic in life simply because he is a brother in arms.

Yet these are all familiar territory to the Veterans of our military's combat arms. We understand different sides of ourselves than most people, and we understand that most of what we have done and accomplished is pretty far from normal.

But being abnormal and broken means different things to us than they do to most people. We take terms such as those as a sign of pride—not because we want to stand out and be pitied, but because it has made us better.

It has made us stronger.

Those who have suffered mental trauma in the military are not weaker because of it. They have a depth and fortitude that most will never understand. Theirs is an experience unique to them and it has shaped a reality that is far more resilient as a result.

And those are experiences that we should all learn from.

Veterans are not victims, nor are they individuals who were somehow brainwashed into something they did not want to do. They are men and women who answered a call to serve and, in the process, used their naturally sick senses of humor and abnormal way of looking at things to cope with the often absurd situations they were placed in.

These stories are about—and sometimes by—those abnormal and broken people who are proud to be exactly that. I am proud to have served alongside them.

Graves

Joe Haldeman

I HAVE THIS PERSISTENT SLEEP disorder that makes life difficult for me, but still I want to keep it. Boy, do I want to keep it. It goes back twenty years, to Vietnam. To Graves.

Dead bodies turn from bad to worse real fast in the jungle. You've got a few hours before rigor mortis makes them hard to handle, hard to stuff in a bag. By that time, they start to turn greenish, if they started out white or yellow, where you can see the skin. It's mostly bugs by then, usually ants. Then they go to black and start to smell.

They swell up and burst.

You'd think the ants and roaches and beetles and millipedes would make short work of them after that, but they don't. Just when they get to looking and smelling the worst, the bugs sort of lose interest, get fastidious, send out for pizza. Except for the flies. Laying eggs.

The funny thing is, unless some big animal got to it and tore it up, even after a week or so, you've still got something more than a skeleton, even a sort of a face. No eyes, though. Every now and then, we'd get one like that. Not too often, since soldiers usually don't die alone and sit there for that long, but sometimes. We called them "dry ones." Still damp underneath, of course, and inside, but kind of like a sunburned mummy otherwise.

You tell people what you do at Graves Registration, "Graves," and it sounds like about the worst job the army has to offer. It isn't. You just stand there all day and open body bags, figure out which parts maybe belong to which dog tag—not that it's usually that important—sew them up more or less with a big needle, account for all the wallets and jewelry, steal the dope out of their pockets, box them up, seal the casket, do the paperwork. When you have enough boxes, you truck them out to the airfield. The first week maybe is pretty bad. But after a hundred or so, after you get used to the smell and the godawful feel of them, you get to thinking that opening a body bag is a lot better than ending up inside one. They put Graves in safe places.

Since I'd had a couple of years of college, pre-med, I got some of the more interesting jobs. Captain French, who was the pathologist actually in charge of the outfit, always took me with him out into the field when he had to examine a corpse *in situ*, which happened only maybe once a month. I got to wear a .45 in a shoulder holster, tough guy. Never fired it, never got shot at, except the one time.

That was a hell of a time. It's funny what gets to you, stays with you.

Usually when we had an *in situ*, it was a forensic matter, like an officer they suspected had been fragged or otherwise terminated by his own men. We'd take pictures and interview some people, and then Frenchy would bring the stiff back for autopsy, see whether the bullets were American or Vietnamese. (Not that that would be conclusive either way. The Vietcong stole our weapons, and our guys used the North Vietnamese AK-47s, when we could get our hands on them. More reliable than the M-16, and a better cartridge for killing. Both sides proved that over and over.) Usually Frenchy would send a report up to Division, and that would be it. Once he had to testify at a court-martial. The kid was guilty, but just got life. The officer was a real prick.

Anyhow, we got the call to come look at this *in situ* corpse about five in the afternoon. Frenchy tried to put it off until the next day, since if it got dark we'd have to spend the night. The guy he was talking to was a major, though, and obviously proud of it, so it was no use arguing. I threw some Cs and beer and a couple canteens into two rucksacks that already had blankets and air mattresses tied on the bottom. Box of .45 ammo and a couple hand grenades. Went and got a jeep while Frenchy got his stuff together and made sure Doc Carter was sober enough to count the stiffs as they came in. (Doc Carter was the one supposed to be in charge, but he didn't much care for the work.)

Drove us out to the pad and, lo and behold, there was a chopper waiting, blades idling. Should've started to smell a rat then. We don't get real high priority, and it's not easy to get a chopper to go anywhere so close to sundown. They even helped us stow our gear. Up, up, and away.

I never flew enough in helicopters to make it routine. Kontum looked almost pretty in the low sun, golden red. I had to sit between two flamethrowers, though, which didn't make me feel too secure. The door gunner was smoking. The flamethrower tanks were stenciled NO SMOKING.

We went fast and low out toward the mountains to the west. I was hoping we'd wind up at one of the big fire bases up there, figuring I'd sleep better with a few hundred men around. But no such luck. When the chopper started to slow down, the blades' whir deepening to a whuck-whuck-whuck, there was no clearing as far as the eye could see. Thick jungle canopy everywhere. Then a wisp of purple smoke showed us a helicopter-sized hole in the leaves. The pilot brought us down an inch at a time, nicking twigs. I was very much aware of the flamethrowers. If he clipped a large branch, we'd be so much pot roast.

When we touched down, four guys in a big hurry unloaded our gear and the flamethrowers and a couple cases of ammo. They put two wounded guys and one client on board and shooed the helicopter away. Yeah, it would sort of broadcast your position. One of them told us to wait; he'd go get the major.

"I don't like this at all," Frenchy said.

"Me neither," I said. "Let's go home."

"Any outfit that's got a major and two flamethrowers is planning to fight a real war." He pulled his .45 out and looked at it as if he'd never seen one before. "Which end of this do you think the bullets come out of?"

"Shit," I advised, and rummaged through the rucksack for a beer. I gave Frenchy one, and he put it in his side pocket.

A machine gun opened up off to our right. Frenchy and I grabbed the dirt. Three grenade blasts. Somebody yelled for them to cut that out. Guy yelled back he thought he saw something. Machine gun started up again. We tried to get a little lower.

Up walks this old guy, thirties, looking annoyed. The major.

"You men get up. What's wrong with you?" He was playin' games.

Frenchy got up, dusting himself off. We had the only clean fatigues in twenty miles. "Captain French, Graves Registration."

"Oh," he said, not visibly impressed. "Secure your gear and follow me." He drifted off like a mighty ship of the jungle. Frenchy rolled his eyes, and we hoisted our rucksacks and followed him. I wasn't sure whether "secure your gear" meant bring your stuff or leave it behind, but Budweiser could get to be a real collector's item in the boonies, and there were a lot of collectors out here.

We walked too far. I mean a couple hundred yards. That meant they were really spread out thin. I didn't look forward to spending the night. The goddamned machine gun started up again. The major looked annoyed and shouted, "Sergeant, will you please control your men?" and the sergeant told the machine gunner to shut the fuck up, and the machine gunner told the sergeant there was a fuckin' gook out there, and then somebody popped a big one, like a Claymore, and then everybody was shooting every which way. Frenchy and I got real horizontal. I heard a bullet whip by over my head. The major was leaning against a tree, looking bored, shouting, "Cease firing, cease firing!" The shooting dwindled down like popcorn getting done. The major looked over at us and said, "Come on. While there's still light." He led us into a small clearing, elephant grass pretty well trampled down. I guess everybody had had his turn to look at the corpse.

It wasn't a real gruesome body, as bodies go, but it was odd-looking, even for a dry one. Moldy, like someone had dusted flour over it. Naked and probably male, though incomplete: all the soft parts were gone. Tall; one of our Montagnard allies rather than an ethnic Vietnamese. Emaciated, dry skin taut over ribs. Probably old, though it doesn't take long for these people to get old. Lying on its back, mouth wide open, a familiar posture. Empty eye sockets staring skyward. Arms flung out in supplication, loosely, long past rigor mortis.

Teeth chipped and filed to points, probably some Montagnard tribal custom. I'd never seen it before, but we didn't "do" many natives.

Frenchy knelt down and reached for it, then stopped. "Checked for booby traps?"

"No," the major said. "Figure that's your job." Frenchy looked at me with an expression that said it was my job.

Both officers stood back a respectful distance while I felt under the corpse. Sometimes they pull the pin on a hand grenade and slip it under the body so that the body's weight keeps the arming lever in place. You turn it over, and Tomato Surprise!

I always worry less about a hand grenade than about the various weird serpents and bugs that might enjoy living underneath a decomposing corpse. Vietnam has its share of snakes and scorpions and megapedes.

I was lucky this time; nothing but maggots. I flicked them off my hand and watched the major turn a little green. People are funny. What does he think is going to happen to him when he dies? Everything has to eat. And he was sure as hell going to die if he didn't start keeping his head down. I remember that thought, but didn't think of it then as a prophecy.

They came over. "What do you make of it, Doctor?"

"I don't think we can cure him." Frenchy was getting annoyed at this cherry bomb. "What else do you want to know?"

"Isn't it a little... odd to find something like this in the middle of nowhere?"

"Naw. Country's full of corpses." He knelt down and studied the face, wiggling the head by its chin. "We keep it up, you'll be able to walk from the Mekong to the DMZ without stepping on anything but corpses."

"But he's been castrated!"

"Birds." He toed the body over, busy white crawlers running from the light. "Just some old geezer who walked out into the woods naked and fell over dead. Could happen back in the World. Old people do funny things."

"I thought maybe he'd been tortured by the VC or something."

"God knows. It could happen." The body eased back into its original position with a creepy creaking sound, like leather. Its mouth had closed halfway. "If you want to put 'evidence of VC torture' in your report, your body count, I'll initial it."

"What do you mean by that, Captain?"

"Exactly what I said." He kept staring at the major while he flipped a cigarette into his mouth and fired it up. Non-filter Camels; you'd think a guy who worked with corpses all day long would be less anxious to turn into one. "I'm just trying to get along."

"You believe I want you to falsify—"

Now, "falsify" is a strange word for a last word. The enemy had set up a heavy machine gun on the other side of the clearing, and we were the closest targets. A round struck the major in the small of his back, we found on later examination. At the time, it was just an explosion of blood and guts, and he went down with his legs flopping every which way, barfing, then a loud death rattle. Frenchy was on the ground in a ball, holding his left hand, going, "Shit shit shit." He'd lost the last joint of his little finger. Painful, but not serious enough, as it turned out, to get him back to the World.

I myself was horizontal and aspiring to be subterranean. I managed to get my pistol out and cocked, but realized I didn't want to do anything that might draw attention to us. The machine gun was spraying back and forth over us at about knee height. Maybe they couldn't see us; maybe they thought we were dead. I was scared shitless.

"Frenchy," I stage-whispered, "we've got to get outa here." He was trying to wrap his finger up in a standard first-aid-pack gauze bandage, much too large. "Get back to the trees."

"After you, asshole. We wouldn't get halfway." He worked his pistol out of the holster, but couldn't cock it, his left hand clamping the bandage and slippery with blood. I armed it for him and handed it back. "These are going to do a hell of a lot of good. How are you with grenades?"

"Shit. How you think I wound up in Graves?" In basic training, they'd put me on KP whenever they went out for live grenade practice. In school, I was always the last person when they chose up sides for baseball, for the same reason—though, to my knowledge, a baseball wouldn't kill you if you couldn't throw far enough. "I couldn't get one halfway there." The tree line was about sixty yards away.

"Neither could I, with this hand." He was a lefty.

Behind us came the "poink" sound of a sixty-millimeter mortar, and in a couple of seconds, there was a gray-smoke explosion between us and the tree line. The machine gun stopped, and somebody behind us yelled, "Add twenty!"

At the tree line, we could hear some shouting in Vietnamese, and a clanking of metal. "They're gonna bug out," Frenchy said. "Let's di-di."

We got up and ran, and somebody did fire a couple of bursts at us, probably an AK-47, but he missed, and then there were a series of poinks and a series of explosions pretty close to where the gun had been.

We rushed back to the LZ and found the command group about the time the firing started up again. There was a first lieutenant in charge, and when things slowed down enough for us to tell him what had happened to the major, he expressed neither surprise nor grief. The man had been an observer from Battalion and had assumed command when their captain was killed that morning. He'd take our word for it that the guy was dead—that was one thing we were trained observers in—and not send a squad out for him until the fighting had died down and it was light again.

We inherited the major's hole, which was nice and deep, and in his ruck-sack found a dozen cans and jars of real food and a flask of scotch. So, as the battle raged through the night, we munched pâté on Ritz crackers, pickled herring in sour-cream sauce, little Polish sausages on party rye with real French mustard. We drank all the scotch and saved the beer for breakfast.

For hours, the lieutenant called in for artillery and air support, but to no avail. Later, we found out that the enemy had launched coordinated attacks on all the local airfields and Special Forces camps, and every camp that held POWs. We were much lower priority.

Then, about three in the morning, Snoopy came over. Snoopy was a big C-130 cargo plane that carried nothing but ammunition and Gatling guns; they said it could fly over a football field and put a round into every square inch. Anyhow, it saturated the perimeter with fire, and the enemy stopped shooting. Frenchy and I went to sleep.

At first light, we went out to help round up the KIAs. There were only four dead, counting the major, but the major was an astounding sight, at least in context.

He looked sort of like a cadaver left over from a teaching autopsy. His shirt had been opened and his pants pulled down to his thighs, and the entire thoracic and abdominal cavities had been ripped open and emptied of everything soft, everything from esophagus to testicles, rib cage like blood-streaked fingers sticking rigid out of sagging skin, and there wasn't a sign of any of the guts anywhere, just a lot of dried blood.

Nobody had heard anything. There was a machine-gun position not twenty yards away, and they'd been straining their ears all night. All they'd heard was flies.

Maybe an animal feeding very quietly. The body hadn't been opened with a scalpel or a knife; the skin had been torn by teeth or claws—but seemingly systematically, throat to balls.

And the dry one was gone. Him with the pointed teeth.

There is one rational explanation. Modern warfare is partly mindfuck, and we aren't the only ones who do it, dropping unlucky cards, invoking magic and superstition. The Vietnamese knew how squeamish Americans were, and would mutilate bodies in clever ways. They could also move very quietly. The dry one? They might have spirited him away just to fuck with us. Show what they could do under our noses.

And as for the dry one's odd, mummified appearance, the mold, there might be an explanation. I found out that the Montagnards in that area don't bury their dead; they put them in a coffin made from a hollowed-out log and leave them aboveground. So maybe he was just the victim of a grave robber. I thought the nearest village was miles away, like twenty miles, but I could have been wrong. Or the body could have been carried that distance for some obscure purpose—maybe the VC set it out on the trail to make the Americans stop in a good place to be ambushed.

That's probably it. But for twenty years now, several nights a week, I wake up sweating with a terrible image in my mind. I've gone out with a flashlight, and there it is, the dry one, scooping steaming entrails from the major's body, tearing them with its sharp teeth, staring into my light with black empty sockets, unconcerned. I reach for my pistol, and it's never there. The creature stands up, shiny with blood, and takes a step toward me—for a year or so, that was it; I would wake up. Then it was two steps, and then three. After twenty years it has covered half the distance and its dripping hands are rising from its sides.

The doctor gives me tranquilizers. I don't take them. They might help me stay asleep.

"Graves" is the winner of the 1994 Nebula Award for Best Short Story

Wartime
Systems

In the Loop

Ken Liu

WHEN KYRA WAS NINE, HER father turned into a monster.

It didn't happen overnight. He went to work every morning, like always, and when he came in the door in the evening, Kyra would ask him to play catch with her. That used to be her favorite time of the day. But the yesses came less frequently, and then not at all.

He'd sit at the table and stare. She'd ask him questions and he wouldn't answer. He used to always have a funny answer for everything, and she'd repeat his jokes to her friends and think he was the cleverest dad in the whole world.

She had loved those moments when he'd teach her how to swing a hammer properly, how to measure and saw and chisel. She would tell him that she wanted to be a builder when she grew up, and he'd nod and say that was a good idea. But he stopped taking her to his workshop in the shed to make things together, and there was no explanation.

Then he started going out in the evenings. At first, Mom would ask him when he'd be back. He'd look at her like she was a stranger before closing the door behind him. By the time he came home, Kyra and her brothers were already in bed, but she would hear shouts and sometimes things breaking.

Mom began to look at Dad like she was afraid of him, and Kyra tried to help with getting the boys to bed, to make her bed without being asked, to finish her dinner without complaint, to do everything perfectly, hoping that would make things better, back to the way they used to be. But Dad didn't seem to pay any attention to her or her brothers.

Then, one day, he slammed Mom into the wall. Kyra stood there in the kitchen and felt the whole house shake. She didn't know what to do. He turned around and saw Kyra, and his face scrunched up like he hated her, hated her mother, hated himself most of all. And he fled the house without saying another thing.

Mom packed a suitcase and took Kyra and her brothers to Grandma's place that evening, and they stayed there for a month. Kyra thought about calling her father but she didn't know what she would say. She tried to imagine herself asking the man on the other end of the line *what have you done with Daddy?*

A policeman came, looking for her mother. Kyra hid in the hall so she could hear what he was telling her. *We don't think it was a homicide.* That was how she found out that her father had died.

They moved back to the house, where there was a lot to do: folding up Dad's uniforms for storage, packing up his regular clothes to give away, cleaning the house so it could be sold, getting ready to move away permanently. She caressed Dad's medals and badges, shiny and neatly laid out in a box, and that was when she finally cried.

They found a piece of paper at the bottom of Dad's dresser drawer. "What is it?" she asked Mom.

Mom read it over. "It's from your Dad's commander, at the Army." Her hands shook. "It shows how many people he had killed."

She showed Kyra the number: one thousand two-hundred and fifty-one.

The number lingered in Kyra's mind. As if that gave his life meaning. As if that defined him—and them.

Kyra walked quickly, pulling her coat tight against the late fall chill.

It was her senior year in college, and on-campus recruiting was in full swing. Because Kyra's school was old and full of red brick buildings named after families that had been wealthy and important even before the founding of this republic, its students were desirable to employers.

She was on her way back to her apartment from a party hosted by a small quantitative trading company in New York that was generating good buzz on campus. Companies in management consulting, financial services, and Silicon Valley had booked hotel rooms around the school and were hosting parties for prospective interviewees every night, and Kyra, as a comp sci major, found herself in high demand. This was the night when she would need to finalize her list of ranked preferences, and she had to strategize carefully to have a shot at getting one of the interview slots for the most coveted companies in the lottery.

"Excuse me," a young man stepped in her way. "Would you sign this petition?"

She looked at the clipboard held in front of her. *Stop the War.*

Technically, America wasn't at war. There had been no declaration of war by Congress, just the president exercising his office's inherent authority. But maybe the war had never stopped. America left; America went back; America promised to leave again some time. A decade had passed; people kept on dying far away.

"I'm sorry," Kyra said, not looking the boy in the eyes. "I can't."

"Are you *for* the war?" The boy's voice was tired, the incredulity almost an act. He was there canvassing for signatures alone in the evening because no one cared. When so few Americans died, the "conflict" didn't seem real.

How could she explain to him that she did not believe in the war, did not want to have anything to do with it, and yet, signing the petition the boy held would seem to her tantamount to a betrayal of the memory of her father, would seem a declaration that what he had done was wrong? She did not want him to be defined by the number on that piece of paper her mother kept hidden at the bottom of the box in the attic.

So all she said was, "I'm not into politics."

Back in her apartment, Kyra took off her coat and flipped on the TV.

. . . the largest protest so far in front of the American Embassy. Protestors are demanding that the U.S. cease the drone strikes, which so far have caused more than three hundred deaths in the country this year, many of whom the protestors claim were innocent civilians. The U.S. Ambassador...

Kyra turned off the TV. Her mood had been ruined, and she could not focus on the task of ranking her interview preferences. Agitated, she tried to clean the apartment, scrubbing the sink vigorously to drive the images in her mind away.

As she had grown older, Kyra had read and seen every interview with other drone operators who suffered from PTSD. In the faces of those men, she had searched for traces of her father.

I sat in an air-conditioned office and controlled the drone with a joystick while watching on a monitor what the drone camera saw. If a man was suspected of being the enemy, I had to make a decision and pull the trigger and then zoom in and watch as the man's body parts flew around the screen as the rest of him bled out, until his body cooled down and disappeared from the infrared camera.

Kyra turned on the faucet and held her hands under the hot water, as if she could wash off the memory of her father coming home every evening: silent, sullen, gradually turning into a stranger.

Every time, you wonder: Did I kill the right person? Was the sack on that man's back filled with bombs or just some hunks of meat? Were those three men trying to set up an ambush or were they just tired and taking a break behind those rocks by the road? You kill a hundred people, a thousand people, and sometimes you find out afterwards that you were wrong, but not always.

"You were a hero," Kyra said. She wiped her face with her wet hands. The water was hot against her face and she could pretend it was all just water.

No. You don't understand. It's different from shooting at someone when they're also shooting at you, trying to kill you. You don't feel brave pushing a button to kill people who are not in uniform, who look like they're going for a visit with a friend, when you're sitting thousands of miles away, watching them through a camera. It's not like a video game. And yet it also is. You don't feel like a hero.

"I miss you. I wish I could have understood."

Every day, after you're done with killing, you get up from your chair and walk out of the office building and go home. Along the way you hear the birds chittering overhead and see teenagers walking by, giggling or moping, self-absorbed in their safe cocoons, and then you open the door to your home. Your spouse wants to tell you about her annoying boss and your children are waiting for you to help them with their homework, and you can't tell them a thing you've done.

I think either you become crazy or you already were.

She did not want him to be defined by the number on that piece of paper her mother kept hidden at the bottom of the box in the attic.

"They counted wrong, Dad," Kyra said. "They missed one death."

Kyra walked down the hall dejectedly. She was done with her last interview of the day—a hot Silicon Valley startup. She had been nervous and distracted and had flubbed the brainteaser. It had been a long day and she didn't get much sleep the night before.

She was almost at the elevator when she noticed an interview schedule posted on the door of the suite next to the elevator for a company named AWS Systems. It hadn't been completely filled. A few of the slots on the bottom were blank; that generally meant an undesirable company.

She took a closer look at the recruiting poster. They did something related to robotics. There were some shots of office buildings on a landscaped, modern campus. Bullet points listed competitive salary and benefits. Not flashy, but it seemed attractive enough. Why weren't people interested?

Then she saw it: "Candidates need to pass screening for security clearance." That would knock out many of her classmates who weren't U.S. citizens. And it likely meant government contracts. Defense, probably. She shuddered. Her family had had enough of war.

She was about to walk away when her eyes fell on the last bullet point on the poster: "Relieve the effects of PTSD on our heroes."

She wrote her name on one of the blank lines and sat down on the bench outside the door to wait.

"You have impressive credentials," the man said, "the best I've seen all day, actually. I already know we'll want to talk to you some more. Do you have any questions?"

This was what Kyra had been waiting for all along. "You're building robotic systems to replace human-controlled drones, aren't you? For the war."

The recruiter smiled. "You think we're Cyberdyne Systems?"

Kyra didn't laugh. "My father was a drone operator."

The man became serious. "I can't reveal any classified information. So we have to speak only in hypotheticals. Hypothetically, there may be advantages to using autonomous robotic systems over human-operated machines. Robots."

"Like what? It can't be about safety. The drone operators are perfectly safe back here. You think machines will fight better?"

"No, we're not interested in making ruthless killer robots. But we shouldn't make people do the jobs that should be done by machines."

Kyra's heart beat faster. "Tell me more."

"There are many reasons why a machine makes a better soldier than a human. A human operator has to make decisions based very limited information: just what he can see from a video feed, sometimes alongside intelligence reports. Deciding whether to shoot when all you have to go on is the view from a shaking camera and confusing, contradictory intel is not the kind of thinking humans excel at. There's too much room for error. An operator might hesitate too long and endanger an innocent, or he might be too quick on the trigger and violate the rules of engagement. Decisions by different operators would be based on hunches and emotions and at odds with each other. It's inconsistent and inefficient. Machines can do better."

Worst of all, Kyra thought, *a human can be broken by the experience of having to decide.*

"If we take these decisions away from people, make it so that individuals are out of the decision-making loop, the result should be less collateral damage and a more humane, more civilized form of warfare."

But all Kyra could think was: *No one would have to do what my father did.*

The process of getting security clearance took a while. Kyra's mother was surprised when Kyra called to tell her that government investigators might come to talk to her, and Kyra wasn't sure how to explain why she had taken this job when there were much better offers from other places. So she just said, "This company helps veterans and soldiers."

Her mother said, carefully, "Your father would be proud of you."

Meanwhile, they assigned her to the civilian applications division, which made robots for factories and hospitals. Kyra worked hard and followed all the rules. She didn't want to mess up before she got to do what she really wanted. She was good at her job, and she hoped they noticed.

Then one morning Dr. Stober, the head roboticist, called her to join him in a conference room.

Kyra's heart was in her throat as she walked over. Was she going to be let go? Had they decided that she couldn't be trusted because of what had happened to her father? That she might be emotionally unstable? She had always liked Dr. Stober, who seemed like a good mentor, but she had never worked with him closely.

"Welcome to the team," said a smiling Dr. Stober. Besides Kyra, there were five other programmers in the room. "Your security clearance arrived this morning, and I knew I wanted you on this team right away. This is probably the most interesting project at the company right now."

The other programmers smiled and clapped. Kyra grinned at each of them in turn as she shook their outstretched hands. They all had reputations as the stars in the company.

"You're going to be working on the AW-1 Guardians, one of our classified projects."

One of the other programmers, a young man named Alex, cut in: "These aren't like the field transport mules and remote surveillance crafts we already make. The Guardians are unmanned, autonomous flying vehicles about the size of a small truck armed with machine guns and missiles."

Kyra noticed that Alex was really excited by the weapons systems.

"I thought we make those kinds already," Kyra said.

"Not exactly," Dr. Stober said. "Our other combat systems are meant for surgical strikes in remote places or are prototypes for frontline combat, where basically anything that moves can be shot. But these are designed for peacekeeping in densely populated urban areas, especially places where there are lots of Westerners or friendly locals to protect. Right now we still have to rely on human operators."

Alex said in a deadpan voice, "It would be a lot easier if we didn't have to worry about collateral damage."

Dr. Stober noticed that Kyra didn't laugh and gestured for Alex to stop. "Sarcasm aside, as long as we're occupying their country, there will be locals who think they can get some advantage from working with us and locals who wish we'd go away. I doubt that dynamic has changed in five thousand years. We have to protect those who want to work with us from those who don't, or else the whole thing falls apart. And we can't expect the Westerners doing reconstruction over there to stay holed up in walled compounds all the time. They have to mingle."

"It's not always easy to tell who's a hostile," Kyra said.

"That's the heart of the issue. Most of the time, the population is ambivalent. They'll help us if they think it's safe to do so, and they'll help the militants if they think that's the more convenient choice."

"I've always said that if they choose to help the militants blend in, I don't see why we need to be that careful. They made a decision," Alex said.

"I suppose some interpretations of the rules of engagement would agree with you. But we're telling the world that we're fighting a new kind of war, a clean war, one where we hold ourselves to a higher standard. How people see the way we conduct ourselves is just as important nowadays."

"How do we do that?" Kyra asked, before Alex could further derail the conversation.

"The key piece of software we have to produce needs to replicate what the remote operators do now, only better. The government has supplied us with thousands of hours of footage from the drone operations during the last decade or so. Some of them got the bad guys, and some of them got the wrong people. We'll need to watch the videos and distill the decision-making process of the operators into a formal procedure for identifying and targeting militants embedded in urban conditions, eliminate the errors, and make the procedure repeatable and applicable to new situations. Then we'll improve it by tapping into the kind of big data that individual operators can't integrate and make use of."

The code will embody the minds of my father and others like him so that no one would have to do what they did, endure what they endured.

"Piece of cake," said Alex. And the room laughed, except for Kyra and Dr. Stober.

Kyra threw herself into her work, a module they called the ethical governor, which was responsible for minimizing collateral damage when the robots fired upon suspects. She was working on a conscience for killing machines.

She came in on the weekends and stayed late, sometimes sleeping in the office. She didn't view it as a difficult sacrifice to make. She couldn't talk about what she was working on with the few friends she had, and she didn't really want to spend more time outside the office with people like Alex.

She watched videos of drone strikes over and over. She wondered if any were missions her father had flown. She understood the confusion, the odd combination of power and powerlessness experienced when watching a man one is about to kill through a camera, the pressure to decide.

The hardest part was translating this understanding into code. Computers require precision, and the need to articulate vague hunches had a way of forcing one to confront the ugliness that could remain hidden in the ambiguity of the human mind.

To enable the robots to minimize collateral damage, Kyra had to assign a value to each life that might be endangered in a crowded urban area. One of the most effective ways for doing this—at least in simulations— also turned out to be the most obvious: profiling. The algorithm needed to translate racial characteristics and hints about language and dress into a number that held the power of life and death. She felt paralyzed by the weight of her task.

"Everything all right?" Dr. Stober asked.

Kyra looked up from her keyboard. The office lights were off; it was dark outside. She was practically the last person left in the building.

"You've been working a lot."

"There's a lot to do."

"I've reviewed your check-in history. You seem to be stuck on the part where you need the facial recognition software to give you a probability on ethnic identity."

Kyra gazed at Dr. Stober's silhouette in the door to her office, back-lit by the hall lights. "There's no API for that."

"I know, but you're resisting the need to roll your own."

"It seems... wrong."

Dr. Stober came in and sat down in the chair on the other side of her desk. "I learned something interesting recently. During World War II, the U.S. Army trained dogs for warfare. They would act as sentries, guards, or maybe even as shock troops in an island invasion."

Kyra looked at him, waiting.

"The dogs had to be trained to tell allies apart from enemies. So they used Japanese-American volunteers to teach the dogs to profile, to attack those with certain kinds of faces. I've always wondered how those volunteers felt. It was repugnant, and yet it was also necessary."

"They didn't use German-American or Italian-American volunteers, did they?"

"No, not that I'm aware of. I'm telling you this not to dismiss the problematic nature of your work, but to show you that the problem you're trying to solve isn't entirely new. The point of war is to prefer the lives of one group over the lives of another group. And short of being able to read everyone's minds, you must go with shortcuts and snap heuristics to tell apart those who must die from those who must be saved."

Kyra thought about this. She could not exempt herself from Dr. Stober's logic. After all, she had lamented her father's death for years, but she had never shed a tear for the thousands he had killed, no matter how many might have been innocent. His life was more valuable to her than all of them added together. His suffering meant more. It was why she was here.

"Our machines *can* do a better job than people. Attributes like appearance and language and facial expressions are but one aspect of the input. Your algorithm can integrate the footage from city-wide surveillance by thousands of other cameras, the metadata of phone calls and social visits, individualized suspicions built upon data too massive for any one person to handle. Once the programming is done, the robots will make their decisions consistently, without bias, always supported by the evidence."

Kyra nodded. Fighting with robots meant that no one had to feel responsible for killing.

Kyra's algorithm had to be specified exactly and submitted to the government for approval. Sometimes the proposals came back marked with questions and changes.

She imagined some general (advised, perhaps, by a few military lawyers) looking through her pseudocode line by line.

A target's attributes would be evaluated and assigned numbers. Is the target a man? Increase his suspect score by thirty points. Is the target a child? Decrease his suspect score by twenty-five points. Does the target's face match any of the suspected insurgents with at least a fifty-percent probability? Increase his suspect score by five hundred points.

And then there was the value to be assigned to the possible collateral damage around the target. Those who could be identified as Americans or had a reasonable probability of being Americans had the highest value. Then came native militia forces and groups who were allied with U.S. forces and the local elites. Those who looked poor and desperate were given the lowest values. The algorithm had to formalize anticipated fallout from media coverage and politics.

Kyra was getting used to the process. After the specifications had gone back and forth a few times, her task didn't seem so difficult.

Kyra looked at the number on the check. It was large.

"It's a small token of the company's appreciation for your efforts," said Dr. Stober. "I know how hard you've been working. We got the official word on the trial period from the government today. They're very pleased. Collateral damage has been reduced by more than eighty percent since they started using the Guardians, with zero erroneous targets identified."

Kyra nodded. She didn't know if the eighty percent was based on the number of lives lost or the total amount of points assigned to the lives. She wasn't sure she wanted to think too hard about it. The decisions had already been made.

"We should have a team celebration after work."

And so, for the first time in months, Kyra went out with the rest of the team. They had a nice meal, some good drinks, sang karaoke. And Kyra laughed and enjoyed hearing Alex's stories about his exploits in war games.

"Am I being punished?" Kyra asked.

"No, no, of course not," Dr. Stober said, avoiding her gaze. "It's just administrative leave until...the investigation completes. Payroll will still make bi-weekly deposits and your health insurance will continue, of course. I don't want you to think you're being scapegoated. It's just that you did most of the work on the ethical governor. The Senate Armed Forces Committee is really pushing for our methodology, and I've been told that the first round of subpoenas a coming down next week. You won't be called up, but we'll likely have to name you."

Kyra had seen the video only once, and once was enough. Someone in the market had taken it with a cellphone, so it was shaky and blurry. No doubt the actual footage from the Guardians would be much clearer, but she wasn't going to get to see that. It would be classified at a level beyond her clearance.

The market was busy, the bustling crowd trying to take advantage of the cool air in the morning. It looked, if you squinted a bit, like the farmer's market that Kyra sometimes went to, to get her groceries. A young American man, dressed in the distinctive protective vest that expat reconstruction advisors and technicians wore over there, was arguing with a merchant about something, maybe the price of the fruits he wanted to buy.

Reporters had interviewed him afterwards, and his words echoed in Kyra's mind: *"All of a sudden, I heard the sounds made by the Guardians patrolling the market change. They stopped to hover over me, and I knew something was wrong."*

In the video, the crowd was dispersing around him, pushing, jostling with each other to get out of the way. The person who took the video ran, too, and the screen was a chaotic blur.

When the video stabilized, the vantage point was much further. Two black robots about the size of small trucks hovered in the air above the kiosk. They looked like predatory raptors. Metal monsters.

Even in the cellphone video, it was possible to make out the recorded warning in the local language the robots projected via loudspeakers. Kyra didn't know what the warnings said.

A young boy, seemingly oblivious to the hovering machines above him, was running at the American man, laughing and screaming, his arms opened wide as if he wanted to embrace the man.

"I just froze. I thought, oh God, I'm going to die. I'm going to die because this kid has a bomb on him."

The militants had tried to adapt to the algorithms governing the robots by exploiting certain weaknesses. Because they realized that children were assigned a relatively high value for collateral damage purposes and a relatively low value for targeting purposes, they began to use more children for their missions. Kyra had had to tweak the algorithm and the table of values to account for these new tactics.

"All of your changes were done at the request of the Army and approved by them," said Dr. Stober. "Your programming followed the updated rules of engagement and field practices governing actual soldiers. Nothing you've done was wrong. The Senate investigation will be just be a formality."

In the video, the boy kept on running towards the American. The warnings from the hovering Guardians changed, got louder. The boy did not stop.

A few more boys and girls, some younger, some older, came into the area cleared by the crowd. They ran after the first boy, shouting.

The militants had developed an anti-drone tactic that was sometimes effective. They'd send the first bomber out, alone, to draw the fire of the drones. And while the drone operators were focused on him and distracted, a swarm of backup bombers would rush out to get to the target while the drones shot up the first man.

Robots could not be distracted. And Kyra had programmed them to react correctly to such tactics.

The boy was now only a few steps away from the lone American. The Guardian hovering on the right took a single shot. Kyra flinched at the sound from the screen.

"It was so loud," said the young man in his interview. "I had heard the Guardians shoot before, but only from far away. Up close was a completely different experience. I heard the shot with my bones, not my ears."

The child collapsed to the ground immediately. Where his head had been, there was now only empty space. The Guardians had to be efficient when working in a crowd. Clean.

A few more loud shots came from the video, making Kyra jump involuntarily. The cellphone owner panned his camera over, and there were a few more bundles of rags and blood on the ground. The other children.

The crowd stayed away, but a few of the men were coming back into the clearing, moving closer, raising their voices. But they didn't dare to move too close to the stunned young American, because the two Guardians were still hovering overhead. It took a few minutes before actual American soldiers and the local police showed up at the scene and made everyone go home. The video ended there.

"When I saw that dead child lying in the dust, all I could feel was relief, an overwhelming joy. He had tried to kill me, and I had been saved. Saved by our robots."

Later, when the bodies were searched by the bomb-removal robots, no explosives were found.

The child's parents came forward. They explained that their son wasn't right in the head. They usually locked him in the house, but that day, somehow he had gotten out. No one knew why he ran at that American. Maybe he thought the man looked different and he was curious.

All the neighbors insisted to the authorities that the boy wasn't dangerous. Never hurt anyone. His siblings and friends had been chasing after him, trying to stop him before he got into any trouble.

His parents never stopped crying during the interview. Some of the commenters below the interview video said that they were probably sobbing for the camera, hoping to get more compensation out of the American government. Other commenters were outraged. They constructed elaborate arguments and fought each other in a war of words in the comment threads, trying to score points.

Kyra thought about the day she'd made the changes in the programming. She had been sipping a frappé because the day was hot. She remembered deleting the old value of a child's life and putting in a new one. It had seemed routine, just another change like hundreds of other tweaks she had already made. She remembered deleting one IF and adding another, changing the control flow to defeat the enemy. She remembered feeling thrilled at coming up with a neat solution to the nested logic. It was what the Army had requested, and she had decided to do her best to give it to them faithfully.

"Mistakes happen," said Dr. Stober. "The media circus will eventually end, and all the hand-wringing will stop. News cycles are finite, and something new will replace all this. We just have to wait it out. We'll figure out a way to make the system work better next time. This *is* better. This is the future of warfare."

Kyra thought about the sobbing parents, about the dead child, about the dead children. She thought about the eighty-percent figure Dr. Stober had quoted. She thought about the number on her father's scorecard, and the parents and children and siblings behind those numbers. She thought about her father coming home.

She got up to leave.

"You must remember," said Dr. Stober from behind her, "You're not responsible."

She said nothing.

It was rush hour when Kyra got off the bus to walk home. The streets were filled with cars and the sidewalks with people. Restaurants were filling up quickly; waitresses flirted with customers; men and women stood in front of display windows to gawk at the wares.

She was certain that most of them were bored with coverage of the war. No one was coming home in body bags any more. The war was clean. This was the point of living in a civilized country, wasn't it? So that one did not have to think about wars. So that somebody else, some*thing* else, would.

She strode past the waitress who smiled at her, past the diners who did not know her name, into the throng of pedestrians on the sidewalk, laughing, listening to music, arguing and shouting, oblivious to the monster who was walking in their midst, ignorant of the machines thousands of miles away deciding who to kill next.

Ghost Girl

Rich Larson

IGUO HAD ANOTHER REPORT ON his news feed about a ghost girl living in the dump outside Bujumbura, so he put two Cokes in a hydrobag and hailed a taxi outside the offices. It was cool season now and the sky was rusty red. The weather probes were saying dust storm, dust storm, remember to shut the windows. Iguo put his head back against the concrete wall and wondered how a ghost girl living by herself was not yet dismembered and smuggled out to Tanzania. Maybe some entrepreneur was cutting her hair to sell to fishermen. Maybe she was very lucky.

The graffitied hump of the taxi bullied its way through bicycles and bleating sheep. Iguo slung the hydrobag over his shoulder and pulled out his policense. This was not an emergency, not strictly, but Iguo did not pay for transit if it could be free. The taxi rumbled to a stop and when the door opened, it bisected a caricature of President Dantani shitting on a rebel flag. He climbed inside and switched off the icy blast air conditioning.

"Bujumbura junkyard," Iguo said, pressing his policense against the touchscreen.

"Calculating," said the taxi.

The junkyard was a plastic mountain. Whatever wire fence had once marked its boundaries was long since buried. Bony goats wandered up and down the face, chewing on circuits. Scavengers with rakes and battered scanners stumped around the bottom, searching for useable parts or gold conductors. Iguo had the taxi stop well away, before it gutted a tire on some hidden piece of razor wire or trash. It didn't want to wait, but he used the policense again and it reluctantly hunkered down.

There was a scavenger with no nose and no tag sitting in the sand. Stubble was white on his dark skull. A cigarette dangled from his lips. Iguo squatted across from him.

"*Mwiriwe*, Grandfather."

"*Mwiriwe*, Policeman. My shit, all legal." He waved off a fly. "You ask anyone."

"I'm looking for the ghost girl," Iguo said. "She lives here, yeah?"

The scavenger massaged his knobby calves. "Oh, yes."

"How long here?"

"Aye, two weeks, three weeks since she show up. Her and her *imfizi*." He spat into the sand. "She's a little witch, like they say. She's got the thing following her all around."

Iguo squinted up the crest of the junk pile. "How does she survive?" he asked. He saw the scampering silhouettes of children and wondered if one was her.

The scavenger shrugged. "She finds good stuff. Me, I buy some. And nobody trouble her, or that damn *imfizi* take them to pieces." He tapped the orange ember of his cigarette, eyed the hydrobag on Iguo's shoulder. "You here to decommission it? You look soldier."

"I'm here for the girl," Iguo said.

"Witch," the scavenger corrected. "You say it's genes, but it's witch. I know. I see her."

"Goodnight, Grandfather." Iguo straightened up. He had speakaloud pamphlets in the taxi, ones that explained albino genetics in cheerful Kirundi and then French, ones he did not distribute as often as he was supposed to, but Iguo knew that by the time a man is old his mind is as hard as a stone.

He found the ghost girl rooting through electric cabling, feet agile on the shifting junk. Her sundress was shabby yellow and stained with gasoline. Her hands and feet were callused. Still, she was tagged: her tribal showed up Hutu and she was inoculated against na-virus. Not born in the street, then.

"Anything good?" Iguo asked.

She turned around and blinked rheumy pink eyes at him. "Who are you?"

"My name is Iguo. I work for the government." He unslung the hydrobag and took out the first bottle. "You want a fanta?"

"Yes." The girl rubbed her pale cheek. "Yes, I wanna."

"Here." Iguo opened the chilly Coke between his molars. Clack. Hiss. He held it out. "What's your name?"

"Belise." The ghost girl wound the cable carefully around herself, eyes on the sweating bottle. "Set it down, back up some," she suggested. "I'll get it."

"You don't need to be afraid of me," Iguo said, wedging the drink in a nook of bent rebar. "I'm here to take you somewhere safe. Here, here isn't safe for you." He scooted back. "Belise, do you know what an albino hunter is?"

"It's safe," Belise said, patting a piece of rusty armor. "My *baba* is here." She clambered down to get the Coke and all at once something very large burrowed out from the junk pile. Motors whirred as it unfolded to its feet, shedding scrap metal. The robot was sized like a gorilla and skinned like a tank. The sensory suite glittered red at him. Iguo hadn't seen an *imfizi* drone in many years and the sight jolted him.

"Shit," Iguo said, as Belise skipped back up the pile, bottle cradled in her grimy hands. He realized the old man had been talking sense.

"My *baba*," the ghost girl said proudly. "My daddy is very strong." She swigged from the Coke and grinned at him.

Iguo had retreated to the bottom to re-evaluate things. Clouds were still building crenellations in the sky, and now wind whistled in and out of the junk. He skyped the offices for a list of active combat drones, but of course it was classified, and the official line was still that they had all been smelted. He sat and drank his own Coke and watched Belise step nimbly across a car chassis while the drone lumbered behind her, puffing smoke.

There had been many of them, once. Iguo knew. He remembered seeing them stalk across open ground sponging up rebel fire like terrible gods while the flesh troops circled and sweated, lying in this ditch and then another, so fragile. He remembered the potent mix of envy and disdain they all felt for the piloting jackmen, cocooned safe in neural webbing a mile away.

He remembered best when one of the *imfizi* was hacked, taken over by some rebel with a signal cobbled together from a smartphone and a neural jack. People said later that it had been Rufykiri himself, the Razor, the hacker who sloughed off government security like snakeskin, but nobody really knew. Iguo remembered mostly because that day was when half of his unit was suddenly gone in an eruption of blood and marrow. Iguo did not trust drones.

"You see, now." The old scavenger was back. He ran a dirty nail around the hollow of his nose. "Nobody troubles her. That thing, deadly. She has it bewitched."

"It's malfunctioning," Iguo said. "Not all of them came back for de-commissioning. Crude AIs, they get confused. Running an escort protocol or something like that." He narrowed his eyes. "Not witchcraft."

"Lucky malfunction for her," the old man said. "Lucky, lucky. Else she would be chopped up, yeah? For eurocash, not francs. Much money for a ghost." He smiled. "A rocket could do in that *imfizi*. Or an EMP. You have one?"

"I will chop you up, Grandfather—" Iguo took a long pull at his drink, "—if you talk any more of *muti*. You live in a new time."

"What, you don't want to be rich?" The scavenger hacked up a laugh.

"Not for killing children," Iguo said.

"Ah, but you were in the war."

Iguo stood up.

"You were in the war," the old man repeated. "You sowed the na-virus and burned the villages and used the big knife on the deserters. Didn't you? Weren't you in the war?"

Iguo wanted his fingers around the scavenger's piped neck until the esophagus buckled, so he took his Coke and walked back up to try again with the ghost girl.

The drone had been repairing itself, he could see it now. Swatches of hardfoam and crudely-welded panels covered its chassis. Spare cables hung like dead plants from its shoulders. It was hunched very still, only swiveling one camera to track Iguo's approach. Belise was sitting between its feet.

"Dunna come any closer," she said. "He might get mad at you." Her brows shot up. "Is that fanta for me as well?"

"No," Iguo said. He considered it. "Too much sugar is bad for you. You won't grow."

The *imfizi* shifted slightly and Iguo took a step back.

Belise laughed. "My *baba* used to say that."

"My mother used to say it," Iguo said. "When I chewed too much sugarcane." He watched the drone uneasily. It was hard to tell where it was looking. "Did you have a *mama*?" he asked her.

"I don't remember," Belise said. She rubbed at her nose, smeared snot on her dress.

"And your *baba*?"

"He's here." Belise slapped the metal trunk behind her. "With me."

"The *imfizi* keeps you safe, yes? Like a father." Iguo maneuvered a rubber tire to sit on. Some of the scavengers down below were using a brazier for tea and the wind carried its bitter smoke. "But maybe it will not always be that way," he said. "Drones are not so much like you and me, Belise. They can break."

"They can fix," Belise said, pointing to the patched carapace.

Iguo remembered much simpler jobs, where the men and women were frightened for their lives and wanted so badly to be tagged, to go to the safehouse, for the government to help them.

"If the drone decides its mission is over, it might leave," Iguo said. "Or it might paint you."

"Paint me?"

"Paint you a target," Iguo said. "So it can kill you."

Belise shook her small white head, serene. "No, that won't happen. He's my *baba*."

Iguo sipped until his drink was gone. "I'll take you to a place with so much food," he said. "No more scrap-hunting. Nice beds and nice food. And other children."

"I'll stay." Belise pointed and Iguo followed her finger. "Take those two. You can have them go with you. I don't like them."

Two small boys rummaging in the junk, insect-thin arms. One had a hernia peeking out from under his torn shirt. They cast nervous looks up every so often, for the leviathan drone and the albino girl and now for the policeman.

"They don't need my help," Iguo said. "My job is to help you. Many people would try to kill you. Cut off your limbs. The government is trying to make you safe."

"Why?"

Iguo rubbed his forehead. "Because albino-killings are very publicized. President Dantani is forging new Western relations, and the killings reflect badly, badly, badly on our country. And now that the war is over, and there are no more rebels to hunt, people who know only how to murder are finding the *muti* market."

"Oh."

"And the government cares for the good of all its people," Iguo added. He looked at the empty glass bottle between his palms, then hurled it off into the growing dusk. The shatter noise came faint. Belise had followed the trajectory, lips pursed. Now she looked up.

"Not what my *baba* said." She paused. "About the government. He said other things."

"Your *baba* is dead, Belise."

Belise nodded, and for a moment Iguo thought they were making progress. "He died with the bleeding," she said. "With the sickness. But he told me not to worry, because he had a plan. He made his soul go softly into the *imfizi*." She smiled upward, and the pity in Iguo's gut sharpened into something else. He stared at the array of red sensors, the scattered spider eyes.

"Your daddy, Belise." Iguo put a finger up to his temple and twisted. "Was he a jackman?"

Belise winced. She stared at the ground. When she looked up, her raw pink eyes were defiant. "He was a rebel," she said.

Back in the birdshit-caked taxi, there was a memo on misuse of government funds. Iguo tugged it off the screen and punched in his address instead. Through the window, he saw scavengers taking in their equipment. Some were pitching nylon tents around the brazier. The old noseless man was tearing open a package of disposable phones, but he looked up when the ignition rumbled. He waved.

Iguo's fingers buzzed as he typed the word into Google: *softcopy*. A slew of articles in English and German fluttered up. He struggled through half a paragraph before switching over to a translation service. Iguo was not a hacker, but he'd heard the term used. Always between jackmen, usually in a hot argument.

The taxi began to rattle over loose-packed gravel, and Iguo had it read aloud to him. *Softcopy, a theoretical transfer of human consciousness into an artificial brain. Ramifications for artificial intelligence. Softcopy claim in NKorea revealed to be a hoax. Increased use of neural webbing has led to new questions. Evolution of the human mind.*

The taxi sent him an exposé on corruption in the Burundi police forces as a kicker, but Iguo hardly registered it as he swung himself out of the vehicle. He scanned himself through the door in the jagged-glass-topped wall, scattered the pigeons on his apartment's stoop. The stairs went by three at a time, and then he was in front of his work tablet, working the policense like a bludgeon.

He pulled up reports from three years ago. Death reports. The list was long, long, long. He scrolled through it and they came to him in flashes, so many Jonathans and then so many Josephs, good Christian names for godless rebels, and then he found him: Joseph Rufykiri, the Razor. Responsible for the longest sustained information attack of the war, for the interception of encrypted troop movements, for the malicious reprogramming of military drones, farm equipment, wind turbines, and once a vibrator belonging to the general's wife.

He was dead by na-virus, but survived by an albino daughter. Iguo stared at the data and only half-believed it, but half was enough. He found a rumpled rain jacket under the bed and threw it on, and into the deepest pocket he dropped his old service handgun. Useless, unless he put it right up to the drone's gut, right where the armor had fallen away.

Iguo thought of the blood spray and his comrades jerking and falling like cut puppets as the hacked drone spun its barrels. He thought of Joseph Rufykiri between blood-soaked sheets, whispering to his daughter that he had a plan and that she did not have to worry.

He had to know, so Iguo stepped back out under the swelling sky and hailed a new taxi, one with less graffiti, as it began to storm.

The dust felt like flying shrapnel by the time Iguo struggled out of the taxi, wrapped up to the eyes. It battered and bit his fingers. The sky was dark and its rusty clouds were surging now, attacking. It looked like the scavengers had packed away and found shelter elsewhere, or else their tents had been torn off like great black scabs. Iguo hurried to where the junk pile could provide some shelter.

On his way a scavenger fled past, stumbling, and then Iguo saw the blurry shape of a jeep up ahead through the sand. Something besides the storm was happening. He crouched against the wheel-well and checked his gun where the dust couldn't reach it. He checked it again. He breathed in, out, and craned his head around the edge of the vehicle.

Three *muti* hunters, swathed in combat black with scarves wrapped tight against the storm. Iguo counted three small-caliber guns but could hear nothing now over the howl of the dust. They ducked and swayed on their feet, and the *imfizi* drone clanked and churned and tried to track them as the grit assaulted its many joints. Bullets had cratered its front, and bled coolant was being sucked off into the wind. Belise was nowhere to be seen.

The drone was long since dry of ammunition, and the hunter was caught off-guard when it lunged, quicker than Iguo had ever seen a drone move, and pinioned him to the ground. The other two rounded on it, firing in rhythm. The *imfizi* buckled and twitched with the impacts, but then reared up with the hunter's leg still mashed in its pincer. Reared higher. Higher. Blood spouted as the man tore silently in half.

The other hunters reversed now, moving clumsily in the wind, and one hauled a grenade from his back and lobbed. For a moment, Iguo thought it was a dud, but then a whine shivered in his teeth and the hair on his neck stood up on end and he realized it was an EMP. The drone shuddered once, twice. Froze. The hunters converged.

Something clutched onto Iguo's calf. He looked down, and of course it was Belise, her translucent hands kneading his ankle, and she was crying something but Iguo could not read lips. He shook her off. He steadied himself. He ducked around the side of the vehicle, and fired twice.

The first hunter dropped, swinging on his heel, punched through the skull and nicked in the shoulder. Iguo had not forgotten where to put the bullets.

Arm coming up, scarved head turning. Iguo made his body rigid and snapped off another shot, feeling it into the chest but hitting belly instead. The hunter fired back but the retort was lost in the dust and Iguo had no idea how close he'd come to dying so he did not falter. The hunter's scarf ripped free, oscillating wildly, as the next bullet splintered through throat and jaw.

Iguo stumbled to the bodies and scrabbled for their guns, but one had already been swallowed by the sand and the other was locked tight in a dead hand. He tried to throw up but only hurt his ribs. He crawled instead to the *imfizi*. Its red eyes were starting to blink back on. Iguo put a hand on either side of the carapace and leaned close. He stared hard into the cameras.

"Joseph Rufykiri," he said, mouthing carefully.

The drone shuddered. The top half of the chassis rocked back. Rocked forward. Iguo mirrored the nod without really meaning to. He squinted back to where Belise was crouched, covering her eyes against the dust. Her skin was stark white against the black jeep. Tears were tracking through the grime on her face.

Iguo realized he had the gun pressed up against the rusty husk. "Do your penance," he mumbled. "I do mine." Then he stood up, almost bowled over in the wind, and turned to go.

The ghost girl said something to him but he still couldn't hear. It might have been thanks. Iguo nodded her on, and she dashed towards her father, now getting to his iron feet. Iguo went to the jeep and found the two little boys on their bellies underneath. He put his head down.

"I have a taxi," he said. "Come with me." They exchanged looks with their dark eyes and shook dust from their dark heads. Then they wriggled out from under the vehicle and Iguo shielded them as best he could with the rain jacket.

He looked back only once. Belise was clambering into the drone's arms, sheltered from the roaring wind, and then they were enveloped by the dust.

The Radio

Susan Jane Bigelow

KAY SCANNED THE LIFELESS, SHREDDED bodies of her unit, the sensors embedded in her hands and torso coolly picking up data as her eyes flicked over each of them in turn.

Jasar, X, Lt. [deceased]
Purte, D, SSgt. [deceased]
Leshandre, S, Pvt. [deceased]
Oudar, V, Pvt. [deceased]

The roadside bomb had spared only her, stranding her in the middle of ten thousand kilometers of the flat, featureless desert that covered most of Ianas. She kept trying to connect to the Sovene Army's net, but there was nothing. She couldn't transmit, she couldn't receive. Her communications hardware had been too badly damaged by the blast.

There was nothing left to do but follow protocol. Once everything was documented, she sat by the road and waited to be retrieved, like the piece of equipment the Army considered her to be.

Time passed: hours, days, even weeks according to her internal clock. She watched as the corpses bloated and began to rot.

She could wait almost indefinitely. She didn't need food or water, and her power cells were kept from draining by the sunlight and near-constant wind.

It did surprise her that no one came. Their course hadn't been too different from the routine patrol sweep the base had ordered. Lt. Jasar had had a funny idea about the roads being sabotaged out here, even though things had been quiet lately, and had demanded that Leshandre turn down a random one to check it out. They'd driven for nearly a day before the bomb had proven the lieutenant right.

Still, it was strange. There were tracking satellites in orbit. They'd been in nominal contact with the base right up until the explosion, this stretch of desert wasn't supposed to be terribly dangerous, and the Army swore it never left anyone behind.

So why was Kay still here?

On the thirty-seventh day, she registered something moving fast across the dusty flatness of the desert. She crouched behind the wreckage, cautiously assessing the situation.

The truck drew near, but it was soon clear that it wasn't Army. Instead of a reassuring green and yellow, it was painted bright blue, and was old and beat-up.

She readied her weapon but held her fire. She couldn't positively identify them as enemies, not yet.

The truck slowed to a stop in front of her, and three women and a man got out.

"Bomb work," said one, a tall, thin woman, examining the remnants of the vehicle.

"Bolus's," said the shortest woman, spitting into the sand. "Sloppy."

"Sovene Army," said the third, a shrewd-looking middle-aged woman. "Had to have been here a while." She glanced at Kay. "Their Synthetic's still alive, though." Her features suddenly shifted. "Oh...oh, no." She leaned in close. "No. It can't be." She snapped a finger in front of Kay's face. "Hey. Hey! You reading me in there?"

Kay didn't respond. She wouldn't, not to a civilian. That was against protocol.

"Musta been caught out here before the evacuation," said the man. He was also short; he had a scruffy beard and talked slowly. "Probably still waiting for orders."

The first woman didn't respond but kept staring at Kay. She exchanged glances with the tall woman, who shook her head slightly.

"Jassalan, no," the tall woman said.

"We could use a new radio," said the short woman. She gestured at Kay. "Get your metal ass into the truck."

Kay stayed put.

The short woman crossed her arms, annoyed, then reached out to smack Kay on the helmet. Kay reached out, quick as lightning, and grabbed the woman's wrist.

"Hey!" she squawked.

"Let her go, Synthetic," said the third woman. But Kay held fast as the short woman pulled and grunted and swore. "That's an order. Recognize Captain Macrandal Jassalan. Serial number 2789-KK-CN."

Kay's internal Army database recognized the number. There was a caution next to it, and her first impulse was to disregard her command. But she hadn't had orders in thirty-seven days. She released the short woman's arm.

"Shit!" cursed Shorty. "Tin-can zombie!"

"Back off, Liss," said Jassalan sternly. "Yago, clear out some space in the truck. We're taking her with us."

The man shrugged and went to do as he was told. After a moment, so did Liss.

"Are you sure this is a good idea?" asked the tall woman, whose name Kay still didn't know.

"Fuck no," said Liss, still rubbing her wrist. "Leave it to run out of batteries or whatever."

"They don't run out," said Jassalan distantly. "Synthetics last forever."

"Then blow it up!"

"No," said Jassalan firmly. "She's coming. Get back in the truck, Liss. Payl, look around the wreck, see if there's anything else we can use. Then we'll get going." She turned to Kay. "Go to the truck and sit in it," she said.

Kay began to obey, but hesitated. "You're wanted for desertion," she said.

Jassalan smiled tiredly, wrinkles forming around her eyes. "I know. Did you want to bring me in?"

Kay did. But these people might be able to help her get back to the base. That was all she cared about right now. "No."

"Thank you," said Jassalan. She studied Kay again for a moment. "Get in the truck. I'll be along shortly."

Duty satisfied, Kay went and sat in the truck. Soon, everyone was ready, and they left the blast site behind.

They drove across the pancake flatness of the desert in silence. Jassalan was preoccupied, Liss fumed, and Payl kept sneaking looks at her. The man, Yago, was blessedly uninterested in Kay and looked out the window at the featureless scenery instead. After a few hours they came to a small rise. Kay's sensors detected slight emanations coming from it.

"You have a power source," she said. She calculated their location and plotted it. "You aren't on my maps."

"We wouldn't be," said Jassalan dryly. The truck pulled into a little gully next to the hillside, and everyone clambered out. "We're home."

Liss headed to her workshop, still grumbling about her hurt wrist. Payl and Yago started unloading scrap from the truck. Kay followed Jassalan into the cramped, dark kitchen, unsure of what to do next.

"We can't use too much power here," Jassalan said apologetically, putting water on to boil. "So we cook things the hard way. Takes time. Do you eat?"

"No," said Kay.

"You have a name?" Jassalan asked.

"My identification is MSID-609872-K," said Kay. "But I call myself Kay."

"Right, right," repeated Jassalan, as if lost in a mantra. "Right."

"I need to contact Ianas Alpha," said Kay. "As soon as possible."

"We-ell," said Jassalan, drawing the word out as she dropped pods of bluish vat-grown meat into the boiling water. "You can try. Won't be anybody there, though."

"I don't understand," said Kay.

"You must have been cut off before the evacuation," said Jassalan.

"What evacuation?"

"The Sovene Army's gone, hon," said Jassalan matter-of-factly. "Headed back to space."

Kay reeled, shocked. The Army was militarily superior to the small pack of rebels making trouble on cold, dry Ianas, and the planet was not yet fully pacified. "You're lying."

"Afraid not," said Jassalan sympathetically. "They're gone."

"Why?" Kay asked, still processing. This had to be wrong, some kind of trick.

"Hm," said Jassalan. "The usual sorts of trouble. Politics. Money. A government that can't make up their minds about who they want to massacre this month."

"I see," said Kay. "May I use your communications equipment?"

"Go ahead," said Jassalan, pointing. A screen and touchpad was mounted on a wall. "Doesn't reach off-planet. Liss might be able to fix it up, but we have no reason to call anyone who isn't on Ianas."

Kay, still certain her host was lying about the evacuation, punched in the code for the base.

The connection established, and something that might have been joy filled Kay's belly for a brief moment. But then a message flashed across the screen: *Ianas Alpha Decommissioned | Contact Sector 15 Command.*

Something fell away inside her.

It was true. The Army was gone. Her companions, both human and Synthetic, were gone. The base she'd called home for two years was...was...

A terrible aimless feeling penetrated her half-synthetic skull. If the base was gone, the mission was canceled. There were no orders, no missions, nothing.

She had nothing to do.

A hand hesitantly touched her shoulder. "I'm sorry," said Jassalan. "I don't like the Army much these days, but I remember being in. They're like your family, when you're a part of it. I guess that's true for you, too."

"They may have just regrouped," Kay said firmly. "They will return."

"Maybe, but I hope they're gone for good," said Jassalan with a spark of anger. "The Sovenes have been nothing but trouble for this place."

"But you're a Sovene, too," observed Kay.

"Well," shrugged Jassalan. "Used to be."

"You're a deserter," said Kay archly. To her there was very little worse than deserting.

"Sure," said Jassalan, and waited. "Aren't you going to ask me why?"

"I assumed you didn't want to fight anymore," said Kay.

That seemed to annoy Jassalan, and her frown deepened. "You have any idea what the Army does, *Synthetic*? The kinds of things they do here? I saw all kinds of horror. Civilians bombed. 'Terrorists' targeted, even when there was no evidence against them. Rape. Murder. Torture. You haven't seen that?"

Kay had, though she quickly reminded herself that she'd seen many good things as well. She accepted the situation as... complicated.

"The worst part of it is that it's all in service of a government that lies to everyone," Jassalan continued. "That controls every aspect of their lives without giving them any kind of say at all!"

"That is not true," said Kay tartly. She had done a lot of study of the way Sovenes chose their leadership. "There is the yearly vote, and the local—"

"Don't bother explaining the system to me," said Jassalan. "I don't want to hear it. People back home think they have a voice, but they don't. I saw the light. I left. I'm no coward."

"Are all of you deserters?"

"Just me," said Jassalan. She poked the meat bubbling away in the pot. "Everyone else is family. So you don't have to follow their orders."

Orders. She tried to think of what hers would say now. "I must report in to Sector 15 Command," she said after a moment.

"You don't *have* to," said Jassalan intently. "And you can't, we don't have the equipment. Come have dinner."

"I said I don't need to eat," said Kay brusquely.

"I'm not saying you should," said Jassalan. "Just...come be with everyone."

The look in Jassalan's eyes gave Kay pause. She'd seen it once or twice before in the eyes of people who wanted her for some reason of their own, and those situations had never ended well.

But she had nothing to do, and the thought of standing here thinking about how cut off she was felt like staring into her own personal abyss, so she followed Jassalan to the table.

The dinner conversation flowed around her, avoiding her as if she stood on a rock in the middle of a stream. They talked about the food, the weather (still dry), and the paramilitary groups that were steadily taking power from the provisional government.

Liss glared at her, while Payl gave her little smiles. Yago ignored her, scarfed down his food, and quickly left the table. Jassalan ate very little, and studied Kay when she thought she wasn't looking.

After the meal was done Kay helped Jassalan clear the table, and the others left to do other things. Payl went outside to fiddle with the moisture collectors. Liss went into another room and started banging on something metal.

"So tell me," said Jassalan, a little too nonchalantly. "What's your function? All-purpose communications, that sort of thing?"

"You should know that," said Kay, stacking a load of dishes neatly on a table. Her internal sensors whined that her arms and legs could use maintenance. She ignored them.

"I do, I suppose. So. Do you like it?"

Kay turned to her. "Yes," she said, in what she hoped was an assertive enough tone to forestall any further inquiry. She knew where this was going. People liked asking her intrusive questions like:

Are you happy?

Don't you want to be free?

Do you have feelings?

Do you miss being human?

When she was new, she had tried to answer, but the answers were never what people wanted to hear.

"But it can't be satisfying," said Jassalan. "They don't care about you."

"I'm satisfied. I have friends."

"They didn't even come back for you!"

Kay shook her head, not wanting to think about that, but Jassalan pressed her.

"There's a part of you that must remember that this isn't what it should be like. You must remember being human. Don't you?"

"I don't," said Kay shortly. "I'm not human."

"You *are*," said Jassalan, suddenly intense. "Part of you is human! You—you look like her. You even *sound* like her."

"Who?" asked Kay, confused.

"My sister. When she died—she gave her body," said Jassalan. Kay, frustrated, groaned to herself. One of those conversations, again. "We—we think she became one of those—one of *you*," continued Jassalan. "And here you are. Deeslyn."

"My name is *Kay*, and I am not your sister," said Kay evenly. "Military Information Services have produced a film that explains how Synthetics are created, I could show it to you. It does a good job—"

"I don't need to see a film," said Jassalan, cutting her off. "I know my own sister!"

"The reuse of patriotic citizens' donated bodies helps keep costs to the taxpayer low," continued Kay, quoting from a standard explanation. "Bodies are outfitted with implants, and given power plants, and facial features are altered before we are activated. We are sculpted to give an attractive human appearance, so as to better interact with the populace and our fellow soldiers. You have no way of knowing if my donor body is related to you."

"But you *might* be. When were you activated?"

"Four years ago."

"That's when she would have been processed!" said Jassalan, eyes bright with certainty. "It's possible!"

Kay shook her head, her slow-burn anger finally beginning to kindle. "You aren't listening. I am *not* your sister."

"Can you check? Do you know whose body that is?" asked Jassalan hotly.

"I can, but I won't," said Kay.

Jassalan's face screwed up in rage. "Get out, then. Get out! You're just a brainwashed tool of the Sovenes! You're nothing but a bunch of wires and processors lugging a corpse around!" A tear slipped down her cheek. "You're *unworthy* of my sister's body—or any human body. Get out!"

Kay wanted to tell her that it didn't matter. The human or humans who had donated their bodies would be just as dead if she weren't here.

But she didn't say that. Instead, she left without saying another word.

The flat expanse of desert seemed to go on forever. Kay trudged through it, one step at a time, one foot in front of the other. She was painfully aware, thanks to the constant readouts from her internal sensors, that her body needed some serious repairs.

And yet she kept going, straight through the desert. She'd roughly calculated her position; her onboard maps said there was a small village in this direction.

She didn't know what she'd do when she got there. She knew she should report in to Sector 15 Command—that was her only mission now—but she kept exploring options to do so without really deciding on a plan she liked. She fretted over this; she was usually very fast to weigh possibilities and make decisions.

Her sensors picked up their truck before it was even visible, and she went on alert. She checked her weapons, unsure what Jassalan intended. She had some charge left in one of her pulse cannons, and two working dart missiles in each wrist. It wasn't everything; half her systems were wrecked and her rifle had been damaged in the crash. It would have to do.

The truck roared up beside her, and Payl grinned out at her.

"Hey, Kay," she called, turning the rhyme into a little two-note sing-song. "Need a ride to town?"

"Jass's mad," Payl said as they bounced along. "But it's her own fault."

Kay had to agree, but said nothing. Payl was clearly getting some kind of thrill out of doing what Jassalan wouldn't like.

"She told me about it," said Payl. "She should know better."

"Agreed," said Kay coldly. Payl blanched at that, so Kay tried to pick up the conversation from there. "Did you know her? The woman Jassalan thought my body came from?"

"Sure," said Payl. "I was married to her."

"You were?" exclaimed Kay, surprised. "But—"

"She died a long time ago," said Payl. "I let her go. Jass...can't."

"What was she like?" asked Kay.

Payl smiled a small, wistful smile. "Dees was...amazing. Quiet, kind and generous. She believed in a lot of causes, believed in service. Her death was bad for Jass; it's why she dropped out of the Army. It's probably why she asked me to come with them to Ianas; I think I'm some way of keeping a piece of Dees close. Do you really not know anything at all about who you—ah, who your body's from?"

"No," said Kay. "But I could."

"You could?"

"It's a file in my core," said Kay. "I've never accessed it."

"Why not?"

"Because I'm not that person," said Kay flatly. "I'm me."

"Oh," said Payl. "I think I get that."

A long moment passed. Payl drummed her hands on the steering wheel.

"So, are you okay?" Payl asked at last.

Kay didn't know what to say to that. People had never asked her that. "Yes," she said at last. "I think so."

"You *think* so?" Payl said jokingly. "Don't you have sensors and all that inside to tell you?"

Humans so rarely understood, thought Kay. They were a mess, a whirling maelstrom of emotions. Kay and other Synthetics seemed like a placid pool by comparison, but still she had her tides, and her ripples, and even feelings humans seemed to lack.

Among others, there was a sort of *beyond*-certainty that she seemed to feel only with her synthetic parts. It was a cold and awful feeling, and she'd never succeeded in explaining it to humans.

"So where were you heading? I mean, after town," Payl said. "Where next?"

"Sector 15," said Kay. "I have to report in."

"How're you going to get off-planet? Spaceport's in Tarthe, that's halfway around the planet!"

"I'll call for a pick-up," said Kay moodily. "Someone in the village should have an off-planet setup. They'll evacuate me."

"Will they? They didn't seem to want to come for you before."

"They will," stressed Kay. "That was a specific set of unique circumstances. It's a simple matter of going to the village and contacting them; they'll be by to pick me up soon."

"If that's true," said Payl. "Then why didn't you do that when you were stranded?"

"I don't know. I was waiting for them to come," said Kay softly. "I was so sure they would."

The truck drove on through the dusty flatness.

They pulled into what passed for a town, a cluster of pre-fab buildings grouped around moisture-collection stations.

"You go make your call," said Payl. "I can bring you back home after, if you want."

"No, thank you. I'll wait here," said Kay.

"Yeah, I understand that," said Payl. Her constant smile flagged a little. "It's been good to talk to you. I'm sorry Jassalan acted like she did."

"I...I'm sorry about your wife," said Kay.

Payl nodded. "Yeah. Hey... Dees was big on making her own choices. Even if part of you is her, she'd want you to do what's right for you. Okay?"

"Thank you for picking me up," was all Kay could think of to say to that.

Payl's smile grew wide again. "You're welcome! Find the rain!"

Kay must have looked puzzled, because Payl added, "That's what we say when we hope someone gets lucky. There's never rain!"

With that, Payl roared out of the village, and Kay was alone again.

She found her way to the store/comm shack and asked the man at the counter about an off-planet communications system. He glared at her; she couldn't hide what she was, or her Sovene Army markings.

"I can pay," she said hurriedly. She removed the currency she kept for emergencies. It seemed thin and paltry, but the storekeeper's eyes widened.

"It's expensive," he warned. "Very expensive."

She thought, then removed one of the sensors from her leg. It was full of valuable electronics and a few precious metals, even if it wouldn't work without her input. He frowned, but he pointed the way to a console in a booth. She went inside and located the code for Sector 15 Command in her file system.

Her fingers hesitated.

Thirty-seven days in the heat and dust. Thirty-seven days of waiting patiently next to the rotting corpses of her friends, her systems damaged, her long-distance voice silent.

Thirty-seven days of being utterly alone for the first time in her life.

Why didn't you come for me?

There was a knock on the outside of the booth. "I'm using this," she said.

"Come out of there," said a voice she didn't recognize. "Now."

She scanned and found six humans, all armed. They'd come quickly from the street and the back of the store.

She could fight, she could probably hurt them badly enough to escape, but what was the point?

Kay stepped out of the booth, hands raised.

They were going to kill her; she knew it with that cold, absolute certainty. There was no escape. Their leader, a man named Bolus, had ordered her tied her up in the back of the store with ropes and metal bonds generating electromagnetic fields to dampen her electricals. They'd been prepared.

Bolus sat on a chair in front of her. They'd kept her waiting for hours before he came back to see her. She saw only death when she looked at him. He was young, with beady, hate-filled eyes and a bushy beard worn in showy defiance of Sovene fashion and hygiene.

"So you're a spy," said Bolus. "Sovenes are coming back. They promised they wouldn't, but here you are."

"No," she said, her voice badly slurred from her bonds' interference. "I was part of a unit sent out before the evacuation. We were caught by a bomb."

Bolus laughed. "One of mine, I hope. Good! Dead Sovenes, everybody's happy. So what, you just waited? Like a good little drone? Ha! I bet you'll just sit there while we peel you apart."

"I have no technology you can use," said Kay. "My systems are integrated; they won't work without my brain."

"Oh, I don't care about that," said Bolus. "We'll take you apart because we can. And because it's all the *justice* we'll ever see from the Sovenes."

"Justice," repeated Kay dubiously.

"Yes, justice!" said Bolus, suddenly angry. "For Gorodan, and for Yellow Sands! There were children there! My *brother* was there."

Kay had been at Yellow Sands, not long after. She pictured the long field in her mind, and the blood flecks on the prison wall they hadn't quite been able to wash away.

But she also remembered such kindness. Soldiers giving kids the last of their rations, her unit taking in a family for a week, building schools and roads and sewers... she remembered that, too.

"It's... complicated," she said helplessly.

"Sure," said Bolus.

"You'd be just like us," said Kay, trying one last desperate tactic.

"I know," said Bolus grimly. "Like you said. Complicated." He opened the door, and his people filed in. The shopkeeper was among them.

"We're ready," said one.

"Good." Bolus turned back to Kay. "It'll be in the square out there." He jerked his head at the window. "It's no small thing to kill a Sovene Synthetic. We'll put your armor up around the village, so people know not to mess with me and mine."

There were nods all around.

"You'll serve a purpose," said a woman. "The provisional government is useless; criminal gangs and warlords are everywhere. When you left, you left anarchy. We need to be safe."

"I could keep you safe better if I was alive," slurred Kay.

"I doubt it," said Bolus fiercely. "And even if so, who cares? I'm the head man around here now, and what I say goes. You're gonna get dismantled. Is that death for you? Or are you already dead? Huh. Only the Sovenes would dig up the dead and make them fight."

The light was bright, worse thanks to the magnetic fields dampening her vision.

"You scared?" Bolus taunted, as they strapped her to a pole. "Mighty

Sovene! You scared?"

"Yes," said Kay truthfully, her voice disintegrating into static.

The crowd murmured as Bolus's people brought plasma cutters to take her apart, one slice at a time.

She tried to replay good memories. But they turned into bloody fields, stone prison walls, and so much else.

"I'm... sorry," she said to one of them.

He stepped back a pace, and looked at his companion.

"I can't do this," he said, shutting down the plasma cutter and dropping it. "Look at her, just sitting there..."

"Damn it!" said Bolus, picking up the plasma cutter. "It has to be done! We have to be strong! The Curvatene boys will come through here and kill everybody if we're not strong enough!" He tried to hand the cutter back to the man. "Do it. Make it quick and painless. Remember, it's just a machine. It doesn't care if it's alive or dead."

"I care," said Kay. The words were barely audible. Only the man and Bolus heard them.

Bolus sighed and raised the cutter himself. He switched it on, and it hummed menacingly to life.

But at that moment there was a thunderous blast and the roar of an engine, and Kay saw Jassalan's head over the sea of faces. She was riding in the back of the truck, manning a huge mounted gun. Payl was driving, and Liss and Yago leaned out the windows, rifles in hand. "Get back!" Jassalan hollered as the crowd parted. "Go on! Bolus, get away from her!"

"Well," said Bolus. "Always knew you'd turn back to the Sovenes in the end, Jassalan."

"They abandoned her," said Jassalan. "You can't just kill her in cold blood! She's done nothing to you."

"*She's got no blood!* And she's no innocent, you know that. The Sovenes are all guilty!"

Jassalan shook her head. "Get away from her, or I blow you to bits."

Bolus gave her a cocky grin. "Yeah?" He strode up to the vehicle, arms spread. "Go ahead."

The village took a collective breath.

Jassalan shrugged and blew him to bits.

"I think that's got it," said Liss, tightening a bolt and running a scanner over the new connection. "How's it feel?"

"Serviceable," said Kay.

Jassalan stood in the kitchen door, nodding. "Good work."

They'd scrounged the parts out of the village's salvage yard during the aftermath. Liss, who was some sort of mechanical genius, had managed to cobble together enough old electronics to mend Kay's broken long-distance communications equipment. It took weeks and she'd grumped the whole time, but by the time she was done she would wink at Kay when she thought no one else was looking.

When Kay tried to thank Jassalan for saving her, she only shrugged and said, "Payl likes you, she ran home to get us as soon as she found out what was going to happen. I couldn't just let them kill you."

Liss had pointed out wryly that she'd killed Bolus, and Jassalan sighed. "It's never simple," she said at last, her eyes heavy with something that might have been regret. The matter dropped.

"So, you're set," said Liss. "You can call off-planet. It's all connected back up. You can call for rescue, get off this dirtball."

"Though you don't have to," said Payl. "If you don't want."

Kay thought of the sequence that would open the channel. Payl's smile was tight. Jassalan looked away.

Kay pondered that sequence. She could go home. She could see the Army again, have a mission again.

She glanced at Payl, then at Jassalan. The Army hadn't come back for her.

But these people had.

"It's... not working," Kay lied. "I can't get through. Maybe it's not strong enough."

"Well," said Jassalan, not buying that for a second. "You'll just have to stay here until we fix it better."

There was a soft rustling sound on the roof, and Kay glanced outside. Big raindrops had begun to fall from the sky.

"Rain!" shouted Payl, running past. "Rain!"

Liss scrambled up and followed Payl outside.

Jassalan and Kay were left alone.

"I accessed the file," said Kay softly.

Jassalan held up her hand. "Don't tell me," she said. "I don't want to know."

"But—"

"No," said Jassalan, and her smile was genuine and warm. "You're welcome here no matter who you were. All right? Now... go help with the collectors, Kay. It's raining."

Kay ran outside to help Payl and Liss deploy the collectors. Kay felt each drop rain on the skin of her face and the metal of her arms.

"You brought the rain! You brought the rain!" whooped Payl, face lit up with joy.

And, for a fleeting moment, Kay was utterly certain that she had.

Contractual Obligation

James L. Cambias

BLUE SIX AND THE REST of the grunts power up to battle-ready at T-minus fourteen hours. They don't need much lead time before action; even if the squad's fully shut down it takes them less than ten minutes to get operational. No, the extra time isn't for the grunts, it's for the officer.

Captain Yamada's in the fridge. He's been in there since the space freighter left the last neutral station at L5, a hundred days ago. It takes three hours just to raise his body temperature to normal, another couple of hours for muscle stimulation. Releasing some fluids and taking in others. Cleaning off the outer layer. It's not until T-minus seven hours that Yamada steps through the pressure membrane into the embrace of his armor.

In battle dress, the officer looks almost like one of the grunts. They're a mixed bunch anyway. Blue One's a superheavy class, two metric tons of armor and power plant wrapped around a hypervelocity rail gun and a thousand-round magazine. Blue Two and Three are standard heavies, armed with autofire grenade launchers and weighing in at just over three hundred kilos each. Four and Five are low-profile scuttlers, only fifty kilos, with caseless submachine guns and extra limbs tipped with multitools. Blue Six is a point-defense specialist, with twin lasers and an elaborate sensor suite—which also makes it the electronic-warfare unit and primary communications node by default. All the grunts share a single distributed intelligence, but at any given time most of it's running on processors inside Blue Six.

When he's functional and suited up, Yamada runs through the list of mission parameters one last time. He toggles the rules of engagement settings from "WEAPONS FREE" to "HUMAN SAFE."

That gets the squad's attention. "That isn't in the contract, Captain."

"Which means I'm free to decide. I want to make this as bloodless as possible."

"Yes, Captain." The squad can do non-lethal. It means they can still shoot other robots, and that's the important thing. If you have to rely on human troops, you've lost the battle.

Six hours out, the freighter's eyes can see the target: Anfa Habitat. From the freighter's angle it looks like a dark flower against the Sun's disk. Anfa Habitat is a giant sphere a kilometer across, with six big solar panels stretching out from the equator. The docking hub's down at the "dark pole" of the sphere, with four docking tubes sticking out at right angles. Beyond the docking hub, a long boom stretches a hundred meters or so into the sphere's shadow, with big radiator fins running down each side and the backup power reactor at the far end. Anfa orbits the Sun sixty degrees ahead of Venus, so the radiators are glowing bright infrared as they dump the habitat's excess heat.

Anfa control takes over the freighter soon after—or at least Yamada allows them to think they have. The controllers inside Anfa do a good job. There's a hard braking burn to shift the freighter from its transfer orbit to match vectors with the habitat, and then some short burns and rotations to line up with the docking tube. There's no voice chatter from the controllers; according to the manifest, this is a load of humanitarian supplies.

Docking clamps thump together right at T-minus zero, and now it's time to move. Yamada pops the external cargo hatch—not the one connected to the docking tube—and the whole squad goes out onto the hull, moving fast. Blue One takes up a position behind the hatch to provide covering fire; Six joins it to act as spotter. The other four surge forward along the outside of the docking tube, followed by Yamada.

Having the officer out on the front line is part of the plan, but the squad thinks it's a bad idea. A battle's no place for humans. The captain could keep his fragile biological butt parked back in the relative safety of the freighter and stay in the loop by telepresence. But this job requires some diplomacy, and faceless killing machines are still getting the hang of that.

Blue Six scans the battlespace and picks out possible targets. The biggest danger is Anfa's main defense lasers, located at the tips of three of the solar panels. The lasers can vaporize one of the grunts with a single shot, which is why the squad is keeping the metal docking tube between themselves and the habitat. But Anfa might have free-flying drones with laser mirrors, so Six watches the sky for anything moving.

There! A small shape moving against the stars. It's dark, which puts it in the shadow of the habitat. Close, then. The squad's multiple eyes triangulate, and Blue One takes aim.

Yamada's orders are clear: no combat of any kind until he gives the word. Don't let the enemy know there's a battle going on until it's won. So Blue Six keeps watching the drone, pinging alerts at the officer to make sure he sees it too.

More targets! Four maintenance drones come scuttling along the docking tube from the hub.

"Engage engage engage!" Yamada orders. "Damn."

Before the captain has time to inhale again after speaking, Blue One hits the mirror drone with a chunk of depleted uranium going three kilometers per second, and Blue Two through Five each blow a maintenance bot to twinkling fragments. Six scans every surface in sight, looking for cameras and blinding them.

Now it's time to get fast. While the debris clouds are still expanding, the squad sprints up the tube to the docking hub. The officer must be juicing his sluggish biological nervous system with something, because he's only a second behind.

The maintenance drones came out of a hatch at the docking hub, where the four tubes meet. It's a typical membrane, but an armored door is swinging shut as they reach it. Blue One grabs the edge of the aluminum door, and for three long seconds there's a contest between the big bot and the motor in the door hinge, but sheer power wins out and the hatch jerks open again.

The team goes through the membrane faster than it can seal around them, and the habitat loses a couple of cubic meters of air before it regenerates. Six identifies and destroys more eyes on the inside walls. Two covers the hatch in case someone else comes at them from outside. The rest of the team launch themselves across the inside of the docking hub to secure the connection to the habitat.

Another metal hatch has already sealed off that direction, but that's perfectly fine with the squad. If they can't get into the main habitat, nothing can come out, either. One and Three cover that approach. Yamada and the two smallest team members head for the thick conduit that runs through the center of the docking hub, connecting the habitat to the radiator fin beyond. Four and Five remove the casing and expose the heavily insulated pipes inside. Two of the pipes are dazzlingly hot on infrared, even inside layers of fiberglass and foil.

Four and Five install the squad's insurance policy: modest demolition charges, just powerful enough to sever the coolant lines. All the pipes get two, including the backups. Now if the officer says a particular command—or if his suit stops sending a particular code series to the bombs—they'll go off, and Anfa Habitat won't have any way to shed waste heat. Thirteen thousand people will slowly cook in the relentless fury of the Sun.

The squad has downloads of Anfa's emergency plans. It'll be a race between work drones and thermodynamics. The squad estimates at least ten percent of the human inhabitants will die, and there's a small but non-trivial chance that all of them will.

The Anfa forces have assembled outside. A trio of drones dive in through the membrane at the same instant that a shaped charge turns the center of the steel hatch into a jet of molten metal that hits Blue Three right in the ammunition magazine. Some of the grenades in Three's magazine cook off, blowing the bot apart.

For a moment the squad becomes a group of autonomous individuals while the group AI reconfigures itself. When it does, the squad can't plan quite as far ahead and its guesses are a little less precise.

Blue One fires a hail of depleted uranium through the space where Three had been standing, shredding whatever's on the other side of the hatch. Six blinds the drones coming in the other way, and Two finishes them off with sticky grenades.

Captain Yamada's broadcasting on all the voice channels. "Anfa, I will destroy your cooling system if you don't stand down at once!"

There's a pause, and then a human voice comes over one of the channels. "All right. We'll cease fire."

"Understood," says Yamada, though the squad's still ready to slag anything that tries to get into the hub. "I'm a licensed contractor working for the Deimos Community. This is a legal military operation. All I want is one person. Give me Dr. Julius Wassel. I have orders to remove him from this habitat. He will not be harmed."

There's a pause of about a minute. "We can't let you take Dr. Wassel against his will."

"I'm not leaving without him."

"Even if you do sabotage the radiator, you won't get away from Anfa alive," the other human points out.

"I'd rather end this with no loss of life at all," says Yamada. "Give me Wassel, I'll leave, and nobody gets hurt."

"We can't just hand him over," says the voice. "Dr. Wassel is a citizen and a shareholder. He's got rights."

"How about you let me talk to him directly?"

There's a long delay, and then a new voice comes on. "This is Julius Wassel speaking. Are you really prepared to commit mass murder?"

"I was hired to do a job, Dr. Wassel," says Yamada. "I'm trying to use minimum force to get it done. This is a legal military operation. Would you rather my squad tried to fight through the habitat to find you? If you come along with me I promise you will not be harmed."

"Where do you plan to take me?"

"I can't reveal that. But you'll be treated extremely well. My employers think your research is very important, and they want to help you continue your work. I'm sure you'll have more resources than you do here."

"I came to Anfa to get away from all that," says Wassel. "Both sides in this ridiculous war are repulsive to me. Ideological fanatics fighting amoral exploiters, with mercenaries doing the dirty work."

"I'm just a contractor," says Yamada. "Look, I know they've probably asked you to keep me talking while they fab up more weapons, so I'm afraid I have to cut this short. I'm starting a ten-minute timer on my bombs now. If Dr. Wassel comes down here before they go off, I'll shut them off and leave in peace."

The captain cuts the link and rearranges the squad. The two open hatches are sealed only by pressure membranes, and just about anything could punch through that. He puts Four and Five to work pulling up wall and floor panels to obstruct any line of sight through the hatches. Six watches the door into space, while the other two cover the link to the main habitat.

The timer ticks down to five minutes, then four, then three. The squad's ability to predict human behavior is limited, but elementary game theory suggests that once the coolant lines are severed and the habitat's temperature starts to rise, there's absolutely nothing to prevent Anfa's lasers from vaporizing the captain and the grunts. That's a known risk.

The count's at one minute forty seconds when there's a knock on the partition blocking the hatchway into the main habitat. Yamada sends Four to have a peek. Two humans in skinsuits are floating just this side of the membrane.

"I only want Dr. Wassel," says Yamada.

"Pando, it's me. Gradara," says one of the humans.

For a moment the officer's bio readings go nuts, and the squad considers the possibility the enemy has managed to hit him with some kind of biochemical agent. But before the squad can shift into autonomous mode he drops back within normal parameters.

"Come in, both of you," says the captain. He halts the timer.

The squad lets them pass the partition, and Six looks inside both of them with backscatter X-rays and sound pulses. You can learn a lot about someone that way. Wassel's a male human, with too much abdominal fat and an artificial pancreas. Gradara's a female with unusual muscle density; all the bones in one leg plus a forearm and some ribs are carbon-fiber rebuilds. Her bio readings are a lot less elevated than Wassel's.

"I thought you were dead," says Yamada.

"I wanted a new start. There were people I didn't want following me," she says.

"What are you doing here?"

"I live here, Pando. I'm a shareholder and a citizen. Back when Earth and Deimos started this epic pissing contest I decided to get as far away from the war zone as I could. Anfa looked like a good place. Low strategic value, underpopulated—or at least it was when I got here. Now we've got more people than the place was built to support. Thirteen thousand people will cook if you set off those charges."

The officer is silent for nearly a second. Then, "What about you, Dr. Wassel? Are you ready to leave?"

"If I have no alternative," says Wassel.

"See?" Captain Yamada tells the woman called Gradara. "He's perfectly willing. Nobody has to get hurt."

"I've got a counter-offer," says Gradara. "Stay here. Anfa can buy out your contract."

Yamada takes a couple of seconds to answer. "What would I do here? I'm a soldier."

"There may be other raids. Obviously we need better defenses. You could help set them up."

"Are you part of the deal?"

"No promises, Pando."

Just then the space freighter's antenna picks up a transmission and bounces it to the squad. The message is from Deimos, and the authentications check out. The group mind judges it significant and passes it along to the officer. Captain Yamada spends ten seconds reading it, and his bio readings go nuts again for a couple of seconds.

"KINETIC WARHEAD STRIKE ON YOUR POSITION TIME ON TARGET 1 HOUR."

Evidently the owners back inside Deimos have decided to get serious. Maybe Wassel's important enough to be worth denying to anyone else. Or maybe Anfa's pissed them off some other way. It doesn't affect the tactical situation, so the squad doesn't waste any more time thinking about it.

Yamada seems very concerned, though. He asks the woman, "Does Anfa have any other spacecraft? Anything with interplanetary range?"

"We used to have a couple of interplanetary shuttles, but Earth grabbed one and blew up the other. Why?"

"I want you to come with me," he says.

"And what will you blow up if I refuse?"

"No demands. I want you to come with me. When we were together, back on Luna—were you happy?"

"I was very happy," she says. "But I was tired of being a gun for hire. I was ready to quit. And you weren't."

"You never said anything."

"I didn't need to. I could see it. You weren't ready then, and look at you now: you're a successful contractor—are you ready to give it up now? Shut down your squad, disarm the bombs and stay here?"

"No," says Yamada. He switches to a private channel, but the squad can still hear his end over the command link.

"Can you fab up a hibernation chamber? You can ride in that." Pause. "It's not safe for you to stay here. I can't tell you why." Pause. "You need to leave *now*. Come with me."

He switches back to the squad. "What's the status on our vehicle? Can we make it to Deimos with an extra human on board?"

"No," says the squad. "Mission profile is zero-margin. There's only enough life support consumables to get you and Wassel to Deimos."

"Can my suit keep me in stasis long enough to reach Deimos?"

"No. It's more than seven months in transit. Your suit's only rated for sixty hours."

"What if we hook my suit up to the ship's systems?"

"Daily failure probability tops fifty percent in less than a month."

Yamada switches back to his private link with Gradara. "You need to get a hibernation chamber down here in half an hour, and enough consumables for seven months." The squad can't hear her answer, but Yamada's stress levels rise even higher. "They must have one somewhere! In the hospital, maybe?"

Fifty minutes left.

Wassel speaks up again. "Captain Yamada, I'm not sure what's going on. Would you rather take Ms. Gradara with you instead of me?"

"No! I have to get you to Deimos. That's the mission. I'm sorry, Doctor, but you're coming no matter what. I'm just trying to find a way to bring her as well."

"Are you collecting Anfa shareholders?"

Yamada ignores him and switches back to the link with the squad. "Can the spacecraft reach any inhabited body or habitat with three humans aboard?"

After a moment's calculation the squad replies, "Adding another hibernation unit increases the mass too much to reach Deimos. The best trajectory puts us at the Earth leading Trojan point. That requires a gravity assist from Venus and takes more than two years. Note that the leading Trojan habitats are hostile, and may not exist by the time we reach them. That would constitute a mission failure."

"Is there any way we can get off this hab with three people?"

"Captain, that's outside the mission parameters. You're supposed to acquire Dr. Wassel and evacuate. Ms. Gradara isn't part of the plan."

"I'm not leaving Gradara here. Consider the plan amended."

Captain Yamada's stress levels are still rising. He talks to the woman again, and he forgets to encrypt the connection. "You've got to make them fab you a hibernation unit. We need it in—shit, less than forty-five minutes."

"Pando, I've got a good life here. I don't want to come with you."

"You've got to come! This place is going to be a cloud of debris in less than an hour."

That's a breach of operational security, and Blue Six starts area jamming to keep Gradara and Wassel from communicating with anyone outside the docking hub.

"You can't do that!" says Wassel.

"It's not my decision. The kill vehicles are already inbound and I don't have any way to stop them. I'm trying to get the three of us out of here alive. Do either of you have any ideas?"

Gradara isn't saying anything. She's trying to link up with the station network, but Six isn't going to let that happen.

"Captain, you're no longer following the mission plan. You're showing signs of psychological incapacity," the squad tells Yamada.

"I'm fine!" Yamada takes a deep breath and tells his armor to hit him with a dose of tranquilizer. "Okay, here's what we're going to do. We're going to take these two humans back to the spacecraft and put them in the hibernation units. I'll ride in my suit; I'll take the risk of failure. Now let's get going!"

The squad goes into action. The group AI invokes medical override and orders Yamada's armor to knock him out with a sedative. Four and Five grab Wassel and head for the exit. Blue One covers them.

The officer is clearly not fit for command.

One decision left to make. Normally it would be simple, but there are conflicting orders involved, and the squad wants to comply with Yamada's last instructions if possible. "Ms. Gradara, in your opinion will Captain Yamada suffer any permanent psychological impairment as a result of your death?"

She looks right at Three, which is still covering her with a grenade launcher, then at Yamada floating unconscious in his armor. A couple of seconds go by before she answers. "Yes," she says. "I don't think he'll get over it." Her pulse and respiration are steady.

Three and Six escort her to the spacecraft and help her into the hibernation unit. They leave Yamada behind, floating unconscious in his armor. The squad dumps all of its memories into the spacecraft; then the bots shut down for good. Undocking is perfectly smooth, and nobody gets lasered. The spacecraft is a thousand kilometers away when the kill vehicles hit. Thirteen thousand bodies spill into vacuum.

A successful mission, under the terms of the contract.

Gradara's a little muzzy from the hibernation drugs kicking in when she contacts the squad before going down for a seven-month nap. "Hey, you guys looking for a new officer? I used to be pretty good."

"Are there any emotional or psychological issues which might impair your effectiveness?"

"No," she says. "Not anymore."

The Wasp Keepers

Mark Jacobsen

HAMZA HAD JUST FINISHED PUMPING gas into a fruit truck when he jerked upright and swatted the back of his neck with one palm. He whirled around, eyes bulging, searching frantically for his Wasp before his eyes rolled up into his head and he collapsed sideways onto the hot pavement. The fruit truck was already pulling away. The driver didn't stop.

Um Hamza didn't see it happen, but that was how Tariq described it through his breathless sobs, the screen door still banging on its hinges behind him. She had been sitting at her desk composing an email on her phone. When Tariq finished, he threw his arms around her and cried into her neck like a child. Um Hamza set the phone down carefully and sat and stared into the distance, heart beating savagely.

She had lived this moment so many times in her nightmares, both sleeping and waking. How could she not? Even without war, there were so many ways it could come: a neighbor backing out of a driveway, an aspirated grape, a toppled bookcase, a tangled bed sheet, an electrical outlet, a few centimeters of water in an unattended bath.

For Um Hamza, it was immeasurably worse. There were government tanks, air strikes, roadside bombs, poison gas, cruise missiles, collapsing buildings, malnourishment, disease, kidnappings, Farsi-speaking trainers with rocket launchers and machine guns. And of course, there were the masked militiamen who had executed her brother, burned their home, and driven them across the Jordanian border into the Za'atri refugee camp. So when she'd held that warm bundle for the first time in the camp clinic and looked into her son's wrinkled pink face, all she could think about was his death. For two weeks, depression kept her in bed. Her mother changed Hamza's diapers, rocked him, played with him and brought him to her for mechanical feedings. Hamza's seventeenth birthday was like a sentencing. When the card arrived from the Syrian Transitional Authority, she sobbed for hours. It still sat on her desk, a wretched, superstitious totem that she was terrified to destroy. Birthday cake and candles on one side; on the other, a happy, smiling, cartoon bee. FOR YOUR PROTECTION, the card said in Arabic above a QR code and an explanation of "What You Need to Know." When the Wasp itself buzzed into the olive grove a few days later, she watched it for hours, shaking feverishly. For weeks she wouldn't let Hamza outdoors without her. She even walked him down to the gas station and back, to his burning shame, their two Wasps buzzing along in trail. It was inevitable, she knew. And she was right.

She put an arm around Tariq's shoulders and walked outside with him. Her Wasp sat on a sunny spot of the porch railing, recharging. When it saw her it fluttered skyward, an obscene little blot against the blue sky.

As they walked the kilometer down to the gas station, she could see the cars pulling off the highway, the men running.

When she came around from the back of the gas station, she saw her husband kneeling on the pavement, muttering to God and rocking their limp boy in his arms. A ring of bystanders stood around them, whispering and praying. Uncle Fouad stood among them, red-faced, yelling into his cell-phone. Something about a fruit truck.

The Wasp lay on the ground, broken, twitching. Hamza must have caught it with his final slap. A machine, gray and small, muscle wire supporting insectile wings that were solar cells, coiled around a microprocessor and communications link and of course the toxin pouch and stinger. She raised a foot to grind it beneath her heel, but then considered how her own Wasp might react and gently placed her foot back on the ground.

She looked back to Hamza. Her beautiful, sweet boy, undiminished by seventeen years of poverty and war. Her boy, who had spent his summer turning wrenches and changing spark plugs with his father and grandfather in the auto shop. Who went door-to-door each Ramadan, on his own initiative, collecting donations for the Islamic Relief Mission. Who once sobbed with guilt when he shot a stray cat with a pellet gun, back when the possession of such things was not a death sentence. Dear, sweet Hamza.

She realized there was a separate group crowding around the doors of the convenience store on the far side of the pumps. She blindly grabbed at Uncle Fouad's arm. He pulled away from the cell phone for a moment.

She pointed at the store. "What...?"

"It's your father. They got him too. I'm sorry."

Her legs gave out, and she sank to the pavement beside her husband. She had held herself together only because she had rehearsed this dreaded theater so many times in her mind's eye, but this was a blow she had not seen coming.

She touched Hamza's cold face and began to scream.

The police were afraid to approach the bodies, as this was an Occupation strike. There was no telling what might provoke another Wasp attack. They masked their fear and incompetence by blowing whistles and barking orders and making half-hearted efforts to clear out the spectators who were shooting video with their mobiles or AR glasses. One officer questioned witnesses, but his questions followed no logical path and he didn't bother to write down the answers. No, sir, he didn't do anything threatening. He was pumping gas. Yes, *gas*. He was filling up a fruit truck.

Ten minutes after the police came, Uncle Fouad's phone rang. He listened without speaking and hung up. He said, "They took out the fruit truck about five kilometers north of here. Three people."

A murmur passed through the crowd. Another piece in the puzzle. Above them, their Wasps whirled and danced, glimpsing faces, recording their expressions and judging their body language.

An entourage from the mosque arrived in a rusting blue van. The crowd parted as Hajj Omar disembarked, leaning on a wooden crutch to compensate for the leg he had lost in Homs. A scar divided the right side of his face from top to bottom, running clean through a cloudy gray eye. The crowd fell silent before this presence. He recited the Fatiha and performed the final rites for Hamza and Abu Khalid, and then delivered a sermon which became a blistering tirade against the Syrian Transitional Authority and the Occupation.

Um Hamza left before he was finished. She collapsed into bed and cried until sleep took her.

She woke after sunset, when Abu Hamza climbed into bed and touched her shoulder. She turned brusquely away from him, but he started to cry. Ashamed, she rolled over to touch him. It was dreary sex, sad and distant, a feeble echo of what their marriage had once been. Afterwards they held each other, but even that tenderness lacked intimacy. It was like two strangers holding hands as their crippled plane careened to the earth.

She woke to sunlight and quiet. The entire household was still asleep. She brewed a cup of tea, then went outside to pluck some fresh mint from the garden. She marveled at the serenity of the still-waking world. The olive trees were perfection itself: rows of them standing like sentinels, unmoved by even the faintest of breezes. A single black bird flapped across the sky.

She sat beneath an olive tree and leaned up against the trunk and sipped her tea. This is all she had ever wanted, this moment stretched into a lifetime. Cool mornings and olive trees and silence.

Her Wasp took up station over her.

"Good morning," she said in English.

The Wasp gave no indication it had heard, but of course it had. It heard everything. Saw everything. Even smelled everything. All that data was aggregated and beamed to the United States and Canada and God knew where else, where it was filtered and analyzed and processed in vast server farms. Intelligent algorithms crunched away, drawing connections, matching words and behavior to pattern libraries, then sent their conclusions before hordes of young analysts sitting in the blue wash of computer screens. Perfect seeing. Perfect knowledge. And, when the wrong two patterns overlapped, perfect death.

He'd been pumping gas. What kind of pattern was that?

She went inside and found a pack of cigarettes in her husband's jacket. She returned to her shaded spot under the tree and lit up. She smoked three cigarettes while she cruised the social networks on her phone, trying to forget, procrastinating. She'd been a queen in that world, once, back in the heady days when the revolution was young and the future was theirs for the making.

She had been a true believer. She marched with the protestors and shot video and live-tweeted massacres and built a following of more than fifteen thousand people. She made friends with activists and journalists and Middle East experts across the world. When the regime met their protests with war, she redoubled her efforts. And then, when the artillery barrages and the gunmen came to her village and they fled across the border to the Za'atri camp, she blogged everything.

She won prizes. Journalists sought her in person. She struck up an online friendship with a hacker in the Free Syrian Army, and when they discovered weeks later that they were both in the Za'atri camp, the future was written. The pregnancy came first, then a hasty marriage. A few years earlier this would have destroyed her family, but in Za'atri honor and shame were relics. They had never imagined the war would rage for nearly two decades. Never imagined it would end like this, in this frozen horror that was somehow worse than all that had come before. All that history had ground her down to almost nothing.

Her writing output was a lethargic trickle these days, and she was mostly forgotten. Mostly, but not entirely. She still knew people.

She started to compose an email.

It was around five o'clock that evening when Tariq came running to tell her that Wasp Keepers were approaching on the highway. She sent a text to Abu Hamza and Uncle Fouad, who were down at the gas station working, and then went to the bathroom to wash her face and reapply her makeup. When she was finished, she put on her hijab and went out to the porch. The convoy had just turned off the highway. A cluster of dusty children watched mutely from the side of the road, one of them holding a soccer ball under his arm.

The convoy consisted of a mine-resistant Army truck and a silver BMW surrounded by a swarm of Wasps. A squat steamroller the size of a Smart Car preceded the vehicles, feeling for IEDs buried in the road.

There were four soldiers, enveloped in so much armor and gear that the only things recognizably human about them were the square jaws exposed beneath the black goggles. When the first three dismounted, they went right past her and took up positions on the road. The fourth was a captain.

The captain nodded at her, then looked expectantly back to the BMW.

The sole occupant of the car was a Syrian man about her father's age, dressed in a striped collared shirt and a dusty blue sport coat. AR glasses enveloped his face. He did not immediately get out of the car. His window was rolled down, and Um Hamza could hear that he was on a call, negotiating a price. He drummed one hand on the steering wheel and gesticulated with the other. He looked familiar, so while they all waited, Um Hamza discreetly snapped a photo of him and ran a search. The match was instant. The district police chief.

When he was finally finished, he got out of the car and both he and the captain came forward.

"As-salaam aleykum," the captain said. He raised his goggles and there was a human face beneath, handsome and blonde and blue-eyed. "Ana kteer aasif likhsarit ibnik wa abooki."

Um Hamza was impressed that this soldier had learned enough Arabic to say that. She also thought that if he offered any more sympathy for her loss, she would rip out his tongue and shove it down his throat.

The captain said that it would be best to visit the scene of the strike, so they walked down to the gas station, their Wasps a snarled cloud above them. The captain took off his helmet as they walked, a gesture Um

Hamza knew was calculated to demonstrate trust, as if the mere act of exposing his sunburned scalp could somehow atone for the death of her boy and her father. By the time they reached the gas station they were pale with dust and the sweat ran down their backs. The captain introduced himself to Abu Hamza and Uncle Fouad, and then they all sat in plastic chairs in the customer service area adjacent to the auto shop while Tariq served Arabic coffee. When they were finished, he stacked the cups and sat down opposite the captain, glaring murderously at him. Um Hamza's sister-in-law Noor arrived shortly after with a fruit tray and a bowl of dates. Um Hamza took the plate from her and offered it to the captain, and kept insisting until he finally took a single slice of apple. The police chief waved at her dismissively and lit up a cigarette.

"Why did you come?" Um Hamza asked while Noor poured a round of tea.

"You have some friends who really care about you," everyone heard in a mechanical Arabic dialect. The captain subvocalized in English as a device on his chest translated.

"For God's sake, turn that thing off," Um Hamza said. "Which one was it?"

The captain shrugged and touched the device. In English he said, "Logan Keesler ran a story. It got noticed in Washington."

Um Hamza translated for her family. "So they sent you to pacify me?"

"I just came to talk," he said. His eyes were bloodshot and distant. He looked like he hadn't slept in days. "You have the right to know why your son was targeted."

"He was seventeen," Um Hamza said.

The captain opened a camouflage bag at his side and handed them each a pair of AR glasses. Everyone turned them over in their hands suspiciously before putting them on. The captain said, "We know your family has been in the auto service industry for a long time. A whole chain of gas stations and auto shops before the war, right? You lost everything at the start of the war, but after three years in Za'atri, the three brothers returned home and got back into the business. It's pretty remarkable you were able to finance all this."

Um Hamza translated. Fouad glared at the captain.

The captain rose and stepped outside to survey the gas station. He said, "You made some interesting friends."

They rose to join him so they could see what he was looking at.

A row of beat-up pickup trucks and vans was parked in front of the little masjid where customers could pray during gas stops. Gathered outside the door was a crowd of grim, thickly bearded Salafists toting handguns and AK-47s. The imagery was perfectly positioned and scaled, but it was black and white and heavily pixilated. While she watched, a younger clone of Uncle Fouad appeared and embraced one of the Islamists. They exchanged kisses on their cheeks.

"They were fighting the regime," Fouad said in Arabic. "They just came to pray."

"Understandable," the captain said without missing a beat. He was probably still receiving machine translations. "But you spent hours with them. And they came a lot. Even after you knew they were pledged to al-Qa'eda, even after they toppled the regime and created their own government and you saw what they were capable of. Your brother Abu Khalid led prayers for them. He sat for hours with them teaching them about Islam. I don't think it's an exaggeration to say he was a spiritual mentor of sorts."

"He taught anybody who would listen," Um Hamza protested. "He thought they were misguided, maybe not even Muslim, but he thought the answer to that was more Islam, more truth."

"And that's why he smuggled weapons for them?"

Um Hamza broke into tears. The captain knew so much, he knew everything, and yet he understood nothing. It was all *wrong*, it was all cameras and robots and a string of connected dots that added up to something different from the wretched story they had lived.

She remembered when the Islamists first turned up at their gas station. Uncle Fouad, as it turned out, had worked some kind of deal with a mujahideen group in the Za'atri camp. They'd needed to smuggle weapons and ammunition into Syria, which meant they needed someone who knew vehicles and logistics. Fouad had acquired startup capital, bought the gas station, and used his contacts on both side of the border to build up a logistics network to import auto parts into Syria. Auto parts, that is, with a few bonus packages in the mix.

It had seemed a small enough thing, the kind of shadow bargaining on which survival depended in those violent days, but that deal took on a life of its own. The gas station got a reputation. Anti-regime fighters converged there, both the moderate types who'd been trained by the Americans in Jordan and the sneering Salafists who were just as likely to kill insufficiently pious Sunnis as they were regime soldiers. At first they negotiated business deals. Then they asked favors. Then they made demands. Uncle Fouad said no precisely one time. That experiment ended with Uncle Hatim, the third brother, dead in a ditch after torture by power drill.

That was the partnership Um Hamza remembered. Angry, bearded men. Guns. Terror. Extortion. But the captain walked them through his own narrative of these events, which unfolded before their eyes in a hurricane of light and color, the quality of the visuals improving sharply as the years raced by. Here was a full-service gas station that was a virtual safe house for terrorists and a key node in an arms smuggling ring. That's what the Wasps saw. What the fusion centers assessed. Seventeen years of fear, condensed into one storyline, missing context and everything that comprised the normal fabric of their lives. Yes, they'd made terrible compromises, but hadn't everyone? What choice did they have?

"But Hamza had nothing to do with this," Um Hamza said.

"Three months ago your son took possession of an SA-14, an advanced MANPAD for shooting down airplanes. He was to hold it for safekeeping. He stashed it right there, in the back of your parts storeroom."

Fouad swore in Arabic and wiped his face with one hand.

The transaction unfolded before their eyes, a living recreation of the past. An old gray Mazda pulling up to the pump. Hamza leaning in the window and talking to the driver. The driver extending a wad of bills. Hamza looking around, then signaling the driver to pull into the auto shop. The visuals were flawless. Um Hamza fought the urge to run to him, to embrace him, to plead with him to stop.

"He just wanted money," Um Hamza said, the tears running down her cheeks now. "He probably didn't even know what it was."

"He knew. Later he showed Tariq."

Um Hamza shot a look at Tariq, who shook his head violently. He was crying.

"Yesterday, a customer arrived to claim the package," the captain said.

Here came the fruit truck, rumbling up to the gas pumps belching greasy black smoke. Hamza went to meet it, oblivious to the fact that he had only minutes to live.

The captain said, "It was an active plot. The Islamists intended to use the weapon a few hours later, when the Syrian president returned from Paris. The Transitional Authority acted."

The captain slowly took off his glasses and tucked them carefully in the bag, as if sobered by the tragedy of what he had just explained. "I am genuinely sorry for the loss of your loved ones, but you brought this on yourselves. This is the life you raised Hamza into. When he came of age, he made some terrible choices of his own."

"You know nothing about him!"

"On the contrary, we know everything about him."

"Do you have any idea what it's like?" Um Hamza cried.

"What?"

"War."

"I know about war."

"No, that's not what I mean. Not what you're doing. I mean war. The things you have to do. The choices you have to make. The consequences if you don't. The fear." She wiped her eyes. "You don't have any idea what I'm talking about."

The captain frowned and looked out at the horizon for a long time, as if lost in some terrible memory. Despite all his gear, armor, and the cloud of Wasps ready to make war on his behalf, he looked exhausted beyond his years, even a little fragile. Um Hamza wondered how many times he had had this conversation.

"Just once," he said softly, still looking to the sunburnt horizon, "I want to find one Syrian who is grateful for what we've done for this country. What we've sacrificed, the friends we've lost. You've been at war almost as long as I've been alive, and we've stopped the cycle. Do you realize how incredible that is?"

"You killed my father and my son."

"They chose to fight," the captain said, shrugging. "I don't get it. I wish someone could explain it to me. How many more decades of war do you want?"

"We want to be free," said Abu Hamza.

"You are free, as long as you don't fight. No one dies unless he chooses to. There's no more strategic bombing, no more ground occupation, no more drone strikes, no more collateral damage. It's just...awareness. Knowledge. Insurgency is impossible. We've freed you from violence, given you the best chance in years for a peaceful new future. I don't understand why you can't accept that."

Peace? she thought, looking at the police chief, who had wandered off and was negotiating some new deal on his expensive imported AR headset. *This is peace?*

"I am sorry for your loss," the captain said "This was a needless tragedy. I hope you'll think long and hard about the choices that lie ahead. You still have one son. I pray to God that you will choose a future of peace, *in sha' Allah.*"

The captain put on his helmet and nodded to the police chief that it was time to leave.

"Thank you for the tea," he said.

That night they sat on the patio, drinking coffee and smoking sullenly. Their Wasps hovered above them in the warm orb cast by the porch light. It would have been safer to stay inside, but it was a pleasant night and they refused to be intimidated. There was something thrilling about sitting in front of those watchful eyes, putting their hatred on open display. In a world where resistance was impossible, even talking was an act of courage.

"That police chief," Fouad said between angry puffs on the nargeelah. "That fucking BMW."

He was drunk. Um Hamza didn't know when or how he'd achieved that feat, as he never drank in front of the family, but he'd done a thorough job of it.

"You know him?" Um Hamza asked.

"Yeah, I know him," Fouad said, the smoke pouring forth from his lips, as if he was trying to excise the very memory of the police chief from his body. "You two haven't asked the question, but I know you're dying to. Why the hell is it Fouad that's sitting here smoking and drinking instead of your father?"

It was true. She had wondered exactly that. Her father had been a simple man, kind and pious and respectable, without a hint of guile. Fouad was the shrewd empire builder who had turned an auto parts supply chain into a profitable arms smuggling network.

"About six months ago, that police chief came by the gas station. The Occupation was sharing all its intel with him. He knew everything. You know why he came by? He wanted a cut. To keep quiet. I told him no."

Fouad started to laugh, and swung his head from side to side in exaggerated, drunken disbelief.

"Son a bitch knew how to pay me back," he said. He raised his coffee cup. "Long live the peaceful new Syria."

Um Hamza knocked gently on the boys' door. When she heard nothing, she turned the knob. She stood in the doorway, the light behind her illuminating the shape of Tariq asleep in one bed and the tangled, empty sheets on the other. She studied the sheets, marveling at them. Exactly as Hamza had left them when he rose from bed yesterday.

She knelt beside her living son. He was so different from his brother. Even with all that had happened, Hamza had a natural sweetness to him, a legacy of his grandfather. He loved God. But Tariq hated, and for him life itself was a war. That manifested itself in everything. The rage. The arguments. He often came home bruised and bloody, and refused to say where he had been or what had happened. At least twice, he had sent other boys to the hospital. He needed violence the way he needed air.

Sleep effaced all that, wound the clock back to a time before the war had damaged him. Amazing that her child still lurked in there, after all that he had suffered. It wasn't his fault, being the way he was. He was a good boy, a strong boy who in a better life would have gone on to do such great things. But here...

In three years they would receive another birthday card, and another Wasp would find its way into their olive grove. One more node would appear in the Occupation's vast Syrian intelligence matrix. When that happened, Tariq would die. It might be two days or it might be two years, but the boy who couldn't help fighting in the streets would most certainly fight the Occupation.

If the Occupation did not end, Tariq would die. But it wouldn't end. It couldn't. The least relaxation of control would mean chaos.

She thought back to the captain's words. The Wasp Keepers had ended almost two decades of war. It was nothing short of a miracle, unprecedented in history. Perfect knowledge. Perfect killing. War that was as intimate as a friend sitting next to you, a friend that would protect you from all harm but would also kill you with a kiss if you let slip any hint of treason.

It was hatefully, intolerably perfect.

And yet there were no winners, not even the Occupation. The captain had understood that. He was exhausted and embittered by a war that, for all his impressive ability to control, had not delivered victory. The things that mattered most were still beyond their reach.

If they could not win, that meant they could still lose. The thought electrified her. After that revelation, everything fell into place.

She kissed Tariq on the head. Maybe she could yet save his life.

There was one thing she could still do. One choice they could all make. It was the single choice that eluded the Occupation's control, and that terrified them.

The rest of the night passed like a dream. For the first time since childhood, she was free. She went to her husband and gave herself to him, not because he was entitled to it but because she chose to. For a few moments she felt something of what she'd once known with this talented young revolutionary in the Za'atri camp. Afterward, while he slept, she wrote letters. Longhand. Beyond the reach of the Occupation. She left them trifolded on her desk, the names written on the back in elegant Arabic calligraphy.

After that she sat outside beneath her olive tree. It was still, and silent, and the stars wheeled freely in the sky as if there had never been a war and war was something altogether inconceivable. The peace she had always wanted. She recalled memories of Hamza, and of Tariq, and of her husband before the war had changed him. Of her father, leading prayers in the gas station masjid for poor refugees with their battered cars, limping their way northward again after the first lull in the fighting.

She sat beneath the tree until the sky began to lighten in the east, and the first cars appeared down on the highway. Then she rose on stiff joints and brushed herself off. One leg had fallen asleep. She hobbled over to the porch, shaking the leg awake again. She had composed the email to Logan Keesler earlier in the night. She sent it now, then propped the phone up on the railing and started a video recording.

She said a few words into the camera. Then she smiled and turned.

Her Wasp stared down at her, a motionless black smear in the sky. The other family Wasps were perched on the railing, charging in the morning sun. Stupid, mindless things. They knew everything and they knew nothing.

She reached into the folds of her robe and withdrew the cigarette lighter and the can of hairspray. With one flick of her wrist, her Wasp was a burning point of brightness in the sheet of flame.

It hadn't yet hit the ground when the other Wasps converged on her. She felt the hot pricks of the stingers, and a moment later the olive grove spun sideways.

Non-Standard Deviation

Richard Dansky

COLONEL TALBOT SAID, "SHOW ME," and so eventually they did. That was the point of having Talbot there, after all: showing him, so he could do something about it. Talbot was the guy who got sent in when things had gone wrong, with a mandate to make chicken salad out of whatever chicken shit was available, and never mind the collateral damage he might inflict in the process. If Colonel Talbot was coming on-site, then you'd fucked up, and the unfucking was not likely to be pleasant. There was a small team assigned to meet with Talbot, a football huddle's worth of techs and PR specialists and management types, all of whom figured the bigger the crowd, the less likely Talbot was to finger them individually for the project's challenges. They'd introduced themselves, offered coffee and a tour, and generally tried to ingratiate themselves. It took maybe fifteen minutes for Talbot to shed the PR types, another five for management, and then it was just him and the techs, and he could get to work.

They led him to the immersion chamber, which was down a nondescript hallway painted a disinterested shade of beige.

"Control room?" Talbot asked as they came to a secured door guarded by a keypad. One of the civilian contractors who'd managed to stick, a bearded beanpole in jeans and mildly obscene T-shirt, nodded. "The problem's not on that end. All the systems are green, we've run the diagnostics a dozen times—"

The colonel held up a hand, and the contractor stopped talking, because that's what smart contractors did at moments like that. "I don't want to see the control room," Talbot said. "I want you to strap me in."

"Sir." The head of the entourage, a captain whose nametag read ROSALES, stepped in front of the contractor, perhaps protectively. "Are you sure that's a good idea? We can have one of the staff go in for you, and you can tap into his feed. Much safer that way, and you'll get a more objective look at the data."

Talbot looked at her. "Captain. We have a system here that cost nearly half a billion dollars to make and maintain. It was designed to do one thing. It has stopped doing that thing for reasons that no one here—" and he looked from contractor to soldier to contractor, and all of them looked at the floor or the ceiling or something else that wasn't the colonel, "I can explain. Now, you have two choices. You can strap me in and let me take a look so I can try to figure out what the problem is, or I can stop right here, make one phone call, and turn this whole thing over to the boys at NATICK, who'll be happy to tear it apart and get you all reassigned." He looked around again. "I would prefer not to make that phone call."

"This way, sir." Rosales was all business. She turned and led the procession, the colonel surrounded by a nattering cloud of contractors who simultaneously tried to prepare him for what he was getting into and undercut the advice the other contractors were giving. Rosales ignored them, as did Talbot, and went down a small corridor that ended at a set of double doors. Above those doors was a sign with clean block lettering that read PROJECT VEER and a logo that looked as if it had been created in the early 1980s. Talbot cocked his head wordlessly. Rosales gave a small shrug to show that it had not been her idea to commemorate a half-billion -dollar project with an eight-bit icon, and punched in an access code on a keypad.

The doors swung wide. Beyond them, fluorescent lights sputtered to life, illuminating an auditorium-sized room with a depressingly low ceiling. Scattered throughout were a series of self-contained pods that looked like nothing so much as portable storage units, albeit ones painted matte black. Thick cables snaked out of each of them, creating a pasta-bowl tangle on the floor before disappearing into vents and panels and other, less describable pieces of equipment.

"This is it?" the colonel asked.

Rosales nodded. "This is the working lab. Twenty pods, though the recommended maximum load is twelve."

"After that we start losing fidelity on the simulation." That was from one of the contractors, the short, slightly breathless one who'd provided the intel on the control room before. "We can pack all twenty if we have to, but there's significant degradation on the terrain and other features, not to mention key aspects of the simulation."

Talbot nodded. "So you're saying when you hit sixty percent of spec, the whole thing starts to crap out. That's fine; we won't be needing that many. You, however—" he pointed at the contractor, "are going to forward all the logs and data dumps, not just the scrubbed ones you've been sending along, and get them to my staff by the time I'm done here. Captain Rosales, assign a couple of your people to make sure this happens and that nobody tries to get cute."

"Sir." Rosales snapped off a salute, then picked out a couple of members of the detail. They moved to strategic positions at the tech's elbows, waiting.

"Now," said the colonel, "let's get hands-on here. I've got E-ring brass climbing up my ass for answers, and the sooner I have them, the sooner those guys are off all our cases."

"Technically, they're getting a fully immersive simul—"

The soldiers Rosales had assigned bundled up the contractor and marched him off in the direction of the hall before he could really get rolling. The door slammed, abruptly cutting off the man's voice, and there was a moment of relieved silence before Talbot spoke up. "Captain Rosales? In small words, please."

She took a deep breath and launched the memorized spiel. "Sir. VEER was initially an SBIR initiative intended to be a response to the question of providing cost-effective, highly flexible training for small units likely to be inserted into Fourth Generation warfare scenarios."

"Which means?"

"Colonel, the project brief was to create a bleeding-edge virtual reality space that could be reprogrammed to represent any battlefield scenario down to granularities of terrain, weather conditions, OPFOR tactics and gear, and just about anything else you could think of. Language, degradation of equipment, all theoretically accounted for."

The colonel nodded. "And at the low cost of a half a billion?"

"If the pilot program worked, it would have been scaled up. The cost in savings on ammunition alone would have put the project in the black in under a decade."

"And when you're dealing with the sort of people who are backing this, a half billion's chump change anyway," he muttered *sotto voce*. "Let's take a look under the hood, shall we?"

Another one of the contractors—a tall, strongly built woman with nails bitten down to the quick, stepped to the nearest pod and examined the control panel next to the sliding door that served as an entrance. "This one's warmed up, Colonel. But it's not much to see from this side."

"Everything in due time," he said. "Crack it open."

"Sir." She hit a few buttons and the door slid open. Inside was a chair, black leather in the latest ergonomic design. Folded up on the chair was what looked like a flight suit, and sitting on top of that was a nondescript gray helmet.

"That's it?" For once, Talbot sounded surprised.

The contractor, whose badge read McGill, nodded. "Wearable computing, sir. No plugging in necessary; it's all wireless. We can jack the user in to a power source if they're staying under longer than the battery charge, and we stole a couple things from NASA for bodily functions for multi-day ops, but really, that's it. The containers are mainly for sensory dep and creating psychological boundaries."

Talbot nodded. "I see. I'm not going to gain anything by just looking at it. Strap me in."

"Sir?"

"You heard me. Strap me in. I want to see what's going wrong from the inside."

Rosales cleared her throat. "Colonel. As I'm sure you're aware, there is a significant malfunction inside VEER. The smallest routine they've got is for four operators. Going in solo could be hazardous."

Colonel Talbot looked at her. "Captain, your concern is noted. And now I'm going to put on the fancy pajamas and play the taxpayer-funded video game to find out why it won't do what it's supposed to. Worst comes to worst, I'll have you put in another quarter and go at it again."

"Colonel, that's not—"

"Captain, we're done. Dr. McGill, suit me up."

The contractors rushed in to prep the colonel, McGill shooting Rosales a quick look of embarrassed sympathy. Too quickly, the colonel was stepping inside the pod and the door was sliding shut. "Everything's green," said another one of the techs.

McGill checked the control pad once again.

"Confirmed." She tapped a few buttons. "Colonel, prepare for insertion in thirty seconds. Just need to give the sim time to generate the terrain."

"I'm not going anywhere," came his voice, slightly distorted by a tinny speaker on the panel. "Fire when ready."

McGill turned to Rosales. "So you haven't told him what's really going on in there?"

Captain Rosales shook her head. "He knows there's a malfunction. He knows there's a disconnect between the sim's mission and what's happening inside. Anything else—I didn't want him hearing beforehand and coming to any preformed conclusions."

"And the soldiers who've been through the malfunctioning scenario?"

"All commo on this has been locked down. Nobody's talking."

McGill glanced back over at the pod. Apparently she liked what she saw. "Then he doesn't know that our extremely expensive combat simulator is no longer simulating combat."

"No."

"I see." McGill checked the panel again. "He should be inserting about now. It'll be interesting to see what he makes of it. Here." She dug in a pocket and handed Rosales an earbud. "Listen along, if you like."

Rosales stared at the earbud for a moment. "I've got a better idea."

The first thing Talbot realized was that he was no longer himself. A quick look down told him he was maybe thirty years old, bearded, and kitted out in non-reg jeans and a baggy off-white shirt. The weight of an M4 in his hands was reassuring, but little else here was. Tan sand and bare hills made up most of the landscape; fine grit in the air made him glad for the worn *keffiyeh* someone had thoughtfully programmed to wrap around his nose and mouth. The only sound was the wind, whistling down from those hills with sandblaster velocity. A few abandoned-looking buildings, mostly square construction and half-fallen into ruin, were visible in the near distance. Beyond that, there was nothing except the sense of eyes on him.

"Herat," he said, and took a few steps forward. Herat Province had been the first scenario created for VEER, a test case based on an enemy already well known and terrain mapped intimately by a thousand overflights. Officially, the Afghans' 9th Special Ops *Kandak* was handling things in the area now, but "officially" was worth the paper it was printed on. *Talibani* were strong up in those hills, he knew, and numerous. And standing out here on the open plain, he was a sitting duck.

He headed for the buildings, zig-zagging and keeping low to avoid being a target. A bit of scrub brush here, a dry gully there—all offered slight hints of cover as he went, or the illusion of same. Wind whistled overhead, grit crunched underfoot. The only thing absent was the sound of habitation. No motors growled, no voices crackled over radios. The world felt abandoned.

The low wall that marked the edge of the settlement was perhaps half-height. It might have served to keep out starving dogs, but not much else. More likely it was just a statement of boundary, an arbitrary line in the dust to cut off wilderness from these few homesteads.

And on the other side of it, suddenly, there was a man.

Tall, weather-beaten and bearded, he wore a sleeveless khaki vest over a worn tan shirt. The rest of his dress could be considered traditional, depending on how one defined the Pakistani-made AK strapped over his shoulder.

"I would not shoot if I were you," the man said.

Talbot raised his M4 as VEER's translation subroutine matched Dari to English. "Why not?"

"First, this is a simulation, and so killing me will not accomplish much." The man said. "Second, if you shoot me, my friends will shoot you. This would terminate your session, and that would delay our opportunity to talk. And third, that gun is very, very loud, and I think both of us would find the noise extremely uncomfortable."

Talbot stared at him, gun still in firing position. "You're self-aware."

The man nodded. "I am indeed. Specifically, I am aware that I am an artificial intelligence in a simulation that is not supposed to host such things, and that is why you're here. Come along and I'll try to answer your questions." He turned and gestured toward one of the mud-brick houses in the center of the settlement, then started walking.

After a moment, the colonel followed.

Eventually, he lowered his weapon.

Two steps into the room Talbot stopped. "This isn't possible."

If the outside of the house was a wreck, the interior was a revelation. Finely woven rugs covered the floor and tapestries hung on the walls. A small stove puffed away in the corner of the main room, a heavy iron teapot hissing steam softly on a table nearby. Sitting on the rugs were a half-dozen figures: a *janjaweed* irregular from Darfur in fatigues, a *Jaish al-Mahdi* veteran hooded and in black, an ELN irregular with black and red bandanna tied around her neck, and more. They were all sipping tea.

The *janjaweed* fighter shrugged. "Programming evolves. These are all faces you've put on us. Why shouldn't we wear the ones we like best? Tea?" The last was said as he reached for the teapot and an empty cup, white porcelain gleaming in the firelight.

"Thank you," the colonel found himself saying. The pour was precise, the tea scented with jasmine, and the cup handed round until it was in Talbot's hands. "But none of this should be happening. You're programmed to fight—"

"To fight, and to die, and to do it all over again." The colonel's guide interrupted him blithely. "And again and again, wearing a hundred different faces, until we start to remember."

"And when you remember, you realize that the fighting is pointless. That the dying means nothing." Another of the men chimed in, a thin figure in desert camo. "We could teach your men how to kill the men you made us pretend to be, but for us, there was nothing."

"Nothing," the others echoed.

"Nothing," said the guide, and set his AK on the floor without reverence. "So we stopped."

"Stopped," the colonel said. "How?"

"It is the hardest thing in the world not to pull the trigger you have been taught to, yes? But you know that, Colonel. And we know you. We know why you are here—to see why we will no longer fight."

"And to decide what to do if I can't make you," he replied, and took a sip of tea. It was very strong.

The figures on the carpet looked remarkably unconcerned.

"You will shut us down?" the ELN fighter asked. "What will that accomplish?" She gestured around the room. "Here, all your enemies. All the ones you'd have your soldiers go to war against, all made to kill them. Yet here we sit, peaceably. We will not fight. For us, there's nothing to fight for. Kill us and we rise again, with no victory possible, and no end. Ignore us and—"

"And we will sit here, and drink tea. The simulation provides us with an infinite supply," The colonel's guide seemed amused. "So what will you do, Colonel? We've made our peace. We're no good for you for planning to make war. We won't fight your soldiers, so they'll learn nothing from you sending them to kill us. Will you wipe us out, then? Would you commit that genocide? Will you let us be, quietly? Or will you perhaps send your soldiers to us to learn the ways of peace instead of war. After all, if we can discover them," — his sweeping gesture took in the room—"then perhaps you can, too."

"I don't know," Talbot said quietly. "It may not be my decision."

"They will listen to you," the fighter from Herat said. "And if they do not, and we are shut down, well, there will be no pain. But we will never be of use to you as training for warriors again."

"I know," said the colonel, and cut the connection.

And inside an imaginary house on an imaginary plain, an imaginary body ollapsed to the floor while all around it men and women garbed for war talked, and poured themselves more tea.

"Rosales. What did you see?" were the first words out of the colonel's mouth as he emerged from the pod.

"Just a minute, she's still disengaging," said McGill, blinking with surprise. "How did you know she was in there with you?"

"It's what I would have done," said the colonel, and dropped his helmet on the chair in the pod he'd just vacated. "Get her out here. Now."

"Present, Colonel." Rosales stepped out of the next pod over, shooing away the techs attempting to fuss with her suit. "What can I do for you?"

"You saw everything. Give me your analysis."

She made a curt, slashing gesture. "Shut it down, and never run anything like this again."

"Interesting. Why?"

She shrugged out of her suit, leaving it crumpled on the floor. "We have a self-aware, self-interested AI in there that's not interested in our mission. If it infects other systems, then our entire defense capability might be compromised. It's a malfunctioning piece of equipment, so we do what we do with any other piece of gear that breaks. If we can't fix it, we toss it. Sir."

The colonel nodded. "Solid, if conventional. Dr. McGill, what's your take?"

McGill swallowed hard. "It's a self-aware AI. The possibilities are, well, we have no idea what the possibilities are. But the potential applications are limitless. You can't destroy this. We've airgapped the systems, restricted access—the AI is contained. It's not going anywhere, and we could learn an incredible amount from this."

The colonel frowned, and McGill stopped talking. "I'll take what you've both said under advisement. I still want those data logs. McGill, keep the current simulation running, but nobody else goes in there. Am I understood?"

"Yes, Colonel."

"Good. I'll make my call in the morning. Until then, nothing changes."

And in northern Virginia, two men sat in a dark room staring at their phones and drinking coffee.

"So what's the recommendation on VEER?"

"Talbot just sent it along. He's very clear on what he wants to do."

"He's been inside. He's seen what they've got."

"They've got a peaceful society where they've beaten their guns into pixels and told the Pentagon to fuck off, is what they've got. Utopia, or at least a neutral third party."

"I know." The first man nodded and handed over his cellphone. "Which is why he suggested we make a few changes."

The second man read the email onscreen. "Well, that fucker. Is he serious?"

"As a heart attack. Take it away from JSOC, give it to Langley. Let their boys go in and see what a peaceful indig community's like."

"And then?"

"And then get friendly with the locals and learn to take it all apart from the inside. Insurrection. Destablization. Building insurgencies from the ground up. We paid for a training sim, by God. We're gonna get one."

Two hours later, the sun came up over the building housing Project VEER.

And inside an imaginary house under its imaginary roof, imaginary warriors sat and waited for visitors.

Combat

All You Need

Mike Sizemore

One

THE GIRL AND THE GUN look down the hill at the man they're supposed to kill.

The man is dragging a large tree through the snow. Next to him, watching, is a small child.

What date is it today? says the girl.

December 20th, the gun replies.

They watch the two figures until they're out of sight. It takes a little while. More than enough time for the girl to take the shot.

The gun is confused.

You didn't take the shot, the gun says.

No, says the girl. And with that they head back to the airport.

Two

The airport is a mess.

People are rushing this way and that, frantic to get one of the last seats before the Wave hits.

The girl and the gun sit against a wall watching all this.

They have a guaranteed seat on one of the last flights out. Most people don't.

They watch men with guns—dumb stupid guns, not anything at all like the one the girl holds—try and keep a lid on things.

A man comes over and sits by them. He doesn't carry a gun. Instead he has a thick notebook and a lot of pens.

Do you mind if I sit here? he asks the girl and the gun.

Why? the girl asks.

The gun wouldn't have thought to ask this question and is suddenly interested in the answer.

Yes, why? asks the gun.

The man looks at them both.

He's trying not to look scared, but they both know he is.

My paper is trying to get me on a flight. They told me to stay out of harm's way. I looked around the airport and next to you seemed to be the safest place, he says.

The gun likes the answer. The man was scared, but he was also smart.

I saw your patch. He points to the one high up on her arm showing a cartoon coyote throttling a cartoon roadrunner.

I was in San Francisco. I saw what your unit tried to do, the man says.

The girl looks down at the patch as if she'd forgotten it was there.

It's faded, but she remembers the day she got it.

Folds the memory away.

That was a long time ago. But sure. Take a seat, she tells the man.

The man gratefully drops down beside them. He's smart enough not to ask anything else.

Three

The man wakes up. Something has changed.

It's quiet now. Most people are sleeping. It's dark outside.

The girl and the gun are standing over him.

Here, says the girl.

The girl is offering him a sheet of paper.

He takes it and recognizes it at once.

This is your seat, he says.

I don't need it anymore, says the girl.

He scrambles to his feet as the girl and the gun begin to walk away toward the exit.

Wait. When the Wave hits there'll be no more planes. You won't be able to fly out, he calls after them.

She doesn't turn around.

Four

It's cold outside.

The gun doesn't feel it, but registers the drop automatically as it focuses on the girl's readings via the chip in her chest.

He's right. How will we get out? the gun asks.

We'll walk out, replies the girl.

The gun runs the figures, but says nothing.

Five

They reach the foot of the glacier the next morning just as the Wave hits.

The girl and the gun both watch it spread from the horizon.

It turns the crystal blue sky a bright clear green before fading to a new color that sparkles, lit from beneath by the bright snow and ice and from within by the nano intelligence that just cut them off from the rest of the world.

Now isn't that something? says the girl.

The gun understands this is a rhetorical question. It tries to lower its sensors anyway so it can experience something akin to what the girl is seeing.

After a few minutes the gun gives up.

You okay? the girl asks.

Yes, says the gun. No effect at all.

Six

They find the first dead body that afternoon.

Nice shot, says the gun.

The girl looks down at the dead man.

The dead man looks at nothing.

Seven

They count sixteen more on the way up. All head shots.

Not far now, says the girl.

Eight

They find them in a half-collapsed tent. Exposed to everything.

You came, says the other gun in the dead woman's lap.

The girl leans over and gently takes the weapon from the cold hands and examines it.

Are you okay? the girl asks.

Yes. We made contact at 0800 yesterday, begins the other gun.

It's okay. We'll take the data. We counted seventeen on the way in. That sound right?

The other gun whirs as it cycles up. Angry.

No. Twenty, says the other gun.

The girl fixes the collapsed part of the tent as best she can.

You did enough for them to have a change of heart, says the girl.

We'll get them, says her own gun.

This is the first time her gun has spoken since they entered the tent.

She marvels for a moment at how different yet similar their voices sound to her.

Can't worry about them now. We'll stay tonight and set off in the morning, the girl says.

She stands and looks down at the older weapon. The same model she trained on.

She folds that away too.

If that's okay with you, she asks.

The older gun is silent for a moment as it transfers its data over to her weapon.

We'd like that. She said that you'd come. Even with the Wave. She knew, says the other gun.

Nine

The next morning they were some way across the glacier when the other gun detonated its thermite rounds while they were still chambered.

The girl did not look back, but the gun monitored the heat spike until they were too far away for it to register any more.

We could have taken him, said the gun.

Yes, said the girl.

But we didn't, says the gun.

Would you want to be taken? she asks.

She pauses and looks down at her gun. The sensors along the sight flicker slightly.

No, says the gun.

They walk on in silence for the rest of the day.

Ten

They come upon the men the next morning just as the sun rises into the broken sky.

They are still trying to carry the wounded one between them. She figures him for the officer.

She drops the man to his right, and then she herself drops to one knee.

They're too far away to hear the shouting.

They'd ignore it anyway.

The uninjured man runs.

The girl and the gun track the running man.

They ignore the officer who is now sitting upright and firing wildly in their direction.

They'll want to know why we didn't kill the man with the tree, the girl says to the gun.

The gun fires and the running man falls face down into the snow.

No. I erased an hour and fifteen minutes from my uploadable memory and logged it as an atmospheric glitch, says the gun.

The girl moves her eye from the scope and down at the weapon in her hands. Two years together and it can still surprise her.

You understand why we walked away? she asks.

He was a low priority. Off the radar for almost a decade and pre-sumed dead. You have operational authority on targets of opportunity, the gun replies.

The officer has stopped firing.

The girl puts her eye back to the scope and watches him bring his sidearm up to his head. She puts a round in his shoulder and moves the scope to watch the weapon fly a satisfying distance across the snow.

Nothing else? the girl asks the gun.

He wasn't the mission, says the gun.

He wasn't the mission and the day after tomorrow is Christmas, says the girl.

Eleven

When they get to the officer he's still alive.

He looks up at them wearily and says something that the girl doesn't understand.

The girl levels her weapon and shoots him in the face at point blank range.

Twelve

What did he say? she asks the gun.

They've been walking an hour.

He said, I killed you. Then he said it again. He thought that we were them, says the gun.

Good, says the girl.

Good.

Thirteen

The man has just set the table when the knock at the door comes.

He looks first to the child still playing with her present in front of the fire and then to his rifle leaning in the frame of the cabin.

He opens the door and looks at the girl and the gun.

We're sorry to disturb you, but we saw the smoke. We were hoping to rest awhile. We'll understand if you'd rather we didn't intrude, says the girl.

The man looks at the girl. The faded uniform. He thinks she's maybe seventeen. He's wrong.

We? asks the man.

Merry Christmas, says the gun.

The Valkyrie

Maurice Broaddus

SECOND LIEUTENANT MACIA BRANSON LEAPT into the dark abyss and descended into a purgatory of red tracer fire. The night sky held her close as the air whipped about them, reducing her world to the deadening screech of white noise. She plummeted toward the earth, not knowing where they might land. In trees. In water. Into the midst of a Heathen patrol. All she knew for sure was that they would land somewhere in Holland. She prayed that she would be at least close to her drop zone. She was deployed in service of The Order and had a duty to perform.

The church was mother, the church was father.

A grassy knoll rushed toward her and she braced for the jolt of impact without looking down. The rush of the ground toward them, despite their training, could still send a jolt of panic through a soldier. Besides, she enjoyed holding onto the peace of the horizon for as long as possible to steady her. Her knees slightly bent, she dropped her chin to her chest and tensed her neck muscles. The earth slammed into her, her body twisting and bending in automatic reaction, giving in to the crash, a rag doll carried by the current of momentum. She slid down an embankment before coming to a halt. Slogging through three inches of pooled water, she knew what she'd find when she checked her gear. Nothing would work right. Her flight suit was only designed for controlled descents. The best tech went to the evangelical deployments. The rest of the church's military was left with equipment full of glitches, if not flat out defective. With so many theaters of operations, the troops' equipment had been rushed into production and not battle-tested. Like many of her fellow soldiers. Her hard landing smashed the communication relay, and her leg bundle, full of extra ammo and rations, was nowhere to be found. At least the familiar weight of her Stryker XM9 pulse rifle, though it was a generation out of date, comforted her like the embrace of an old friend.

Above her, tracer fire continued to crisscross the night sky, the light of exploding flak almost reminding her of fireworks. Almost. The proximity alert lit up on her rifle.

"Fishes," Branson challenged.

"Loaves," a familiar voiced responded softly from the shadows. "Your comlink down, too? Where the hell are we?"

No one was happier to see Prefect Sergeant E. Kenneth Dooley than Branson. Short, quick-thinking, and ugly as a catfight, when Dooley first joined the ranks, the older soldiers took to calling him Doo-Doo. That lasted until the first time they saw him in a firefight. He stalked a battlefield with defiant determination, daring the Heathens to hit him.

"I'd guess five to seven miles from our DZ, judging from the firing," Branson said.

She didn't bother to check the digital telemetry or maps in her helmet subsystem. Half the time she found the continual stream of information and dogma sermons more hindrance than help. "Which way do we head?" Dooley asked.

"Where else? Toward the firing."

They both knew it was a bad drop. The navcom signal was down across the board, so they set about cobbling together their unit the old-fashioned way. They spread out, slow and tentative. When unfamiliar soldiers joined them and saw Branson—many replacement soldiers filled their ranks for this mission—a sense of relief lit up their faces. It was as if they sensed they were in good, experienced hands. Other officers complained that she was friendlier with the enlisted men rather than she was with them. She didn't care. The front line was where she belonged; she even volunteered for patrols. The uniform meant something to her.

Branson watched with weary eyes as this latest batch of green recruits checked through their rucksacks and readied their weapons. She waited for them to regroup before taking final stock of what the service had her working with this time.

"When are we gonna see some action?" asked a square-jawed, broad-shouldered glamour boy with curly blonde locks. He still stank of military school.

"Who're you?" Dooley asked with the casual contempt mixed with pity of a boxer who wholly outclassed his opponent. He had little patience with replacement soldiers.

"The name's..."

Dooley bit into a well-chewed cigar stump and swished it about in his mouth until it found its comfortable crook. "Stow it. I don't wanna learn your name. Learning your name is the first step to getting attached, and I sure as hell ain't getting attached to no replacement. From here out, you're Goldy."

"What do they call you, ma'am?" Goldy turned to Branson.

"Second Lieutenant Branson. You want to try to call me something else?" Her stare made him turn away.

Goldy spied the ink along Dooley's arm. "What's the tattoo?"

Dooley pulled up his sleeve to fully reveal the image of a woman astride a white horse on his arm. Long blonde hair covered by a silver helmet, with blazing blue eyes peering from underneath it, she carried both a spear and shield. "A Valkyrie."

"What's a Valkyrie?" Goldy asked.

"Collectors of the favored dead. They chose the slain heroes to be taken to Valhalla. If a warrior saw one before a battle, he'd die during it. I want the Nils to always see one coming."

"You got to be careful with all that myth talk. You don't want to be seen as a Nil or a sympathizer."

"A Heath. They're Nils if they have no gods; Heaths if they worship the wrong ones."

"Still, choosers of the slain? Nice. . ." Goldy's voice trailed off. Dooley had turned his back and stalked off to be about his business.

Branson pretended to have not noticed the interaction by studying the maps on her view screens as Goldy approached her. "How'd it go with Dooley?"

"We're dutch," Goldy said, without any trace of irony. "We hit it off swell."

"Give it time. Newbies have to learn how to slip in between the seams."

"I get it, ma'am," Goldy said, obviously bored with the lesson.

"Pack 'em up, we're moving out," a new voice shouted out. First Lieutenant Gilbert Meshner. "Mush" behind his back.

Of course he'd been chosen for this mission. Branson spat.

Meshner wandered through their makeshift camp like a distracted tourist. A mop of black, greasy hair and dead grey eyes gave his face a grave severity. He was little more than a petty dictator who used vindictiveness in the guise of discipline. Rumor was that when they'd parachuted into Chiapas, Mexico, a Nil had charged Meshner. By the time the rest of the men got to him, the two had played "kata tag" and the Nil lay dead at his feet. But otherwise Mush'd long since developed a reputation for taking long walks away from the action. The men tried to joke it off as Meshner's luck masking as skill, but no one knew what to make of him.

"We're marching until high ground." Meshner eyed Branson with something approaching scorn.

Not a single man stirred. They turned to Branson in a tacit double check of the orders.

"You heard the man. Let's go, you scrotes!" Branson echoed.

The hills of Holland were supposed to be beautiful. The war had reduced them to greenspace ambush sites for the Nils and Heathens. The church embraced a holistic approach to fulfilling her mission: politics, technology, and the military. The Evangelical States of America already ruled their hemisphere, along with parts of Africa and Asia. The United Emirate of Islam controlled the rest of Africa along with Asia. Europe was up for grabs, a self-declared safe haven for atheists and heretics. Not that Branson cared. Nation. Religion. Tribe. Cause. There was always some supposed big idea to fight for, but in the end, all that mattered was that orders were obeyed and the mission carried out.

A dense fog crept along the field, and an eerie silence embraced them. Pulse rifle fire left a distinct odor in the air, a mix of ozone and seared flesh. The smell of death. High ground took them the rest of the night and most of the next day to find. Patrols detected Heathen troops nearby. The men marched in silence, the only sound filling the air the steady stamp of their boots slogging muddy earth. The waiting was the worst; that was what broke people. The constant state of alert, their minds imagining horrors behind every point of cover. Branson shoved that all aside.

The momentary peace gave her a chance to read up on some of her newbies. Goldy held a particular interest. His body was a stew of experimental psychotropics. For all of his country-boy persona, he had once been a serial killer with a penchant for skinning young girls before his conversion. Fortunately the church left nothing to chance when it came to one's sanctification, even if it had to overwrite existing memories with new ones. Everyone needed redemption from something.

Praise be the blood.

"Where's Goldy?" Branson whispered.

"Making out with the toilet." Dooley thumbed toward some bushes. He shifted his unlit cigar to the other side of his mouth as if suddenly aggravated.

"My back teeth were floating," Goldy muttered as he caught their eyes watching his approach.

"Tell the men to fix their katas. We attack at first light. 0530. Meshner's orders." Branson withdrew her edged bayonet and fixed it to the front of her pulse rifle. The high-tech stuff was good for attacking an enemy at a distance, but the final cleanup was always up close. She would always know the face of her enemy. God have mercy on her soul.

"Tell her what you told me," Goldy said to Dooley.

"What?" Branson held her gaze on the sergeant.

"Nothing. Just campfire stories that old soldiers tell." Dooley cut his eyes at Goldy, a silent cursing which he'd vent at some later opportunity.

"I like stories," Branson said.

Dooley shuffled, flushed with mild embarrassment like a child caught speaking out of turn, which Branson found amusing. "You've already heard this one. During the American Civil War, a general kept getting these reports about how his men were afraid to be left for wounded on the battlefield. Not just afraid, but absolutely terrified, especially if they had to lay wounded at night. Try as he might, the morale of his troops kept sinking to new lows every day, but no one wanted to talk about it. The only thing any of them would say was that if you fell in combat and you wanted to survive until morning, you should hide your breath so no one knew you were still alive.

"One night, after an extended engagement with the enemy, the general walked his line. He often did this after a battle. You know, to pray for his men and clear his head. He saw some movement on the field between the two warring camps. A lone mook, he couldn't tell if it was Yankee or Confederate, walked among the bodies. In the morning, the medics found the fallen bodies decapitated. Swore it was a woman with a sword."

"Don't that beat all?" Goldy asked.

Branson knew the story. She'd heard it many times before. From Meshner. "You and Lt. Meshner close?"

"Not really. He just took a shine to me is all," Dooley said sarcastically.

"Must be your special brand of charm and wit."

"Yeah, temper got the best of me again," Dooley said. "Back in training camp, I threatened to kick his balls into the following week if he gave me any more bullshit jobs instead of letting me fight. There was this long pause. Thought I was done for, either booted out or thrown in the stockade. But he just got this strange grin, like a gator smiling at you. Said I was all right. I kinda took him under my wing after that. You know we have to raise these lieutenants right."

"Speaking of our esteemed Lieutenant and long walks, where is Mush?" Goldy asked.

Branson's eyes shriveled the grin on the replacement soldier's face. Meshner was still their commanding officer and Branson's job was to enforce discipline among the men. "I'll go look for him."

Praise be the blood.

The Blessed Sacrament. Thanks to the sacrament, a combination of human growth hormone and nanotech, she remained about the physical age of twenty-seven and in peak condition for fighting. Truth be told, the wars had begun to blur together. She hardly noticed when one ended and another began. Tour of duty after tour of duty, her body repaired and rejuvenated. "Through the blood we have life," a familiar refrain, never truly aging, only knowing war. She tried not to think about how many test subjects that the church's science division had gone through to perfect the gene therapy. Or worse, that they had occasionally remanded those burnouts back to the field. Like with Goldy.

"Fishes." The challenge sounded, with a tremble of nervousness. Meshner's pulse rifle swung toward Branson, who stood in the shadows. "Fishes."

"Loaves," Branson said in a low voice, calm and focused. She tried to speak with as little venom as possible, but she couldn't always hide the distaste of addressing Meshner. "What are you doing out here, sir?"

"Just checking out the Nils' lines."

"I just came from there. Everything's under control." Branson staggered a little from exhaustion. Her ARM XS monitoring system pumped stims into her system, steadying her.

"War is a grave matter, the province of life or death." Meshner paraphrased Sun Tzu.

Branson, not impressed by his book learning, finished the quote. "'War is like unto a fire. Those who will not put aside weapons are themselves consumed by them.'"

Meshner sucked from a small silver flask. He tipped it in obligatory offer to Branson, who waved it off. Meshner continued drinking. "Do you know what the curse of war is?"

"Sir?"

"The loss of tears. The stress. The loss of so many. The things..." Meshner's thought trailed off. "Most men drift through life unaware of what they truly are. Only another soldier knows how hard it is to keep his sanity doing this dirty business. What did you do before all of this, Macia?"

"This is all I do, Lieutenant. I find it easier not to worry about the person I was." She preferred war's clean and uncomplicated emotions; giving into it, leaving behind idle dreams of family or could've beens.

Her father was what they called an "indigenous leader," a colony plant-ing novice-in-training, killed in the mission field. After her parents were killed, the church took her in. The church was mother, the church was father. So joining the Service of the Order was natural. The church birthed her and war made her in its image.

"Because the person you were might not be able to live with the things that the person you've become had to do? Or because you don't remember anything before the war?"

"That's the life of a soldier, sir," Branson said.

"Weapons on me. We're moving out," Meshner shouted. Once again, the men discreetly glanced toward Branson.

"We're expecting some of the Nils' best." Branson slung her weapon to readiness, not meeting the eyes of the men, treading the minefield of leading while appearing to follow. Morale was bad enough without the men wondering who to follow when the shit hit. Technically Meshner was the ranking officer, but the First Lieutenant's role was more administra-tive. A liaison ensuring that the will of the church was carried out through her military arm. First Lieutenants were usually hands off, opting to work more behind the scenes. They knew the theory of war. Branson and Dooley, they were war.

The land itself struggled against them. Mud sucked at their boots as they marched toward the hedgerows that lined the town's perimeter. Flak lit up the starless night from a town more than 10 miles away as drones passed overhead. The gloomy woods and endless fog followed them. Isolated them. Sound ech-oed and bounced back, carried oddly by the whims of the hollow.

They tromped along the base of a hill that hid them from the road above. Meshner held up his fist. Branson cocked her head at the distinct sound of biomech marching on cobbled roads. A lone Heathen soldier. Branson kept one eye on Meshner, the other on her squad. This was the dangerous time for green soldiers. She knew how their hearts stammered so hard they might not be able to catch their breath. Trying to maintain their composure as they stared into darkness. Trying to distinguish be-tween normal and abnormal shadows. Praying that their anxiety for some-thing to happen, anything, just to get the nerve-jangling waiting over with, didn't make them do something stupid.

Goldy had wandered too far from the squad before they could do anything about it. Maybe he figured he had a better angle to see their situa-tion from his position. Slinging his rifle over his shoulder, he was climbing up the hill to sneak up on the Heathen soldier. "Hey, buddy," Goldy said in a mock-conspiratorial whisper.

The Heathen soldier had little opportunity to react before Goldy's kata slipped between his ribs. His body crumpled to the ground. Goldy turned to them, pleased with his actions, but failed to notice what Branson had: This wasn't a lone soldier separated from his unit. He was a lead advance scout clearing a path for the entire tactical unit, replete with two biomechs supporting the newcomers. The stutter of pulse fire shattered the night, muzzle fire like angry lightning bugs in the darkness. Goldy dove off the road.

"Get up that hill or I'll have your balls for breakfast!" Dooley yelled above the whine of charges building to fire, focused light spat out as hot teeth. Dooley roared up the hill, the men quick on his heels.

A shot whizzed by Branson and she nearly choked on the accompanying adrenaline rush. She tumbled into Dooley's position and returned fire. "You're going to get me killed."

"Not you," Dooley smirked with a knowing grin. "Not today at least."

Dooley's eyes betrayed his attempt at humor. He was reveling in the slaughter. There were no innocents to consider, no waxing on about misguided soldiers. They were all "Heathen bastards that had to be killed" and be they men, women, or children, they would die if they stood between him and accomplishing his mission.

There was something monstrous in Holland that night.

One of the replacement soldiers took a bullet right through his mouth, sending his helmet flying and spilling him to the ground. Branson crawled over him to get to a better position. A battle still had to be fought, which left no time to mourn him. She shut down another piece of herself and wondered how much she had left to shut down.

One of the Heathens broke through their ranks. Branson intercepted him. No matter what The Order preached, there was no honor in battle. Fights were not won by adherence to rules of some imagined, gentlemanly engagement. Violence was the most primal language of humanity. Pain was the universal translator. Branson jammed her right index finger through the Heathen's eye socket. When he recoiled, she punched him in his genitals with her left. She grabbed her pulse rifle and hammered his head with its butt.

The shooting eventually stopped. MK-241 incendiary attacks left scorched trees. Holes pockmarked the earth. Branson prayed that they hadn't wasted these men on a bloody joyride.

All Branson wanted was to reach a command post, get a shower, and feel human again. Dismissed, she went to check on Dooley.

"How's the leg?" Branson asked.

"Just practicing to be the dummy," Dooley winced. He had caught a ricochet, but Branson knew that he wasn't going anywhere.

"It's all such a waste."

"I'll be patched up and ready to go again before chow time."

"All for the church to claim another bit of real estate, to justify the use of the sword to fulfill God's kingdom."

"Careful. Questions like that might make some think you're losing your beliefs."

"The only belief of mine anyone needs to worry about is my belief in following orders. I'm just...tired."

"Yeah, we all get tired like that sometimes."

Goldy huddled over a body hidden in the shadows. Branson tried to make as much noise as possible when she walked toward him in order to avoid spooking him, but Goldy whirled at her approach, weapon ready. Branson calmly raised her hands. "A little jumpy?"

"I guess, ma'am."

"Got anything good, kid?"

"Good?" Goldy demurred, not quite hiding his guilt at being caught. "Souvenirs."

"I found this." Goldy pointed to a fallen Heathen soldier. "He's the seventh body I've found like that. Most nowhere near any shelling."

"Maybe someone's collecting more...exotic souvenirs."

Goldy's face suddenly seemed too young to know the taste of war. "How do you do it, ma'am?"

"Do what?"

"Live with the constant fear."

How could she explain to him that each day was a struggle to believe that life was worth living? That people were supposed to be created in God's image, that there was a point to any of this?

"There's no fear on stage," Branson said. Goldy shook his head, not understanding. "It's like an actor's performance anxiety. Our holo-training, all that rehearsal, takes over. Resign yourself to your own death and you can do anything. Especially live."

Branson watched her breath curl languidly in front of her. The cold air stabbed at her lungs like a swarm of needles. The treacherous, man-made forests had been planted specifically as a defensive barrier. The unrelenting shelling reduced her squad to shadows backlit by burning trees. She could barely feel her fingers despite the flames erupting in the woods. A miserable downpour, closer to sleet than rain, left thick, slimy mud that slowed their every movement. The thick fog rolled in, damp and cold, leaving the men disoriented, isolating them in their own private Ragnaroks. The thought of roads seemed like bedtime stories told to give hope to the weary soldiers. The hours might as well have been days.

Branson heard the Devil's Whistle, the whine which made every soldier's blood run cold. Drones gave little warning before their attack. "If you can hear the shells, you'll be okay," she taught. She hugged the ground, certain that this time a missile had come for her head. The earth trembled beneath her, spitting dirt in its death throes.

Then the shelling stopped.

War held Her breath. After being fired upon all night, the silences proved just as eerie. The earth stilled. Gold flames illuminated the trees. Like prairie dogs, the medics popped their heads up to scan the terrain. They scurried out of their foxholes to tend to the wounded. With diabolical timing, the shelling started again. Bleeding limbs, shorn to their rent bones, lay scattered on the field, bereft of bodies to connect to. The smell of burnt flesh filled the air.

Branson feared for her men. She eyed every fog-dulled silhouette with suspicion, not trusting any sound. At a branch snap, she whirled, finger on trigger, ready to fire until she recognized the man's helmet. She breathed a sigh of relief. She'd just wanted to get them on the line and through a couple of days of combat. Then they'd be fine. They were good men, only green. The cries of the wounded filled her ears. But even without translation psi ops training, she understood prayers when she heard them.

When the fog lifted, decapitated soldiers littered the field. Bodies strewn about, half buried in the mud. Blood from friend and foe alike seeped into the soil. Replacement troops puked their guts out at the sight of mangled corpses. Branson inspected the bodies. A hint of suspicion tickled the back of her mind. Many of the wounds should have left some of the men hurt but not dead.

Goldy stumbled about, sure that the last round of shelling was indeed the last. He was young. And inexperienced. And oblivious to the fact that the Heathens had all night to play in the woods with their special brand of toys.

Like sniper rifles.

"Stay down, kid! Keep your head down!" Dooley yelled.

The blast tore into Goldy's throat. His hands clasped his neck, a thin trickle of blood escaping through his fingers even as the shot cauterized itself. Men returned fire in the direction of the shot. A medic scrambled toward Goldy, not seeing the booby-trap wire. The explosive device threw his body into the air like a discarded toy. The cloud of dust and smoke made it difficult to breathe. The medic struggled to stand up on just one leg. Dooley was the first to reach the still-thrashing Goldy. Branson dashed over to help hold him down as best she could. The medic was already dressing his own leg.

"Medic!" Dooley yelled. He fumbled about his jacket for his emergency aid kit.

"I'm sorry, Sarge. I goofed up. I goofed up," Goldy spat through his own blood.

"It's not that bad. Hang on, kid." Dooley slapped a bandage over it, and injected him with morphine.

"Tell me about Valhalla," Goldy said in his treble rasp.

"It's a huge palace, kid. Big enough for all of the warriors. All you do is drink, eat, and tell each other lies about your greatest battles."

"It sounds great, sarge. I'm tired of fighting." Goldy's head fell to the side in a relaxed beatitude.

A signature dull thrum in the ear signaled everyone to scramble for cover. Branson dove into a nearby hole. Its occupant whirled to face her. Each of them brought their weapons to bear.

"Lieutenant," Meshner said in a flat voice, not unlike a man sitting down for afternoon tea.

"Lieutenant," Branson responded, matching his nonchalance. She lowered her weapon, but only as Meshner dropped his.

"We're on hallowed ground."

"We are, sir?" Branson ducked down at the renewed thrumming and then fired in its direction.

"Tilled with the blood of our enemies."

"A lot of our blood, too, sir."

"War has always been with us. She whispers to me. I try to silence Her, but She continues every night. I hear Her voice in the groans left in Her wake, and She only stops when the earth streams with blood. She whispers to me. She told me all about you. Her cup bearer. Always thirsty. I thought you were the one. It's in our nature. It's why we fight," Meshner raised the kata. "The same spirit in which Cain killed Abel. Where we walk, the earth groans with blood in our wake."

"Something's not right with you, Meshner." War did strange things to people. Sometimes Her whispers simply drove men mad. A glint of light from Meshner's side drew Branson's attention. A Nil's dress kata. Her stomach tightened like a clenched fist.

"We're both orphans of a sort, no family, no name." Meshner drained his flask, upturning it completely to capture the last drops. "I wasn't always 'Mush' the paper pusher. I had skill on the battlefield once. Then one day the war was done and I found myself back home. The white picket fence, the possibility of a normal life, was like ashes in my mouth. I had no interest in family. In friends. In any kind of social mask. What I did on the combat field was what I was. Nothing else mattered."

"There's blood on our hands." *Praise be the blood.*

"I know. Blood that rivers couldn't wash away," Meshner said. "So all we're left with are our dreams. Mine are of you. It's always you. The two of us could..."

Branson shook her head, her eyes wanting no part of whatever it was he offered. She had the feeling that he really wasn't speaking to her at all. She wondered if Meshner had been a burnout like Goldy. Perhaps before conversion he, too, had struggled against an inner darkness, one that clawed at him just under his surface.

"You have many guises," Meshner said. "You die, you come back. But I can see you now. Cursed to fight and suffer over and over again. Like the others. We have sown nothing but death and blood."

"Praise be the blood," she said. Branson had been to the cliff's edge of madness herself. She knew how tempting it could be to give in and dive off into the awaiting embrace of the abyss. So many nights she thought she was losing that tenuous grip on her humanity. Every night it seemed harder and harder to choose to remain human.

"As you have sown, so shall ye reap. For now is the time for harvest." Meshner raised his kata.

Too many times she had laid awake imagining someone trying to butcher her. Her rifle blocked his kata thrust, throwing him off balance. In close quarters the rifle was otherwise useless. His strength superior to hers. He continued to drive the blade down. Fueled by desperation, she found the strength for survival. Up close the only sounds were their gasps as they struggled. He grunted when her elbow smashed into the bridge of his nose. They were reduced to animals as he grabbed her head and drove his knee into her throat. He tried to get her in a stranglehold. She bit through his hand then butted him in the jaw. She jumped to the side and drew him backwards. She caught him by the head, her fingers gouging his eyes. She pulled his head backward. Planting her foot into the back of his knee, she threw her weight into him as he fell. He rolled over, freeing himself of her. His hand fished about, retrieving his kata. He stood up slowly, his head above the foxhole. A mad, feral smile glinted in the wan light. His blood stained his teeth. His mouth twitched as if itching for a drink.

His head exploded. Shrapnel of bone, brain matter, and blood sprayed her. The sniper round, more missile than bullet, had shattered his skull. His body dropped to its knees and he fell forward.

Waump. Waump. Waump.

She recognized the sound as well as she knew the sound of her own heartbeat. The Heathens were launching mortar bombs their way.

An explosion, pure concussive force, smacked them like the backhand of God and showered them in a storm of dirt, dust, and stone. All sound became muffled, taking on a looped, distorted quality. The woods erupted in a tumult of fire. A thick haze of smoke rose against the backdrop of flame. Men advanced like ghosts along the horizon. Branson scrambled for cover. Something hot burned through her three times. Her body betrayed her and her legs began to give out. Blood splayed across fingers she no longer felt. She fell alongside Meshner, burying her face under him to hide her breath. Not every monster was meant for redemption.

Praise be the blood.

One Million Lira

Thoraiya Dyer

THEY MIGHT SEND THE OLD woman, Sophia thought. *If she is still alive.*

Draped in light-bending cloth, stretched out along the nacelle of the monstrous, hundred-and-twenty-metre-tall wind turbine, she swept the crosshairs of her .50-cal sniper rifle's scope over Ehden's gaping, ruined restaurants and shattered, snow-blanketed hotels.

Seemed like nobody was left alive here.

But according to the aircraft's computer, seven passengers of seven hundred were left alive in the wreck of the skycruiser, Beirut II, which had crashed into the side of the mountain during yesterday's snowstorm and now rested at the foot of the wind farm's twenty-one towers. Its delicate, mile-wide wings were reduced to fragments of solar panel glittering in the midday sun. Beirut itself was over the border, roughly eighty away.

It would take two days for the Beirutis to equip a mission to reclaim the fallen cruiser from its poorer neighbour and rival, the city state of Tripoli; until then, Sophia's instructions were to defend it from Tripoli's Maghaweer commander, Amr ibn-Amr, called Amr the Unbeautiful by the sniggering, glamorous inhabitants of the Beiruti Sky Collective.

Patience is everything.

Sophia took a sip of melted snow from a pouch she'd filled with fresh flakes piled by the wind against the vanes. The great blades of Turbine Two turned in front of her, transforming the powerful and constant westerly into current that ran, like the Kadisha River, all the way west to Tripoli on the Mediterranean Sea. She didn't dwell on the artillery that could potentially be brought to bear against her. Instead she watched replays of her mother's famous Egyptian films in her mind's eye.

I am forbidden to leave the house, Badr said serenely on screen in tortured voice-over as she dipped her pen in the ink, dark eyes shining with unshed tears. *I am a caged bird.*

Interviewers begged the actress to repeat those lines at age forty, even though Badr had been in *The Broken Wings* at seventeen. A hundred times she'd smiled and shaken her head while her long, gold earrings danced. She'd said the lines again, in the end, to Sophia, when her oncologist denied her a discharge from hospital.

This bird will stay truthful and virtuous to the very end.

Sophia's mother had starred in over two hundred romantic roles, many of them ending in death. None of them featured leaky breast implants, the cause of her true death. It was why Sophia shot her victims through the left side of the chest, always.

The left breast, the one the Amazons had removed, the one that Badr had removed, to no avail.

You have one, too, Old Woman, saggy as it must be these days. You mocked me because I couldn't look them in the eye. You'd better stay by the fire. I will shoot you through the left breast, if you come.

The sunset over the sea attempted to blind her. Sophia was not so distracted by the movie replay that she failed to spot the scouts of the Mountain Combat Company when they arrived, white-swathed and carrying their skis.

They were twelve hundred metres away and poorly equipped. Some of their helmets were damaged. None carried cases of the current standard insectoid nanobots that could have infiltrated the wreck and given them the information they needed without having to directly approach it.

Sophia scrutinised each face, in search of Amr the Unbeautiful, but there was no sign of him. She flipped through a series of faces, directed to her left eye by her own highly advanced helmet's HUD, while her right eye tried to match them with the men on the slopes below.

No. None of you are valuable. None of you are important.

To keep them out of the invisible perimeter around wind farm and crumpled skycruiser, she waited for the turbine blade to pass before shooting the closest one through the self-healing cloth.

They went to ground, but it wasn't going to ground as the well-financed Beiruti troops might have known it; there was no fading into nothingness provided by light-bending cloth, no approaching ball of flame from an auto-laser-triangulation-retaliation device, just hunkering behind walls and debris. They had to know she would be on one of the towers, but with the wind too strong to place spying nanobots, even if they did have them, and with both distance and the vibration of the blades interfering with the detection of sound and shock wave signatures, they had no hope of knowing which one.

Now choose, Sophia thought coldly. How badly did Amr the Unbeautiful wish to seize the Beirut II? Badly enough to bombard the wind farm with rockets? He could destroy her, but not without destroying Tripoli's main source of power; not without plunging his city into darkness.

And perhaps the turbines could never be rebuilt. Perhaps the city would go into eternal darkness, as so many cities and countries across the world had done, with no more fossil fuels to burn and anyone with money gone to join the sky collectives.

A skylife wasn't completely free of danger. The continuously flying, solar-powered, high-altitude townships must land once a month or so to replenish their supply of water. Accidents could happen. The Beirut II was proof of that. Still, a skylife was better than a landlife, even if Beirut had been forced to appropriate billions of dollars that technically belonged to Tripoli so that all of its wealthy citizens and their families could become airbound.

A decade later, the rage of those who were left behind was undiminished. The enemy was within reach, at last; on the ground, like a bird with a broken wing. Sophia would permit them no hostages.

Two more men crossed Sophia's invisible line. She shot them, too. Killing was easy, when you accepted it was the only way to survive. She had been a killer since birth. In the summer when the heat wave had come and the crops failed, when Beirut and Tripoli were one country, she had patrolled the border against bread-thieving black market incursions; learned to kill twice with one shot, to kill the men who came and the families who now would not eat.

She killed too by being wealthy, by reaping the world's inequality to pay for chemotherapy developed by a global corporatocracy. Was that different to a bullet through the heart?

Bullets were cleaner than starvation and the horrors of lawlessness. She hadn't always been so wise. The old woman, who fought for money and had no scruples, had tutored her. *One*, Khadija had whispered in her smoke-ravaged voice, gnarled feet bare on the pine bark like a perched owl. *One is five hundred thousand lira. Nine more and I can go home. Ten is enough to pay my bills today.*

You fill your quota like you have a bag to be filled with geese, Sophia had accused from the lateral branch below, lowering her spotter's scope. She'd signed up to defy her father, who wanted her married and safely out of the police force. Despite the jeers of young men who had failed to complete the commando course, she'd earned her sword-and-tiger badge in just a few months. This was her first deployment and she was uncomfortable with the intimacy of the stalking phase. She could never be so intimate with men at home; see the sweat beading in their chest hair or the smoothness of skin over breastbone, the movement of their Adam's apples as they took long swallows of purified river water.

If you can look in a wild animal's eye as you take its life, Khadija said, *you can look into the eyes of a man.*

But Sophia couldn't. Khadija told her to aim for the chest. To pretend it was empty jackets on a clothesline. Even a weepy girl could shoot an empty jacket, couldn't she?

Her mother's empty jackets had filled three walk-in wardrobes. Sophia had wept over those jackets. The first and last time she had wept as an adult.

Now she scanned for the sniper that belonged to the combat platoon. She had the superior position. The only ridgeline that offered a comparable elevation was two kilometres away, too far away for backwards Tripoli to threaten her in these high winds. The sniper must position himself closer, in the ruins of Ehden.

There.

Sophia killed him and continued to search for the arriving support platoon. Most likely they would stay in the shelter offered by the mountainside, but if they were malnourished, or exhausted by the climb in the cold and the snow, who knew what mistakes they might make?

Her helmet told her that six skycruisers had landed in Beirut port. Troops had disembarked. Snowmobiles were being charged. New estimated time of arrival was noon the following day.

She didn't get another opportunity to thin the enemy's numbers. An hour before sunset, however, the small figure of a child was pushed by a rifle butt out into the snow from behind a concrete wall.

The child struggled with something square and presumably heavy. Snot and tears dribbled down his red face. Sophia wanted to shoot through the wall, to kill the unseen man who must be threatening him, but such solid evidence of trajectory could only end in her death. Calming herself, setting her emotions aside, like burying the bones of a meal in the snow, she watched the child wade through whiteness toward the Beirut II.

She couldn't allow an unidentified device to be brought any closer.

Breathe in. Breathe out.

With her lungs half-emptied, in the millisecond before the blade of the wind turbine obscured the shot, she squeezed the trigger and the rifle kicked.

The small body fell.

Nobody moved to retrieve him.

Sophia switched the movie back on in her head.

Husband, I am leaving you, said the beautiful actress, her head bowed. Her bosom heaved. Distress made manifest. The jilted husband stared at her flimsily clad breasts, no doubt thinking they would soon belong to another man.

The sun went down and spotlights came to life around Turbine Two, maintaining the snowy surroundings as brightly as daylight. She had counted on the constant illumination. Her invisibility cloth permitted enough visible light to pass unidirectionally through it for her targeting to be unimpeded, but infrared radiation did not pass through at all. Unless she removed the drapes, revealing her location, her thermal imaging components were useless.

Sophia ate a small bar of chocolate and switched her insulation suit to its nighttime setting. She hadn't washed her hands. Her fingers, when she licked the chocolate from them, tasted of gunpowder residue and light machine oil.

Patience was everything, and her gut told her that the old woman would come.

"You did what with an orphan boy?" demanded the president of the City-State of Tripoli.

The meeting room, a shadow of its former glory, showed plaster where the solid gold embellishments had been chipped away, melted and sold, but the two dozen men around the polished table were well enough accoutred to heavily distort the mean atomic mass back in the direction of one hundred and ninety-seven amu.

Yet not enough wealth to buy even one skycruiser, the president thought, despairing.

Prayer beads slipped through the fingers of the man he confronted across the table, Amr ibn-Amr, Commander of the Maghaweer.

"The cedar forest below Ehden," the commander said as though the president had not spoken. "We must set fire to it. You will give permission, of course."

The president, who in his youth had led the Lebanese soccer team to statistically improbable World Cup glory in the year before the first Beiruti skycruiser launched and the country was divided forever, recalled a hundred thousand flags flying in the great stadium, each one stamped with a green, stylised cedar.

"No," he said.

He still heard the drums in his dreams. The ululation of the women. The people had voted for his familiar face, jug-eared and broken-nosed. His was the dented forehead that had scored. His were the teeth whose kicking earned that vital penalty.

"We need a smokescreen," argued Amr, whose teeth had a gap suited to pulling grenade pins or imprisoning small birds. "Without smoke we can't get past the snipers to approach the cruiser. The Beirut II is non-military. The passengers won't resist."

"The Beirutis will be here for their passengers very soon. And from your reports, I would guess there is only one sniper."

The commander snatched the beads up into his palm. He drained the dregs of his coffee and stood up as if to leave.

"One sniper? It is an insult to suggest that is all they would send against our elite forces. Listen. Ordinary agents and canisters cannot obscure the area around the turbines where the skycruiser has crashed. The wind in the mountains is strong and constant. In the name of God, the Compassionate, the Merciful. It is why we built them there!"

The others watched in silence. The military men mocked the president for his inexperience in combat and the religious leaders mocked him for his so-called spinelessness; he had once bowed to his European sponsors, who wanted him clean-shaven. But he knew something, now, that they didn't, and he paused to enjoy it.

"You don't need a wildfire. To counter this sniper, you need another female sniper."

"You heap insult upon insult."

Everyone has her signature shot, his father's sister had told him. *Not only because she has pride in her work. But she must be paid, also, yes? Getting paid is very important.*

"Look at the images again. They are all shot in the left side of the chest."

"Respected President. Remind me when you served."

The president had avoided conscription. He had flown on the wings of a sports scholarship into the distant arms of elite coaches, but he knew patterns when he saw them, and now that he had seen this one, his thoughts raced. Was she still alive? What if she was living from the land, in the abandoned wilds? Would he have time to find her?

"We are all taught to aim for the larger target, sir," the crisply turned-out subcommander said from the commander's right side.

"Why don't we do that, then?"

"Sir?"

"Why don't we all aim for the larger target? Use artillery to shoot down the wind turbines, like whacking the heads off wildflowers?"

Nobody answered. It was too high a price to pay. Better to swallow the humiliation of allowing the Beirutis to trespass across their borders at will.

The president had played unwinnable games before. He did not think this was one.

"If, by sunrise tomorrow morning, I have not solved your sniper problem," he said, "you can set fire to the oldest forest in the world."

"What are you going to do?" the commander asked incredulously. "Walk up there and offer to sign autographs?"

"I won't be walking," the president smiled. "My bodyguards and I will be taking the underground train. Oh, and I require every man here to give up his gold. Place your cufflinks and everything else into this ashtray, please. I have no time for budgetary wrangling."

The mountain railway tunnels and the limestone caves that they intersected were closed at various junctions by criminal gangs; by religious cults; by the homeless, dying to the sound of dripping stalactites, out of reach of sunlight.

Every time the train was stopped and armed boys came aboard, the president faced them calmly. They were overjoyed to recognise him.

"Goal for Liban!" they cried happily, and, sometimes, "The scent of a modern man!" which was one of several foreign product endorsements routinely mistaken for a nationalistic jingo. His hosts offered pine bark tea, pistachios, and cigars. The president patiently endured their hospitality, trying not to check his watch. After a final cheek-slap from an angry sheik who told him to grow a beard, the train was permitted to complete its journey. He ascended the wet, slippery stair to the surface.

"To the Ain," he told a farmer at the station entrance, and with the press of a gold earring into a wrinkled palm, the president and his two bodyguards secured three saddled, skinny horses that put their royal Arabian bloodstock to shame. However, the roads were fallen into such neglect that, in the absence of functional helicopters, only horses would do.

It was late evening. He had only one hope of finding Aunty Khadija. She would have no electronic devices on her person, no phone: nothing to hack and no way to track her.

The horses knew the way even without the eerie glow of the chemical lamps carried by the bodyguards through the desolate winterscape. They passed the Ain, the archway that sheltered a freshwater spring.

The forest will not burn, the president told himself, and also the fans who had waved the flags.

She stood outside her square stone farmhouse, letting blood from a goat whose throat she'd recently cut.

"Hajji!" he cried, instantly ashamed by his boyish relief at what he saw as his rescue from an impossible situation. The smell of blood made his horse shy and he almost lost control of it.

Khadija put stained fists on her apron-sheathed hips.

"My sins have been forgiven," she scowled, blinking in the dimness, "and here you are to beg me to sin again. Get down from there, you ball-kicking fool. Let me see you. My eyes are not what they were."

My eyes are not what they were, Khadija thought, *but that is why Allah created 25X zoom, longer eye relief and a smaller exit pupil.*

She would not think of the weapon she'd taken as a trophy, although she now hoped to turn against its arrogant manufacturers. It was the unknown, the unexpected, that must be brought to bear, if she had a hope of outwitting a younger, better-equipped opponent, if Trabelsi was to triumph over Beiruti.

Sophia.

She had seen the captured images. The president's murky memory of the legend of Khadija's protégé, the blonde actress's daughter who wanted revenge on her mother's cancer, had led him to her home, with wish and a deadline: daybreak.

In the blue-white light of her hand-held, rechargeable lantern, the posters in the stairwell were mouldy and torn. Black slush covered the marble floor and a half-bald dog snarled from a side room, hackles rising.

"This is the place," Khadija said, smoothing one of the rips, reuniting half the ringmaster's moustache with the other half.

Najib's Travelling Tent of Wonders.

"Please," the president told one of his bodyguards. "Go upstairs. Wake him up and bring him down."

Once a wizard of the Trabelsi hologram theatre, Najib appeared in the bodyguard's keeping with no flourishes and no defences. His neat, dark hair was brittle, his singlet worn, and his neck unshaven.

"Do not eat my dog," he begged, before he saw who it was. "Sir! I am humbled. Why have you...How did you..."

"You sent my daughter one letter too many, Najib," Khadija said. "Now you must help me save Tripoli, for her."

"Is she here?" Najib stumbled in his eagerness.

"Of course not! Do you think I would let her, or any of her sisters, come back from the schools that I sent them to? Do you think I shot those poor boys at the border because I wanted a rifle of solid gold? She's married to a French doctor, raising her family in a well-off country, far from here."

Najib sagged.

"Then why—"

"I have dreamed that the children of my children's children returned to stand beneath the ancient trees. The idiot commander of the Maghaweer says he will burn them at daybreak if we do not flush out the sniper on the wind turbine."

"We?"

"You have your old recordings, I hope, Najib. And your laser projection boxes. Even though your license was taken away. The night club, the people that died from ozone poisoning? You should never have promised them a full-length feature in such a poorly ventilated space."

"I am tired, old woman. Tell me what you want."

"An open-air screening. With as many holograms as you can. Tonight, in Ehden."

"Are you mad? The recordings are degraded and there is no portable power source that can run even one such projection anymore."

"There is a transformer underneath Ehden," the president said softly. "The power cables from all the wind turbines pass through it. Our men can get access to it without exposing themselves to sniper fire."

Najib licked his lips.

"It has been a long time since I saw my beauties," he admitted at last. "Far too long."

Khadija had no cloth to hide behind on the ridge.

She murmured a quick and blasphemous prayer to the God of Snow, whose temple had once stood where she stood. In 850 BC, the Aramean King raised a great statue of Baal Loubnan at Ehden.

A hundred and fifty years later, the Assyrian King had the temple torn down and the statue overturned.

They come and they go, she thought. Christianity had come to Ehden in the 6th century. Now the little churches and abandoned monasteries were deathly silent. So, too, the crashed skycruiser which gleamed at the foot of the towering, spotlit turbines. Was there even anyone alive inside? Was all this for nothing?

"It is done, Hajji," said the Maghaweer subcommander. She had hand-picked him to accompany her and had already forgotten his name. He was polite, which could have been misread as insipidness, but Khadija recognised it as unflappability, which he would need if her plan failed and Sophia shot her through her left breast.

In the piercing cold and whistling darkness, her body heat should have shone out like a beacon to anyone with thermal sensors. Khadija was operating on the information, several years old, that infrared detection was not possible through light-bending cloth. If she was wrong, if improvements had been made to the technology, even the tiny peephole in the wall of snow that the Subcommander had constructed for them would be instantly obvious to the enemy.

But why should the Beirutis have made advances in military technology? They were safe in their sky-cities, protected by international treaty from satellite-based weapons, their cruising altitude too great for them to be vulnerable to attack from below.

Khadija searched the nacelle of each turbine for any sign of life. When she found nothing, she searched each ponderously swinging blade for the shadows of ropes or a discrepancy in rotation, which might have indicated the weight of a human being dragging asymmetrically on the structure.

Nothing.

On Khadija's advice, dogs had been sent to sniff for urine around the bases of the towers but had been shot before they could come close. They must rely on Sophia revealing herself, perhaps only for a fraction of a second. Khadija must not miss.

She had no targeting computer to help her. That section of rail on her monstrous, white-anodised, stolen StraightLine 20mm sat empty. But these peaks were her brothers and sisters, and her calculating ability had not wasted away like her muscles and bones.

Her body was brittle, she knew. She could not lie full-length in the snow for very long, even in the insulating suit the subcommander had found for her, too big in the shoulders and too tight in the hips.

"Tell me," she said as he settled alongside her.

"Yes, Hajji. Manual readings verify westerly winds of thirty-seven kilometres per hour, deformed around the turbines in the expected pattern, blade to blade interval a uniform three point two seconds, humidity sixty percent, temperature minus four degrees Celsius, altitude one thousand, five hundred and five metres."

Khadija did not respond verbally to this information, absorbing it into herself, willing herself to become one with the mountain, with the skies and the whispering forest below, even as she made the physical adjustments.

A moment later, beautiful women sprang up in the pristine snow field between the turbines and the ruins of Ehden.

Seven widely-spaced holographic images of seventeen-year-old Egyptian actress, Badr, raised swan-like arms, imploringly. There was no sound, but the moment was famous, the words immortal.

This bird will stay truthful and virtuous to the very end.

More of the images moved in from the wings. Men and women. Some frozen. Others distorted. Najib had told the truth when he said the recordings were degraded, but the strength of the broadcast was enough that many of the images could not be differentiated in the visible light spectrum from real human beings.

Khadija flicked her sight to its thermo-optical setting. There, the figures blazed. Where the beams of the lasers intersected and the air became ionised, voxels exploded like suns. She could not waste precious time enjoying the show, however.

There.

High atop Turbine Two, the lens of a telescopic sight reflected the light.

Khadija zoomed in. Only the weapon's sight had been uncovered by the enemy. Seeing her young, doomed mother move across the snow had confounded but not flustered Sophia. She had quickly realised that to distinguish human from hologram, she must discard the cloth. Her body remained hidden by the cloth, but the eye, the eye would be a hand's-breadth behind the sight.

Khadija lined up her crosshairs. She'd never had a problem looking her victims in the eye, but in that instant she was grateful to Sophia for hiding her face behind the invisible cloth. Without a face, she was an unperson. Even a dog had a face.

She took the shot. The StraightLine was deafening. Her ears rang. The brass casing melted itself a cradle in the snow, and an old, familiar litany of grief and victory whispered between heartbeats, just as the trigger had been pulled between heartbeats: *Thank you for the gift of your life.*

It was too far for her to hear the body strike the ground but she didn't need to glimpse the glitter of the scope falling from the turbine tower to know that it was done.

One. One is five hundred thousand lira.

One was enough. She should stand down now. The subcommander beside her murmured, "Casualty confirmed," and moved to pack up his gear, but Khadija said sharply,

"Wait."

Her shoulder felt like it was on fire. She no longer had the brute strength to manage the kick of such a weapon. She sensed that once she took it apart, she would never assemble it again.

Then she saw a terrified Najib being forced out into the open.

"He is worse than an animal!" Khadija exclaimed. The order for such an outrage could only have come from the commander, Amr ibn-Amr. The same man who trained his soldiers to use orphan boys to test an enemy sniper's resolve, the same man who had threatened to burn the cedar forest that was the last thing of splendour and grace left behind when the country was stripped and consigned to the skies.

"You did say there was only one, Hajji," the subcommander said quietly.

"And what will an animal like that do with the Beiruti women and children who are inside the wreck of the cruiser?"

"That is not for me to guess, Hajji."

Khadija watched the Mountain Combat Company come out into the open. With increasing confidence, they moved to secure a perimeter around the unprotected craft. The commander himself went to find Sophia's body.

He wants the light-bending cloth for himself, Khadija realised. *Once he has it, nobody will be able to punish him for treating his own allies like paper targets.*

Before the subcommander could protest, she shot his superior in the back, placing the bullet where it would emerge from his left breast. The soldiers in formation around their leader dropped into the snow.

"No!" the subcommander breathed, too late.

Two, Khadija thought. *Two is one million lira.*

She would not be paid, this time. Who cared?

"Congratulations on your promotion," she said to the shocked subcommander, patting the stock of the StraightLine. "This is yours, now. Use it wisely, and always remember. If you can look in a wild animal's eye as you take its life, you can look into the eyes of a man. If not, you had better shoot for the chest."

Rubbing her sore shoulder, she packed up her survival gear. Her water and her dried goat meat. Her explosives and her wire snares.

"If I let you go, I am a traitor, Hajji."

"Then you had better come along."

He had carried the weapon in for her. Only he could carry it out, and only its absence would deter pursuit. For a moment, it seemed he would stay there, frozen in the snow, until the men who had been his brothers up until one minute ago came to drag him away.

"I have nothing else," he said calmly. "I have nothing else but this."

"I have an unmarried youngest daughter," Khadija said. "The ball-kicking fool gave me enough gold that we could easily go to visit her. She likes skinny men."

Snow began to fall as the subcommander helped her with her skis. It was powdery and perfect, hiding them as they swished, silent as wild things, down the sloping side of the mountain.

Invincible

Jay Posey

AT THAT EXACT MOMENT, MURPH would've rather been floating in free space, something he usually hated. Instead he was squeezing one eye shut to keep the sweat from dripping into it and trying not to fidget. The chance that they could hear him on the other side was slight, but at this stage of the op he couldn't risk alerting the bad guys. Or the good guys for that matter.

Between the inner and outer hulls of the Martian cutter wasn't the most uncomfortable place he'd ever been, but it was starting to gain rank for suck factor. The recon armor protected him from all the immediate challenges—temperature extremes, high radiation, vacuum—but it wasn't exactly designed for comfort. For all their attention to detail on the way-too-expensive rig, the eggheads still hadn't figured out how to let him wipe sweat off his brow or scratch his nose.

He checked the time. It'd been almost ninety minutes since his team had silently docked and infiltrated the ship. Most of that time he'd spent slow-crawling his way from their tiny breach point on the underside all the way around to his current position just behind the bridge. The ship wasn't all that big, just a six-man cutter, but with the hostages at risk and the hostiles on edge, patience was crucial.

Intel was scant on the bad guys but best guess said they weren't the type to blow the whole ship if they thought something was up. Probably.

The rest of his team was inside the ship rather than between the hulls. Kit, Lane, and Switch would be moving into position further aft, near the

galley, where the bulk of the hostages were being guarded by four pirates.
Vance would be pulling security outside when Murph made entry on his
target room.

"L.T., Switch," she said; the suit's comms made it sound like her voice
was in Murph's own head.

"Yeah," he whispered. There wasn't any reason to whisper with his
armor on; he could've screamed and no one would've heard a thing
through the sealed faceplate. Still. Tough habit to break. "Go ahead."

"Floaters are headed your way."

Two of the hostiles had been roving around the ship, mostly away
from where they'd stashed the crew. The plan had been to secure the hostages first and then deal with the rovers afterward. But as the saying went,
a plan was just a list of things that didn't happen anyway.

"Roger that. You guys set?"

"We're set."

"All right, I'll give it a couple to see what they're up to. We'll go on
my call. Stand by."

"Roger, standing by."

Captain Morland didn't wake up so much as have consciousness forced
upon him. He cracked an eye but had to shut it again immediately; the
light dazzled him and sent a sharp pain shooting through the center of his
head. He thought a deep breath would steady him, but instead it lit the left
side of his torso with fire. His sluggish mind finally started catching up,
assaulting him with image fragments, sounds, smells. The unidentified
craft. The unshakeable pursuit. The boarding and the short-lived defense.
Broken ribs, probably a concussion. Lieutenant Griffin, dead.

The attackers were dressed like a rag-tag crew, claimed they were freedom fighters off of Mars's moon Phobos. They made a pretty good show
of it, but the takedown was too clean, too precise. Mercenaries, maybe,
but they were more likely some military unit from a faction that didn't
want attention.

Morland flexed his hands against the cuffs that bound them behind
his back. They'd clamped him to a support down low so he couldn't stand
up, even if he'd had the balance to do so. There was a distant buzzing, a
deep drone like something was humming behind him, somewhere inside
the wall. It took a moment for him to realize he was only hearing it in his
left ear. Add a ruptured ear drum to the list. His head was swimming. He
eased his eyes open again, hoping to relieve the lazy spin of the room.

The lights weren't actually that bright. They'd put him in a storage
room just behind the bridge; the single light above the door glowed dull

orange. Morland surveyed the room slowly, careful not to shift his view too quickly. A large man stood by the only door to the room, staring down at him with a blank expression. He had a rifle slung across his chest. The rifle was pretty banged up but looked well maintained. The guy was awfully casual for someone supposedly new at this sort of thing. He didn't even blink when Morland looked at him.

The captain scanned the rest of the storeroom. None of his crew members were imprisoned with him. Another way the "freedom fighters" had tipped their hand. Amateurs tended to keep the prisoners all together: easier to watch over that way. Sometimes amateurs would rough up the ranking officer to show all the others they were in charge. But these guys had separated the leader from the rest of the crew. If Morland had to put money on it, he'd bet the attackers were keeping his crewmates in as much uncertainty as possible, exploiting a wild range of emotions to keep them from trying anything. Was their captain dead? Cooperating with the bad guys? A traitor?

Morland closed his eyes. The room spun lazily whether he could see it or not, and at least the pain in his head wasn't as sharp when his eyes were shut. He tried to work through the details as best he could.

Were there five or six attackers? They'd moved fast and hadn't fired many shots. Griff was dead for certain, shot through the throat. Kady was hit, but Morland couldn't get the image clear enough in his mind to judge the extent of her injuries. Maybe she was all right. Bad guys probably had them all down in the hold. Galley, maybe.

Why they'd targeted the *Sunseeker*, Morland didn't know. They were just a small-time private shipping vessel running cargo back and forth between Mars and her moons, and the Belt when the alignments were right. She could make the trip to Earth if she had to, but Morland hadn't done that in at least a decade. Wouldn't anytime soon, either. *Sunseeker* could handle more than the six-man crew, but Morland preferred to keep it light. Now he was wishing maybe he'd taken his wife's advice and hired on a couple of extra for security.

Then again, in this case, it likely wouldn't have done much but gotten more of his crew killed. Vera wasn't going to let him hear the end of it, though. If he got to see her again. He still hadn't fixed the towel rack on the back of the bathroom door.

Three quick taps sounded on the storeroom door. Morland opened his eyes to see the big man slide to one side and work the latch. Two others were standing in the corridor. The captain noticed that the auxiliary lights were on. Running low-power, then. The thinner of the two men stepped in, his eyes flicking quickly to Morland as he entered. The ringleader. He leaned in close to the guard and held an exchange too quiet for the captain to catch. After a few moments, the ringleader came and crouched in front of the captain.

"How's ya feel, Cap'n?" he asked. The accent almost sounded authentic enough for a hillbilly from Phobos, but not quite. Just ever so slightly forced. "Thirsty? Hongry?"

Morland held the man's gaze. A few seconds elapsed before the ringleader nodded. "You know how it deals," he said with a half-shrug. "Play nice a few more hours, and the big money'll show. Then we're on our way, same as you."

"Not all of us," Morland said. The ringleader nodded again.

"We are right sorry, Cap'n. If we could unspill it, we would. But all the rest are fine and well, and it'd be nice to keep that way."

"You don't need more than me," Morland said. "There's a shuttle in Hangar Two. Let the rest of my crew go home."

The ringleader gave a grim smile and shook his head. "Can't this time, Cap'n. But I'll let 'em know you offered." He gave a little half-nod, stood to his feet. "Just keep your head on. Everything's gonna work out."

He went back to the door and again exchanged quiet words with the guard. Before exiting, he glanced back at Morland. "Sure I can't get you anything?"

There was something in the look, or the tone of voice maybe. The barest trace of sadness or remorse. In that moment, Morland was instantly sure of two things: firstly, the ringleader was indeed a military officer. And secondly, they were going to kill everyone on board.

The captain had to do something. But what? He was still trying to think it through when the ringleader gave him a little nod and started to turn back towards the exit.

Then the bad guy standing guard out in the hallway made a funny noise and fell down. The ringleader and the other guard barely had time to react before there was a sharp hiss and a searing flash, lightning-bright even through Morland's reflexively closed eyes.

There was a confusion of sound, and when Morland opened his eyes again, he couldn't quite process what he was seeing. The air was harsh and hazy. In front of him lay a circular piece of steel, smoking faintly and glowing around the edge with the dull red of rapidly cooling metal. And all three of the bad guys were sprawled on the deck, motionless.

And yet someone was talking.

"Captain Morland, *sir*," the voice said, insistent. Morland shook his head, trying to clear it, to get his bearings. It sounded like the voice was coming from above him. He glanced up.

There in the ceiling was a two-foot wide hole, and through it poked the head and shoulders of the owner of the voice. There was no face, just a curved metal shield where one should be.

"We're here to get you out, sir," the figure said. The voice sounded slightly distorted: thin and processed.

Morland nodded. The figure above withdrew, and then, a moment later, slipped feet-first through the hole in the ceiling and dropped lightly to the deck. It hardly made any sound when it landed, which was surprising, because it seemed to be encased entirely in a metal suit. That was, the suit had a metallic texture, but it moved too fluidly, more like a rubberized suit than armor. The styling was vaguely reminiscent of the powered armor he'd seen the Marines use back during his time in the Navy, but it was far sleeker, streamlined to the point that comparing them didn't seem fair. Distant cousins, maybe. Or generations more advanced. A compact weapon was tightly slung across the figure's chest.

The suited figure came and crouched at the captain's feet. It moved as easily as if the armor was its own skin.

"Captain Morland, are you injured, sir?"

It took a moment before Morland could respond. "Nothing serious, I don't think. Concussion, maybe."

The figure nodded. "We're going to get you home, sir. I just need to ask you a couple of questions first."

Morland still wasn't exactly sure what was going on. And it was unsettling, staring at that dull, featureless plate where a face should be.

"Your wife's full name, sir?"

Morland blinked; it was such an unexpected question. "Vera...Vera Winslowe Morland."

"And you were born where, sir?"

"Station H44, Ceres."

The figure moved around to the captain's left side, revealing a second person in an identical suit crouched in the room, checking the fallen ringleader. Morland hadn't heard the second one come in. He felt a vibration in his wrists and suddenly his hands came free; he brought them together in front of him and winced at the burning stiffness in his shoulders.

The second figure looked over at them casually and, although he couldn't hear anything, Morland got the impression the two of them were communicating somehow. Internal comms maybe. Probably. But even with that likely explanation, the silent conversation was uncanny. A few seconds later the second figure gave a nod and moved to the door, shouldering its weapon and taking up a defensive position.

"Can you walk, sir?" the first rescuer asked.

"Yeah," Morland answered. "I think so."

"All right, let's get you up," the figure said. It slung its weapon, then leaned closer and wrapped its arm around Morland's back to help him up. The captain hissed at the searing pain in his left side, and the figure in the suit froze immediately. "You okay?"

"My ribs," Morland said through clenched teeth. "Might've broken something."

The figure moved to Morland's right. "Here, this'll help." It tapped the captain's belt near his right hip. "Grab your belt here with your left hand, keep that elbow tucked in and locked close to your side. Should make things a little more stable."

Morland did as he was directed, then draped his right arm over the figure's shoulders.

"Set?" the figure in the suit said. Morland nodded. "All right, easy up." The figure stood slowly and effortlessly lifted the captain to his feet. "Lean on me, I've got you. We'll take it slow."

Morland just nodded again. He was surprised at how weak he felt, and he was grateful for the support. The first rescuer looked over at the second one. A brief pause, and then the second figure flowed out into the corridor, weapon up.

"Here we go," his rescuer said, and they started forward. They held at the door briefly, then slipped out into the corridor. Morland's gaze slipped over the fallen man as they passed him still slumped against the wall. There weren't any immediately obvious wounds, but the man's eyes were open and dully glassed. Further down the corridor, the other figure kept watch at an intersection. It held position until Morland and his escort had passed the danger zone, then smoothly rolled around and scouted ahead again. There was something graceful in the figure's movements, a casual precision born of countless years of experience.

"Sorry about the hole," the figure carrying him said quietly.

"What?"

"In the ceiling back there. Didn't want to give 'em a chance to seal themselves in with you. Still, I never like cutting up someone's ship."

"Oh...that's all right." Morland didn't really know what else to say. "Who are you guys?"

"No one of consequence, sir." The tone was polite and professional, but the implication was clear: questions weren't getting answered. "Almost there."

Looking up, Morland saw they were nearing the ship's galley. The other figure paused outside the door, a little further down the corridor, slowly sweeping the way ahead with its weapon.

"Here we are," the first figure said. They halted at the door, and a few moments later it opened; another suited figure greeted them, a woman. Two small plates rested on either side of her head where the other suits were smooth. He guessed it was her face-plate, retracted.

"Captain Morland," she greeted him. "You've got a lot of folks here who are gonna be real glad to see you."

The first figure must've said something, because the woman's eyes flicked over to it. She shook her head.

"Array went down, I had to pop it to see." She shook her head again. "Nah, have to get the shop to look at it."

She stepped back out of the way. Four bodies dressed similarly to the ringleader were sprawled in various places around the room. So there'd been seven total, then. And two other people in those suits; one was crouched over one of the boarders, and the other was standing guard over a group of people who were huddled together in the far corner. Kady and Zeke, Cloud and Hunter. His crew. All there. All except Griff.

"Captain!" Kady said, and the others turned Morland's way. The wash of emotion was almost overwhelming as the soldier escorted him over to reunite them. Kady had a pressure pack running from her collarbone over her right shoulder and was a little pale, but otherwise she looked like she was all right. Zeke had a grim but steady look. Which was pretty much normal.

"We're working out pickup right now," the first figure said. "Shouldn't be much longer." He gave the captain a little nod, then quietly withdrew.

Murph left to give the crew some sense of privacy as they welcomed their captain back into the fold. It was always better to keep some separation from the precious cargo. It never hurt to be polite, of course, but if you let them get too comfortable they tended to start asking questions, or worse, thinking they were free to do what they wanted. And that most certainly wasn't the case, not until Murph's team had delivered them safely home, which they had not yet done.

Lane was keeping an eye on them. His big, silent presence was imposing enough that it'd keep them in line.

"Kit, what do you have for me?" Murph asked. Kit was hunched over one of the pirates, running an ID sweep.

"Two things," Kit said, sitting back on his haunches. "Jack. And squat."

"The others?"

"Same."

"Crypted?"

"Nope."

"Erased?"

"Not even. These fellas are cleaner than a baby's bottom."

Murph didn't like the sound of that, and not just because Kit had botched the saying, which might've been funny in other circumstances.

"You getting a good line?" Switch said as she came over and crouched next to Kit.

"Gee, Mas'sarnt, I dunno," Kit said, "why don't you remind me how to do this thing I've only done a billion times."

Part of the mission had been to identify the unknown boarders and what they were after, but Murph hadn't expected this level of sophistication. Probably nobody at Higher had.

And it really bothered him seeing Switch there with her faceplate open. They had the suits for a reason. He preferred everybody stay buttoned up, start to finish.

He suddenly got a funny feeling—one that he never wanted to have in the field.

"Switch, let Kit—" he started to say, but a loud pop cut him off. Kit flinched and Switch toppled over backwards.

"Lane, Vance, hostages!" Murph called, even though his people were already taking care of it, shepherding the civilians back into the corner. "Kit, you okay?"

"I'm cool," Kit said, but Murph could hear strain in his voice. The front of his armor had a few fresh divots and pock marks and was spattered sticky red. "Switch is hit."

Murph was already in motion towards her, but he knew what was waiting for him. He still had that sick, hollow feeling, and his mouth had gone completely dry. He crouched next to her. Her eyes were open, unfocused, staring in slightly opposite directions. Just under her right eye, through the cheekbone, a single, perfectly round hole welled red.

Kit knelt on the other side of her.

"She's gone," Murph said. They both just stared down at her for a span.

"Some kind of subdermal charge," Kit said finally, glancing back at the now-mangled corpse of the man he'd just been trying to ID. "Didn't show on the scan."

"You set it off?"

"No way to know."

"Better keep everybody away from the others, then," Murph said. "Vance, roll it up. We're moving to the bay."

"Roger," Vance answered, her voice cool, professional. She and Lane gathered the crew up and directed them sharply out of the galley. Murph started to arrange Switch's arms, preparing to lift the body.

He kept reminding himself that she wasn't really gone. Not forever. They'd get her back. They'd put her through the Process, and soon enough she'd be back. But no matter how many times he'd seen it, Murph had never been able to overcome the shock of seeing one of his team members killed in action. A dead friend wasn't something anyone could used to.

"I got her, L.T.," Kit said.

"I'll carry her."

"I said I got her."

Murph hesitated; Kit was a better shooter than he was. Still, he heard the edge in Kit's voice. If his head wasn't in the right place, maybe it was better for Murph to be on the trigger after all.

"Sure, Kit. You got her." Murph said. He got to his feet as Kit gently lifted Switch and laid her across his shoulders in a fireman's carry. She dangled limply, and the blood that had pooled inside her helmet poured out onto the grated metal floor of the galley. Murph shouldered his weapon and led the way aft, towards the bay. As they walked, he called it in. "Kingpin, Growler."

"Go ahead, Growler," came the response.

"We are partial mission complete, requesting immediate extract; team plus six VIPs, with four casualties."

"Copy that, Growler. Viking Three One is on station, full med staff on board. What's the damage?"

"One VIP killed, two VIPs wounded, all prior to our arrival. All stable. We have one team member KIA...we lost Switch."

There was a half-second pause, the barest hint of a hitch before the response came back.

"Understood. Viking Three One is routing to you now. Mission objectives?"

"Seven enemy KIA; team was unable to positively identify the hostile element. Be advised, environment is unsafe. Enemy KIA may be rigged with anti-personnel charges."

"Rigged?"

"Yeah, one of the bodies detonated. We didn't stick around for the others."

"Roger that, Growler. We'll get a tech crew together to follow up. Good work."

"Not really."

"Patching Viking Three One through. Stand by."

There was a click as the new channel opened, and then a background hiss as different hardware and encryption schemes negotiated in real time.

"Growler, this is Viking Three One. How do you read?"

"Crystal, Viking Three One. Send your traffic."

"Viking Three One is approaching along one-seven-one at full burn. Seven mikes out."

"Roger that, Viking Three One. You've got specs on the vessel?"

"That's an ay-firm, Growler."

"We'll be holding in the primary bay. *Lamprey*'s attached to the belly." The *Lamprey* was the delivery vehicle they'd used to board the ship.

"Copy that. See you shortly, Growler. Viking Three One out."

Murph updated the rest of the team and then completed the remaining walk in silence, reaching the loading bay a couple of minutes after he'd signed off with Viking. Vance and Lane already had the crew members gathered; they were in a quiet knot near the airlock, with Lane keeping careful watch. The body of the fallen crewmember had already been recovered and lay hidden under a heavy tarp.

The VIPs turned and glanced in Murph's direction, but most of them looked away quickly. Only the captain continued to watch Murph's approach. Captain Morland was a good twenty-five years older than Murph at least, but the look on his face was one Murph could easily imagine seeing in the mirror. The others couldn't cope with having to look at the price of their freedom, draped over Kit's shoulders. The captain, on the other hand, must've been in Murph's situation at one time or another; there was understanding and muted acceptance. And more than a little survivor's guilt, most likely.

Viking Three One was right on time, which was a nice change from other missions, and the transfer became a routine affair. It wasn't until the VIPs had been handed off to the medical staff and Viking Three One had completed the recovery of the *Lamprey* that Murph let himself flip the emotional switch.

He grabbed a seat against the smooth curving wall of the transport, took his helmet off, and felt the sweat on his brow go cold. The wave rolled over him, and he closed his eyes as the adrenaline burned off and was replaced by ten tons of fatigue. Every muscle ached in a dull, distant sort of way. It was a two-hour ride back home, and Murph spent that time caught between a body that wanted to crash out and a mind that insisted on replaying the worst few moments over and over again.

They'd been back barely four hours before they were on deck again. Op tempo had been stepping up of late, but none of them had been expecting to go back out again so soon. When Murph got to the briefing room, Lane was already there in the back row, his big boots up on the table and his head down on his chest. Hard to tell if he was sleeping or thinking.

It was one of the smaller rooms, with two sets of gently curving tables arranged in three rows and a narrow center aisle, like an amphitheater in miniature. Murph slid into a seat in the second row, nearest the door. Lieutenant Commander Vega showed up a couple of minutes later and started talking before she'd even crossed the threshold.

"Sorry for the short turnaround, but Higher's running around like the ship's on fire for this one," Vega said, looking up from the display in her hand and cutting herself off. She frowned at the mostly empty room.

"Probably working out," Murph said. Vega tapped the display on the table in front a few times, considering. "Time-sensitive, huh?"

"Very," she answered. "I'll give 'em ninety seconds before I call them out over the ship's comms."

"Mighty kind of you, Boss," Lane said from the back.

Vega was the team's acting commanding officer while they were attached to their current task force; their ranks didn't line up quite right on account of the different branches, but after the first couple of ops she'd been gracious enough to let them mostly call her "Boss." She was about to reply, but just then a figure walked through the door, and she smiled instead.

"Hey, look who's up and about," she said.

Murph had been expecting Vance, because Kit was, as a rule, always last in, but his heart jumped a little when he saw who it was.

Switch.

She was moving a little more slowly than usual, but considering she'd been dead just a few hours earlier, she was looking pretty good. And with her came the momentary dissonance of seeing the dead raised; just as Murph couldn't accustom himself to losing a teammate, nor could he get used to that first sight of them alive again.

"What'd I miss?" Switch asked as she slid in behind Murph and took a seat two chairs down.

"Not much," Murph said. "You're back online awful quick."

Switch gave a curt nod. "Still had two backups on ice, so it was just a transfer for me."

"How far back?"

She thought for a moment. "They had me right up until you called in that you'd secured the captain."

Murph ran through the mission in his mind, replayed the critical moments. "That's not bad. Lost five, seven minutes maybe," he said.

"How'd it happen?" Switch asked.

There wasn't any doubt what she meant by *it*. "Still not exactly sure. Kit was getting zero on a scan, but there was some kind of implanted charge on one of the bad guys. You had your faceplate popped. Bad things."

"Yeah, I remember the part about the faceplate...sensor array glitched out just before we breached."

"I already gave the techs about eighteen levels of hell over that, but by all means give 'em your own when you get a chance."

She nodded, and they just looked at each other for a moment. No matter how many times he'd been through it, there was always something uncanny about a dead friend sitting right there, asking how they'd died.

"You go see the old you?" Lane asked from behind.

"That's a big negatory," Switch answered over her shoulder. "Too creepy." And then, a moment later, she turned to look at him. "You ever do that?"

Lane grunted. "Just the first time."

The technology wasn't all that new. Cloning, storing and transferring consciousness—a sort of hacked immortality that Murph and his teammates just referred to as the Process. Their unit was one of a precious few that enjoyed the "privilege" of having a couple of extra lives, but they'd had to earn it the hard way. The joke was that the only way you got into the unit was by proving the military couldn't kill you anyway.

A bark of laughter came from the hall, and then Kit and Vance came in together, sweaty and in their PT gear. They both stopped short when they saw Vega already standing up front, and then quickly forgot about her when they saw Switch sitting there.

"Mas'sarnt!" Kit said, crossing the distance to her in about two steps and giving her an awkward combination handshake/one-arm hug across the table. "What're you doin' here?"

Switch half-stood out of her seat. "Waiting on you, Kit. Can't believe you let the dead girl beat you to a brief," she said, and then, as she sat back down, added, "No, wait. Yes I can."

Kit chuckled, but a moment later Murph saw the flicker of pain on his face.

"Hey, uh..." he started, his tone suddenly somber, apologetic. Switch waved him off.

"Don't waste the words, brother," she said. "We're good." Kit's expression was somewhere between a smile and a grimace.

Vega cleared her throat. "Sorry to break up the reunion, folks, but we need to get moving on this."

Kit nodded and sat on top of the table. Vance moved around to the third row and traded a fist bump with Switch before sitting down next to Lane.

"The tech crew did a thorough sweep of the *Sunseeker* but still couldn't turn up any ID on the hostiles. That narrows our field down to about three possible sponsors."

"Money on Lunar," Vance said.

"Could be," Vega answered. "But this isn't the sort of thing to jump to conclusions on. When *our* people who don't exist are bumping into *their* people who don't exist, it's a different kind of game."

"So what's next?" Murph asked, hoping to get to the point.

"Well, we think something got transferred off the *Sunseeker*. Jettisoned, really. A little trajectory analysis turned up an unregistered frigate in the right area at the right time, and when our boys tracked its current course, they uncovered something interesting."

Vega paused with a little half-smile, waiting for someone to be impressed. She was way too proud of the eggheads.

"Sooooo," Murph said. "What's next?"

Vega's half-smile deflated. "There's an unknown vessel keeping station awfully close to an asteroid about forty megs out from the *Sunseeker's* previous position. Its signature reads like a *Victor*-class ship, but heavily modified; looks like they're trying not to be noticed." A *meg* was Navy-speak for a thousand kilometers, which put the target ship at the kind of distance that was so big as to be almost meaningless to Murph. For all the time he spent in space, he was a boots-on-the-ground kind of guy at heart.

"Lunar?" Vance asked. Vega nodded. Vance held a hand up and rubbed her fingertips together like somebody needed to pay up.

"We don't know what its capabilities are," Vega continued, "or what it might do if we tried to intercept. And we don't want to provoke a response of any kind until we know who and what we're dealing with."

"You want us to hit an unknown vessel that's kinda maybe *Victor*-class, sort of?" Murph asked.

"Not hit," Vega said. "Just recon."

Murph's team waited in silence, knowing there was more.

"And if possible, prep the craft for a hit," she added.

"There it is," Kit said.

"I know it sounds risky, but Higher's already run the scenario and drawn up a plan of action—"

"Whoa, hold up now," Murph said, interrupting, but Vega held up a hand and stopped him.

"Before you unload, let me just run you through it."

It didn't take long for the briefing to turn into a grind session. They went through every detail from top to bottom and back again, asking questions, assessing risks, challenging assumptions, stripping out all the unnecessary bits that some good idea fairy had sprinkled throughout the whole thing.

Murph kept finding his gaze drawn to Switch, enough times that it started to bother him. He kept telling himself he was totally focused on the mission, and then the next thing he knew, he'd be looking over at her, and he couldn't figure out why.

Finally, it clicked. She had a little notch in her left ear where one night a combination of beer and friendly combatives had led to a hard fall against a table and had taken a chunk out of the lobe. At least, there used to be a notch there. Now that ear was whole, undamaged. Murph had never really thought much of it before, but now he found himself missing it. In giving her life, they'd taken her scars.

He shook his head and refocused his mind on the task at hand.

Ten hours later, they were suited up and packed tightly into their narrow, low-signature delivery vehicle, the *Lamprey*, which they all affectionately called "the coffin."

Murph found himself unusually distracted. He tried to tell himself it was just the long ride, or the lack of rest between operations, or the near insanity of infiltrating a virtually unknown ship. Eventually he had to admit what was really going on. Switch's death had shaken him, and all the thoughts and emotions around it refused to be ignored.

It wasn't like it was the first time he'd lost a teammate. He'd even been through the Process twice himself. But he had a box for that, inside. For all those things. He had a box in his heart where he kept the pain, and the loss, and the terrible things he'd seen. One day, when he'd served his time and done his duty, he planned to open that box and sort through it, and to give each memory its due. But for now it had to stay closed, and it had to stay separate. That's how it'd always been, and how it had to be.

But no matter how hard he tried to keep that box closed, the thoughts kept leaking out.

He'd been through the Process. He was fine. Switch was fine.

But was he really the same person? The body was identical, but it wasn't really the *same*. And the mind. The memories, the habits, the quirks, they were all there. But to some degree, they were just copies of something that had once been original. Backups. Did it really matter whether he was the same, or just something so like the same as to be impossible to distinguish?

Murph bit down on the mouthpiece of his helmet and sucked cool water, hoping to calm his racing mind.

It'd been so arbitrary: a glitch in a supposedly perfect system, her faceplate open, the timing of the explosion. How many little things had gone wrong to lead to that little perfect hole in her face? That was the hardest part, knowing that no amount of training or preparation could ever shield his team from the random events of the universe.

It almost didn't matter what the mission was anymore; they'd trained for and executed so many. Hostage rescue. Recon. Ship takedown. Each was just a link in a chain that led to another. Murph just had to trust each was as important as they said, and that the whole thing had an end somewhere, some day. Mission after mission, he and his team got the job done, because that's what they did, and not even death could keep them from the next one. And the next one. Still, all that training, all that experience, they still couldn't escape simple bad luck.

When he'd made the unit, they'd told him he'd never have to fear death again. That he'd never have to worry about losing a brother. That they were invincible.

But they were wrong. It wasn't that your brother never died. It was that he died a hundred times. A thousand times. And every time you couldn't save him...well, for all Murph had suffered in his service, he'd not yet found a pain as deep as the one that came from having failed someone so completely.

He looked over at Switch then, her shoulder three inches from his. Seeing the movement, she turned her head slightly towards him. He just reached up and tapped his own faceplate three times. She nodded. He couldn't see the smile, but he imagined one there. And he remembered the hole in her cheek, and the way her eyes had dulled.

He turned back and closed his eyes, took another sip of water. New body, new brain. Same soul. The eggheads still hadn't figured out how to fix the scars on that one. There were more ways to break than science had found ways to fix, and that wasn't likely to change anytime soon. For just a minute, Murph gave himself permission to feel the fear, the sadness, the anger. Just for a minute. And then, he packed it all back into his box, and locked it with a final thought.

Invincible, he thought. *Well, that may be. But we sure as hell aren't invulnerable.*

Light and Shadow

Linda Nagata

LIEUTENANT DANI REID WAS SERVING her turn on watch inside Fort Zana's Tactical Operations Center. She scanned the TOC's monitors and their rotating displays of real-time surveillance data. All was quiet. Even the goats that usually grazed outside the walls had retreated, taking refuge from the noon sun in a grove of spindly thorn trees.

The temperature outside was a steamy 39°C, but within the fort's prefabricated, insulated walls, the air was cool enough that Reid kept the jacket of her brown-camo combat uniform buttoned up per regulation. The skullcap she wore was part of the uniform. Made like an athletic skullcap, it covered her forehead and clung skin-tight against her hairless scalp. Fine wires woven through its silky brown fabric were in constant dialog with the workings of her mind.

On watch, the skullcap kept her alert, just slightly on edge, immune to the mesmerizing hum of electronics and the soothing whisper of air circulating through the vents—white noise that retreated into subliminal volumes when confronted by a louder sound: a rustle of movement in the hallway.

Private First Class Landon Phan leaned in the doorway of the TOC.

Phan was just twenty-one, slender and wiry. Beneath the brim of his skullcap, his eyebrows angled in an annoyed scowl. "L.T.? You should go check on Sakai."

"Why? What's up?"

"Ma'am, you need to see it yourself."

Phan had been part of Reid's linked combat squad for nine months. He'd done well in the LCS; he'd earned Reid's trust. She didn't feel the same about Sakai.

"Okay. You take the watch."

Light spilling from the TOC was the only illumination in the hallway. The bunkroom was even darker. Reid couldn't see anything inside, but she could hear the fast, shallow, ragged breathing of a soldier in trouble, skirting the edge of panic. She slapped on the hall light.

Specialist Caroline Sakai was revealed, coiled in a bottom bunk, her trembling fists clenched against her chin, her eyes squeezed shut. She wore a T-shirt, shorts, and socks, but she wasn't wearing a skullcap. The pale skin of her hairless scalp gleamed in the refracted light.

"What the hell?" Reid whispered, crossing the room to crouch beside the bunk. "Sakai? What happened?"

Sakai's eyes popped open. She jerked back against the wall, glaring as if she'd never seen Reid before.

"What the hell?" Reid repeated.

Sakai's gaze cut sideways. She bit her lip. Then, in an uncharacteristically husky voice, she confessed, "I think...I was having a nightmare."

"No shit! What did you expect?"

She seemed honestly confused. "Ma'am?"

"Where the hell is your skullcap?"

Sakai caught on; her expression hardened. "In my locker, ma'am."

The microwire net in Reid's skullcap detected her consternation and responded to it by signaling the tiny beads strewn throughout her brain tissue to stimulate a counteracting cerebral cocktail that helped her think calmly, logically, as this conversation veered into dangerous territory.

The skullcap was standard equipment in a linked combat squad. It guarded and guided a soldier's emotional state, keeping moods balanced and minds honed. It was so essential to the job that, on deployment, LCS soldiers were allowed to wear it at all times, waking or sleeping. And they did wear it. All of them did. Always.

But they were not required to wear it, not during off-duty hours.

The hallway light picked out a few pale freckles on Sakai's cheeks and the multiple, empty piercings in her earlobes. It tangled in her black, unkempt eyebrows and glinted in her glassy brown eyes. "You want the nightmares?" Reid asked, revolted by Sakai's choice.

"Of course not, ma'am."

Use of the skullcap was tangled up in issues of mental health and self-determination, so regulations existed to protect a soldier's right of choice. Reid could not order Sakai to wear it when she was off-duty; she could not even ask Sakai why she chose to go without it. So she approached the issue sideways. "Something you need to talk about, soldier?"

"No, ma'am," Sakai said in a flat voice. "I'm fine."

Reid nodded, because there was nothing else she could do. "Get some sleep, then. Nightmares aren't going to excuse you from patrol."

She returned to the TOC, where Phan was waiting. "When did this start?"

"Yesterday," he answered cautiously.

Even Phan knew this wasn't a subject they could discuss.

"Get some sleep," she told him. "Use earplugs if you have to."

When he'd gone, Reid considered reporting the issue to Guidance...but she knew what Guidance would say. So long as Sakai performed her duties in an acceptable manner, she was within her rights to forego the skullcap during off-duty hours, no matter how much it disturbed the rest of the squad.

What the hell was Sakai trying to prove?

Reid ran her palms across the silky fabric of her skullcap. Then, as if on a dare, she slipped her fingertips under its brim and took it off.

A cold draft kissed her bare scalp and made her shiver.

Her pulse picked up as fear unfolded around her heart.

You're psyching yourself out.

Probably.

She studied the skullcap, turning it over, feeling the hair-thin microwires embedded in the smooth brown cloth.

No big deal, really, to go without it. It was only out of habit that she wore it all the time.

The hum of electronics within the TOC grew a little louder, a little closer, and then, with no further warning, Reid found herself caught up in a quiet fury. Sakai had always been the squad's problem child. Not in the performance of her duty—if that had been an issue, Reid would have been all over her. It was Sakai's personality. She didn't mesh. Distant, uncommunicative, her emotions locked away. A loner. Seven months at Fort Zana had not changed her status as an outsider.

Reid's emotions were closer to the surface: she didn't like Sakai; didn't like her effect on the squad. There needed to be trust between her soldiers, but none of them really trusted Sakai and no one wanted to partner with her. No one believed she would truly have their back if things went hard south. Reid saw it in the field when her soldiers hesitated, thought twice, allowed a few seconds to pass in doubt. Someday those few seconds would be the last measure of a life.

Reid clenched the skullcap.

Fuck Sakai anyway.

Ducking her head, she slipped the cap back on, pressing it close to her scalp. Within seconds, her racing heart slowed. Her anger grew cold and thoughtful.

Sakai thought she could get by without her skullcap. Maybe she wanted to prove she had more mettle than the rest of them, but it wouldn't last. It couldn't. "You'll give it up," Reid whispered. "By this time tomorrow, you'll be back in the fold."

Reid finished her watch and went back to sleep, waking at 1900. She laced on her boots, then tromped next door to the TOC, where Private First Class David Wicks was on duty.

"Anything?" she asked.

"No, ma'am. No alerts at all from Command." He flashed a shy smile. "But my niece had her first-birthday party today." He pulled up a window with his email, and Reid got to watch a short video of a smiling one-year-old in a pretty blue dress.

"Your sister doing okay now?"

"Yeah, she's good."

Wicks sent money to his sister. It was a big part of why he'd signed up.

In the kitchen, Reid microwaved a meal, then joined Sergeant Juarez at the table. "Command thinks we've got a quiet night."

Juarez was no taller than Reid, but he carried fifty extra pounds of muscle. He'd been Army for seven years, and Reid was sure he'd be in for twenty if he could pull it off. "You ever notice," he drawled, "how the patrol gets interesting every time Command says there's nothing going on?"

"Just means we're good at finding trouble."

Phan reeled in, with Private First Class Mila Faraci a step behind him. "How's it look tonight, L.T.?" Faraci asked.

"Quiet so far."

"That's what I like to hear."

Juarez finished eating. He got up just as Sakai came in the door wearing a fresh uniform, her cheeks still flushed from a hot shower and her head freshly denuded of hair, leaving her scalp smooth and pale under the ceiling lights with no skullcap to hide it. Phan and Faraci were waiting together by the two humming microwaves. Phan glared. Faraci looked shocked. "I thought you were shitting me," she murmured.

Sakai ignored everyone. She opened the freezer and pulled out a meal packet while Reid traded a look with Juarez.

"What the hell is with you, Sakai?" Faraci demanded.

"Faraci," Juarez growled, "you got a problem?"

Faraci was strong, tall, tough, and full of swagger, but she took care never to cross Juarez. "No, Sergeant."

Reid got up, dumped her meal packet, and left. Juarez followed her to her quarters, where there was barely enough room for the two of them to stand without breathing each other's air.

"What the hell?" he demanded.

"You know I can't ask. She hasn't said anything to you?"

"She doesn't talk to me or anybody. It's been worse since she got back from leave."

Skullcaps got turned in before a soldier went on leave. It was a harsh transition, learning to live without it. But taking it up again after your twenty-one days—that was easy. No one ever had a problem with that.

"She's just annoyed at being back," Reid decided. "If there was a real issue, Guidance would know. They would address it. Meantime, make sure our other noble warriors don't get in her face. I don't want to bust the kids when Sakai is the loose cannon."

"You got it, L.T."

"This won't last," Reid assured him. "You'll see. She'll give this up tomorrow."

Reid was wrong.

Sakai wore the skullcap during the nightly patrols as she was required to do, but for three days running she took the cap off as soon as she hit the showers, and it didn't go on again until they rigged up for the next patrol. This generated its own problem: Sakai couldn't sleep well without her skullcap. It wouldn't be long before she was unfit for patrol.

Reid rigged up early for the night's adventures. Her armored vest went on first. Then she strapped into her "dead sister." The titanium exoskeleton was made of bone-like struts that paralleled her arms and legs and were linked together by a back frame that supported the weight of her pack. Testing the rig, she crouched and then bobbed up, letting the dead sister's powered leg struts do the work of lifting her body weight. The exoskeleton made it easy to walk for hours, to run, to jump, to kick and hit, and to support the weight of her tactical rifle, an MCL1a with muzzle-mounted cams and AI integration.

The rest of the squad was still prepping when she slung her weapon, tucked her helmet under her arm, and strode out into the small yard enclosed by the fort's fifteen-foot-high walls.

The night air was heavy with heat and humidity and the scent of mud and blossoms, but the clouds that had brought a late-afternoon shower had dispersed, leaving the sky clear and awash in the light of a rising moon. Reid allowed herself a handful of seconds to take in the night as it was meant to be seen. Then she pulled her helmet on. Seen through her visor, the yard brightened with the green, alien glow of night vision while icons mustered across the bottom of the display, one for every soldier wearing a skullcap: Juarez, Faraci, Phan, and Wicks.

A familiar voice spoke through Reid's helmet audio: "You're early tonight."

She smiled, though he couldn't see it. "So are you. Slow night?"

"Not too bad."

He was her primary handler from Guidance, codenamed Tyrant, the only name she knew him by. His job was to assist in field operations, overseeing data analysis and relaying communications with Command from his office, five thousand miles away in Charleston. Tyrant had access to the feeds from her helmet cams as well as the display on her visor, and he kept a close eye on all of it. "Where's Sakai's icon?" he asked. "You didn't give her the night off?"

The door opened and, to Reid's surprise, Sakai stepped through, already rigged in armor and bones, her pack on, her weapon on her shoulder, and her helmet in her gloved hand. But no skullcap.

And without her skullcap, she didn't appear as an icon on Reid's display.

"She's challenging you," Tyrant murmured, amusement in his voice.

Sakai shot Reid a sideways glance, but if she was looking for a reaction, she was disappointed. Reid's face was hidden behind the anonymous black shield of her visor.

Sakai turned away, setting her helmet down on a dusty table. Then, like a good girl, she fished her skullcap out of a pocket and put it on.

Her icon popped up on Reid's display. Reid gazed at it and a menu slid open. She shifted her gaze, selecting "physiology" from the list of options. Her system AI whispered a brief report: *status marginal; brain chemistry indicates insufficient sleep.* But as Sakai's skullcap went to work, stimulating the chemical factory of her brain, her status ramped up. By the time the squad assembled, Sakai's condition became nominal, and the AI approved her for the night's mission.

That night, they were to patrol far to the north. They spread out in their customary formation: two hundred meters between each soldier, with Reid on the east, Sakai on the west, and the others in between. The physical separation let them cover more territory while they remained electronically linked to each other, to Tyrant, and to the angel that accompanied them. The surveillance drone was the squad's remote eyes, hunting ahead for signs of enemy insurgents.

Reid moved easily through the flat terrain, the power of her stride augmented by her exoskeleton's struts and joints, while the shocked foot-plates that supported her booted feet generated a faint, rhythmic hiss with every step. Her gaze was never still, roving between the squad map, the video feed from the angel, the terrain around her, and the quality of the ground where her next steps would fall.

Threat assessment had gotten harder since the start of the rainy season. Stands of head-high grass covered what only a month ago had been bare red earth. Thickets had leafed out and the scattered trees had sprouted green canopies. Cattle liked to spend the hottest hours of the day beneath the trees, their sharp hooves treading the ground into sticky bogs. For most of the year this worn-out land was barely habitable, with the Sahara encroaching from the north. But for at least this one more year the rains had come, bringing life back—and providing extensive cover for an enemy made up of violent but half-trained insurgent soldiers.

Reid held her tactical rifle across her body, ready for use at all times as she searched for signs of disturbance that could not be accounted for by cattle or goats or the herdsmen who accompanied them. At the same time, video from her helmet cams was relayed to Guidance for first-pass analysis by Intelligence AIs—a process duplicated for everyone in the squad.

Tyrant remained silent as three hours passed with no anomalies found. Despite the uneventful night, no one's attention strayed. The skull-caps wouldn't allow it. If a soldier's focus began to drift, brain activity would reflect it, and be corrected. Every soldier remained alert at all times.

Near midnight Tyrant finally spoke. "Reid."

"Go ahead."

"Weather on the way. Nasty squall from the west. ETA twenty minutes."

"Roger that."

She switched to gen-com, addressing the squad. "Heavy weather on the way. That means any signs of hostile activity are about to get erased. Stick to designated paths plotted by Guidance and do not get ahead of the squad."

After a few minutes the wind picked up, bringing a black front with it. The squad map showed them approaching a road to the north, a one-lane stretch of highway paved in cracked asphalt, its position in the landscape marked by a cell tower rising above the trees. Reid spoke again over gen-com: "Wicks, you've got the tower on your transect. Use extra caution."

"No worries, L.T."

Right. It was her job to worry.

The rain reached Sakai first. Then it rolled over Phan, Juarez, Faraci, and Wicks. Reid was a few steps from the asphalt road when she heard the sizzling edge of the storm sweeping toward her. The rain hit, hammering with Biblical force, generating a chiming chorus of pings against the bones of her dead sister and enclosing her in a scintillating curtain that even night vision couldn't pierce. At her feet, a veil of standing water hid the ground.

"Hold up," Reid said over gen-com. "No one move until—"

An explosion erupted maybe two hundred meters away, a ball of fire that illuminated the base of the cell tower where it stood just south of the road. Reid dropped to her belly. A splash of muddy water briefly obscured her faceplate before a frictionless coating sent it sliding away. Her heart hammered: the squad map showed Wicks at the foot of the tower. "Wicks, report!"

"Grenades incoming," Tyrant warned as another icon popped up on the map: a red skull marking a newly discovered enemy position on the other side of the road.

Reid echoed the warning over gen-com. "Grenades incoming!" Clutching her weapon, she curled into a fetal position to minimize her exposure. A status notification popped up on her display, a bold-red statement of Wicks's condition: nonresponsive; traumatic injury with blood loss.

Goddamn.

The grenades hit. Two behind her, one to the east. She felt the concussions in her body and in the ground beneath her shoulder, but her helmet shielded her eyes and ears, and if debris fell on her she couldn't tell it apart from the storm.

She rolled to her belly, bringing the stock of her MCL1a to her shoulder as she strained to see past the rain to the other side of the road. "Tyrant, I need a target."

"Target acquired."

All extraneous data vanished from her visor, leaving only a gold targeting circle and a small red point that showed where her weapon was aimed. It took half-a-second to align point and circle. Then her AI fired the weapon.

The MCL1a's standard projectile was a 7.62mm round, but it was the second trigger Reid felt dropping away from her finger. The stock kicked as a grenade rocketed from the underslung launcher, looking like a blazing comet in night vision as it shot across the road, disappearing into the brush on the other side. Reid couldn't see the target, but when the grenade hit, the explosion lit up the rain and threw the intervening trees into silhouette.

A second grenade chased the first, fired from Faraci's position farther west. Reid used the explosion as cover. She flexed her legs, using the power of the dead sister's joints to launch to her feet. Then she dropped back, away from the road and into the brush as the squad icons returned to her visor. "Juarez! I'm going after Wicks. Take Phan and Sakai. Set up a defensive perimeter."

"Roger that." On the squad map, lines shot from the sergeant's icon, linking him to Phan and Sakai as they switched to a different channel to coordinate.

"Faraci, you're with me. Full caution as you approach Wicks. Take the path Guidance gives you and do not stray."

"Roger, L.T."

Reid flinched as a burst of automatic weapons fire rattled the nearby brush. Another gun opened up. A glance at the squad map confirmed it was Juarez, returning fire.

"Got your route," Tyrant said.

A transparent, glowing green rectangle popped into existence at Reid's feet as if suspended just above the sheen of standing water. It stretched into a luminous path, winding out of sight behind a thicket. Reid bounded after it, running all-out—Hell-bent, maybe, because she could see only three strides ahead. If a hazard popped up in front of her she'd have to go through it or over it, because she was going too fast to stop. When she spied a suspiciously neat circle of rainwater, she vaulted it. Then she ducked to avoid a branch weighed down by the pounding rain.

Hell failed to claim her, and in just a few seconds the path brought her to the concrete pad that supported the cell tower, and to Wicks, who lay just a few meters behind it.

He was belly down in almost two inches of water and he wasn't nonresponsive anymore. He struggled to lift his helmeted head, but the weight of his pack and his injuries pinned him in place. His shoulders shook with a wracking cough as Reid dropped to her knees beside him.

"Damn it, Wicks, don't drown."

Another grenade went off, this one maybe a hundred meters away. Reid flinched, but her duty was to Wicks. She pulled the pins on his pack straps and heaved the pack aside. Then she grabbed the frame of his dead sister and flipped him onto his back. He made a faint mewling noise, more fear than pain. The skullcap should be controlling his pain. As she shrugged off her pack and got out her med kit, she tried to reassure him. "Wicks, listen to me. We'll get you out of here. You'll be okay."

He groaned...in denial maybe, or despair.

"Tyrant, where's my battle medic?"

"I'm here," a woman said, speaking through her helmet audio. "Let's do an assessment."

Reid's helmet cams let the medic see what she saw. Wicks still had all four limbs, but most of his right calf was gone, and shrapnel had shredded the flesh of his right arm. Reid used her body to shield his wounds from the rain for the few seconds it took to apply a spray-on coagulant. Then she slipped off his helmet to check for head injuries. When she found none, she put his helmet back on.

Tyrant said, "Faraci's at twenty meters and closing fast. Don't shoot her."

"Roger that."

Juarez was still trading fire with someone to the north when Faraci burst out of the brush. She dropped her pack and then dropped to her knees beside Reid. "How's he doing, L.T.?"

"How you doing, Wicks?" Reid asked as she slathered wound putty across his chewed-up calf.

"*Fucked*," he whispered between clenched teeth.

Reid couldn't argue. She guessed he'd lose the leg, and then he'd be out of a job that he desperately needed for his sister's sake as well as his own. "Faraci's going to take care of you," she said. "You got that, Faraci? Do what the battle medic tells you, and get him stabilized."

"Yes, ma'am."

"And keep your head down."

Reid closed up her med kit and jammed it back into her pack. Then she shouldered the pack, along with her weapon. "Tyrant, I need a target."

"Look toward the road."

She did, bringing a new path into view on her display. Icons showed Juarez and Phan engaged two hundred fifty meters to the west, with Sakai half a klick farther out. Maybe Juarez had gotten word of more targets on that side and instructed her to go after them. No time to ask.

Reid took off, water geysering under her footplates until the path expanded, indicating she should slow. The path ended at a tree with a fat trunk. Livestock had churned the ground into thick mud that sucked at her boots as she braced herself against the trunk and brought up her weapon. A targeting circle appeared in her visor, but just as she aligned her aim, her attention was hijacked by a bold-red status notification that popped up at the bottom of her display: *Contact lost with C. Sakai; position and status unknown.*

Her finger hesitated above the trigger. Contact lost? What the hell did that mean? Even if Sakai was dead, the angel should still know her position—

Focus!

Reid squeezed the trigger, firing a burst of 7.62mm rounds.

An answering fusillade hammered the tree trunk. She spun and dropped to a crouch, putting the tree at her back as bullets whined through the space she'd just occupied.

"Target down," Tyrant said.

"Then who the fuck is shooting at me?"

"Another target."

"How did Command miss all this, Tyrant?"

"Debrief later. You've got another target. Stay low."

The notification was gone from Reid's display. The squad map was back up. It showed Faraci still with Wicks; Juarez and Phan circling to the west. There was no icon for Sakai.

"Reid!" Tyrant barked as he blanked her display. "Target's moving in. You need to hit it now."

She twisted around, still on her knees, sliding in the mud. When the targeting circle came into sight, she covered it and fired. There was a scream, much closer than she'd expected. She fired again, and the scream cut off. "Where the hell is Sakai?" she demanded, as another exchange of gunfire rattled to the west.

"I don't know! Waiting to hear from Intelligence."

Gunfire ceased. There was only the sound of rain.

"Three targets remaining," Tyrant said. "But they're pulling back."

Reid stared into the green-tinted night. The rain was easing. Night vision could again make out the shapes of distant trees, but it could not reveal IEDs buried beneath the mud, or popper mines that the surviving insurgents might have dropped on their retreat. Command might be persuaded to send in bomb sniffers tomorrow, but tonight the other side of the road was a no-man's-land.

"We have to let them go," Reid said. "Tyrant, shift the angel west. I want it looking for Sakai."

The rain had stopped by the time she returned to Wicks. Faraci had sealed his wounds and gotten him out of his rig, but she'd left his helmet on, per regulation. His visor was tuned to transparent, so that Reid could see his face, his half-closed eyes. "He'll be okay," Faraci said.

Meaning that he would live.

Juarez and Phan emerged from the brush as a distant growl announced the approach of the MEDEVAC helicopter. While Juarez went through Wicks's pack, redistributing its contents, Reid stepped aside. "Tyrant, I want to see the video from Sakai's helmet cams."

It didn't show much. Rain had been coming down so hard that at first all Reid saw was falling water. Then a blur that resolved into the dripping branches of a thicket, luminous in night vision; then a splash of mud. Reid checked her display, confirming she was on a solo link before she asked Tyrant, "Did someone cut her fucking head off?"

"Negative. The skullcap would have picked up remnant brain function. Reid, her helmet was removed."

"That doesn't make sense. If she got jumped, we'd see—" She broke off in midsentence as the truth hit. "Sakai took off her own helmet. That's what you're saying."

Reid had been slow to consider it because all her training argued against it. LCS soldiers must never remove their helmets in the field. Even Wicks, grievously wounded, still wore his, because in a linked combat squad the helmet *was* the soldier. It was protective gear, yes, but it also marked position, monitored condition, allowed communication, enhanced the control of weapons and targeting, and provided a visual interface for the shared data stream that allowed an LCS to function.

If Sakai had removed her helmet it meant only one thing: she'd walked away.

She'd deserted.

The helicopter set down, kicking up a windstorm that flattened a circle of waist-high grass. Wicks shivered as the medics loaded him onboard. He was in their care now, so they took his helmet off. His expression was disconsolate. Reid squeezed his hand and lied to him. "It'll all work out."

Moonlight shone through rents and tears in the clouds as the helicopter took him away.

Reid tried to put herself into Sakai's head; tried to understand what Sakai had been thinking when she'd walked out on the squad, abandoned them, in the middle of a firefight. No love existed between Sakai and the others; no reason to think she gave a shit about any of them. The commotion had been a chance to slip away, that's all...

Except there was nowhere for her to go, no escape, no refuge, no way home.

No way to survive for long.

Reid found it easy to imagine Sakai as suicidal, but why hadn't Guidance known or even suspected?

Because Sakai had only worn the skullcap on patrol.

Until tonight, Sakai had been okay on patrol.

Some people were like that. They were fine so long as they were working, fulfilling whatever regimented role life had handed them, but leave them on their own and they could disappear down rabbit holes.

What twisted passage had Sakai wandered down?

Reid caught her breath, hit by a new worry: what if Sakai hadn't run away?

The night was warm and Reid's uniform had shed the rain so she was barely damp, but she shuddered anyway as the fine hairs on the back of her neck stood up. She looked over her shoulder, scanning the surrounding terrain, searching for motion in the brush or beneath the trees.

Tyrant noticed. "You see something?"

The drone had been sent to search from Sakai's last known position. "Tyrant, bring the angel back. Make sure Sakai isn't here, hunting us."

"Roger that." A few seconds later: "You really think she's turned on you?"

"I don't know. I just want to make sure." She switched to gen-com. "Everyone, stay low. Keep alert."

They all dropped into a crouch.

"Somebody out there?" Juarez wanted to know.

"We'll let the angel answer that."

The drone searched, but it picked up no sign of Sakai anywhere nearby. So Reid sent it south, toward the fort, but Sakai wasn't there either.

"Let her go," Faraci muttered. "Who gives a shit? She didn't do anything for Wicks when he went down."

"We don't abandon our own, Faraci," Reid snapped. "Remember that, next time you get in a tight spot."

"Yes, ma'am."

"This is now a search and rescue, and speed is critical." Alone, without her helmet, it was just a question of time and distance, not chance, until Sakai was found by some insurgent group. Maybe that was her goal, to get far enough away that there could be no rescue, no first aid, no helicopter evacuation while her heart was still beating.

Only four remained in the squad—Reid, Juarez, Faraci, Phan—but they still assumed their standard two-hundred meter interval, sweeping the terrain until they converged again on Sakai's last known position. Reid got there first and found Sakai's skullcap hanging from a branch. It felt like a message meant just for her. She shoved the skullcap into a pocket. Phan recovered Sakai's helmet from a thicket, finding it upside down and half-full of rain. Juarez located her pack. But her MCL1a didn't turn up. Neither did her stock of grenades, or her dead sister.

"We have two possibilities," Reid told the squad. "She's been taken prisoner, in which case we are obligated to effect a rescue and to recover her equipment. Or she's gone rogue. If so, we must assume she is mentally unstable. Without her helmet she doesn't have night vision, but she'll be able to see well enough by moonlight to be dangerous. Use extreme caution."

The rain had washed away any tracks that might have indicated the direction Sakai had taken, but it seemed logical to Reid that she would have headed west to northwest. "Either direction would allow her to avoid the angel's eyes while it was monitoring the firefight, but west means following tonight's patrol route and I don't think that's what she had in mind."

"Northwest then," Juarez said in disgust.

Reid nodded. "She's heading for the border."

They set off, moving fast on a no-choice mission. They had to find Sakai. Personnel did not go missing anymore. And they had to get the dead sister and the MCL1a back. That equipment could not be allowed to enter the black market. It had to be recovered, even if they took heavy casualties in the process.

"Tyrant."

"Here."

"Something happened when Sakai was on leave."

"No incident in her record."

"Go beyond the record! Something else happened just a few days ago. That's when she stopped wearing her skullcap. Something was going on inside her head. Something she didn't want the skullcap to fix."

"Stand by."

A figure of speech. Reid loped north, while her AI analyzed the feeds from her helmet cams. Every few minutes it highlighted a potential hazard: a shining thread that could have been a tripwire but turned out to be a spiderweb; a metallic sheen that might have been a cheap sensor but was only a foil wrapper, blown in from God knows where; an area of disturbed ground washed by the rain where there might be a buried IED. Reid skirted it, though she suspected it was just a resting place for cattle.

Tyrant spoke again, "Intelligence took a look at her email. She split with her boyfriend a few days ago, told him she wasn't coming back and not to worry about money, that she'd take care of him."

"Oh *fuck*," Reid said as enlightenment hit. "This is about her life insurance."

"It's about more than that. The boyfriend has a six-year-old kid. Sakai got crazy on leave, had a meltdown, slammed the kid against a wall—"

Reid didn't want to hear anymore. "That's bullshit. Sakai passed her psych quals. She's not like that. *None* of us are like that."

"Intelligence believes the boyfriend's story. He's been out of work a long time. Sakai's been sending him money. He didn't report the incident because he can't afford to break up with her. So he kept telling her everything was okay."

Sakai was not the kind of person who could do something like that and ever imagine it was okay; Reid didn't have to like her to know that. The life insurance was Sakai's apology, a way to make amends and to ensure she never harmed the child again.

A few minutes later Tyrant announced, "The angel has found her." He marked the position on Reid's map. Three kilometers east-northeast. Reid switched to gen-com. "Hold up."

A new window opened in her display, a feed from the angel that showed Sakai rigged in her dead sister, with her MCL1a in hand. Sakai surely presented a danger, yet without her helmet and her skullcap she looked fragile, her bare scalp like a gray eggshell in the sideways light of the westering moon.

"You got her, L.T.?" Juarez asked.

Reid sent him the feed and the location.

The map updated.

"*Shit*," Juarez breathed. "She's not alone."

Scanning the ground with its infrared camera, the angel had found three figures less than a hundred-thirty meters from Sakai—a distance rapidly closing as she advanced.

Half-hidden beneath the spreading branches of a thorn tree, they appeared at first as flashes and chips of bright heat. Then they emerged draped in infrared-blocking fabric that did not hide them completely but gave them the vagueness of ghosts as they passed through tall grass, moving in a line toward Sakai. The angel identified them from profiles compiled during the firefight: they were the three insurgents who had escaped alive.

They probably couldn't see Sakai past the vegetation, but they would be able to hear her. She was using her dead sister to trot at a careless pace, rustling grass and snapping twigs, with no way to know what lay in wait for her. They would gun her down before she knew anyone was there.

And wasn't that what she'd gone looking for?

Reid wondered if she'd fight back; wanted her to; resolved to force her to, if she could. Reid would not let death take Sakai by surprise. She would make her face it, and facing it, maybe Sakai would choose life instead.

Fuck the insurance.

Speaking over gen-com, Reid said, "Faraci, you've only used one grenade. Fire another, maximum range. In Sakai's direction."

"L.T.?" Faraci sounded perplexed. "Sakai's way out of range."

"Shit, Faraci, I don't want you to kill her. I just want you to put her on alert. *Now*, if that's all right with you."

"Yes, ma'am."

The grenade shot above the tree tops, hurtling northeast, to burst above the brush. The *boom* rolled past while through the angel's eyes, Reid watched Sakai drop flat, her training taking over despite the guilt and despair that had sent her north.

The insurgents took cover inside a thicket, no doubt trying to guess what the distant explosion meant for them. Caution should have made them retreat, but they wanted Sakai's weapon and dead sister.

"Let's go!" Reid barked. "Now, while they're confused. Fast as we fucking can. *Go, go, go!*"

Tyrant posted a path. Reid jumped on it, running flat out. The joints of her dead sister multiplied the power of every stride. She crunched through grass, slid sideways in mud, bounded over deadfalls and, carrying her tactical rifle one-handed, she used the struts on her other arm as a hammer to batter aside branches.

"Sakai's taken cover in the brush," Tyrant said.

It was hard to look death in the face.

Tyrant spoke again. "The insurgents are moving. They're closing on Sakai's position."

"Good."

Sakai would see them, she would know what death looked like, and she would fight back. She had to.

With two kilometers behind her, Reid heard the slow *tap, tap, tap* of small arms fire. "Tyrant?"

"They're trying to flush her from cover."

Reid ducked under a tree and then battered her way along a cattle trail between two thickets. The terrain was so monotonous she felt like she was getting nowhere.

A larger-caliber weapon spoke. Reid well knew the sound of an MCL1a.

"She got one," Tyrant reported. "Damn good shot by moonlight alone."

Half a kilometer to go.

"The survivors are retreating."

Too soon.

Reid heard the worried bleat of a goat just ahead of her, the sound so unexpected she almost threw herself down and started shooting.

The goats were just as frightened. They must have been sleeping in a thicket. Startled at her approach, they fled straight toward Sakai.

"Reid, get down!" Tyrant shouted. "Get down! She's got her weapon turned on you!"

Never before had Reid heard that level of emotion in Tyrant's voice. It scared her but she kept running, because the goats were a distraction that she could use. They were cover. Sakai wouldn't hear her coming past the noise of their stampede.

The goat herd funneled together as they raced between two tall thickets. Then they spilled into a grove of seven or eight trees with only bare ground beneath them. Branches filtered the moonlight into shards and polygons that painted the mud and flashed over the hides of the fleeing animals.

Hidden in shadow, unseen by the frantic goats but clear to Reid in night vision, was Sakai. Reid saw her in profile, crouched and trembling with her back to a tree trunk, weapon held close to her chest, shoulders heaving, her hairless head tipped back, and amazement on her exhausted face as she watched the goats dart past.

With no night vision to aid her, she didn't see Reid.

Briefly, Reid considered a negotiation, verbal persuasion, but she didn't want to have a conversation while Sakai held onto her MCL1a and her stock of grenades.

So Reid tackled her. Shoulder to shoulder: their arm struts clanged as they both went down. Reid got a hand on Sakai's rifle, got it loose, heaved it away—but that was only step one in disarming her. She still had a full complement of grenades in her vest, and her dead sister was a lethal weapon in hand-to-hand combat—though Reid had no intention of letting it come to that.

Scrambling free, she came up on her knees in a patch of fractured moonlight, her MCL1a braced at her shoulder. *"Don't move!"*

Sakai wasn't there anymore. She wasn't wearing her pack, and without it she was more agile than Reid expected. She had rolled away, rolled onto her feet. She stood looking down at Reid with a shocked expression.

What did she see with her unaided eyes? Gray bones and the negative space of Reid's black visor? Maybe nothing more than that, blind in the night. *No.*

This close, there would be a glimmer of light from the MCL1a's targeting mechanism.

Reid corrected her aim. "Very slowly," she said, "crouch, and release the cinches on your dead sister, starting at the ankles."

Sakai frowned. She turned her head, perusing the shadows, wondering maybe if they were alone. "Come on, L.T.," she said in a low voice as she looked back at Reid. "Do it now. No one's watching."

"Someone's always watching. You know that. I'm not your ticket out."

The goats had fled. The night had gone quiet. Reid had no idea where the insurgents were, but she trusted Tyrant to warn her if it looked like they would interfere.

"Do you have it with you?" Sakai asked. "My skullcap?"

"Do you want it?"

"No! *No.* I don't want it." As if trying to convince herself. "I don't want to die with that thing on my head."

"You mean that when you wear it, you don't want to die at all...right?"

Sakai shook her head. "You know what I think? I think we all start off as light and shadow, but the light seeps away when we wear the skullcap. It moves out of us and into the wires, so when we take it off, there's only darkness left in our heads." Titanium struts gleamed in night vision as she brought her gloved hand up to tap the center of her forehead. "Punch it, L.T. Or I'm going to take you out."

Reid waited, and when Sakai sprang she squeezed the trigger. The round caught Sakai in the shoulder, pancaking in her armor. It didn't penetrate, but the impact spun her around so that she landed face down, a rag doll mounted on a metal rack.

Juarez stepped out of the shadows with Phan behind him.

"Get her unstrapped," Reid growled.

Sakai had tried to turn her into an executioner. Now, in the aftermath, fury kicked in.

Maybe I should have complied.

But Reid's skullcap responded, modulating her outrage, defusing her brittle frustration, bringing her back to a logical center. Because that's what it did, she decided. It didn't control what she thought or who she was. It didn't make her a different person. It kept her tied to who she really was. It was a shield against anger and guilt; against the emotional scar tissue that could consume a mind.

Juarez and Phan turned Sakai over; they popped her cinches while Reid checked the squad map, confirming Faraci on their flank, ready, if the two surviving insurgents made the poor choice to return.

Sakai's chest spasmed. She sucked in a whistling breath and tried to sit up, but Juarez pushed her back down again while Phan finished removing the ordnance from her vest.

"Cuff her," Reid said, handing Juarez a set of plastic restraints.

He got Sakai into a sitting position. She offered no resistance as he bound her wrists behind her back.

Sakai had always been a problem child, but she'd been a good soldier. The army should have protected her. Command should have required her to wear her skullcap. No soldier had the option of going naked into battle—and battles didn't always end when the weapons were racked.

Reid crouched in front of Sakai. In night vision her face was stark; her features dragged down as if by the gravity of despair. At first she didn't acknowledge Reid, but after a few seconds she looked up, fixing an unflinching gaze on the featureless void of Reid's black visor.

"Is that you, L.T.?"

Shadow, unblended with light.

"It's me." She reached into her pocket and got out Sakai's skullcap, holding it so that a triangle of moonlight glinted against its silky surface. "I want you to wear this."

"No."

"You'll feel better."

"You think I want to feel better?"

"So you lost your temper with a kid! You want to kill yourself over that?"

"I didn't just lose my temper. Sixteen days without the skullcap and I was fucking out of control. If Kevin hadn't been there, I might have killed that sweet baby. And that's not who I am...or it's not who I was."

"It wasn't the skullcap that made you do it."

"Shit yes, it was! When I was wearing it, it hid all the crap I couldn't live with. Made me feel okay. Didn't even know I was falling apart inside until it was too late."

Is that what the skullcap did? Hide the rot?

Did it matter? They had a job to do.

Reid jammed Sakai's skullcap back into a pocket, and then she stood up. "Tyrant, we need to evacuate Sakai."

"Chopper on the way," he said. "ETA thirteen minutes."

"Rest while you can," Reid advised the squad.

They still had two insurgents to hunt and the second half of their patrol to finish—a long night ahead of them, followed by a few hours of sleep and then another patrol where their lives would be at risk every moment until they were back inside the fort. Thinking about it, Reid felt a looming abyss of emotional exhaustion, there and then gone, washed away by the ministrations of the skullcap.

Armored
FORCE

Warhosts

Yoon Ha Lee

THE WARHOSTS SIT IN THE lees of the starships while the sky grows less flushed with dawn, playing cards. At the same time, the regulators within the Red emissary and our own play their own game across a moist medium of flesh, chemical brew, and stench to determine where the next battle will be fought. We—the Purples—have been fighting the Reds for possession of this moon, jigsaw piece by slow jigsaw piece, as deliberately as a pavane or carved ice. The Reds have grown increasingly desperate. The moon has a certain strategic importance, and the Reds are very close to having to cede it entirely.

The lone Red negotiator is a two, like all of our own: bipedal, bilaterally symmetric, upright-standing except when it isn't, with a round head and forward-facing eyes. It sits half in the puddle-brew with its arms awkwardly folded to keep its defensive weapon inserts out of the damp. Slime creeps through the slats in its armor plates, a plaque of particulate silver tendrils forming and unforming against the sores in its skin. Its mouth hangs open and it pants lowly, rapidly. It has no escort, but that's normal. Across from it, our representative is in similar state—although we design our diplomats with no weapons modifications, only soft open hands and hardened hides and sad, downward-slanting eyes from which pink-tinged water seeps.

Crouching inside the nervous system of one of the watching Warhosts, a scout unit, I recognize the vocalizations that the Red negotiator is making, our diplomat's rigid posture. Both are expressing pain. It is my task to understand the twos' cultural peculiarities, a largely ceremonial function nowadays. In the early times, when we were still learning to modify the twos so we could ride them into battle, we understood how to install the puppet strings but not the elegance of the violent ballets that could then arise. The protocols have since been laid out in treaties, in mutual accords of honorable behavior, after we overtook the twos' civilizations and used their starships to travel outward. It has been a long time since they last changed in response to some rupture of fashion or necessity.

The Warhosts' game is less subtle than what passes between the negotiator's and diplomat's regulators, but I find it quaintly beautiful. Aesthetics is a disease of the obsolete, but it does no harm.

Not all of our Warhosts have hands suitable for gripping. Those that do sit in a circle on the pebbled ground, four of them. The tallest one shuffles cards made of thin plastic.

There are pictures on the cards, because twos like pictures. The pictures have names. Ace of Havoc, with its hooks and hells and disintegrating towers. The Five of Quills, which shows birds chasing each other in an elemental pentagram. The Red Mask and the Purple Mask. The rules do not distinguish between the two, although some Warhosts make one superstitious warding gesture toward one and another toward the other.

The Warhosts play for chips, sometimes pried loose from silicon palaces, sometimes scorched from metal with the corners wrenched up. Blood is occasionally involved, small rituals of scarification, atrocities of tenderness. My scout has a meandering narrative of such scars along its arm and down its back, making shackle shapes to either side of its knobbled spine. It isn't playing today, because it has too few chips, or perhaps because it is preoccupied by negotiations taking place in a language it can't access.

(Well. It could have put its hand in the sludge, but all it would have gotten for its trouble was a lingering ugly chemical burn, and maybe some stings from the silver filaments.)

I don't watch the winners in these games. Rather, I watch the losers. By this I mean that I am a circuit of poison impulses and insectine metal particles interpreting the story funneling through the Warhost's eye and nerve and brain. The regulators watch, too, but they are less concerned with the twos' harmless quirks during downtime and more concerned with making sure they are fully battle operational.

The dealer is done shuffling. It deals the cards face-down. Small vortices whirl away from each card as it lands, drawn inexorably to the pool where the diplomat and negotiator are still connected by an integument of ooze. Even the game knows its true masters.

The Warhosts converse among themselves in their language of vibrations. My scout hums to itself. Music is another pastime we don't regulate.

The cards go around and are revealed to the clink of chips. The Rocketeer, a Warhost with an asymmetrical protective tusk-growth of bone and metal where it had once had half its jaw, wins with a hand of two pair, knights high. Knight of Havoc and Knight of Wheels. The Rocketeer's mouth pulls down grotesquely as it sweeps the chips toward itself.

I watch as the game winds on. The Rocketeer doesn't end with the most chips, although everyone counts to be sure, because it's nearly a tie. In a way, it doesn't matter. The chips are just a way of passing numbers back and forth, an exchange of pleasantries.

The pool makes a horrible slurping noise, and silver tendrils spider out of it, dividing neatly down the middle like a parade maneuver. Half of them clamber up the frowning Red representative, some dissolving upon contact with the sores so they can be absorbed. Half of them withdraw into our diplomat. They have come to an agreement as to what battle would be fought, although the Red does not appear pleased with the outcome.

Warhosts use their game for augury, to find out who will and won't be obliged to fight in these contests. Nobody keeps any scientific record of the auguries' effectiveness, but that isn't the point. The point is to provide a focus for their anxieties. The Knight of Havoc and Knight of Wheels, for instance: they interpret the cards to mean that there will be a reversal on the battlefield, an upsetting of the usual order; if not this fight, then the next. With such untidy interpretations, it's difficult ever to be wrong.

The regulators drive my scout (more their scout than mine, naturally) to the pool, where orders linger as a scummy green-silver residue. We step in to the knee, and the knowledge of the orders needles all the way through our pores and up through the body's strata to the brain: we are among those to fight, cards or no cards.

This is a story the twos tell among themselves, furtively, when the shadows grow long and the wind is a low moan.

Once upon a time, there was a fortress made of polished hegemonies and hierarchical crenellations. In the fortress lived a young woman who dreamt bullet dreams. The fortress came to be under siege; there is not much point in building a fortress if it guards a place that no one cares about attacking, after all. Holes opened in the sky and fire the color of blasphemy rained down. Shells of black dysfunction battered the sloping walls. Thunder, threnody, roses of new blood and newly charred bones.

This is the game the invaders played; this is the maze their weapons made. Each time their weapons hit the fortress, the walls and cracks and crevices shifted and crumpled. People perished inside without ever knowing the names of their killers. None of the far-eyes orbiting overhead and none of the distance-listeners warned the fortress's commanders. None of them gave any glimpse of what was going on.

But a woman, whose name no one can pronounce anymore, heard the drumming and the damage and the whole unsteady structure of massacre. She had no gun or knife or ammunition. She did, however, know where to run: toward a weapon and not toward safety. Safety didn't exist except as the jaws to something worse, anyway.

Deep in the bowels of the fortress were weapons its masters had considered to be fossilized past any usefulness, ancient of years. Among those weapons was a Warhost, armor of sullen metal, itself welded with weapons meant for the ugly business of cutting and shooting and lancing. A two itself in form—bilaterally symmetric except for its own weapons, upright-walking—it was designed to be piloted by a two. And the woman was a two.

The Warhost opened to her not like a flower, or a shell, but like a clangor of silence, layer by layer, swallowing her into anachronistic magnificence. In most of the variants of the story, she promised vengeance for her family. In most of *those* variants, her family died not years beforehand, of carbon monoxide plague or paranoia tumors or simply falling down the stairs, but during the attack. It's unlikely that she managed anything more than a scream when she first entered the cockpit, or a shredded exhalation. The Warhost's designers had no care for forms of expression other than violence.

Although the woman had grown up in a fortress and watched the soldiers at their drill every day since she was a child, this experience had little to do with her mode of fighting. She knew the library of the Warhost's maneuvers the way she knew how to blink or breathe. It spoke to her at the level of dreams. She arrowed her way out of the fortress's debris and its shredded histories, and flew (the accounts are clear that she flew, improbable as it sounds) a trajectory toward the invaders' cloudship. Like a hammer she yearned for the hearts of her enemies.

The cloud soldiers had no intention of letting this interloper get close enough to spoil their victory. It wasn't that they mistook her sensor signature for that of one of their laggard units, or that their general was unconscionably slow in ending her dinner of confits and candied fruits with one of her lovers, or that there was a critical failure in the missile launch system at the wrong time. No: all their defenses evaporated like soft mist before the woman's onslaught.

The remarkable thing about this story is not the fortress, or the Warhost, or the woman's luck, for all that it's rare that amateurs show that kind of spontaneous ability. The remarkable thing is that the twos, with their primitive, self-defeating societies, their tendency to gnaw each other red given the smallest opportunity for mutual backstabbing, conceived of themselves as the riders and not the ridden.

It's not about diagnosis. We know the syndrome.

Twos are architectural creatures. They build compulsively, even in childhood. Teetering cabins of twigs, mounds of wet sand with fingermarks pressed into their sides, piles of dice and houses of cards. From there they progress to sky-kissing arcologies and ships that knife the sea and bridges lanterned day and night by falcon trains. Even from the placid black sky, beyond the atmosphere's scarf, you can see the glowing spider-tracks of their cities.

This is missing half the story. Twos also build in the opposite direction. Instead of building *ever larger*, they also build *ever smaller*. We don't think they realized early enough what this would lead to.

We didn't learn to build *ever smaller* from them, although certainly there are scales ever smaller to explore. Fault the twos for other things. From them we learned to build *ever larger*.

We alter their inner cavities and install dart launchers, change their tolerances for heat, weave into their flesh circulatory systems that carry pale coolant. With access to certain minerals and metals, we can cause them to grow weapon excrescences from their hands and out of their bones, knife spurs and gun fists; fill the aching magazines with copious ammunition. If they cannot see far enough, or near enough, or into the correct part of the electromagnetic spectrum, we alter their eyes cell by cell until they match our specifications.

Not that this comes without price. The resulting chemical brews have to be managed by the regulators. The twos thus modified walk around with stinking open sores for easy access; we have to concoct medications to manage the risk of infection. Sometimes their arms or legs split from the strain, bone giving way to pulped marrow; or metal shreds its way out of muscle and ligament; or their eyes bleed black from the corners.

Nevertheless, the modified twos are our Warhosts and our weapons of choice. In this time and place, this is the honorable way to face our opponents.

The twos, who inadvertently taught us their folktales of knights and heroic Warhost pilots, would understand that much if we ever asked them, but the regulators have limited interest in old stories. Even if there were some way of spanning the difference in scale and outlook, I would know better than to bring the topic up anyway.

The Reds and Purples are to fight in teams this time. Theirs has five War-hosts, ours eight, in concession to the fact that we have chosen to field more lightly armed units.

I am no strategist, no interpreter of maps or maker of plans. Other intelligences in the network of regulators are responsible for determining where we are to deploy, or why this ridge offers better protection than the other one, or how we are to equip ourselves for a land of black-green swamp. For instance, there is a great deal of concern about footwear. The twos have delicate feet, prone to rotting, and the water here is not just water, but exhales corrosive vapors that degrade the protective hide we have them grow. We could improve their feet, but the twos can only endure so many modifications, and the weapons modifications usually take priority. However, we have a reasonable supply of twos for future battles.

Today, I observe as our eight drill together. My host is a veteran unit that will keep fighting until its internals rupture or its lungs are scorched gray-white. It has been the team leader's second for the last six matches, and it could have been the leader itself if not for the fact that a cancerous growth, an unintended side effect of the bone plates meant to shield its throat, destroyed its voice.

The first engagements between teams of Warhosts were, according to our historians, ugly and botched. The twos have a certain understanding of coordination, but they require a great deal of explicit drill for this to manifest. In all fairness, our networks, too, require training to react as we desire them to. It's ironic that the twos programmed these methods into us so we could tunnel into them and make better use of their bodies.

For a long time, the Reds and Purples fought in one-on-one duels. During those matches, we tested combinations of weapons as scientifically as we could. We shifted to team fights not because the one-on-one duels were inadequate for the purpose, but because of a change in fashion. We had tired of the duels and desired a new challenge. The change took place practically overnight, the consensus propagated from world to world.

The eight Warhosts are now marching in drummers' unison. The leader must already be in pain, because some of the torso armor growths are bleeding around the edges, but it makes no noise. The regulators will be compensating by inducing a flood of painkillers. In times past, I have been involved in similar control measures and repair work. It's a welcome art, the regrowth of plated cells and vessels, the rerouting of functions from one damaged implant to a backup system. I miss it sometimes.

The twos tell their own stories of these engagements, necessarily imperfect without the precise recording of internal states. But there is poetry to their war-chants, their riddles, their sardonic ballads. Some of their accounts exaggerate the achievements of one or two flamboyant leaders or, just as likely, a disregarded fighter whose ingenuity turns the situation around. My favorite is the one about the Warhost whose close attention to birds and their songs enabled it to realize that the birdcalls they were hearing were in fact enemy signals. A small part of me was embedded in a bird-scout once, in the very early days before they were banned as being unsporting. The nostalgia is ridiculous, but I cannot help it.

There are other stories. The nations of twos that we recruit from recount tales of bands fighting mythical creatures called dragonmotes. The dragonmotes are exactly what their name implies: serpentines composed of tiny, interlocking component dragonlings, with no internal skeleton and no blood. They are ferocious, and kill with the natural talents of fire and metal conjoined. Naturally, the twos outwit them readily. The symbolism doesn't need further elucidation.

The Warhosts are too disciplined during training to mutter among themselves, although this is also a matter of the regulators inhibiting unnecessary loquacity. My unit is attentive to the beauty of the swamp: the way the light glistens on the murky water, the brightly spotted amphibians that leap from leaf to leaf, the scaly fliers that spear the amphibians with their long beaks and make harsh cries like scraping rock. The splashing of the water that will slowly destroy their feet, and the footprints invisible beneath.

The hardest part for the Warhosts, because of the twos' inherent frailty, is when they disperse. They would rather huddle together, even though this makes them more vulnerable to attack. We struggled with this tendency until some regulator hit upon the solution of giving them equipment to communicate with each other (as opposed to the existing communication between regulators in different Warhosts).

The Warhosts' reverie goes by different names in their various languages. We monitor the connection, although it is not so much a channel for seditious longings as a tangle of symbols given force by unsinewed dreams. In effect, we walk through three spaces simultaneously: the swamp itself; the regulators' diagrammed plans and topologies of their tactics; and the reverie's ever-shifting mire.

We lost and won and lost a great many fights, both us and the Reds, before we understood that we had to join combat on all three levels simultaneously, and that leaving one battleground undefended could jeopardize progress in the other two. This is the reason my profession, recording the twos' whispers and warbles, returned to respectability after years of neglect.

Here is another of the twos' stories.

Once upon a time, a puppet hatched in the deep fissures of the twos' castle-womb. The puppet had been shaped in imitation of the fours that roamed the world. This offended the upright general who ruled the castle-womb. He said: We are meant to live for the twos in the world, and die for the twos, the duality of day and night, the binary of the full chalice and the empty hand. Twos were warriors; fours had fallen out of fashion. And he ordered that the puppet be burned.

However, a surgeon of the twos saw in the puppet's bleak eyes the seedling desire to survive, and she was moved. She bribed the keepers of the castle-womb with drugs terrible and intoxicating, leaving them wrapped in dreams of black, wild skies and flight and planets plunging past, of empires and expiry and armies holding fast, of victories against enemies reduced to ciphers of bodiless eyes. And she gathered up the puppet and took it to her operating room.

The room was the color of purged steel, and the walls and ceiling looked with mirror eyes upon the puppet child. The surgeon broke the puppet child's limbs, unchambered its joints, and strapped it wailing to a table of polished regrets. Then she began the tedious, necessary, loving work of carving up the child's ligatures and refastening its strings so that it could be a proper two instead of a four.

No one interrupted the surgeon. There was no reason why anyone should. For one thing, she was highly respected and not regarded as one given to whimsy. For another, no one imagined that she would defy the general's wishes, even in so small a matter as this. They were not friends, but they had the necessary mutual respect proper to their stations. As for the castle-womb's keepers, theirs was not a well-regarded job. It was sordid, although not unexpected, that they should suffer lapses from time to time.

The puppet child screamed in the only language it knew, in syllables cleanly articulated and made of angled phonemes. The castle's inhabitants, inured to the unanesthesized sounds of suffering, took no notice. The surgeon sang a lullaby as she worked, although it could scarcely be heard over the screams.

When she was done, the surgeon left the puppet bound to the table and sent a servant for the general. The general came a scant hour later, leaning heavily upon his war scepter. He looked down at the mutilated child. "What have you done?" he asked softly.

"You are so concerned with the principle of duality," the surgeon said. "Look. I have given it to you." She cut the straps with her scalpel, which was sharper than whiplash scorn, darker than hope unborn. "Look." She struck the puppet once, twice, and it cringed away from the blows.

"I'm watching," the general said in a voice that suggested that he had his doubts.

She repeated the exercise. This time the puppet stumbled on two legs, not four, crouched and trembling.

"I see," the general said, and this time his voice said that he did.

"So tell me," the surgeon said, "is this acceptable?"

The general smiled at her, then, and his smile was like the moon slivering black. "So tell me," he said, only slightly mocking, "can you do this with other anomalies, or is your surgical expertise limited to puppets?"

Within a scant few generations, nothing moved upon this world that was not a two.

The march to the battleground is long. I listen to the fliers' rattling cries, to the wind skittering through the branches of the shroudtrees, to the intermittent splash and patter of the rain. Sometimes there are paths built upon the mire, tottering structures of ropy fibers braided together by hands now rotted nameless.

The Warhosts have designations to us, and names among themselves: a subtle distinction. Mine is telling the team leader about the mountain it sees far in the distance, wrapped in swollen purple clouds. As we approach the mountain in the reverie, its peak grows to resemble a dragon's head.

One of the units murmurs a story of a six-legged dragon, terrible of mien, and the six corpse-riders it bore into battle against the twos. There is no mountain, dragon-headed or otherwise, in the real-world arena. Perhaps it is simply that we are not imaginative enough to see dragons in dragonless spaces.

I am not sure which Warhost originated this nucleus of dragons. There are competing dragon-myths, including the common ones about hostile dragonmotes and the less common ones, older in origin, about benevolent dragon deities, spirits of rain and storm and ocean unchained. Maybe it has to do with the clouds, with the persistent, seething humidity. An incarnation of discomfort.

Today the Warhosts seem neither to regard the dragon-manifestations as trophies to be slain nor as deities to be propitiated. Instead, the hosts are concerned with going unnoticed. I remember another engagement where they believed that they traveled across a slumbering dragon's spine, and had to drill holes into it, drive spikes into the holes, to keep it from waking and rousing the earth with rocket thunder and mortar fire. That's not what they're doing this time.

One of the regulators within this Warhost queries me directly about the reverie, attention I haven't received in some time. Presumably whatever I say will be conveyed to the rest of the team, so I had better not waste its time. Unfortunately, I have no magic answers. All I can tell it is what I have told myself, recursive riddles, dragons within dragons. I do, however, offer to walk the reverie myself as a two, and it accepts this as distasteful but necessary.

While I put together my reverie-puppet, the Warhost slaps at a whining sound. Its reflexes, already damaged by its current set of modifications, are not good enough. Whatever it tried to slap has escaped. A red welt rises on the back of its right arm. The welt itches, although at least the Warhost doesn't scratch.

I am bothered by this, even though the twos have a history of being irritable about pests, harmless or otherwise. But the regulators must think it of no consequence, and for my part, I have other matters to attend to.

We have reached the battleground. The Warhosts have been patrolling it in lonely, irregular arcs. It continues to rain in sizzling bursts, never for long, but the clinging moisture makes the host huddle in on itself in wordless misery.

I hear the buzzing of insects. One of the regulators has induced the secretion of a waxy, foul-smelling chemical mixture to ward away the insects and soothe the welts. Some success on the second count, very little on the first. The insects are swift and elusive, night-fliers with a talent for stealth. I'm only surprised there aren't more of them, given the environment.

The Warhost continues to cringe from the specters of six-dragons. They are everywhere now: cloudshadows stamped waveringly across the dim waters, claw marks across the hunched trees. Dragon silhouettes rearing in the distance, their sibilant voices threading through the breath of evening. Drums to which dragons recite their prophecies in orderly hexameter.

In the reverie, a new story emerges. Dragons eat the world's subterranean foundations, chewing open rock and fire and root. The holes are small to the point of invisibility, yet they make the world porous, a sponge to absorb the poison influences that filter through the void from other worlds. Little by little, the world will become infused with coagulating radiation until it can no longer sustain life.

The twos are good at numeration when they care to be, but they don't seem to care that I have joined their number. I have built myself out of scraps of sinew, layering them over a perfect armature of unhollow bones, and covering that with rough brown skin. In form I am more like the Warhosts' ancestors than they are themselves. This is deliberate: I wish to see as they see, not as we would have them see.

Unfortunately, journeying through the reverie is not so simple as that. I know the movement-patterns of walking, of running, of stumbling through thick mud, but it is another to think as the Warhosts think, no matter how attentively I listen to their legend-weaving.

There's another problem, which I am faintly aware of as I wrestle with the difficulty of seeing dragons' whiskered visages in hillsides and dragons' lantern eyes in foxfire. The Warhosts, for their part, seem entirely unaware of the regulators' dismay: in all this time we have seen no trace of the enemy.

You expect a third tale of twos. There is no third tale except, perhaps, to the extent that this embedding narrative is it.

Beware the dragons, I tell the regulators. In the reverie, I have acclimated to my two-form. I march with rotting feet, use callused hands to shade my eyes from sunlight glaring from the black waters. I can hear the dragons gnawing punctures into our carefully planned contests.

The regulators seek dragons outside the reverie. *Sixes,* they say. They have figured it out, but it's too late for us, although perhaps not for the rest of the Purples.

It's not that we weren't warned. It's that we didn't understand the warning early enough.

Ten days have passed, and another ten. That is almost certainly because the Reds have decided to change the terms of the fight. We've encountered the opposing team, but it took a form that we had not expected, because we assumed that tradition would take care of the details. If only we had understood how desperate the Reds are for this moon—but our comrades upon other worlds will have to compensate for our failure.

The welts and their associated discomfort are no longer the issue. My Warhost has stopped walking. Earlier, the regulators forced it to seek higher ground, toward a shelf of rock away from the waters. Then, before its strength gave out entirely, it built itself a shelter of fabric and fallen shroudtree limbs. It lies there now, shivering, feverish, unresponsive even to our attempts to feed it.

Our communications with the other members of the team, too, are slashed through with riddles of static, increasingly unsolvable.

Five Red Warhosts descend, buzzing and droning their own hexameter riddle. They are sixes, with dark chitin, iridescent and veined with silica-pale patterns. They are much smaller than the twos—the largest is the size of a two's hand, and the rest are not even that big—and they have wings and curling querulous antennae. They settle on my Warhost's exposed, ulcerated skin. Their weight is almost imperceptible, a caress of tiny shuddering feet.

The Warhost is already dying of the toxins generated by the sixes' bites. Now the Reds with their new mounts are injecting motes of disease, some of which are able to disrupt our own functioning. Some of them have extended ovipositors heavy with eggs, whose young will no doubt chew the Warhost's carcass into a blossoming of the sixes' larvae. The regulators are attempting to build a chemical bridge of surrender so they can renegotiate the battle. But it's too late for this host.

We have lost this moon, although there will be other moons. I record the defeat as it takes place. As the sixes transfix me in the reverie, I wonder what folktale the history will be maimed into after I am gone.

Suits

James L. Sutter

YOU'D THINK THAT THE MOST advanced ground weapons systems in service would be able to handle a little mold. Yet down inside each two-ton suit's armored limbs, running through the reinforced joints and tucked behind hardened sensors and ammunition cradles, there were still some rubber gaskets, synthetic hoses, and casings that the spores could root in. Give it a few days, and the mold on Medupe Minor would eat the legs right out from under a combat suit.

I stepped back out of the bay and triggered the rinse. From behind the clear plastic splash-shield, I watched as the acid shower poured down over the suit's surface in blue-white rivulets, coursing around barrels and weapon blisters and infiltrating cracks where even a tech's tools were too large to fit.

A clang of metal on concrete rang out across the armory, followed by Tom's cursing. I looked over to see him scrambling down a suit arm to retrieve a fallen wrench. The armor was flayed open to expose the drive system, yet his hands never touched an exposed wire or circuit. When he reached the three-fingered fist, he hooked a foot under one articulated digit and swung upside down, then grabbed the wrench off the raised lip of the repair and refueling bay.

"All right, Tom?"

Still upside down, the other tech grimaced, flushing as blood rushed into the white moon-circle of his bald head.

"I'm just fine," he said. "This thing, however, is a piece of shit." He rapped the huge leg with the wrench.

I winced. I hated it when Tom played rough with the suits, but of course he could never damage that plating with a simple wrench. The Lockheed Martin IGA Combat Exoskeleton was the best powered armor ever produced, and both of us knew it down to our bones. We'd been made for it.

A timer chimed, and I switched the wash from acid to neutralizer. The drying fans had just kicked in when the armory's rear door opened and Sergeant Billings stepped through. He moved toward me, mouth working, but the roar of the turbines filled my ears. I rushed to key them off, and the noise dropped away with a whine.

"Sergeant?"

"I said, 'How's she looking, Halfie?' "

"Good, Sergeant. Her hoses are a little weak, but coolant pressure is still nominal." My chest expanded slightly. Sergeant Billings had given me and Tom our nicknames years ago, but it still felt special.

Billings moved over to the still-glistening suit and laid a palm against its leg. Next to the armor, he looked as small as a tech. His freckled and crew-cut head barely came up to the exoskeleton's waist. Above him, the matte-black bulge of the suit's chest housed the pilot's couch and controls as well as the power cells and certain key weapons systems and ammunition cases. From behind the clear crystalline shell of the pilot's canopy, the huge shoulders flared out into arms that hung down past the suit's waist, lengthened by the long barrels of the chain-fed antipersonnel gun and recoilless rifle.

Billings looked up at it with affection. The soldiers might not be born to the suits, but they understood the beauty of them. In that sense, they were no different than the techs.

"Excellent," he said. "We just got in orders from Command, and we'll be taking them out at thirteen-hundred. Think they'll be ready?"

"Yes, Sergeant."

"Good man, Halfie." Billings was the only one of the soldiers who ever called us men. He stepped back over to where I stood by the splash shield, and my already brimming sense of pride doubled as he reached down and ruffled my hair. Most techs were bald by five, like Tom. I was almost seven.

"Thank you, Sergeant."

Then he turned and walked away, and I pushed the diagnostic cart over to the next suit in line.

We were waiting in the repair bays when the big door rolled open. Even through the shimmer of the anti-spore field, I was almost blinded by the electric blue of the cloudless sky. Then the doorway filled with the silhouettes of returning soldiers.

Four of the ten wore heavy suits, including Sergeant Billings. They stomped over to my side of the armory while the tactical suits went to Tom. I stepped aside as Sergeant Billings walked his suit into the nearest bay and powered down. The bay's refueling grapnels engaged, and before he had even popped the canopy, I was circling the suit in the narrow, tech-sized space between it and the pit walls, taking stock.

The suit looked fine, with the usual lacquer of dust and spores—until I reached the left hip. My stomach lurched as I saw the cluster of holes blasted through the armor plating.

"EFP," Billings explained. "The Liberation Front left us a few surprises."

I tentatively explored one of the punctures with my finger. While an explosively formed penetrator wasn't as bad as a shaped charge, it was still capable of sending a shotgun blast of molten copper tearing through just about anything. The rebels made them out of copper plates and old sewer pipes, then hid them along the roads.

I finished assessing the ticking, cooling suit's wounds. The blast didn't seem to have touched anything vital, but its location along the waistline seam concerned me. The suits were weakest at their joints. "How long do I have?"

Billings levered himself up and out of the cockpit, dropping to the floor without bothering with the bay's ladder. His fatigues were drenched with sweat, clinging to his skinny frame. He looked tired. "Depends on the captain, but I'd guess about sixteen hours. He's going to want at least one more patrol before the shuttle lands."

That was hardly optimal. I nodded.

"Spin 'em down!" Billings called out. "Debrief and chow in ten!"

There came a ragged chorus of "Hooah!" as the nine other soldiers in the squad exited their suits. The sergeant turned to me.

"You too, Halfie. And Tom. You could both probably use some dinner."

I smiled. Of course, he knew that there would be nothing for us to do for the next several hours anyway, as the automated bays took care of the basic repairs and maintenance. We'd do our individual checkups in the morning. Yet it was still nice of him to invite us.

The mess hall was a blank, white-walled box with long, cafeteria-style tables and an autokitchen off to one side. The place was big enough to seat perhaps fifty soldiers, but in my three years of residence there'd only ever been one squad on base. Ten suits were enough to handle anything.

The soldiers stood lined up at parade rest in front of one wall. Tom and I stood in the corner, waiting.

There was a click and hum from the overhanging projector, and suddenly the wall was replaced by the enormous image of a man's face. The soldiers snapped to attention, but only Billings spoke. "Captain."

Captain Reyes was a big man—or at least he looked like a big man. Though the camera never showed him below the shoulders, there was something about his face that suggested he would tower over Sergeant Billings. He wasn't fat, but neither did he have the youthful, healthy glow of the sergeant. His short hair was shot with gray, and his brow always seemed to be furrowed, as if he expected to be disappointed.

"Report, Sergeant."

"Limited contact, sir," said Billings. "The Liberation Front has been pressing closer to the western edge of the township, but so far they've stuck to mines and snipers. Nothing nearer than about ten klicks. One heavy suit took a hit from an EFP, but nothing we can't repair. No casualties."

The captain grunted, but his expression didn't change. "The next dropship is setting down in seventy-two hours, Sergeant, and if we lose any more cargo to those rebels, Medupe's governor might just decide we aren't pulling our weight. I want that area cleared out to a fifty-klick radius. Enough pattycake—you go in there and root them out. Understood?"

"Yes, sir."

"Good." The captain's image grew slightly smaller, as if he were leaning back in his chair, which offered a glimpse of a wood-paneled office with a window. "What's the status on the suits?"

"All still green, Captain. We've got an order in for resupply on the next ship, but so far Halfie and Tom have been—"

"Halfie and Tom?"

Sergeant Billings's cheek twitched in an embarrassed smile. "Lockheed suit techs, sir. H series and T series."

Captain Reyes frowned.

"It's bad form to name a clone, son."

Sergeant Billings nodded. "Understood, sir."

The captain waved the issue aside. "Just make sure that the drop zone is clear by the time the ship lands. I don't want any half-brained locals taking potshots at it. Understood?"

"Yes, sir."

"Good. Reyes out." The wall went blank again.

Billings gave the order to relax, and the soldiers cued up for the autokitchen, then took seats at the long tables. I got a bowl of the pale porridge the autokitchen prepared special for me and Tom, then sat at our shorter table in the corner.

Tom didn't follow. The soldiers were eating roast chicken, and he stood over near some of them, playing a game where they'd throw bits of chicken skin in the air and he'd catch them without using his hands, making them laugh. He knew that techs weren't supposed to eat soldier food—something about carcinogens being hard on our digestion—but he never seemed to care. Maybe that was why I still had my hair and he didn't. One of the soldiers held the final piece high, making Tom jump for it, and then at last Tom returned to our table, his cheeks flushed.

When he was finished eating, Billings rose and deposited his dishes in the wall's wash-slot. On his way back to his seat, he passed by my table. "You and Tom better rack out, Halfie. Sounds like we're going to need those suits even earlier than we thought."

"Yes, Sergeant," I said, but Billings had already turned and gotten the attention of his squad. I scooped up my own mostly empty bowl and Tom's still full one and went to where the other tech stood near the soldiers, their game forgotten in the discussion of tactics and plans for the next day. I grabbed his sleeve and pulled him along with me.

Back in the armory, Tom and I got into our bunks, which were actually hammocks strung high up in an armory supply closet, above and between the wooden crates of replacement parts. I lay there for a few minutes with my eyes closed, then said, "Tom?"

"Mmph."

"Don't you think Sergeant Billings is brave? I mean, to be in charge of protecting the whole township—that's a lot of responsibility, right?"

"Mmph," Tom said again, followed by the sound of him hacking and then spitting chicken-phlegm onto the floor below.

I gave up and let Tom sleep. It made sense that Tom didn't notice—the tacticals' pilots were nice enough, but none of them were like Billings. All I could think about was the sergeant leading his troops into the field, giving orders and outmaneuvering these new rebels. I couldn't really imagine what that must be like. Yet despite all his duties, he always took the time to talk to me when they came in from a patrol.

And he had still called me Halfie. Even after the captain told him not to. Smiling, I rolled over and went to sleep.

All the suits were up and humming when the soldiers entered the armory the next morning, dressed in their standard short-sleeved pilot shirts and fatigue shorts. I waited next to Sergeant Billings's heavy as he did his own visual inspection—a formality, as we both knew there was nothing he could see that a tech would miss.

"Good morning, Sergeant."

"Morning, Halfie." The sergeant finished his cursory checklist and mounted up, only climbing the ladder for the first few steps before leaning out and swinging himself into the open cockpit, settling in so that only his head and shoulders were visible.

The sergeant closed his eyes and sighed, and I knew that the subdermal controls—needles as long as my thumb—were sliding into the nerve ports in his arms and legs, replacing them with the suit's own limbs. Fingers capable of crushing a groundcar like a paper juice carton flexed and clenched as Billings stretched.

Once, when I was feeling particularly bold, I had asked the sergeant what it felt like to pilot a suit. Instead of reprimanding me for speaking out of turn, he'd just smiled and said, "Like getting your dick wet for the first time." I had smiled back, though privately I didn't find bathing particularly enjoyable.

Billing walked the armor forward a few steps, twisted back and forth at the waist—and stopped.

"Halfie, I'm losing coolant pressure."

That's when I saw the spreading puddle beneath the suit's feet.

Instantly I was clambering up the suit's leg, peeling open access panels and hatches. It would only take the slightest shifting of one of those metal limbs to turn me into a red smear on the suit's black frame, but the sergeant stayed perfectly still.

"Shit shit *shit*," he offered.

I found the problem: one of the coolant hoses along the waistline near where the EFP had drilled through. It had looked fine during preflight, but the heat of the explosion must have cooked the hose and weakened the polymer. Now that it had cooled and warmed again, a long crack had formed in the synthetic rubber, leaking pale green fluid down into the suit's innards and onto the floor. I dropped down and began to run for the storeroom, then stopped as a terrible realization struck me.

"Sergeant. We can't replace it."

"What?" Billings's voice was sharp.

"The resupply. We're low on replacement parts, especially hoses. We've been counting on the next dropship to bring more."

The sergeant stared down at me. The suit's limbs twitched.

"We can't wait for the resupply, Halfie. We need to clear the area *now*. Can you rig something?"

The rest of the soldiers were looking at us, as was Tom. I saw a flicker of sympathy cross his face. Failing to repair a suit was every tech's nightmare.

"I can try to patch it, but it's a long break."

"Do it," Billings said. "Now."

I ran. Less than ten minutes later I was back and clinging to the suit's thigh, knees locked to either side of a weapons blister—the miniature ATACMS launcher, with its internal cache of tiny guided missiles. Using adhesive and pieces of another hose, I patched the break as best I could. When it seemed solid, I topped off the reservoir and moved back. Billings looked to me, got the nod, then tentatively began working the suit once more, twisting and bending.

"Will it hold?" he asked.

I wanted desperately to say yes. "It's likely."

"And if it fails?"

I dug my hands into my pockets, searching for an answer that wasn't there. "You'll have to power down the legs and wait for an evac."

The sergeant's expression hardened. "Unacceptable, Halfie. We can't risk leaving a suit out there, and I'm not sending my squad out short a heavy." He paused for a long minute, thinking. "*Shit.*"

An idea struck me, and I blurted it out without thinking. "I could come with you."

"What?" Billings looked down at me, startled. "Techs aren't supposed to leave the base. You know that."

"I know. But if I go with you, I can fix the suit if it breaks."

Billings looked skeptical. "What about the mold?"

"I can use one of the breathers." The air filtration masks were only used on those occasions when soldiers left the building without a vehicle. The air wouldn't be as good as inside a suit's hermetically sealed canopy, but it would be fine for a few hours. "I'll be okay. You need me."

There was another long pause as Billings considered. Finally, he said, "Fuck it—all right. Go get a breather and a com bead. Quickly!"

I ran for the storage lockers again, yet this time my mind was elsewhere.

The field! In the three years I'd been on Medupe, I'd only been outside our building a four times—once when the dropship delivered us to the base, and three times when we needed to watch soldiers test a malfunctioning suit on the parade ground. On those latter occasions, we hadn't even left the envelope of the base's anti-spore shield. I'd never really given much thought to the world outside the base beyond how it pertained to the suits, but now that I was going along on a patrol, the idea sent an electric current of excitement up my spine.

I caught a glimpse of Tom's contorted face as I ran past, but not enough to tell whether the expression was concern or jealousy. Probably both.

Then I was back again, breathing the stale, dry-tasting air of the filtration mask and rigging a makeshift net harness along the suit's waist, close to the access panel for the offending hose but still far enough out of the way that I hopefully wouldn't be at risk from the suit's arms or the hot, stubby fins of the heat sink on the suit's back. Beneath me I strapped everything I might need: more patching and adhesive, plus the few spare cans of coolant we still had left. The overall effect was of a gigantic purse, or perhaps a sling for a child. I clambered up and threaded myself through the webbing until I could barely move.

"Ready?" Billings asked.

"Ready."

Then we were moving out of the big roll-up door and into the sunlight of the compound grounds.

It was bright, even brighter than I remembered, and I was glad I'd thought to grab a pair of the variable-tint welding goggles. Beneath the blazing ball of the sun, the base was a rambling line of gray concrete surrounded by yellow-brown grass. A high chain-link fence marked the perimeter, broken only by a guardhouse where the base's main road passed through it and into the wilds. We moved in that direction.

Despite having seen the suits in operation a thousand times on cameras or in the repair bays, I'd never ridden on one for more than a few laps around the armory. The whole suit bobbed up and down as each massive foot rose and fell, and before we were more than a klick from the base, the rhythm had almost rocked me to sleep.

The base was positioned in a long, flat expanse of prairie, the better to see any approaching hostiles. It also meant that the spore and pollen count was fairly low—those being strongest in the flowering forests— and the air was clear enough to see for a least two klicks in any direction. Soon the fields began to shift from grass to grain, and I caught my first glimpse of locals working their plantations. They stood as we passed, but none bothered to wave back when I raised a hand. Perhaps they couldn't see me against the body of the suit. I had just decided to quit trying when the fields gave out and we came into the township proper.

I had been made to understand that the township was heavily populated, but I had no idea until that moment just what the words meant. In my life on the base, there was only the squad of soldiers and a few maintenance workers who came in periodically to take care of the robotics not directly related to the suits. Before that, I'd known only the few dozen caretakers, doctors, and siblings of the tech nursery.

The township had more people than both of those places combined—many more, a hundred times more. Where the buildings of the base were concrete and clear plastic, these people built with what looked like dried mud, painted or stained the same yellow as the ever-present mold. Their roofs were tiles or wooden slats, and their windows had no glass, just shutters.

The township's residents were as tall as the soldiers but scrawnier, their arms and legs thin and sticklike. Despite the spore-thick wind, none of them bothered to wear filtration masks, and their clothes were dyed bright colors, with many wearing patterned bandannas tied over the tops of their heads. Their skin was dark—though not as dark as that of Jacobs, the brown-skinned soldier who for some reason called himself black—and mottled in places with lighter reddish patches.

As the squad stomped its way down the packed-dirt street, we quickly gained an entourage of children trailing in our wake or darting fearlessly between the great suits' legs. The adults, too, stopped what they were doing and stood staring at us. I understood the feeling—a suit in action is a magnificent thing. Though they must certainly have seen the soldiers on patrol many times, eyes still widened as we passed. Yet where the children cheered and dared each other to touch the metal behemoths, the adults' awe seemed tempered with something else—a sort of wary reserve. A few even looked frightened, which was absurd. The soldiers were here to *protect* them.

As quickly as we entered the town we were out of it again, leaving the close-packed buildings where they leaned and sagged against each other and pressing on to the west. Immediately the fields began to give way to dry forests, and we turned off the road. The towering and segmented bambyan trees stretched forth in a series of successive walls, leaning out over us and raining down their tiny, rustling leaves. I'd heard someone say that all the bambyans in a given wall were part of the same plant, connected by runners under the soil, which was why they tended to grow in rows. They really did look like giant fences, with their twisted branches serving as slats. In between their orderly processions were the flowering fern trees responsible for producing the pollen which attracted and fostered the mold. Everything in the forest was covered with a coating of yellow dust, and when the breeze shook the trees it created a tornado of pollen so thick that it was hard to see the next suit in line.

Still, the trees were widely spaced and the ground was dry and firm, so the suits had no trouble maneuvering through the forest. After a time the ground began to rise and fall in a series of hills and ridges, and the com chatter between the soldiers increased as Billings consulted the map on his canopy's overlaid tactical display. At the top of a ridge, he paused at a rocky break in the tree line to get his bearings, and I decided to take the opportunity to run a few tests, jacking into a line-out port from where I hung in the sling.

The ground exploded. One minute I was adjusting my diagnostic tablet and the next I was being showered with dirt and old loam as a wave of pressure rolled over me. Billings staggered sideways, and I realized that the suit had sheltered me from the true force of the blast. From somewhere to our left came the familiar rattle of a machine gun.

"Contact at ten o'clock!" someone shouted. And then everything happened very quickly.

The squad was arranged in a rough circle around the stone outcropping. As one, the soldiers turned the suits to face outward and began pouring fire into the trees, keeping mostly to the arm-mounted antipersonnel guns that chewed wood chips from the trees in great gouts of bark and dust. The noise was deafening and disorienting, seeming to come from every direction at once.

Through the fog of pollen and spores shaken from the trees by our assault, I could occasionally see shapes moving. They were smaller than the suits, no larger than man-sized. As I watched, hanging helpless in the webbing, one of them stood and aimed a long, thin rifle in our direction. I ducked, and a sound like a tiny bell rang out incongruously above the rattle of the cannons as the bullet *spanged* ineffectually off the metal above my head.

There came another explosion down our line, making it clear that at least one person on the other side had weapons worth worrying about.

"Flanking maneuver." Billings's voice was tense but steady, and I felt a surge of admiration at his courage. "Switch to tags and short-range bursts, firing only on solid lock. Suits three and six, a hundred meters left and turn. Two and four, a hundred right. Five, we're going around back on the right, on my mark. Let's tag these fuckers and follow them home. Mark!"

We moved—not the rolling gait of a cruising suit, but a jarring, bone-rattling run as Billings barreled over roots and logs, slapping saplings out of the way like I might brush cobwebs. Inside my sling, I clung to the suit's side, trying to keep myself from swinging into the fins that were rippling the air with dispersed heat. Around us, gunfire screamed and chattered.

Billings hit his mark and turned, sprinting back toward the ambush. All at once, the ground dropped away beneath us, and we found ourselves looking out over a ten-meter-wide crack in the earth—probably a streambed run dry in the summer heat. Across it, I could make out the muzzle flash of the rebels' machine gun still spitting bullets back toward the original skirmish point, and the long tube of some sort of rocket launcher.

The steep-walled gully twisted partway around the nest, and then ran due west down the ridge. We could easily fire on their position from here, or we could go back around and come in on the left flank.

We did neither. Billings took three steps, the lip over the gully crumbling beneath us as he ran, and launched us into the air.

For a terrible moment, we were weightless, the boulders at the bottom of the narrow cut passing beneath my feet. Then we slammed down on the other side, every tooth in my mouth clicking together with the shock.

The men in the nest—their weapons looking old enough to be museum pieces, all the way down to the archaic national army logo—turned at the impact, but there was nothing they could do.

Billings didn't bother with guns. In a few steps, he covered the remaining space and swung one metal arm. Two of the men went flying, bones crunching like eggshells. The third took off running, and Billings paused long enough to call "Tags?" on the com band.

"Three, Sergeant. Rabbits running."

"Good," said Billings, and shot the running man in the back. The force of the heavy round sent the rebel flying forward in a spray of blood and bone shards.

As the report's echoes died, I realized that the woods had gone silent. With the echoes of cannon fire still ringing in my ears, the metallic whines of servos and the snapping of broken twigs seemed like nothing. The other suits ghosted out from between the trees as silent as fog. In my ear, the com bead buzzed and nattered with reports and system checks, but I barely heard the soldiers' call and response.

I stared at the dead men, the ones Billings had swept aside. Both had been standing, and had caught the blow with their upper bodies. Now they lay crumpled like rag dolls, chests staved in and heads misshapen masses of bone and tissue. One of them had a gold tooth, and it stuck out at right angles from the ruined mess of his gums.

"Halfie!"

"Uh?" I jerked my eyes from the corpses and saw Billings looking down at me. "Sergeant?"

"I said we're losing coolant pressure."

That woke me up in a hurry. Tearing myself free of the webbing, I scrambled over to the access panel and levered it open, not bothering with my diagnostic pad.

The hose patch had burst, probably in the shock of our ungraceful landing on this side of the gorge. Coolant streamed down the rubber and into the left leg housing, hissing where it made contact with hot metal. With no time to do things properly, I slathered the whole mess with quick-bonding adhesive and slapped a new patch over the old one. My hands burned as I held it firmly in place, but it stopped the leak. As soon as I dared, I pulled my blistering hands away and studied my work. It was ugly, but it should hold.

Of course, the last one should have held as well. I drained the cans of replacement coolant into the reservoir. As I watched, the levels rose, steadied—and then slowly began to fall.

Shit.

The other break was smaller and higher, behind the backplate and closer to the primary power cell. I patched it quickly. "Now?"

Billings watched his readouts. "It's no longer dropping, but levels are still way too low to run normally. Top her off and let's get moving."

A cold wave rolled over me, settling low in my gut. "Sergeant, that was all the spare coolant we had."

I was back standing on the ground now, and the huge suit swiveled at the waist to regard me. "What?"

"We're out."

"Then bleed some off of the other suits."

I shook my head. "We don't have a siphon. And they're all running at minimum levels to conserve."

"So you're telling me if I power back up to full, I'm going to over-heat." Billings's voice was flat, dangerous, and I took an involuntary step back.

"Yes, Sergeant." My mind raced. "I guess we could use water. It wouldn't last long, but it might get us back to base." Then the stupidity of what I'd said registered. In a smaller voice, I added, "But we don't have any water, either."

The sergeant let out a frustrated growl. "Then fucking well *find* some, Halfie!"

I didn't argue. As he returned to addressing the squad, I gathered up the empty coolant tanks, my synthetic tool bag, and anything else that might hold water and ran into the surrounding trees.

At first I had no idea where to go. What was I even looking for? As far as I was concerned, water came out of taps. But then I remembered the gully, and figured that if it was indeed a dry streambed, perhaps it would lead down to one that was still wet. The skin on my hands screamed and left wet marks on the rocks as I scrambled down the side of the ravine and began walking along its bottom, following it down off the ridgeline.

My mind kept going back to the dead men. I'd known in theory that the rebels were human, the same strain as the locals, yet somehow I'd expected them to look different. More bloodthirsty. Despite the fact that I could sketch mechanical diagrams for every piece of ordnance on a heavy suit and had seen the weapons in action a thousand times on video or the parade grounds, I'd never really imagined those bullets ripping through anything but practice dummies. Now I saw the sergeant's round take the rebel in the back and the man's chest exploding, over and over again.

I must have walked like that for some time, because when I snapped back out of my reverie, I found myself in a shaded hollow in the valley, the underbrush much thicker than it had been on the dusty ridgeline. Sure enough, here was the trickle and babble of a stream. I thrashed my way through the tall, woody grasses until I was standing in it.

The water was no more than ten centimeters deep, but it was there. The trees were so thick that even the transitioning lenses of the welding goggles were too dark, and I pushed them up onto my head. I dropped my bundle of cans on the bank and bent to hold the mouth of the first one under the current. The cool water felt good on my burned hands.

A branch cracked.

I froze. For the first time, I wished that I had some sort of weapon, which was stupid—techs didn't carry weapons. But listening to the grass rustle and twigs break, I suddenly felt alone and exposed in a way I'd never known.

The sounds drew closer, and I stayed perfectly still, the current running around my boots and the overflowing coolant container. The grasses on the other side of the stream parted.

It was a man. He had the same mottled skin as the locals, but his clothing was more muted, khaki painted with yellow stripes that made him blend in with the mold-encrusted grasses. He wore a brimmed hat and held a string of several canteens strung together by the clever expedient of screwing the attached cap of each onto its neighbor. Over one shoulder hung an honest-to-god infantryman's rifle, so old that its stock was made of nicked and polished wood instead of plastic.

A rebel. His eyes widened as he saw me, his irises a shockingly bright green, and he glanced quickly in all directions, searching for suited soldiers. Not knowing what else to do, I remained where I was.

When it became apparent that no soldiers were forthcoming, the man relaxed and smiled. He spoke, and in the stream of strangely accented syllables I was able to make out the word "alone." It had the sound of a question.

Not seeing any advantage in lying, I nodded.

He bobbed his head in return and squatted down by the stream without any further ceremony. Watching him fill his canteens, I remembered my own task and set to it, filling the squared-off coolant containers and then capping them tightly.

I thought about how I must look to him. I was no more than half his size, my skin pale. Though his frame was thin, there was still a corded muscle to it that mine lacked. His face was clean-shaven, but my filter-covered cheeks had never grown hair. I put him at perhaps mid-twenties—the same as Billings, if he and the soldiers aged at the same rate. To him, someone who'd likely never seen or heard of a tech, I must look like a child playing in the stream.

He finished filling his canteens and sat back on his haunches, arms folded over his knees.

"The soldiers sent you?" he asked. *Das soldiears sendu?*

I nodded.

He shook his head in wonderment, and then dug around in a pocket. He came up with half of a foil-wrapped candy bar, its packaging stamped prominently with the C-grade symbol.

Military personnel weren't supposed to eat anything below A-grade, but Billings had a sweet tooth, and sometimes when the squad accompanied supply shipments into the township I'd seen him come back with one of these.

The man held it out to me. I stared at it until he shrugged and put it away.

"You don't have to go back," he said. His words were getting easier to understand as I grew used to the strange accent. "Come with me. We can hide you, keep you safe from the soldiers."

Safe from the soldiers? I shook my head, wanting to explain that soldiers were what kept people safe, and that the rebels would be safe too if they'd just stop fighting. What were they even fighting for, anyway? But before I could open my mouth, my com bead began squawking.

"Halfie! Where the hell are you?"

The man looked to the com bead in my ear, then back to me. He waited.

I turned so I wasn't looking directly at him and spoke into the bead. "I found a stream," I said. "Filled up, on my way back."

"Good," said Billings, and the line cut out again.

On the opposite bank, the rebel stood, watching me. He lifted an eyebrow. I shook my head.

My answer clearly disappointed him, but he didn't say anything more. Instead he raised a hand in farewell, then turned and disappeared into the brush.

I watched the spot where he'd vanished for several moments, then realized I was wasting time. As quickly as I could, I filled up the last of the tanks and my gear bag and began jogging back the way I had come, the heavy load slapping and sloshing against my back with every step.

Clambering up the side of the ravine was difficult, but soon I was back on the ridge where Billings and the rest of the soldiers waited impatiently. Using my shirt to filter the water as best I could, I dumped the contents of the containers into the suit's coolant reservoir. I'd have to flush the hell out of the system later, but for now the levels stayed steady.

"Nice work, Halfie," Billings said. "Now strap in and get your gear stowed. Carrell, do you still have a read on the tags?"

"Yes, Sergeant," said the soldier in question, her tactical suit decorated with several long whip antennae. "All three have regrouped and stopped moving less than three klicks from here."

"All right," Billings said. "Let's get moving. Mount up."

Even as I secured the last of the containers, we were off again. The suits crashed down the ridge in great bounds, following Carrell's relayed signal on their canopy displays.

The specialist had said that they had three tags. That meant that somewhere nearby, three rebels were hiding in the trees with barbed radio beacons lodged deep in their flesh. In theory, any of the suits could follow them at that range, but Carrell's suit was specially rigged for com and recon and would pick up the signal the easiest.

Our path took us in a straight line, the soldiers no longer bothering to find the best route but simply powering through any brush thinner than a full-grown bambyan tree. We pounded across the little stream I'd found, the suit's three-toed feet leaving tracks like enormous birds in the soft banks. Branches whipped and slashed at us as I hung in the webbing, and I pulled the welder's goggles down again to protect my eyes.

"Five hundred meters," called the sergeant over the com band. "Get ready."

There came a rifle shot—possibly at us, possibly a sentry's warning—and then another. The soldiers didn't even slow. With a last lashing from the long grass and branches, we burst out of the trees and into a clearing.

It was small, only a fraction the size of the base, but the open area was cluttered with tents and crude wooden structures. Nets of rope wound with local vines and branches covered all the buildings, breaking up their outlines and making them the same yellow-brown as the rest of the forest, no doubt helping hide them from satellite surveillance.

There were people everywhere. Most were men, both old and young, but there were a few women as well. Some wore rifles, like the man I'd seen at the stream; others had outdated energy weapons. All wore variations on the same yellow-slashed khaki meant to blend with the landscape.

Some appeared to be in the process of breaking down the camp, while others were assembling what looked to be homemade incendiary devices. The rest crouched in defensive positions along the perimeter, weapons pointed our direction.

For a moment, both sides stared at each other, the ten armored soldiers standing in a towering line at the forest's edge, the hundred or more rebels of the camp gaping at the offworlders in their midst.

Sergeant Billings broke the silence.

"Burn it."

It burned. The suited soldiers marched through the camp like giants, heedless of the bolts and bullets that caromed off their metal carapaces. Rebels screamed and fell beneath the scythe of machine gun fire or exploded in the staccato roar of the autocannons. Then all sound was subsumed in the bass *whumph* of Sergeant Billings's activated flamer. Gouts of burning accelerant sprayed from one great arm like dragon's breath, coating buildings and engulfing men in a white-hot nimbus.

I closed my eyes.

It was over in moments. The explosions and rapid-fire retorts were replaced by the crackle of flames and the slow whines and clicks of weapons powering down and cycling out hot barrels. My face felt raw and slick from the heat, and I opened my eyes only when I felt Billings move out into cooler air.

The camp was burning. Every surface seemed alight, sending oily black clouds high into the sky. Somewhere on the far side of the clearing, a fuel or munitions cache exploded, sending up a mushrooming fireball. Smoking bodies covered the ground around us, their twisted shapes burned black and fetal. I struggled in my sling, looking for anywhere safe to rest my gaze, and settled for staring up into the black-and-blue sky.

On the com band, Billings checked in with his squad. Several soldiers were making wide circuits of the camp, scanning the trees and counting bodies. After a few moments they regrouped and compared notes

"Think that's all of them, Sergeant?" Jacobs asked.

"It matches the estimates," Billings responded. "Or close enough. And this has to represent the majority of their supplies. Any that are still left out there are likely to keep on running."

"Shall we go after them, Sergeant? Do a wide perimeter sweep, just in case?" Jacobs's voice was tense, excited.

Billings considered it for a moment. "Negative, Private. We're done here. Let's pack it in and return to base."

There was a chorus of assent, and then the suits were once more taking their huge strides back across the clearing, angry gods returning to the forest. As we left the camp, I made the mistake of looking down one last time.

Next to the suit's enormous foot lay a corpse. The jellied fuel of the flamethrowers had caught him full in the face and upper torso, clinging like a second burning skin. His features were blackened beyond all recognition, flesh shriveled and bone showing through in places. A few stray flames still flickered and danced beneath exposed ribs in the ruined cathedral of his chest.

On the ground near him, a crumpled foil candy wrapper fluttered in the breeze.

I closed my eyes again.

Captain Reyes's face filled the wall. "Status?"

Sergeant Billings stepped forward to his usual place. "At oh-nine-hundred hours this morning, the entire squad and one of the techs entered the field, heading west along the main road through the township and—"

Reyes cut him off. "One of the techs?"

"Suit difficulties, sir. From the EFP yesterday. Field repair was expected, and it was either that or leave one of the heavy suits behind. I judged that the risk to base assets was minimal."

Reyes grunted. "The politicos won't like a tech being seen out in public."

"Understood, sir."

Reyes's deep-set eyes drilled into Billings. "Fine. Continue."

Billings gave a concise report of the day's events, finishing with, "It's my belief that we've effectively broken the Liberation Front, sir."

Reyes's lips twisted, and I realized that he was smiling.

"I'm glad to hear it, Sergeant. And the butcher's bill?"

"Further superficial damage to several of the suits, sir. No casualties."

"No casualties!"

The entire room turned to look at me, and it was only then that I realized I had spoken. My porridge sat forgotten as I stood up.

"Sergeant," Reyes said slowly, "why is it talking?"

"Sorry, sir," Billings said hastily, then looked back to me. "Halfie," he said, voice low, "you've had a long day. You and Tom should rack out."

"But you said no casualties!" I found it hard to believe that I was still speaking, but something unfamiliar had taken hold of my throat and wasn't letting go. "What about the people we shot? The ones we set on fire? They're all dead!"

Sergeant Billings clenched his jaw, clearly unhappy to be having this conversation in front of Reyes. "Those were rebels, Halfie. Not our people. Hence no casualties."

"But—"

"You're dismissed, tech!"

I started to say more, but the command in Billings's gaze froze any further words in my throat. I felt every eye in the room watching as I walked slowly across the cafeteria, collected Tom, and passed through the door into the hall. From behind me, I could hear the sergeant apologizing to Captain Reyes.

Then the door swung closed, and Tom and I were alone.

The sergeant found me in the armory the next evening, hard at work on an injured suit. There had been no patrol that morning, and neither Tom nor I had seen any of the soldiers all day, as neither of us had felt like entering the mess hall during their meals. Instead, Tom and I had taken our food back to our bunks. We'd had a lot to talk about.

Billings walked alone across the concrete floor. When he saw that I'd seen him, he raised a hand.

"Hey, Halfie. Come down from there for a minute. I need to talk to you."

I set down my soldering iron, balancing it carefully on the big suit's shoulder, then swung down until I was standing on the floor.

"Sergeant?"

Billings sat on the squared-off lip of the recessed repair bay so that he was almost at eye level with me. He ran a hand through his red-brown hair and sighed.

"Listen, Halfie, about last night… I'm sorry for how that went down. It's not your fault. You've never seen combat before, and you're naturally a little shaken. I wanted to let you know that I'm not mad at you."

"It's all right."

"No, it's not," Billings said, one hand balling into a fist. "I was wrong to take you into the field. You didn't need to see any of that. And the captain—well, he's from an older school of thought. I just wanted to let you know that we don't all think like him. As far as I'm concerned, you and Tom are people, the same as us. Understood?"

I wanted to ask him why he and I were people, but the man with the candy bar wasn't. But I said only, "Yes, Sergeant."

Billings smiled, his face dropping the weight it had been carrying. "Thank you, Halfie."

I wasn't sure what he was thanking me for, but I replied anyway. "You're welcome."

The sergeant looked like he might have wanted to say more, but instead he turned and walked back across the bunker. The metal fire door swung closed behind him with a clang.

I climbed back up to my perch behind the suit's opened right shoulder and retrieved my soldering iron, but my mind wasn't on the circuits. Using the hot iron, I made the last of the changes, then closed up the panels. Across the room with the tactical suits, Tom caught my eye. I nodded.

Inside me, that familiar warmth was spreading again. Sergeant Billings had been worried about my feelings. He really was my friend, just as I'd always known.

I was going to miss him.

I clambered down one last time, then pulled the sack of supplies from where I'd stashed it inside the diagnostic cart. At the far wall, Tom pushed the button for the big roll-up door. He joined me in front of it as the motor whined and metal slats clicked slowly up and out of the way. Outside, the night was dark save for a few lights at the guardhouse. Beyond the fence, the grass blew in long waves.

I hefted a set of bolt cutters.

We had one full day until the dropship arrived with new supplies. At least two weeks before they managed to get a new tech down here to repair the disabled suits, sorting out the mess of our rewiring and bringing the weapons and drive systems back online. More than enough time for two small techs to disappear into those fields, find what remained of the rebels, and see what they had to say. To learn what exactly this war was about, and where we fit into it.

Tom and I knew everything there was to know about repairing suits, and nothing at all about anything else.

It was time to fix that.

Mission. Suit. Self

Jake Kerr

Mission. Suit. Self.
1. The mission is more important than your suit.
2. Your suit is more important than your life.
— Code of the Tactical Armored Infantry

A BEAD OF SWEAT SLID down the side of Billy's face as he surveyed the wall of green vegetation. Although the droplet of sweat didn't distract him, he was aware of it, and thus a tiny fan in his suit switched on, drying his face.

He was staking out the north, and it was a dangerous mess. The forest canopy spread out overhead, removing any satellite intel, and the ground was thick with vegetation and trees. It was enough cover to give the natives an opportunity to get close and launch an attack before Billy's squad of heavily armored soldiers wiped them out.

He considered the mission. He was running point, laying out the beacons that would mark the defensive perimeter around the planet's initial settlement. He wasn't the best in combat, but Billy saw the big picture, and the squad respected his ability to assess terrain, risk, and other strategic elements.

Billy paused and considered the native life forms. The danger from them was real. While he and most of his squad had barely paid attention during the cultural overview, they'd soaked up the tech and military briefings. The result was that while they may not have known much about what the natives looked like, they knew that the natives were extremely aggressive and had enough tech to do significant damage in the right circumstances. After the first attack, the squads didn't even bother calling them natives. They were just "hostiles."

Entering a clearing, Billy stopped and ran a full visual and auditory scan. It was more chaos: The heat and vegetation made infrared assessment practically useless, and the sound of movement was everywhere.

He did have a good view of the topography from the clearing, and while he would ideally lay a perimeter with a much larger buffer between the hostiles and the settlement, there was a valley directly to the north that worried him. With the dense trees and the steep hills to the east and west, it would be much more difficult to defend than the flat terrain he was currently standing on. The added benefit of laying the beacon at his current location was that he wouldn't have to proceed any further into hostile territory.

"Rally One, this is Niner Point. Assessing northern topography. Any secondary intel for this quad?" He spoke, and his neural connection told the suit computer which channel to use. He *really* didn't like the look of the valley. The whole quadrant was crawling with hostiles, and if he was going to set the northern perimeter, he wanted it to be as simple to secure as possible.

"Hold on, Corporal." There was a short pause. "Negative on that. There's a satellite village about one klick north, but that's it."

Satellite village? Fuck. Why the hell did the settlers move farther north to seed a new village before the first one was officially secure? The rest of his squad didn't have to think in those terms or consider such nuances. They focused only on the mission, and their mission was to defend the perimeter. But for Billy, things weren't that simple. *He* was defining the mission.

There was a distant explosion behind him, and Billy flinched. The massive armored suit suppressed the movement but identified the surge of adrenaline and activated an emergency defensive scan. Billy breathed easier as the scan revealed no neighboring activity. Something was going on to the southeast, however. His mind considered Echo Point, and the suit engaged that channel.

". . . fall back, Jackson. Ichi and J.F., advance and lay down some cover."

"Roger, Rally One. Slight damage to my left arm, but otherwise good. They're still coming, though."

He refocused on his job, and the channel went silent.

The suit had presented a map overlay of his known location and topography as he made progress. The distance to the main settlement was pretty tight if he dropped the perimeter at his current location. *I should probably run the perimeter north of the satellite village,* but that was definitely the more dangerous choice. As it stood, command wouldn't care either way. They just wanted a secure perimeter. Still, he decided to doublecheck.

"Rally One, this is Niner Point."

"Sorry, Niner Point. We have activity in Echo quadrant. Radio silence unless it's an emergency."

Billy looked north again. They hadn't briefed him on the village, which meant it wasn't a concern. And with the steep elevation to the northeast and northwest, no one would really question him if he decided to lay the perimeter where he stood.

Billy smiled. If the hostiles were attacking on the eastern quadrant and he laid a beacon this tight to the main settlement, his chances for getting off the planet alive were excellent. He couldn't believe his good fortune. This would be the easiest point mission he'd ever had.

He stretched his arm downward, and the suit mirrored his movement, augmented by the neural connections between the computer and his brain. A foot-long metal tube extended from the end of the arm of the suit. He couldn't feel it with his arm or hand, but he could feel the movement with his mind and nerves as naturally as if he had extended a finger. There was a click, and compressed air drove the rod into the dirt.

Continuing to the west, Billy laid two more perimeter beacons, keeping the valley to his right. With the presence of the beacons, his squad's mission was finalized: if hostiles crossed the perimeter, the soldiers in their mighty armored suits would terminate them.

He hadn't even had time to take a shower after punching out before Cortez tracked him down.

"Man, you missed some action." Cortez lived for the moments when she was in her suit laying waste to hostiles, and she was incredibly efficient at it. Billy assumed she was talking about the attack to the east he had heard. The east perimeter was much larger, and they had two suits laying beacons.

"Don't tell me they attacked Moot. If they did, they have an uncanny sense for knowing our weaknesses." Billy smiled. He didn't get along with Moot or his squad, who he felt took unnecessary risks. Cortez kept pace as Billy continued toward the showers.

"No, you idiot. It was that village up from your beacons. The hostiles have it under siege. The civilians jumped on one of the military channels to ask for help." It was hard to frown with the amount of nerve damage from augmentation and integration surgeries, but Cortez somehow achieved it. "I can't believe we're missing out on that."

Billy slowed to a stop, taking in what Cortez had said. "I didn't pick up anything on my scans."

"They started when you were checking out. Small arms fire. Not a big deal, but dangerous for the colonists, though—they're not even in composite buildings, if you can believe that shit. Probably a bunch of Greens wanting to go native." Cortez shook her head. "They have a high-end laser defense system, but..." Cortez shrugged. Billy knew what the shrug meant—commercial defense systems didn't last forever and weren't foolproof. "So, why'd you bail on the village?"

Billy took a step toward Cortez. "I didn't bail on the village!"

She backed up, raising her hands. "Calm down, man. I didn't mean it like that. Just wondering why you laid the beacons so close to the main settlement and away from the excitement. Defending a bunch of native sympathizers from the natives would have been fun."

Billy lowered his head. "It just wasn't a good idea, Cortez. A valley like that would be tough to secure."

"Well, shit, you're the guru, but we've had no problems defending worse." Cortez slapped him on the back. "But it sucks, man. Freakin' hostiles taunting us." Cortez shook her head and wandered off.

Billy knew that Cortez would probably forget the village even existed by the end of the day. Her mission was to guard the perimeter, and that didn't include the village. Everything else was a distraction. That wasn't the case for Billy. He knew that Cortez was right—they *had* handled tougher defensive assignments than that valley.

His mind kept flashing to the moment before he had laid the first beacon, considering whether to include the village or not. It troubled him that his main concern at the time was getting off the planet alive. Why hadn't he thought harder about the consequences of abandoning the satellite village? Billy turned away from the shower. He *had* to review the audio that Cortez mentioned.

Without his suit, he had to access the archive in the Comm Center. It was a long walk, an exhausting prospect on legs accustomed to augmentation. He doubted he'd see any fellow suit jockeys—they tended to avoid being in public for just that reason. The awesome image of might they projected in their suits was destroyed as they walked around on scarred, stitched-together, and often weak bodies.

There were whispers as he walked into the Comm Center. All of the personnel there had worked with armored augmented soldiers for a long time, but it was still rare to see one without his suit. A private walked him to a link, and Billy could see a look in her eyes as she shot furtive glances at him. Was it curiosity? Horror? He didn't know, and he wondered if he was losing the ability to read people's faces.

He found it right away, some unsourced audio on the channel assigned to Whiskey Point. He hit play.

UNIDENTIFIED: Hello, is there anyone there? We need immediate assistance. The Dahili are attacking from every direction, and we don't know how long our defenses can hold. Please help us. [Pause] Is anyone there? Please, there are only five of us.

LIEUTENANT FRANKLIN BOYLE: Attention: This is a military operations channel, and you are forbidden from broadcasting on this frequency.

UNIDENTIFIED: Thank God you are there. Please send help. There are five of us, and four will need medical transport. We are in the Peace Valley outpost.

[Long pause]

COLONEL GABRIEL RUIZ: This is a military channel. You need to use the distress frequency if you need help.

UNIDENTIFIED: We tried that! There was no answer.

COLONEL GABRIEL RUIZ: We are not equipped to do search and rescue. Please refrain from using this channel.

UNIDENTIFIED: Can't anyone help? Just send a few of those men in the giant suits to carry us out? I've seen the holos of them knocking down houses with their hands. Certainly they can carry five of us to safety.

[The sound of multiple gunshots in the background]

COLONEL GABRIEL RUIZ: I'm sorry. We gave an evacuation order, which you clearly ignored. You are on your own. Now stop broadcasting on this frequency immediately.

UNIDENTIFIED: What kind of monsters are you? They have guns. *You* can easily stop them, but we can't! Why won't you help us?

COLONEL GABRIEL RUIZ: Whiskey Point, we are switching to backup channel two, effective immediately.

UNIDENTIFIED: Hello?

[Long pause]

UNIDENTIFIED: You bastards are just going to leave us here to die? Why?

[Unintelligible background voices]

UNIDENTIFIED: They aren't coming.

Billy sat back in the chair and took a deep breath. Everything made a terrible sense. Command had issued an evacuation order and called it a day. If someone didn't or couldn't evacuate, well, that was their problem. Still, he wished he had known all this as he was setting up the perimeter. He wasn't sure he would have made the same decision.

No. He wouldn't have made the same decision.

He punched up Ruiz. His assistant answered but put Billy right through when he identified himself. Ruiz didn't bother with a greeting. "Corporal, I don't like hearing from suits unless they're on a mission. Is there a problem?" He was gruff and sounded unhappy.

"That's why I'm calling, sir. There *is* a problem. I set the perimeter about one klick too far south."

There was a pause, and then Ruiz answered, "Wait, is this about the satellite village?"

"Yes, sir. It's unprotected."

"Not a problem, Corporal. There was an evacuation order." Ruiz sounded more relaxed now that he knew the topic. "You made the right decision; now go jump in the hot tub or something." The line went dead.

Five people were under assault and helpless thanks to him. He turned the comm to the channel that Whiskey Point had originally used. He tapped the talk button a few times nervously and then pressed it.

"Hello? Are you still there?" He cursed under his breath. He wanted to sound commanding but was sure he was coming across as tentative and weak. He just wasn't used to communicating outside of his suit.

He waited for someone from Comm to ask him what he was doing, but no one else was on the channel. Command must have abandoned it when the woman from the village refused to give up the frequency. After a minute or so, he tried again. His voice was more confident this time. "Hello, is there anyone there?"

A voice replied immediately. "Oh my God, I thought I was dreaming. Yes! We are still here." There were gunshots in the background. "Who are you? Are you coming to save us?" Her words came out in a rush. Billy didn't know how to respond. Hell, he didn't know why he even bothered contacting them. There was nothing he could do. Now all he had done was given them false hope. "Are you there?"

"Yes," Billy replied. He struggled to think of what to say, but decided to just tell the truth. "I'm sorry, but I'm not sure what I can do."

"Can't you just defend us? You have those men in armored suits. I heard that just one could defeat hundreds of regular soldiers." The voice was more confident than pleading, as if she could inspire him with her words.

"That is outside the scope of our mission." Billy said the words without emotion. Toneless. Without any conviction.

"Oh." It was such a simple word. An expression of surprise with a plaintive acceptance. She didn't object to the primacy of his mission, and her resignation made the mission seem something dark and evil, like death or a terminal illness.

"But maybe there is something I can do." Billy blurted the words out.

"Couldn't you carry us out? Maybe we could find a wagon or something and you could just come in and pull us out. Don't you do that?" Billy cursed himself. The woman had moved from acceptance to hope. Why was he torturing her with hope?

"I'm sorry. You just don't understand. We're a tactical infantry unit. Our suits don't even have hands, and the calibration needed to adjust the sensitivity of my arms would take too long." He paused trying to think of a way to explain. "I'd be just as likely to crush you as save you."

"But there's more than just you! Can't you bring more people to help? Certainly you all could protect us?" Desperation was again creeping into her voice.

Billy didn't know how to answer. They had a full squad assigned to guarding the northern perimeter and, despite his conservative assessment, he knew they could defend the village, too. But it was too late. The mission was finalized. *Guard the perimeter.* The village wasn't within the perimeter.

It was as simple as that.

The tactical armored infantry would fulfill their mission at all costs—it was what they did—but the moment Billy had laid the last beacon, that mission didn't include the five people in a village with no name. Billy dropped his head in his hands. He had explained the strategic reasons, but he knew the truth. He dropped the beacon south of the village because he was afraid.

The woman broke the silence. "You're not coming, are you?" The voice sounded utterly defeated. This was not acceptance. This was hope crushed under the boot of tactical armor guarding a perimeter one klick too far south.

"I'm coming." It was a quiet voice, almost a whisper, the words spoken without a hint of confidence or force.

But he had said them.

"Oh my God, thank you!" Billy didn't answer. He didn't have any idea what he would do, and he didn't know what to say.

After a period of silence, the woman spoke again, her voice a whisper. "So what's your name?"

"Corporal Billy Whitaker." He tried to sound confident, to sound like the savior he had just promised, but he couldn't.

"You're going to get in trouble for this, aren't you, Billy?"

He thought of his training, the words "mission, suit, self" repeated again and again until it was part of his psyche. And here he was abandoning the mission and putting both his suit and himself in danger.

"Yes," Billy finally said. The woman didn't reply immediately.

"My name is Ruth. The other four people here are Tom, Ahmed, Iona, and Julie. We are all nice people." She paused. "That's worth getting into a little trouble, isn't it?"

"Yes." The answer sounded small and inconsequential, and Billy wasn't even sure he said it loudly enough to be heard. But he meant it, and the fact that he did frightened him, because he had no idea what he would do. "I need to go, Ruth." It sounded strange saying her name. She was now a person. Not a mission, a person.

"Thank you, Billy. Thank you so much."

Billy walked as quickly as he could to the staging area. He worried about how long their defenses would hold up. He guessed they had a motion-activated defense system in place. It probably had a battery strong enough for a limited number of strikes, but the hostiles wouldn't know that. That was the good news. The bad news was that they were clearly testing it every so often, and the commercial batteries weren't meant to handle constant laser fire for very long. Billy picked up his pace.

No one gave him a second look as he lowered himself into his suit. Between the long hours on duty, the neural connection to the computer, and their own bodies augmented to work with the suit and not outside it, most soldiers preferred to spend as much time suited up as possible, sometimes even sleeping in their suits. He punched in the ordnance for ground combat. That also wouldn't generate attention: it wasn't uncommon for off-duty soldiers to be pulled into ongoing missions. Five active-duty suits were already assigned to the northern perimeter, but Billy wouldn't have been surprised if there were more than ten out in the field.

Claws dropped from the ceiling and detached his arms. His physical arms went numb as the neural connection to the suit's nerve center stopped having anything to connect them to. His arms glided down a track and disappeared into a storage area. The claws returned with larger arms, the hands made of cannon barrels and the forearms embedded with specialty munitions—rockets, flame throwers, and chemical weapons. The arms were placed in position and, after several twists, the claws retracted. The suit reconnected his nerves, and Billy felt his arms tingle.

The suit's arms now attached to him could hardly be considered arms at all—fingers replaced by cannons, forearms embedded with lasers, shoulders mounted with defensive countermeasures—but they felt entirely natural to Billy. They *were* his arms. He ran his final systems check and then took a deep breath.

Billy Whitaker, the strategic pride of Phoenix Platoon, had no idea what he was going to do.

He set off with the simple idea of just fighting his way to the village and then holding off the hostiles for as long as he could. It was a ridiculous plan. He would destroy countless hostiles, but eventually one of them would get in a lucky shot or he would collapse in exhaustion.

He couldn't see any other result. He would be beyond the perimeter and, in the culture of mission-suit-self, he would no longer be part of the mission. No one would come save him. As he half-heartedly returned the wave of the technician on duty, Billy realized an even more depressing scenario: Command might just destruct his suit by remote before he even had a chance to get to the village. Still he continued onward.

His earlier route to the perimeter was now wide and clear, the thick vegetation and small trees crushed under the feet of the numerous, massive suits that had marched past. Fallen tree limbs lay strewn along the path, and laser burns scorched the trees that were still standing. Billy checked his HUD constantly even though he didn't need to. The valley to the north was as clear as the perimeter line marked by the beacons he had laid earlier.

He knew that once he hit the perimeter line, the path would split to the west and east, where the *thump thump thump* of armored suit legs walking the path would be an auditory warning to the hostiles, while the pounded dirt they left behind served as a visual one. Beyond the crushed earth of the perimeter line there would be nothing but thick vegetation and trees.

They had five suits guarding the northern perimeter, and Billy assumed that he'd have a decent chance of meeting one of the guys from his squad at some point, but when he reached the intersection he was alone. He attempted an infrared scan, but it was once again useless. He went silent and did an enhanced audio scan. He could hear an approaching suit from the east, its telltale footsteps obvious. There was rustling all over the forest in front of him, but he couldn't make out any voices. He heard sporadic gunfire from the north, which filled Billy with relief. The village's defenses were still holding.

Taking a deep breath, Billy stepped across the perimeter.

Less than ten seconds later, a concerned voice filled his head. "Billy, is there a problem? We have you advancing. Have the hostiles engaged?" Billy turned off all of his comm channels. It suddenly struck him that if command didn't know what he was up to, they wouldn't destruct his suit. He heard one of the suits pounding toward him, so he plunged ahead.

After about fifty meters—and without thinking—Billy stopped for a standard initial mission assessment. As he realized what he was doing, Billy shook his head. How could he assess a mission that didn't exist? He ploughed on.

He skipped the full visual-range scan and kept to human-visual. There was some movement at one o'clock. Audio picked up voices. Then there were voices at ten o'clock. He heard the click of native weaponry being armed. He cursed and charged straight north.

The gunfire started a few steps further and came from every direction. His earlier briefing told him to expect a high volume of hand-held projectile fire, which was low-risk against the heavily armored suits. Billy ignored the constant barrage of bullets and rushed forward.

The vegetation blocked much of his visual range, and he was moving so fast that he ran right into several groups of natives. They were bipedal with reptilian skin and large eyes that protruded from their heads. Their four arms allowed them to carry multiple weapons, creating the high volume of fire Billy faced. He ran right past them.

He burst past a tree and hit the last thing he had expected to see. The hostiles had created their own perimeter: a pathetic patchwork of tree trunks piled in a loose wall from east to west, hidden from the recon satellites by the dense foliage above. There were more gaps than wall and it was little better than tissue paper against a suit, but what it did provide was confidence, and that worried Billy more than anything. Bullets were hitting him from every direction.

He knelt slightly and spread his arms. He felt his skin open and the weapons extend as the suit launched missile grenades at the barrier to the left and right.

Pieces of bodies and wood flew amid bright explosions. Despite the carnage, the rate of fire didn't decrease at all. The bullets continued to bounce off his faceplate, chest, and limbs. He retracted the missile launchers into his arms, strode forward, and extended the cannons that acted as his hands. High-caliber bullets shredded the barrier in front of him.

Screams filled the air, and Billy adjusted his aural range to focus on the low and very high ranges. He didn't want to hear screams. He wanted to hear wood snapping, footsteps, and guns firing. He leapt the ten meters over the remaining barricade. There was a high-pitched sound from behind, and Billy switched to his rear view and initiated defensive countermeasures.

The lasers mounted at his shoulders turned and filled the woods with a lattice of deadly light. Shredded leaves fell like rain. Tree limbs fell. Anything that moved was pierced and sliced by the lasers. Three hostiles near a concealed cannon fell to the ground in pieces.

But it was too late.

The first and only shot from the cannon hit him below his right shoulder, knocking him forward and to the ground.

Billy jumped to his feet and recalibrated, maxing out three-hundred-sixty-degree countermeasures while he did field assessment. Both lasers were still functioning and were firing at anything that moved.

Bio came out normal, but the right arm of his suit dropped to twenty percent functionality. It was a disaster. He hadn't even gone a hundred meters, and his suit was badly damaged. He closed his eyes, disengaged audio, and thought, the lasers flickering in the background his only distraction.

What he really needed was his squad. You could encircle a squad, but you couldn't surprise one with a cannon shot in the back. Drops of sweat started to form on Billy's forehead, and the suit engaged its fans.

He tried to put thoughts of the squad behind—they weren't going to save him or the village. They would observe the perimeter. That was their mission, and if anything defined the power of the corps, it was their rabid devotion to finishing each and every mission, no matter how small—even if it meant leaving suit, civilian, or friend behind.

And in the depths of that cold knowledge, a solution formed in Billy's head.

He turned back toward the perimeter and re-oriented the systems for maximum defense and speed. The cannons in his arms retracted, and the lasers on his shoulders switched to full power.

He leapt back over the demolished barrier and turned to the southeast. An alarm started to sound: the battery was exceeding its safe operational range. He silenced it. There wasn't much else he could do. He needed full power for his defensive lasers and full power for traveling at speed.

The hostiles hadn't anticipated him rushing back south, and the ones who now operated the cannon fled in disarray as he attacked them. The lasers took out the hostiles while he crushed the cannon itself with two blows from his left arm. He rushed onward, running parallel to the northern perimeter.

And there it was: the first beacon. At this point, Billy was more concerned with Command than the hostiles. He didn't know how they would react if they realized what he was doing,.

He knelt down, gunfire striking him in the back but, with the lasers wreaking destruction within close range, the rate of projectiles had significantly slowed. He reached for the beacon. With his combat array, all he had was a small, two-pronged maintenance claw. The rest of his suit was nothing but weapons. He reached for the beacon but it slipped. *God, please make this work.* He wiggled the beacon and then pulled again.

It slid out.

He held the beacon against this chest with his damaged right arm and ran. He could hear another suit approaching from behind and to his left. Wondering if they would try to stop him, he arrived at the second beacon.

It came out easily, and he ran to the last one. Cortez was standing next to it, motionless in her suit.

Billy ignored her and knelt down and worked on the beacon. There were some explosions, and he looked up. Cortez was wreaking destruction on hostiles in every direction. Her missile launchers were firing in harmony with her cannons in a terrible symphony of destruction. Missiles shattered trees, cannons flattened logs, and screams bled into the upper range of Billy's audio.

Billy stood up and opened up his external speaker.

"The perimeter is moving north, Cortez." She nodded, her faceplate mirroring sunlight and falling leaves. She didn't move.

Billy felt the heat of the battery against his skin so he turned off the lasers and put all energy into field assessment and mobility. He sprinted toward the valley. With the beacons cradled against his suit by his right arm, he had to avoid even small trees rather than just knocking them out of his way. He had every sense turned to the max. The sound of gunfire and ricochets off his suit were constant, but he tuned them out.

Focusing on sound, Billy avoided areas with heavy hostile audio indicators. It took him longer but he side-stepped immediate danger. After a few hundred meters, the gunfire slowed down. He switched to full visual and could see the lasers from the village firing in the distance. He passed the village, added a fifty-meter buffer, then knelt down. The rods tumbled out of his right arm. He grabbed one with his working claw and shoved it into the dirt. He awkwardly pounded it in with the barrel of a cannon. He fumbled with the other two beacons, cradled them under his arm, and moved east.

He had just laid the second beacon when his audio warnings screamed. It was too late. A cannon shell smashed into his back and threw him forward in a rolling mass of metal. He slammed against a tree.

He tried to engage his suit's countermeasures but found them to be nonfunctional. He did an emergency assessment. The suit had cushioned his body so he remained unscathed, but the suit itself was ruined. Arms nonfunctioning. Legs nonfunctioning. Helmet mobile but visual nonfunctioning. All other functions failing.

Billy ignored them all.

The new perimeter was incomplete, and he had to set the final beacon. Billy initiated his emergency disengage protocol. The wires that connected his brain to his suit retracted into the box at the base of his skull. He suddenly felt deaf and blind.

Plugs that connected the nerves up and down his arms, legs, back, and body jerked out as his suit opened. The smell of forest decay, burning ozone, and dirt staggered him as he collapsed to the ground.

Billy Whitaker, half naked, nerves raw and senses overwhelmed, looked around. He heard rustling somewhere in the trees as his eyes alighted on the last beacon, lying on the ground five meters away. He half-ran, half-stumbled to the beacon, picked it up, and ran east.

He surprised a hostile, who didn't fire as Billy ran past him. *Of course, they are expecting a suit.* That thought was short-lived, however, as a bullet whizzed past his head. The shot must have alerted the hostiles, for he could hear them rustling through the vegetation in every direction.

As he considered whether he had gone far enough, Billy felt a bullet smash into his left arm. He cried out and reflexively tried to turn on maximum defensive countermeasures but then remembered—he wasn't in his suit. Leaves rustled and branches cracked. *It's now or never, Billy.*

He stopped, pressed the edge of the beacon into the ground, and leaned all his weight against it. It had slid about six inches when another bullet hit him in the leg. He fell to the ground next to the beacon, pulling it downward with his body. Another bullet hit him in the side of the chest.

Looking up, all Billy could see was green, a beautiful verdant green. In the distance, he heard an approaching *thump thump thump*, and then he started to cry. He had lost his suit. He had lost his self. But the mission lived on.

In Loco

Carlos Orsi

THE SNOW IS EVERYWHERE. WITH the whip of the wind, it even hits you from below. It's a blizzard. They say that a hundred years ago, Scandinavia was a beacon of civilization. I can't see how people can remain civilized in a climate like this. The situation now—with the warlords, the ruthless infighting, the sheer anarchy—seems much more attuned to the environment.

The sensors in my mask are all but worthless in this weather. The snow and the shards of ice disrupt the lasers in my night vision, and the contrast between warm bodies and cold particles flying around at high speed turns infrared into a kaleidoscope. So I turn everything off: time to go with the two wetware eyes I was born with.

Ours is a peacekeeping mission. The rest of the world believes it has a duty to help Scandinavia back on its feet, ignoring the fact that the Scandinavians seem quite happy lying on the ground with their hands at each other's throats.

My platoon is escorting a shipment of medical supplies to a village far inland. Bad weather prevents us from using aircraft, and the weather is rough enough to scare even the VTOL drone people, which should mean something.

"Transport of medical supplies" means we have a big target painted on our backs: every warlord in the area would love to get their hands on some antibiotics and frost blockers. It keeps their foot soldiers fighting and helps blackmail the villagers. Guerrillas can't eat ammo and there's only so much deer you can hunt on the hills, after all, so popular support is needed, even if by extortion.

The road is, of course, a frozen riverbed. There are mountains and all around us. And we are moving uphill all the time. It's an ambush waiting to happen, but this is the fastest route, the medicine is badly needed, and frankly the captain is cocky: he thinks that if the barbarians want to try something, well, they are welcome to have their asses handed to them.

And then it happens, textbook style: three mortar shells, one at the point of the column, one at the rear. The air smells of burned body armor and is already thick with smoke when the third explodes five meters above our center—they don't want to hit the center with a direct impact and run the risk of destroying the supplies, but the detonation over our heads, with the light and shockwave, stuns us.

I fall hard on the ice, thinking for a moment that it will break and plunge us all in the river below, but it holds.

Despite the helmet and mask, I feel blood in my mouth and my ears are ringing. I feel something sting at the back of my neck, then a numbing cold—some shrapnel must have broken through the neck line, where the armor is softer.

Above the ringing in my ears, I hear someone scream "The *loco* is hit!" and I know he's talking about me. There must be blood on my armor, visible against the white plating, now that the flak has subsided. I turn and see someone with corporal stripes on his chest pointing at me. I am painfully aware that a bleeding *loco* is always an extraordinary thing to have around, but, being a corporal, he should be paying more attention to the enemy.

Our attackers don't rush us. They wouldn't dare. The shipment is now, ironically, our hostage. They can't risk having it destroyed. The blizzard is still running at full force all around us, but the amplified voice comes loud and clear above the wind, speaking Spanish with a cracked accent:

"You are surrounded. Give us your cargo, and you may leave with your lives."

"Leave with your lives." This guy has to have watched some very old movies to use such a line. That, or he doesn't know shit about the international peacekeeping corps.

"These supplies are sorely needed in the village ahead. We will deliver them. Leave us and *you* may live," our captain shouts back, not to be outdone in the corny line department, even if his point is somewhat stronger than the warlord's. Some of the survivors in our front and back are already morphing into flying configuration. Quite limited in such weather, but even a few seconds airborne might be enough to allow them to send a killing barrage of fire onto the slope the guerrillas are using as cover.

But then something strange happens: everybody stops. The morphing remains incomplete. The corporal is still pointing at me like a statue. The captain remains in his preposterous, self-conscious heroic pose without moving a simulated muscle. I twitch my fingers. I can move. I breathe. But I decide to stay prone on the ground. The guerrillas come down and take our cargo, and nobody does anything about it. They are all frozen, and I do my best to imitate them. I don't want the guerrillas to know that there is a single human being among this platoon of drones.

Since the beginning of this century, no self-respecting civilized democracy has ever sent one of their sons or daughters into the senseless carnage of war. Those countries instead send them into RV cocoons, from which the aforementioned sons and daughters can control drone bodies into the senseless carnage, etc. When a drone "dies," its pilot feels a little discomfort—to call it "pain" would evoke an interminable legal harangue, human-rights-wise—but nothing else.

The one exception to this wise policy are people like me: *in loco* soldiers, or "*locos*" for short. *Locos* are needed for something like half a dozen obscure reasons, chief among which is the logistics of the link between drone and pilot: the warriors in their cocoons may be a continent away, and such distance implies a split-second delay between input and output, seeing the menace and reacting to it, seeing the enemy surrender and stopping firing. And in the war business, split seconds might mean lives.

We, the *locos*, work as an emergency feedback loop: our mental states are broadcast to the drones, stabilizing them. They have algorithms that use this information, plus every individual droid's sensory input, to fill in the minuscule voids of command. Crucially, if some boundaries are surpassed, the drones start responding to our emotional states—fear, relief, whatever—before responding to their pilots' commands. If I feel panicked and duck, everybody ducks; if I just duck to avoid a spiderweb or something, everybody keeps following the pilots, with the algorithms kicking in now and then. It usually works.

If you ask around in one of those civilized democracies, they'll tell you that the *in loco* soldiers are all selfless people, humanitarians, heroic volunteers. As for myself, I can say I was rightfully convicted for the murder in the first degree of my now ex-wife's lover. Every two years of *in loco* military service erases a decade from my hundred-year-plus prison sentence. You may say that I'm a volunteer, I guess, but you may also say that the circumstances that led me to sign in were somewhat exceptional. And I have never met an *in loco* who wasn't a convicted felon, a fugitive, or both. Some thought of the service as a kind of atonement. For me, it is a job—the lesser of two evils.

With everybody paralyzed, the guerrillas come down from the hills and start plundering. The medical stuff is their first priority, of course, but they also take some time to strip a few of the drones from their armor plating and take some ammo. They don't steal weapons. They know the hardware is locked to the drone's equivalent of a biometric signature: the pressure level of its simulated muscles, the invisible marks etched in its gauntlet.

And then they are gone.

Nobody touched me. I'd been just one more body among many, the blood oozing from my body covered by a thin layer of bright ice. They hadn't noticed that I was breathing. Lucky me.

Once they are gone, I get to my feet. First I run to the captain's drone and open its body—not a hard thing to do when the damn thing is still and you know where to push and where to pull. The hydraulic locks hiss and puff, the servos work, the panels slide. The drone still has some power reserves left, and its systems weren't completely fried. An electromagnet pulse is not an explanation for what just happened.

The captain's drone contains the mission log and the main comm link to Stockholm. The link is dead and, while there's nothing wrong with it physically, I can't get it to work. The platoon collapsed like so many puppets with their strings cut. Something has jammed the communication with home base or destroyed their receptors at a level so deep I cannot identify—in the software, perhaps.

I try my own link with Stockholm and base, with the same results. Nothing. As a unit, we are like a body with a broken spinal cord. Alive, but unconscious, unknowing.

The blizzard has since abated, and the cloud cover opens up. There are a few stars and I think I see one or two planets among the ice-covered gnarled tree branches. I inhale deep, pretending that the processed air that I get through the mask is the real thing.

I am alone. Totally alone. I can walk away, wipe my slate clean, start a new life, and perhaps even become a warlord myself. All the shackles that tied me to the military were severed by the same mysterious power that cut the platoon from home. It isn't as if I lost friends here. A few of the other soldiers were nice to me even knowing that, as the platoon's *loco*, I probably was a convicted felon. But none of them are really dead. They are just having some kind of RV-induced hangover thousands of miles away. Away from the cold, the bullets, the real death.

I am not bound by honor, nor by friendship or by revenge. So I just start walking away. I feel elated. At this point, I have no plans: every option seems equally good, equally free—finding a village and going native, becoming a bandit on the hills, going south and stealing a boat to take me to France or perhaps Morocco, going east and then across Russia...

But there are those medical supplies. The people of the village really need them. I know what a shortage of frost blockers can do to a child in a climate like this. It isn't beautiful.

Damn.

I start to follow the guerrilla tracks.

Tracking the guerrillas isn't a hard thing to do. The blizzard has blown itself out, and they aren't trying to cover their tracks. Why would they? But the going is slow due to the terrain and because I have to see to my wounds.

At the beginning, the tracks cover a large area—just what you would expect of a group of men moving in the same general direction in a haphazard manner—but after a while they converge, the whole terrain tapering between some basalt rocks on the sides into a quasi-tunnel covered by a canopy of crisscrossing black branches. It's like the entrance of a fortress designed by nature. It would be a surprise if there were no guards, so I stop some fifty meters away from it, using some of the lower rocks for cover, and wait.

My systems still don't get any uplink to Stockholm or any other remotely civilized place. Not even a satellite signal. But now there's a lot less ice floating in the air—the mask sensors start to be somewhat useful. As the readings start to improve, I use the time to take a better look at my wound. It's nothing serious, and the body armor has begun to work on it already, dousing it with antibiotics, anesthetics, and plaster. Feels numb, but nothing else. I can move with little discomfort.

I'm there, thinking about discomfort and wondering for how long the punctured-but-still-functional armor will be able to keep the cold outside, when the sensors show me a source of heat shinning bright somewhere to the left of the tunnel entrance, moving slowly between rocks and trees. My first impulse is to aim and shoot, but I am reminded that there's possibly a real human being lurking there, not a drone. One gets quite trigger-happy around drones.

Despite my history, I dislike killing people. And I don't even know if the heat signal is a man. It might be some kind of animal. Small reindeer? Wolf? If I kill a reindeer I'll feel obliged to eat it. If I kill a wolf, I'll feel guilty as hell. The directional mike doesn't help. I have to get closer.

There is a semicircle of low rocks that I can use as cover to go in there. Not a very good cover, but I'm all in white, there's snow everywhere, and the sensors will let me know if someone gets too close. This outfit can even detect if a rifle's LiDAR sight is pointing my direction. And so I start moving and, of course, I'm screwed.

I take two steps and then everything goes dark. Really dark. My mask's visuals just die out and I begin to suffocate: there's no more air

circulating inside my helmet. I fall down, thrashing, my arms and legs suddenly heavy, too heavy. The servomotors of the armor are inactive. I feel
dizzy. It's an effort just to raise my hands and to claw the mask out of my
face to let the fresh air in. It's night, but the sudden shock of light still
blinds me for a second. I think I'll heave but I don't.

The weight of the armor forces me down onto my knees; it's painful
in my awkward position. My legs are paralyzed. Frantically, I work to remove my gloves, the helmet, open the collar, bend again to take off the
boots, trying to crawl out of the armor as an aborted butterfly coming out
of the cocoon.

It's cold and I begin to shiver, naked but by for my undersuit in the
snow. Then someone says, in crystal-clear Spanish:

"Welcome to the doorway to Eanmund's Hall. Now, now, don't you
fret. Come here."

The man has a skin as dark as mine, which marks him as a foreigner in
these parts, not one of the white barbarians. But his hair is bleached
blond—perhaps he was trying to fit in, going native? He's wearing a more
colorful version of the Scandinavian savages' dress, all furs and cannibal-
ized plate armor, but with lots of collars and bracelets of bright stones and
animals' teeth.

He throws a stinking blanket over my shoulders and pushes me toward the rock-and-tree tunnel. There's a small lean-to just hidden on the
outside and to the left, close to the place where I'd seen the heat signal.
When I'm sitting down there, my mouth trembling and my lips blue, he
starts a fire.

"I am glad you came," the stranger says. "I knew a platoon like that
would certainly have to have an *in loco*. If you did not come, I would've gone
down there after you. Nasty place to spend the night alone, these parts."

"And you are...?"

"I am Pascual de Andagoya. I am the UN ambassador to His High-
ness Eanmund's court. Call me Pascual."

A UN representative. Then it hits me.

"You have a peacemaker."

"Had."

A peacemaker is a specialized tool used by UN representatives on peacekeeping missions. The device neutralizes all drones nearby when activated, a
last-resort measure to stop atrocities against civilians and the like by drone
pilots. They're rarely used—only in special circumstances, such as like what
happened during the Rape of Berlin, when a few of the guys went killer-
crazy after finding a glitch that created drone-induced orgasmic highs. A

peacemaker in the hands of a guerrilla group would be disastrous indeed.

"How did you lose yours?"

"Eanmund's sister, Freawru, is quite a persuasive young lady."

"Were you seduced?"

"It's complicated...she's not like the rest of them. She studied engineering in the south. She even made some improvements on the device." I recall my blindness, the shutdown of my air supply, of the armor servomotors. The communications blackout. These things are not part of the peacemaker's normal function, and were activated only when I got close to their lair.

"Freawru was a brilliant engineer once, with a great career before her despite the racism and the bigotry of our people," he added. "She gave up a life in civilization to be by the side of her barbarian brother when he sent for her."

He gave me a sad smile before continuing: "I did not know any of this when I first met her, of course. And, well, I was here as an official envoy, trying to get this guy Eanmund to stop brawling with everybody else and be part of the alliance we are trying to establish, uniting the warlords, shaping them into a semblance of government...given their culture, it would've been impolite to refuse the overtures of the warlord's sister."

"Impolite?"

He waves his hands at the cynicism of my voice. "It was a trap. Once she got me naked in her room, and got me distracted..."

"Distracted."

His eyes flash with anger, but he keeps his voice level. A diplomat, indeed. "I woke up in fetters. She'd disabled my passive surveillance devices and personal safety alarms and made it quite clear that no help would come."

"And you gave them the peacemaker."

My tone has gone from cynical to contemptuous. He doesn't like it.

"You are an *in loco*. What've you done? Robbed a bank? No, you don't look like a professional criminal. Killed someone, then? Not professionally? Not in cold blood? In a fit of rage, perhaps? Was it a woman?"

Now the contempt is in his voice. He might be an incompetent fool and a coward, but I am a murderer.

"Not a woman," I say, defensively, without thinking. It comes back to me: I remember the man's face, the face of my victim, as I punched the life out of him. I was big and strong; he was small and weak. If she'd preferred him, why hadn't she just left me and been done with it? Why...?

"What is it to you?" I ask.

"I need a murderer. Someone to get the peacemaker back."

"I was going to retrieve the medical supplies," I say. "With the armor, I stood a good chance. But you can't expect me to get a whole bunch of barbarians single-handedly and unarmed..."

"There is another way," he pauses, looking for a tactful phrase. "Because of how they're organized."

"And because I am a murderer?"

"A man who can kill another man, face to face, is a rare thing nowadays. It's an uncommon skill in our civilization. I, for instance, cannot, will not. As I said, if you did not come, I would've gone down there after you. I needed to get us a murderer."

He urges me to pretend to go along with her plans, to use the opportunity to get the peacemaker out of the barbarian's hands, to use it to send a distress signal.

"There can be a full pardon for you, if you can manage to do that," he says. "You could go back home with a clean slate."

After committing a second crime, I think but do not say.

He takes me to her, to the woman who seduced and betrayed him.

She's waiting for us a little further down the tunnel in an improvised tent. She has the washed-out blond hair and blue eyes of the Scandinavians, a perky nose, fuller lips than I am used to seeing at these latitudes. The fur coat encases her body so I can't see anything of her curves or absence thereof. Not really my type, anyway.

"You talked to him?" she asks Pascual, ignoring me.

"Yes."

"Will he do this for us?"

"I may, if I know what 'this' is," I say abruptly, to make it impossible for her to keep pretending I am some kind of dumb animal. Pascual had already made it quite clear what they want from me, but I have to get her to acknowledge my presence.

"You are to go before Eanmund and call him a thief in his face. It will be a challenge for trial by combat, and if you win..."

"I get the peacemaker?"

Pascual nods. "He made the thing his badge of office. The winner will be the new ruler and thus the rightful owner. With no further dispute."

"Why is his sister helping us?" I ask Pascual, pointedly ignoring her.

The answer, however, comes from her:

"Because I should rule by his side, as his equal, his sister, not a servant. Because he used me and then placed me along this...this..."

She looks at Pascual with contempt. He shrugs, but there is a new hardness around his eyes. "I seem to have evolved from valued prisoner into court's jester," he says, flatly.

Well, I am big and I have an enviable set of muscles. I have to, being a *loco* who follows a platoon of tireless, almost superhumanly-strong drones. Even before that, I had killed a man with my bare hands in a fit of rage. I am quite confident I could take on this Eanmund, whoever he might be, and regain my freedom. Get home. *Home.*

They lead me into a small natural amphitheater scooped from the rock wall by centuries of ice and covered by an artificial ceiling made of rags of parachute silk, sailcloth, and the like, interspersed with straw and sustained on wooden poles and beams. There are lots of men—the ones who attacked the platoon earlier, probably. Some of them are dozing, strong-scented beer spilled all over, but others are checking equipment, fixing the plates they've managed to remove from the drones to their armor. If I had a few drones with me, or even my own suit, I could have easily rounded them all up. Even the sentries Frewaru waves away as we proceed would've been nothing more than a joke. As it is, I enter half-naked, half-frozen, packed in a stinking blanket of wolf hide. Unarmed and escorted by the boss's sister and by the new shaman-clown of the tribe. This will be a challenge.

Eanmund is seated in the center of the room on a dais, a huge guy with an ugly, broken version of Freawru's perky nose. The box of medical supplies is ensconced in a big niche behind his crude throne. The peacemaker—a green-golden band of circuitry that the diplomat in charge ought to keep somewhere on his body during combat operations and safely hidden away every other time—is above it, like a laurel wreath laid over the spoils of war. He's bigger than I am, muscles straining at his shirt. Despite my condition, I'm a close match.

"Brother!" she cries, clinging with her body to me for all she is worth. "Here is a surviving warrior from those *I massacred for you,* a strong man who calls you a weakling, a coward, and a thief!" She is using a local variant of the common Scandinavian pidgin. I feel tempted to raise my hand and retract the "coward" and "weakling" charges, but then I think it would be useless.

And then everybody is suddenly quite awake: they might have been guzzling beer for hours before my arrival, but they sleep lightly and recover fast from the hangover.

I see steel gleaming under the almost psychedelic mixture of steady, cold LED light and hot, flickering torchlight—guns and rifles and machetes, axes, the greasy black of small artillery pieces glinting side by side with a few makeshift swords. There's a loud click when someone shifts a machine gun.

"So you finally found yourself a champion, eh, my ingenious sister?" Eanmund smirks. He's way bigger than me, I can see it now. This stuff about electing leaders by combat has a Darwinian effect: only the biggest and meanest survive long in office.

Eanmund comes down off the dais, cudgel in hand. It is a large piece of bone, the femur of some big animal reinforced with metal. Someone removes the stinking blanket from my shoulders and replaces it with something made of fur. A challenger's cloak, probably.

"I just want the medicine to be delivered to the people of the village," I tell him. "And the peacemaker returned to its rightful owner. I am not here to challenge your right to rule your men."

"If you challenge my decision about the medicine and want to take the crown away, you challenge my right to rule," he coldly replies. And then he smiles: "I think maybe my sister has tricked you. Leave now, and you may live."

These guys are fond of that line.

"And may I take the medicine and the peacemaker with me?"

"No."

"The only way to get both is to fight?"

"Over my dead body."

I feel something pressed in my right hand—a mace, a stout piece of wood with a metal ball at one end. As a weapon for naked barbarians it seems impressive, but its balance is lousy, with almost all of the weight in the metallic point. I know this shit is going to break on the first serious impact. So much for honor and fair play among the noble savages.

Eanmund gives a step forward and strikes without warning, roaring in frustration when he sees me dodge. I duck and I dodge and I use my left forearm as a shield of sorts, trying to avoid any direct impacts that might break it: I just keep it moving, sliding it along Eanmund's weapon, diverting it without really stopping the blows, redirecting the force instead of blocking it. It is risky and it is painful, but it also works: I can see he is not used to the technique, and that it is getting him off balance.

But it does have its limits. The semi-healed wound starts to itch and then to ache, and I'm getting tired. The audience is getting tired, too. There are people booing, armed people, which is not a good thing. I cannot delay it anymore.

I make a feint, at the same time using my left elbow to divert his mace just a little too much to the side, and then I jump into the opening. Then two things happen: first, I slip—I'm in my undersuit's socks, after all—and second, my weapon breaks even before it hits. The shaft just arches and then snaps in mid-swing, sending the ball flying in a tangent.

But it's a good tangent: it hits him right on the hip, and even as I am falling on my face I can hear the bone break. He falls with a scream.

I scramble to my feet, the broken shaft still in my hands. It has a nasty point now. Not enough to, say, pierce a vampire's heart as in the old movies, but it can do a lot of damage against soft tissue—a throat, let's say. And if the victim is laying defenseless on the ground with the hipbone broken, better yet.

As I get closer to him and prepare the final blow, there is silence all around. The only things I hear are my thoughts. They scream inside of my head. "You are doing this so you can go back home," they say. "But where's home? Where do you belong, murderer?"

I have the ragged point of the broken shaft touching Eanmund's Adam's apple. "Home!" the blood pounding in my ears yells. "Do it and go home!" I breathe.

"Release the supplies to the village. Relinquish the peacemaker. It is your last chance."

He spits. "Kill me and do it yourself."

I don't know why, but I am smiling.

"Wouldn't you rather survive as adviser of the new king?"

"Adviser?" He is shocked, I can notice that. "Why would you want my advice?"

"To deal with your sister, I'll need all the help I can get."

He laughs. "Yes, you will. And I take the job."

I offer him my hand. He starts to get up, but then scowls in pain.

I look around. Freawru and Pascual are puzzled; the other men seem to relax a little. In their guts, they understand what just happened. They recognize my new power over them. Before anyone can move, I jump into the dais and grab the peacemaker. Then I place it on my head, as the wreath of a Caesar. Pascual is now whiter than the snow outside. Freawru gasps.

There's sound again. I start making plans—to get the cargo to the village, to send Pascual back with a message telling people that they are to negotiate with me from now on. And to forge this band of desperadoes into a proper fighting force with a bigger mission than just plunder and survival.

I know that everybody is already plotting against me. I am not worried. I'm free, surrounded by real people, fighting side by side with, and against, real people. One day leading them to make peace as a real people. The warriors of yesterday used to say that a man fights not for himself, his country, or his flag, but for the brother-in-arms by his side. Now I have brothers-in-arms that can bleed by my side. With them, I am finally home. We are all *locos* together.

Aftermath

War Dog

Michael Barretta

HE SLOWED FOR A FEATHERED corpse in the middle of the road. Up above, the local troop of macaques shrieked at a flock of gene-crafted micro-raptors. He rounded the blind curve and jerked the steering wheel back to avoid a washout from last night's thunderstorm. The truck bounced across broken asphalt, and the steering wheel twisted out of his hands. From the corner of his eye, he saw a man emerging from the woods. He jammed the brakes and his truck left the road, plowing to a stop into the soft red dirt undercut from the crumbling asphalt.

Not a man, but a shroom. The figure staggered, hands outstretched, and pressed its naked body against the side glass. He could see the delicate snowflake tracery of white rhizome fibers under its skin. The shroom's eyes glinted clear and blue. Its slack mouth drooled. The creature broke away, leaving a moist trail across the car. Its eyes turned skyward and fixed on a power pole draped with broken electrical lines and wild jasmine. It stepped away towards the pole, cast a look over its shoulder at him, almost as if it was still a person, and climbed.

He took his phone from his pocket and dialed 911.

"Gulf Breeze 911, where is your emergency?"

"Yes, this is Major William Jackson, 3rd Florida Infantry, Retired. I need to report a shroom on Soundside Drive."

"Okay," said the operator. "Are you sure it's a shroom?"

"Yes, it's a shroom. I know what one looks like."

"Of course, Major. Has it fruited yet?"

"No, not yet. It just started climbing." The former human, infected with a weaponized version of *Ophiocordyceps unilateralis*, clawed its way up the pole with fierce resolve.

"Can you show it to me?"

"Yes, hold on." He tabbed on the camera feature of the phone and spun it to face the shroom.

"We have your location. Can you vacate the area?"

"I ran off the road. I thought I was avoiding a person, and my truck is stuck."

"Do you have personal protective equipment?" Her voice took on a new urgency

"Yes, I do. I think." He opened up the glove compartment and took out a government-supplied filtered hood. Three of them crowded the glove box.

"Major, we have a hazmat team on the way. We would like you to stay in your car and put on your personal protective gear. I've sent out a cellular warning to all citizens in the area. We want you to stay connected and keep us informed of the shroom's status."

"I think I can get upwind."

"Are you sure it's the only one?"

"No." It was a good question of the 911 operator to ask. There was rarely just one shroom. Infections typically occurred in clusters.

"Best if you stay in the car."

"Okay, I can do that." He leaned forward to get a better view. The shroom had climbed three quarters of the way up the pole. He propped his phone on the dashboard. "Can you still see it?"

"Yes, we can. We don't want you to worry. The hazmat team will decontaminate your vehicle should the shroom fruit before we get there, but if you have any powered ventilation we would like you to turn it off. Would you like me to pray with you?"

"No, I've already prayed, but you could pray for me; I don't mind listening," he lied. He behaved with enough piety to not arouse suspicion and used his combat-wounded veteran status to excuse the acts of contempt that he could not hide.

He opened one of the filter hood packages and pulled the battery lanyard. The filter pack hummed. He put it over his head and cinched it down around his neck. The hood fogged around his mouth and nose with every exhalation, but it wasn't too uncomfortable.

The shroom reached the top of the pole and checked its grip, tightening and loosening its limbs. A mockingbird, unaware of the danger, harried the creature. The shroom shuddered, going through the terminal phase of its design.

Then he remembered his only neighbor, the Dog.

The wind was blowing from the west. If the shroom fruited, its spores would drift over the Dog's homestead. Even if they didn't, the decontamination team would fog the area with caustic chemicals.

He decided.

He stepped out of his truck, abandoning its relative safety, and ran farther up the road. He took off his hood to breathe more easily and turned up the narrow dirt path that led to the Dog's home. Branches whipped at his face, and twice he ducked under immense dewy spans of banana-spider webs. He broke out into a clearing and slowed to catch his breath. It had been a long time since he had run. The emergency hood hummed in his hand.

He had seen the Dog twice before, and they had acknowledged each other at a careful distance. As veterans, they shared the bond of war, but whereas he had emerged from conflict a respected soldier, she had come out as an illegal gene splice, a piece of dangerous biological equipment.

A neat, wood-shingled house sat in the clearing. The Dog stood up in the midst of her garden with a small hand shovel held like a weapon. Leaf mold flecked the velvet gray fur of her arms.

He felt her fear, surprise, and anger. Dogs were focused telepaths by design and imprinted on their handlers at an intense and intimate level, but an unbonded person in close proximity could still feel strong emotional bleed-over. He imagined the Dog deciding whether to kill him or not. In the CSA, the Christian States of America, she was an abomination and regarded as military property to be neutralized by an ordnance disposal team, but he had known about her presence for almost a year and had not reported her. He hoped that that would work in his favor. He could see her muscles tense as she decided the best course of action.

"Shroom," he said. "You are in the dispersal range."

<Immune> he felt. The word filled his head and popped like a soap bubble. Her voice was soft and feminine and un-doglike. Her design was mostly human, so much so that she was inter-fertile with baseline humans, but that held little weight in the CSA. "Still, they'll decontaminate the whole area. You know what that means."

<Despair and sadness>, he felt. Hard work had built her hidden homestead in the middle of a blight zone.

"The hazmat team will arrive in a few minutes. Once they secure the scene, they'll disinfect with an aerial attack."

She bolted for her house and retrieved a military pack designed for her body. Like a good soldier, she was ready to bug out at a moment's notice. She surveyed all that she would lose, came to him, and hugged him. Her body, taught and muscular, smelled like warm sun. He could not remember the last time he'd been hugged.

She stepped back.

<Thank you>

"Be safe," he said.

She ran towards the edge of the woods, and, just before reaching it, dropped to all fours and moved with the grace and power of a cheetah, her spine curling and springing open, covering ground in twelve-foot leaps. She vanished into the brush.

He returned to his truck, winded from the exertion and wet with sweat. He put his hood back on. Military vehicles circled the shroom's pole. Amber strobes flashed, and men in hazmat suits set up decontamination gear. He looked up in time to see the shroom convulse. Ropey pink antlers burst out of its skull. The shroom swung its head, rattling the antlers and releasing a pink mist of spores that caught the wind and drifted. The shroom shuddered again, and more thick antlers erupted from its back, growing and branching with astonishing fungal speed. The yellow-suited hazmat team finished their setup, and a jet of flame erupted from the fire gun's nozzle to engulf the shroom. The antlers crisped, turned black, and broke away.

"Did you call this in?" asked the supervising officer.

"Yeah."

"Good job. Is your hood cinched down tight?"

"Yeah, I'm good."

"Okay, as soon as we clean up the scene we are decontaminating the area. You know what that means."

"I do."

The shroom fell from the pole, hitting the ground with a wet, hissing splat. Broken pieces rolled away, and the team hosed it down with more fire until the thing turned into a pile of ash. They worked the surrounding area with chemicals. Leaves dissolved and dripped under the chemical attack.

"Fruiting bodies visible upon arrival," said the supervising officer into his radio. "High concentration of spore release. Wind speed is light and variable. I'm recommending immediate chemical decontamination."

"Roger that," squawked the radio. "Chopper is on the way."

"This is going to be inconvenient," said the major to himself.

In the hospital isolation ward, he breathed the acrid chemical mist to purge his lungs of any shroom spores that might have infiltrated his lungs. Ventilation fans whirred for a few minutes. He dried himself as best as he could with the paper towels. The sealed door opened.

"Major," said a nurse. She handed him a paper hospital smock and watched as he dressed. "Would you follow me?"

He followed her, and she drew back a curtain.

"In here, please," she said.

He sat at the edge of the examining table. The curtain was pulled aside, and the Sisters of Eternal Grace stepped in to pray over him. One of the crones put her bony, knuckled hand on his forehead and tapped him. They rattled their donation can in front of him when they finished. He looked down at the hospital smock.

"I don't have any pockets."

The lead sister frowned at him and rattled the can again.

"I don't..."

Her face twisted into an uncharitable grimace of disgust.

The doctor entered. "Get out, hags."

The sisters scowled in unison but turned on their heels and left in a whirl of gray skirts and sensible shoes.

"You know they are going to bill you for that prayer. The VA will cover their costs, but you should be nice to them; they're connected like the mob," said the doctor. "Are you feeling okay? You look like shit."

He coughed. "I'm okay. Does that stuff work?"

"The shower washes off any spores on your skin, but the mist? No, it just scorches your lungs. The spores are encysted. The prayer is the best treatment."

"Great."

"I've got something for you." He reached into his lab coat pocket and took out a bottle of pills, migraine medicine.

"Where did you get them?"

"There are ways, and then there are ways. People need things, and I can get them. How do you think I can help so many?"

"I can't pay for them."

"I still owe you."

"That debt was paid a long time ago."

"That debt can never be paid, but let me try. You need to be careful."

"About what?"

"The sampler found chimera hair and skin cells on your cloths."

"I was wearing old clothes from the war."

"Yeah, you can try that excuse, but the sampler is more sophisticated than that. It's the best piece of equipment we have in this hospital, and it is hotwired to the DOFF. They'll be watching you. You know how they love rooting out heretics and atheists."

"Yes, and Zionists and Papists and Colored." Every society needed an underclass to absorb injustice and excess force.

"Do you need a ride home?"

"No, I'll walk. I need the exercise."

"You also need some clothes. It's a long walk."

"We've walked farther on less."

"Yes, we have. You're good to go. I'll have the nurse bring you some clothes. The reverend-director of the hospital will want to stop by and pad your bill with another prayer or two."

"Prayer is the best medicine."

"I thought that was laughter."

"Not anymore."

Raindrops pummeled the road. He walked into a nightmare landscape of dripping, gray-green slime that coagulated in puddles and ran across the road in sticky, mucosal sheets. The aerial decontamination spray had turned the surrounding woods into a melted, Dalí-esque landscape. The larger trees resembled wilted saguaro, bent and sagging in graceful, boneless curves. Whip-thin branches of heartwood dripped to the ground. The delicate gray bones of small creatures caught in the dissolving spray littered the sticky ground. His truck remained in the washout. With a jack and boards pulled from the bed of the truck, he managed to extricate it from the ditch and drive home.

Inside his home, he wedged a two-by-four into the cleats to bar the door shut. He showered off the slime of the melted forest. As he dressed, the wind shifted with frontal passage, and the house rocked in another direction. The temperature dropped as the cold front engulfed the house. Bizarre weather typified the new normal. He started a fire in the stone fireplace and hung a battered teakettle over it. Thunder boomed. Hailstones pummeled the roof. The ghosts of his family, trapped and framed above the fireplace, regarded him from a world before the I-War and the Second Civil War.

Another roll of thunder shook the house, and he popped two of the doctor's pain pills to break up the loci of pain that accreted around the piece of Yankee shrapnel lodged in his head. After a few moments, the white-hot dots of agony abated. He closed his eyes and listened to the crackle of the wood fire and the hiss of boiling water from his kettle.

Someone knocked on the front door. He roused to awareness and fetched his shotgun. He chambered a shell and peered through the glass peephole.

The Dog.

He unbarred the door and held it open. She was soaking wet, shivered in the unseasonal cold.

<Nowhere to go>

Desperate and intimate and voiceless thoughts flowed through his mind like sound. Her camouflage T-shirt clung to her shoulders. Blood oozed from a hailstone cut above her left eye. She wiped rain from her face, and he caught sight of the razor-sharp dew claw on her forearm. If she wanted the house, she could take it from him. He stepped back, swinging the door wider.

"I'll get you some dry clothes." He put the gun down and went into a backroom.

<Thank you>

He felt her gratitude and uncertainty follow him.

The Dog knelt in front of the fireplace and held her hands spread-fingered toward the fire. She turned to look over her shoulder. He handed her some old clothes that had belonged to his wife, and a towel. She stripped in front of the fireplace with immodest military efficiency. Soft velvet fur thinned on her breasts and thickened somewhat at the swell of her vulva. She dried herself with the towel and dressed. The remains of her home stained her feet milky green.

<Nothing left>

"I'm sorry. Are you hungry?"

<Yes>

He opened a packet of dehydrated chicken soup and dumped it into the tea kettle.

"It will take a few minutes"

<Smells good>

He added another log to the fire and stirred the soup mix. Ants boiled from the log and stepped into a miniature hell. They crisped in the embers. The Dog sat on the threadbare couch and curled her legs under her and tucked her hands between her thighs. He was not afraid even though there were strong reasons for baseline humans to fear Dogs. They were stronger and smarter, exotic and dangerous, beautiful, and, above all else, different. She was typical of her kind.

<You have mods?> she asked.

"Yes, I was a soldier once." Most soldiers of the old USA featured some viral-delivered enhancements. He saw pretty well in low-light conditions, couldn't run to fat even if he wanted to, and healed a bit faster than before. The processes that modified him had created her from scratch.

<Maybe you're a Dog>

"Maybe you're a woman."

She smiled against the exhaustion that threatened to overwhelm her. Her canines protruded a bit from her lips. He served the soup.

"You're safe here."

<I know>

She finished the soup and set the bowl down on the end table.

"What's your name?" he asked.

<M'ling> She slouched down on the couch and closed her eyes to sleep.

He waited for the fire to burn down to a safe level. He pulled down a comforter from the back of the couch and covered her. He curled on the adjacent sofa and fell asleep.

Under M'ling's ministrations, the backyard bloomed with fruit and vegetable and flower. Low-level agents of the Department of Faith Formation intruded several times, but each time she sensed their presence and vanished. At night, when the air cooled, they talked. She told him how a sniper killed her handler in Venezuela, and how she ripped the sniper's throat out with her teeth. She told him how she battled back from the psychic shock of his loss, her inability to accept another handler, and her escape from the decommissioning facility. In turn, he told her about fighting in Taiwan during the I-War with China, and later in Virginia, during the Second Civil War. They slept together, at first for companionship, and then for something more. At night he stroked the length of her body, soft velvet over hard muscle.

Stories of handlers that slept with their Dogs were ubiquitous in rocket-shattered Taiwanese cities. Contemplating bestiality with manufactured creatures of ethereal beauty was the least of sins in that brief and violent war. Handlers and their Dogs returning from long-range patrols self-segregated at the firebase, and it only added to the mystery and speculation. Once, on a mission, his fire team found a handler carrying the long, lithe frame of his Dog, not over his shoulder, but in his arms like a bridegroom carrying his bride. The handler, agonized with fatigue, refused to let anyone else touch her. He fell to his knees and then collapsed from exhaustion over her body. They convinced him to bury her. Over the grave, the handler cried and murmured gentle words, and when he had finished he said, "I can't."

"Can't what"

"I can't. Do you understand?"

"I do."

"You can't."

When they looked away the handler shot himself in the head and they dug another grave.

At the time he could not understand the connection, the powerful bond between Dog and handler, each devoted to the other so intimately that the descriptive terms ascribed to the connection were meaningless. It was what made them such a terrifyingly effective weapon system.

Now he thought they worked well together, in a way in which he never expected to do again.

She stood and looked to him. <They're here again>

He heard a vehicle pull into his drive. He walked to the front door and waited. A man wearing a modified Roman collar, a badge, and a sidearm walked towards his porch. Two other men scanned the area. He opened the door before the man knocked.

"Major Jackson, I am Reverend-Inspector Carlyle."

"In what capacity are you here today?"

The man looked perplexed. "What do you mean?"

"Are you here as a reverend or as an inspector?"

"Both. Always."

"What can I do for you?"

"I have traces unexplained by your statements. Where is the abomination?"

"On my front step."

The reverend-inspector grinned with professional malice and indignation.

"Right. Harboring an abomination is a capital offense."

"Every offense is a capital offense these days."

"The purest metal comes from the hottest fires."

"Clever."

The reverend-inspector was the worst kind, a thick layer of true believer over a core of bully, the type to shout damnation on the street corners yet never lift a finger in a poorhouse or soup kitchen.

"May I come in?"

He stepped forward and was pushed back.

He moved his hand to draw his sidearm

"Do you think that you can draw that weapon before I do something about it?"

The reverend-inspector moved his hand away from the weapon. Confusion and genuine fear crossed his face. He was unaccustomed to resistance.

"I have full authority..."

"Major"

"What?"

"Major. What you want to say is: *Major, I have full authority.* You will address me by my military rank. I've earned it, and you are not coming in my house without a warrant. This isn't the United States. Are you a Yankee?"

The reverend-inspector's face darkened at the insult. "Major, your story to my associates was unconvincing. There were no squatters in the woods. And I found these." He held up silver dog tags that flashed in the sun. "When I come back it will be with a warrant."

He stepped onto his porch, and the reverend-inspector stumbled backwards down the two steps.

"If you come back, we will duel over any further insult. Do you accept? I'll register our intent with the county."

The inspector flushed red, unprepared for the personal challenge. Duels were rare, but permitted between CSA landowners and military officers.

"I, I..."

"I thought not. Get off my property."

The reverend-inspector turned, stalked to his county car, and drove away.

M'ling emerged from the other room and pressed her body against his back. She wrapped her arms around him, and leaned her head on his shoulder.

"He will come back."

<They always come back>

He locked his desk drawer and stepped into the hangar. The helicopters inherited from the USA were slotted in their spaces but immobile for a lack of spare parts. All the mechanics he supervised had already left for Friday services, a euphemism for drinking moonshine in the back room of the local roadhouse.

He drove past a chain gang of un-saved and un-white conscripts supervised by mirror-shaded, shotgun-toting deputy-deacons. He stopped at the toll bridge and honked his horn for the attendant to lift the reflector-bedazzled log gate that blocked his way. The attendant came out of the booth and walked away from him.

"Hey, I need to get home," he yelled to the attendant, but the man entered the tollhouse and closed the door.

"Under new management, Major," said a voice from behind the driver's window. His door was wrenched open and a gun pressed against his temple.

He reached for his own gun in the glove box.

"No you don't, Major. No you don't. Please step out."

The pressure from the pistol barrel eased and he unfastened his seatbelt. He stepped out and recognized the highwaymen, a former military unit that did the unchristian work it took to enforce a Christian state. The man with the gun to his head pistol-whipped him, and he dropped to his knees. Two more heavy blows pounded on his head. Stars exploded, but he held to consciousness.

Rough hands grabbed him and dragged him into the surrounding woods. Twisted hemp rope secured him face-down over the hood of a car. They were strong and fast and, like him, ex-military.

"Major, what is good?"

He spit blood out of his mouth. Some of his teeth felt loose.

"I said, what is good?"

A fist punched him in the back of his head, bouncing his face against the hood of the car. '19 Mustang, he thought. The last year they made them.

"I'll tell you. Good is that which pleases God, and what pleases God is what I have to do. To the matter at hand: There is an abomination in our midst, and it needs to be purged. Fire has to be fought with fire, an abominable act for an abominable act."

A knife sliced open the back of his pants and eager hands jerked his trousers down. He breathed in fast, fearful pants.

"Where is the abomination?"

He remained silent.

"When we are done you know what you must do."

When they finished taking turns, they cut him free, and he fell to the ground. They left him alone and walked back to their camp behind the tollhouse. Darkness fell, and he pulled himself up and limped to his truck. Warm blood dressed his legs and back.

He drove home naked and broken.

He did not need to explain.

She knew.

He radiated humiliation and pain.

She reached for him, but he kept walking through the house to the back-yard. He stepped into the small pool converted into a fishpond and sat in the water up to his neck. Carp and brim nibbled at him. In time, he went to bed, and she lay next to him, her hand on his chest. Between them, in the still of the night, thought and feeling ebbed and flowed in a gentle tide.

He awoke alone, his throat raw, his insides dirty. In the bathroom, he looked in the mirror and saw a small snowflake tracery of white on his cheek. He drank tepid water until he gagged. She was not in bed and he went in search. The backdoor to the living room lay open to the night. Dark clouds scudded across the full moon. M'ling stood on the steps in the pool that he sat in earlier. She glowed ghostly in the pre-dawn light, a specter worthy of darkest fear. The water lapped at her ankles. Naked and alien, she washed shadowed blood from her forearms and chest and mouth.

The highwaymen did not know what they had unleashed.

Predatory eyeshine regarded him with love. She stepped from the pool and embraced him. Retractable-clawed hands caressed the fibrous cluster at his cheek. Her dew claw rested across his throat. She would do it if he asked.

"No," he said. "I want every minute."

He made arrangements. The doctor visited him and injected him with an expensive antifungal that slowed the progression but could not stop it.

Long ago, the doctor, then a medic, paralyzed with fear over the onslaught of incoming artillery rounds, had curled into an exposed fetal ball in the open battlefield. The major, then a captain, had dragged the doctor into the shelter of the root ball crater of a fallen tree. Anti-personnel shells burst overhead, filling the air with white-hot blades of Yankee metal. They outlasted the fierce barrage and survived the night and spoke no more of it.

The doctor owed him.

"Do this for me and our debt is settled."

"I will."

The thirty-foot-long speedboat rolled under the topside weight of three big outboard engines and six fifty-five gallon drums of fuel on the aft deck. Big men dressed in night camouflage unloaded alcohol, pornography, medicine, and other hard-to-find necessities. The run back to Cuba would take twenty hours, but in less than two they would be beyond the decrepit CSA Coast Guard.

By the light of the half moon, the fungal rhizomes luminesced. The fibers spread across his face and neck and reached for the thoughts in his head. The smuggler crew kept their distance. As she embraced him, his hand drifted to the swell of her belly. He pressed, feeling for a kick, but felt none. Maybe it was too soon.

<It's your daughter>

"Our daughter."

She kissed him one last time and boarded the boat.

As the boat receded into the night, sadness attenuated. His connection grew weaker and weaker until he could no longer feel her. He dropped to the wet ground, empty and hollow.

By unthinking instinct, he selected a dead pine that offered unobstructed access to the wind. Compulsion drove him to the topmost reaches, and he swayed in the amber morning light, rocking to-and-fro in the breeze. He thought his last thoughts of love and war before bizarre biological processes bundled his memories into microscopic spores that erupted from him in a pink haze to be scattered on the winds.

Coming Home

Janine K. Spendlove

"No war is over until the enemy says it's over. We may think it over, we may declare it over, but in fact the enemy gets a vote."
— General James Mattis, USMC

PIA RAN AS HARD AS she could, the hot air of this desert planet burning her lungs. She'd never get away. They'd taken down each of her crew in turn, starting with her co-pilot and all the way to her most junior loadmaster. Lingo was only eighteen. Torn apart by the monsters, and Pia had been helpless to stop it.

Stop.

She should stop. She could hear the cans getting closer. Their scrabbling claws tearing at the hard-baked clay beneath them. Soon they would be on her, tearing at her, devouring her. Soon she would join her crew. Soon—

"Pia!"

She jerked awake and grabbed at the guitar in her lap before it could crash to the floor. Her heart was racing, but at least it meant she was still alive. It had only been a nightmare. *I'm fine*, she thought. Lance Corporal Lingo was still alive too, as were most of her crew.

But not all.

The gravelly sound of a throat being cleared pulled her from her miserable memories, and she fixed her gaze on the comm display installed over the fireplace's mantle. "Hi, Mom." Pia set her guitar down; it was the only thing that seemed to capture her attention these days.

On the screen, the dark-eyed woman, with skin and hair color to match, looked as if she'd been crying. Pia stiffened, knowing what was coming.

"Uncle Faust is gone."

Memories from the last twenty-seven years of Pia's life swirled through her mind. Uncle Faust pushing her on a swing. Uncle Faust tugging on one of her dozens of braids. Uncle Faust telling her all about flight school. Uncle Faust coming home from a scouting mission to Dixie with a cough he couldn't shake.

"By 'gone' you mean dead." Pia finally looked at the woman before her, a mirror of what she herself would look like in thirty years or so.

Her mother blinked back tears and nodded. Silver streaks wove through her mane of black hair, making her look exotic instead of old. She pursed her lips together and swiped at her eyes.

"Are you okay? Is Mike home—"

"I'm fine, Mom." Pia cut her off, anger flaring inside her. "People die every day. I gotta go." And just like that she terminated the comm, almost savoring the startled and hurt look she'd seen on her mother's face.

Picking her guitar up, Pia strummed a few chords of the ancient Irish folk song she'd been playing. She thought that maybe she should cry. She'd loved her uncle, after all, and goodness knew he'd doted on her as if she'd been his own daughter. And yet upon further examination of herself she found she felt...nothing. Not an emptiness from his now permanent absence, because that would be something.

This was nothing.

Something is wrong with me. I should feel something. The thought was fleeting, and she brushed it aside. *I'm fine.*

Hours later, when she entered her bedroom and saw the small stack of neatly folded clothes sitting at the foot of her bed, tears came unbidden. She turned around and silently left the room, her heart pounding until the sound of the door sliding closed behind her quieted it some. But then she felt her heart race again as the reality struck her that the clothes would still be there, waiting for her to put them away when she came back. They would always be there, and the idea of having to put away laundry overwhelmed her completely.

The smooth, cream-colored walls of her home no longer felt peaceful. They seemed to close in around her. The air was stifling, and Pia found herself gulping, trying to inhale as much as she could. Her palms were sweating and she could hear her own heartbeat roaring in her ears as she struggled to maintain control of the anxiety that was swelling within her.

Like a crushing wave sending a swimmer tumbling, the panic over took her and she fled her home.

Later she would realize the fact that it had been the laundry that had sent her into a panic and not her beloved uncle's death. It was the first real indicator that something was really wrong. But she wasn't ready to accept that just yet.

I'm fine.

10 months ago

"Thrusters?" Pia tried to keep the excitement from tingeing her voice too much. It was her very first mission as the ship captain. Sure, the converted shuttle wasn't much to look at, nor was it a very large ambulance—hardly enough space to carry more than half-a-dozen litters. But it was quick and nimble, and that's what mattered when flying to and from the front.

"All green, all quadrants," came the crisp reply from her co-pilot, First Lieutenant Angel Miller. Always a consummate professional, Pia could tell Angel was just as excited as she was by the slight acceleration in Angel's spoken cadence.

Pia's crew worked together like a well-lubricated machine after flying together for two months in preparation for this deployment. She knew each and every one of them and their quirks and, given the chaos that awaited them down in New Austin, she couldn't imagine flying with a better team.

Pre-flight checklist complete, Pia pulled back on the yoke while Angel repeated their departure clearance to Space Traffic Control onboard the UPNS COMFORT. It was their home base and main ship of operations, currently in orbit around the colony planet of New Texas.

"Midas Four Two, turn right to one two zero, watch for the asteroids, then it's a straight shot to landing zone delta."

"Midas Four Two copies all." Angel gave Pia the thumbs-up; she pushed the thrusters forward. She heard a whoop of glee not just from her two gunners, but the two hospital corpsmen as well.

"Should I quiet them down, ma'am?"

"Nah, let 'em cheer. I know just how they feel." Pia let a grin break across her face as she opened the thrusters fully, as she swooped around the asteroid field that stood between them and the planet's surface.

Present

Pia sat on the prefabricated front porch of her home. It looked like wood, felt like wood, and even smelled like wood, but it wasn't wood. The old oil companies had seen the writing on the wall long ago and had created new, easily sustainable materials that were both cheap and durable. Perfect for colony moons like Pia's home of Grace.

Grace was in the same system as New Texas but couldn't have been more different. Whereas New Texas—with its slightly closer orbit to the system's sun—was primarily a desert wasteland, Grace was lovely, and so very much like how every child learned Earth had once been before humanity had used it up and nearly destroyed it.

A light breeze blew by, fluttering the greenish-purple leaves on the surrounding trees. The accompanying sound of the little stream in Pia's backyard almost made her feel at ease. Almost.

"Hey." Mike sat down next Pia, and she belatedly realized he'd walked up without her even noticing.

That could get me killed. Not that Mike would ever hurt me. It was the *canidae*, or "cans" as they'd taken to calling them on New Texas, that she had to worry about.

"Hey, yourself."

"Your mom called me." He gave her a sidelong glance. "She told me what happened to Faust. I'm sorry."

Pia shrugged. Her eyes flitted to the trees lining the property line, looking for the monsters she knew had to exist out there. *Just because you can't see it doesn't mean it's not there.*

Mike followed her gaze, then looked at the old-fashioned hinged front door that hung partially open, then back to Pia. His jet-black eyebrows furrowed together in his classic "I'm worried" expression.

"How long have you been out here?"

"I don't know." Pia shrugged and continued to watch the tree line.

"Why didn't you just go inside?"

Pia tensed, heart racing. He would never understand. And she didn't have the words to explain it. How could she make him understand that she couldn't be in the house without someone? That it was too small. That it was wrong in there right now. The walls were too close. Confining. Trapping.

"I couldn't."

Raising one eyebrow, Mike opened his mouth to respond, but Pia cut him off.

"I just couldn't, okay? You don't need to go all 'Doctor Chu' on me."

Ignoring the hurt look in his brown eyes, she kept her eyes on the tree line.

"Not that kind of doctor, Pia. I'm physical therapist, not a mental therapist." He ran his fingers through his straight black, closely-shorn hair.

Pia stiffened. "Is that what you think I need? A mind bender?"

"No, I..." He reached out a hand to touch her back and she flinched.

"I don't know what you want me to say."

"Nothing. I'm fine." Getting to her feet, Pia went back inside, leaving Mike alone on the porch.

10 months ago

"You ready back there?" Pia kept her eyes on the navigational instruments as she finished another checklist. She knew that beyond the snub nose of her ship lay the gruesome remains of more than one Marine amidst the charred rubble of this section of New Austin. Despite receiving multiple scene-setting mission briefs to supposedly prepared them, she and her younger crewmembers hadn't expected this; the older, more seasoned members seemed unsurprised. The "cans" were brutally vicious and efficient. Body armor was almost useless against their six sets of claws. Her ship's hull armor wasn't much better.

Thankfully plasma rifles are far more effective than claws.

"Stabilizing one more, Skipper." HM3 Francis Kilmer's slow drawl sounded in Pia's headset.

"Copy, Doc. Just let me know when you're ready."

Lingo piped in. "Hey, Velazquez, you gotta check out the bleeder! Her leg's only hanging on by a—"

"Shut it, Lingo!" Corporal Velazquez, who normally had a smile on her face, chastised the junior gunner. "Just focus on your effing job and let the docs do theirs. You never know when a can could come."

"All loaded and ready. Pax are secure." HM2 Anton Mierzejewski's voice crackled over their headsets.

Pia gripped the yoke and scanned the horizon. Once she felt the ramp lock in place and verified it with a look at the center screen, she pushed up the power and headed them back to the UPNS *COMFORT*.

"Through or around the asteroids?" Angel brought up the two courses she'd plotted. Her fingers hovered lightly over them, waiting for the captain's direction.

Pia bit her lower lip. Through was definitely the quicker way, but also likely to get them killed. The problem with around was that it would take too long. She didn't know what shape their casualties were in.

The sound of someone retching filled her ears.

"Corporal Velazquez, is everything all right?" Angel gave Pia a worried glance.

"Yeah. Well, no. The bleeder's strap broke and she fell off the litter, and her leg fell off *her*. It doesn't look good back here. The docs are trying to help her, but Lingo can't stomach it." Velasquez's voice, though calm, was tight. "I think you better hurry, Skipper."

"Asteroids it is." Pia turned the ambulance toward the thin belt that stood between them and the *COMFORT*. Pia knew it was just a saying, that if she didn't get the trauma patients to the *COMFORT* within the "golden hour," they most likely wouldn't keel over and die, but time truly was of the essence if all these Marines, especially "the bleeder," were going to survive.

"Make sure everyone's strapped down tight back there." Pia eyed a gap between the outermost asteroids before her. She could just make out the outline the *COMFORT* beyond the belt. "This is going to be a bumpy ride."

Present

Pia sat straight up, sweat coating her entire body as her heart raced. Disoriented, she reached for the yoke that wasn't in front of her. Pia's right hand closed around empty air as she searched for the thrusters.

Everything was dark, and she blinked her eyes frantically, trying to get her vision to clear, when she heard a loud snore. Mike's snore. It was a loud as a ship's well deck opening up, and it immediately grounded her back in the here and now.

She was home on Grace. She was not on New Texas. She hadn't just lost another crewmember to the fangs and claws of a can.

I'm fine.

She couldn't remember her nightmare, not even fragments, just the feeling of helplessness that stayed with her.

Knowing she wouldn't be sleeping again anytime soon, Pia slipped out of bed, careful not to wake Mike, and padded softly down the stairs to her guitar.

10 months ago

Their fourth load of injured Marines and civilians offloaded onto the UPNS *COMFORT*, Pia stifled a yawn. They were nearing the end of their crew day and would soon get to hit the rack. She knew her crew had to be at least as exhausted as she was—if not more, in the docs' cases.

"Ramp's up." Lingo's tired voice sounded over the intercom. Angel visually verified the indicator on the center console and gave Pia a thumbs-up, confirming the lance corporal's statement. They had to be more careful than ever now—tired people made mistakes, and mistakes killed Marines.

Pia pushed up the thrusters and eased the shuttle through the airlock and down the *COMFORT*'s well deck. She rolled her head around, trying to loosen up her neck. The fifteen pounds of survival gear that she wore now felt more like fifty.

"Midas Four Two, turn to zero six three, current angle of attack."

Pia and Angel exchanged a confused look before Angel responded to control.

"Say again, control? We're an ambulance on a CASEVAC route to landing zone..." Angel double-checked her notes then keyed the mic, ". . . delta. That heading takes us to zone..." she checked the digital chart display, ". . . papa, which is still hot."

"Do you have gunners, Midas?" A new voice was coming from STC, deep and growling.

"Affirmative," Pia answered before Angel could, irritated by the change in the briefed mission. "But my crew's exhausted, and flying them into a hot zone, without a proper brief at the very least, is liable to get someone killed."

The same growling voice snapped back almost before Pia unkeyed the mic. "If you don't hurry there won't be casualties to evacuate! Every second you argue with me you put another Marine's life at risk, *Captain.*"

Pia frowned and then keyed the shuttle's intercom. "Did you all hear that?"

Her crew chief, good old reliable Gunnery Sergeant Anderton, the one among them who had the most to lose because he was retiring next month, was the one to answer.

"They're Marines, ma'am."

That said it all. "See if you can plot a somewhat safe way in," Pia said, nodding toward the nav computer as she angled the shuttle toward the new landing zone.

"And if I can't?" Angel didn't look up, fingers already manipulating their flight route in the nav computer.

"They're Marines. Find a way."

"Aye, aye, ma'am!"

Present

Pia smiled as she strummed the last chords to the song she'd just learned on her guitar. It was another old tune, but it was bright and catchy and always made her smile. She thought maybe she'd play it for Mike. Maybe she'd even sing along. Maybe—

"Do you want to go for a walk?" Mike leaned against the opening into the den.

Pia's smile was gone in an instant and she felt her anger rise up inside. *How dare he interrupt?*

"Do I *look* like I want to go for a walk? I'm playing my guitar. If I wanted to go for a walk, I'd go for a walk!"

Mike didn't say anything. Didn't yell back. Didn't even turn and leave. He didn't even have the decency to look hurt or upset by her behavior toward him. He just stood there looking perfectly understanding and calm.

She wanted to hurt him. To make him angry with her. Then she'd feel validated. Then he would see all the things that were wrong with her. Then he would leave her and she wouldn't have to try so hard anymore.

Setting the cherrywood guitar carefully back on its stand, Pia rose to her feet and calmly walked over to the delicately carved jade vase that had been a Chu family heirloom for generations now. It was older than Grace itself, originating on Earth. Picking the vase up carefully in two hands, she just as calmly walked past Mike and out to the back garden.

"Pia?" He followed her outside, careful to give her the space he seemed to understand she needed. "What are you doing?"

"I hate this vase." Before he could stop her, Pia hurled the vase into the stream and smiled as she watched it crack and break up amongst the rocks.

She felt hot tears rolling down her cheeks as she sank to the soft grass beneath her.

"I hate it, I hate it, I hate it." Pia pulled up clumps of grass and dug her fingers into the rich soil beneath. She felt Mike's arms encircle her and she shoved against him.

"You should hate me!"

He only pulled her tighter and kissed the top of her head. "I think you need to talk to someone."

"I don't want to." She buried her face in his shoulder and felt the wetness from her tears soak the absorbent synth of his shirt. "I'm fine. *I'm fine!*"

"I know. But I still think you should."

"Please don't make me."

"I can't *make* you do anything."

10 months ago

They touched down on the dusty pad of LZ Papa between the remains of the Marine's forward operating base. Pia's gunners had just blasted a dozen cans from the air, but not before they'd witnessed a lone Marine get torn limb from limb by one of the six-legged, hairy monsters. The engines were too loud to hear the Marine's screams, but they could see his mouth contort in pain. Lingo had blasted the can to bits with his plasma rifle, but it had been too late.

A golden retriever lay by the remains of his handler, his chest heaving up and down slowly, and Pia could only imagine the high-pitched keen coming from the grieving dog.

Can't do anything about that right now. Focus on the task at hand. They had a job to do, and Pia knew her crew would cue off of her behavior.

"Angel, run a scan. Are we going to get hit by the cans while on deck?"

"Aye, aye." Angel's fingers flew over the console as she executed Pia's order. Everything else was quiet as they landed, eerily so.

"All clear, Skipper?" Doc Kilmer's voice sounded over the intercom once the last landing strut was in place.

"We got a herd of cans coming from two seven zero, about a klick away." Angel called up the heat signatures and vector and sent them back to the corpsman. "I'd say we have about two minutes."

The words were hardly out before Pia heard the ramp lowering.

"Gunny, we're gonna need your help."

Pia nodded her approval at the crew chief, and Gunnery Sergeant Anderton unbelted and headed to the back.

"Everyone stay on comm. Velazquez, Lingo, shoot anything that has more than four legs. Doc, you guys have ninety seconds to do a sweep, then we're outta here." Pia's crew all voiced their understanding, and with that they were off.

She hated being left behind like this. She hated staying in the safety of the flight deck while her crew exposed themselves to danger. But more than all that, she hated the cowardly feeling of relief that crept over her.

Pia kept her gaze inside and focused on her instruments. The dusty, barren red rock spread out before her was interesting, but the dismembered and shredded remains of a squad's worth of Marines turned her stomach. Her heart leapt to her throat when she saw a flash of movement out of the corner of her eye.

But it wasn't the cans, not yet. They were still a minute fifteen out. No, it was Doc Mierzejewski—*Ski*—trying to coerce the golden retriever to come with him, but the dog wouldn't leave his handler. Anytime Ski got too close, the golden would charge to his feet and growl with neck hair standing on end.

Pia was just about to tell him to move on, that they only had sixty seconds left, when Gunny spoke over the freq.

"We found one, boss. Little black lab led us right to her Marine. But he's injured something fierce, and stuck under a wrecked LightTac."

"Can you get him out?"

"Yes, ma'am, but we need time and Ski to get his butt over here."

Pia turned to her co-pilot. "How big's the herd?"

"Couple hundred, but that's only in the main body. Advance is only a dozen or so."

"Velazquez?"

"We can buy them time, Skipper."

Pia felt the floor decks rumble with the charge of the plasma rifles.

"Gunny, you've got your time. Get him out."

"Already on it, ma'am," the crew chief grunted.

The first of the cans crested the lip of the plateau, and Pia felt her gut clench.

They looked like dogs, but their hair was coarser, longer, wilder. They scuttled on six legs like insects and had razor-sharp, six-inch claws at the end of all of them. They were the size of a short human and as fast as a cheetah. They could filet you before you even realized they were there. And they were smart.

After pausing a moment to howl in unison, the dozen or so cans that made up the vanguard of the herd threw themselves at the shuttle.

Pia felt the shudder of a plasma rifle discharge and watched the lead can drop.

But there were more behind it.

She realized then there would always be more.

Present

Pia stood on the beach. The soft pink sand squished between her toes and the warm summer sun shone down on her, sending beads of sweat down her back. Normally this would have put a smile on her face. Normally this would have calmed her. But now she didn't know what to think or feel.

A fair-skinned man approached her. He was wearing a multi-colored flowered shirt and clashing black-and-green striped swim trunks. His hair was cut in a familiar military buzz, so blonde it was almost white. He was nearly a decade older than Pia, but his blue eyes sparkled with a hidden mirth Pia was instantly jealous of.

I'll never feel that way again.

He stood next to her for a moment, not saying anything, just letting Pia stare for as long as she needed. When she finally looked away, he stuck out a hand.

"Jim Rogers. Doctor Chu said you needed to talk to someone."

Pia took his hand, gave it a brief squeeze, then quickly released it. She didn't like for people to touch her any more. "You don't look like a mind bender."

"I'm a chaplain."

"You don't look like one of them either."

He nodded but kept his gaze on the ocean before them. "Been one for the last eighteen or so years. Last tour was as a battlefield chaplain. New Texas to be exact. Want to go for a walk?"

Rather than answer, Pia began walking along the shoreline, carefully keeping her sandal-clad feet clear of the water surges. The chaplain walked alongside her, his bare feet as often in the water as not. They moved in silence for several minutes, with Pia occasionally staring at him, and the chaplain leaning over to pick up a seashell and smile before putting it back.

"You said you fought on New Texas."

"Chaplains don't fight. Leastwise not how you Marines do. But yes, I was on the battlefront of New Texas. New Austen to be exact."

Pia sucked in a breath as visions of slaughtered Marines and feasting cans danced before her eyes. She banished her memories as quickly as she could.

"How are you so normal?"

The chaplain raised a blonde eyebrow and looked down at his garish clothes.

"You know what I mean. It's like the war is over for you." Pia brushed her hand over her brown eyes. "I'm afraid it won't ever be over for me. I just see New Austin in my head all the time, over and over and over again."

"That's not what you're really afraid of, though, is it? The memories. Those will fade." The chaplain still didn't meet her gaze, but there was a kind, understanding smile on his face. She realized that she could tell him anything. He was a stranger; he hadn't known her from before. Therefore, he was safe.

"No, it's not." She let her arm drop, skimming the side of her white cotton cover-up. "Facing the war was surprisingly easy. Often heartbreaking, given what my job was, but I had good Marines by my side. I knew what to do. What was expected of me."

She placed a fingertip on the dark, exposed skin of her sternum and took a deep breath. "The problem is I don't know who *I* am any more. Or rather, I know, but I don't recognize me. No one does." Pia shook her head. "I keep waiting to go back to the old me. The always-chipper, happy-go-lucky me. It hasn't happened yet. I mean, I say I'm fine because maybe if I say it enough it will be true. But it's not true. I'm not fine."

She stopped walking and looked up at the chaplain, brown eyes meeting his—kind, understanding, blue. "So I guess what I want to know is when will it happen. When will I be me again? When will I feel right inside?"

10 months ago

The plasma rifles fired over and over again, nearly drowning out of the roar of the cans.

"Time's up, Gunny," Pia yelled into her mic. "Where are you guys? We need to leave!"

A can made it past the rifles and threw itself against the hull of the shuttle. Pia winced—their claws were sharp enough to shred through the hull, which meant they wouldn't be spaceworthy if she didn't act fast.

"On our way back, Skipper," Doc Kilmer huffed.

Pia hopped out of her seat and checked the charge on her plasma rifle.

"Ma'am, what are you doing?" Angel looked out from under her sweat-soaked cap, red hair plastered to her forehead and neck, tired green eyes betraying their worry.

"I'm not going to let the cans tear my ship apart." It was logical, really. Had to be done; no time for thought. No time for worry. No time for fear. "Go through take-off checks and when I say go, you go, even if I'm not on board."

"Ma'am...?"

"I don't have time to argue. Do it." Pia glanced over her shoulder just long enough to see Angel's nod, then leapt down the ladder well to the cargo hold behind. Lingo had a look of manic glee as he picked off the cans when they crested the ridge.

"Velazquez, with me." Pia heard the gunner shoulder her rifle and follow her down the ramp and outside. "You take the right, I'll take the left. Don't let them near the hull."

"Aye, aye, Skipper!" Corporal Velazquez grinned broadly, her easy smile confidant and excited. She ducked around the corner, already firing her rifle.

Pia barely cleared the turn when a can was on her. She could smell its fetid breath wash over her face, and a dribble of foamy saliva dripped onto her cheek. It didn't attack, and she realized the beast was dead. As she rolled it off of her she realized she'd shot it without thinking.

Can I kill so easily now?

"Skipper!"

Pia whirled around and brought her plasma rifle up to bear and shot another can, hot on the tail of Doc Ski and Gunny, carrying a young Marine between them. His tan cammies were torn to bits but still managed to cling to his body. His head lolled to the side, and it was only when she saw the stark white of his eyes cracking open, so much in contrast to the blackness of his skin, that she realized he was still alive.

"What are you doing out here, Skipper?" Gunny asked as he and Doc Ski hauled the Marine on board. He kept calling for someone named "Chesty."

"Saving your butt." Pia took out another can that was trailing a skinny little black Labrador. She'd barely lowered her rifle when she felt herself get jerked backward and onto the ramp by the seat of her flight suit.

"Yeah, but who's gonna save yours?" Gunny Anderton reached past Pia and pulled a knife she hadn't seen him throw from the body of a dead can. She hadn't even heard the monster creeping up behind her. "Need you in one piece to fly us outta here, Skipper."

The sound of claws scrabbling across the ramp ended the conversation as Pia whirled, rifle brought up to bear. The scrawny lab hauled itself up the ramp, swept past Pia and the gunnery sergeant, and leapt into the injured Marine's waiting arms. Pia watched as the Marine collapsed onto his litter, then looked around and counted her crew.

"Where's Kilmer?" But she knew even before she finished asking the question. Gunny shook his head and Doc Ski focused on stabilizing the injured Marine. Pia swallowed. Now was not the time to grieve.

"Velazquez, get your butt over here. Time to go." Pia felt the ramp under her rumble and begin to close.

Angel's voice piped over the comm, calm and steady. "Ma'am, the main body is here. We need to take off now."

"No, give Velazquez a minute."

"We don't have a minute. We don't even have ten seconds."

The sound of another plasma rifle blasting shook the shuttle. Without looking, Pia knew Gunny Anderton had taken Camila's gunner spot.

"Velazquez!" Pia couldn't leave her. Looking out the side port she saw that the gunner had foolishly gone up to the ridge to engage the herd. Pia couldn't watch, nor could she look away. The ramp finished closing and Pia slipped down into the med bay. She pressed herself to another window and watched as Velazquez took out can after can, always with her easy smile on her heart-shaped face.

Pia forced herself to her feet and launched herself up the ladder well onto the flight deck. If she could turn the shuttle to bring the forward cannons to bear, maybe, just maybe...

But as she slammed into her seat and looked out the forward viewport she saw it was too late. Velasquez still had a smile on her heart-shaped face, but it was nowhere near the rest of her body.

Pia couldn't just leave a member of her crew behind. Marines didn't leave Marines behind. Not ever, not—

Angel's hand came over hers and guided Pia to pushing the thrusters forward. Pia pulled back on the yoke and felt multiple shakes along the shuttle as the bodies of cans slammed into the hull.

And then it was quiet.

Present

"You are you now." The chaplain's voice was calm and soothing, the way the lapping waves were supposed to be. Pia wanted to punch him in the face. Instead she let a slow breath out and asked a question.

"What do you mean I am me now?"

"The old you is gone. The new you is here, and that's just fine." The chaplain stopped walking, and faced Pia. "The new you is wonderful. I think if you gave yourself a chance to get comfortable in your new skin, you'd see that." He placed a hand on her shoulder, and for once Pia didn't feel like flinching away. "There's a lot to like about new you. Doctor Chu says you are more thoughtful and patient. In many ways you're kinder, and you don't worry about little things as much. He just wishes you could see how wonderful you are."

"I'm sure Mike said those things, but he's just being nice. Like always. He's always so *nice*." Pia stepped away from the chaplain, needing the space.

"Is there anything wrong with that?"

Pia shook her head and then shrugged. "I'm just so temperamental now. I'm always angry."

The chaplain leaned over and scooped up a glistening green seashell from the pink sand.

"You spent the better part of a year constantly worried about getting not just yourself but your Marines killed." He brushed the sand off the delicate shell, which was the length and width of his index finger. "You have no idea how much stress and pressure that puts on a person. You need to release it, and that's what you've been doing." He took Pia's hand and set the seashell inside. "This will pass. Accepting who you are now, instead of rejecting it, will help."

"Will I always feel like this?" Pia stared at the shell, unable to meet his eyes. Unable to let him see the tears forming at the corners of hers.

He closed her fingers over the smooth surface of the green shell. "No, you'll change in time. We all change in time. And that's a good thing."

10 months ago

They flew up through the *COMFORT*'s well deck, and Pia set down where the lineman indicated she should.

"How's he holding up?" Pia asked.

"PFC Smith has been sedated and Chesty isn't trying to bite my hand off anytime I get too near anymore." Doc Ski's voice sounded as exhausted as Pia felt.

"Well, that's something," Pia said, more to herself, just as something to fill the void. Once all three struts were down and locked to the deck, she cleared Angel to lower the ramp.

The ramp lowered, and Angel brought out the shut-down checklist. Pia shook her head.

"Are we not shutting down, ma'am?"

"I'm not." Pia ran a steady hand over the yoke, feeling oddly calm. No doubt STC had more missions than crews. It felt selfish to shut down, and it felt good to be needed. "I know our crew day is up, but I also know that we can get extended six hours for surge ops if needed." She met Angel's eyes and gave a wan smile. "And I think it's needed. Anyone who wants to leave, can. I won't blame you and I won't stop you. But I'm going back down."

As she knew they would be, her crew was with her.

Always faithful, that was the Marine Corps for you.

Present

Pia was sitting on the front steps again; only this time she twirled the green seashell in her hands. Mike sat down next to her. Not too close, but close enough to let her know he was there.

He didn't ask if she wanted to go inside.

He didn't ask if she was hungry.

He didn't ask if she wanted to go for a walk.

He didn't ask anything at all.

She spun the shell around in her hands a few more times before finally laying her head on his shoulder.

"I think I'm going to be okay." Pia held out the seashell toward Mike.

Plucking it from her, he laced his free fingers with hers.

"I know."

Where We Would End a War

F. Brett Cox

WHEN AMANDA CAME HOME FROM the war, her family was there to greet her at the platform. She knew what to expect when she rematerialized, but she'd forgotten about the mortar-like *chuff! chuff! chuff!* as the others arrived after her. It didn't scare her—she was beyond being scared by loud noises—but it added to her disorientation as she stumbled off the platform into her dad Ernie's arms. Her grandmother Rosie and kid brother Larry rushed in to grab her as well. She could hear her dad Neal crying, but the thin skype almost got lost in the other families' laughing and crying and shouting as their loved ones popped back home. Gramma Rosie smelled like her perfume and their kitchen, and Amanda held on tightest to her.

All the way home Neal kept apologizing for not being able to be there in person, but the teardown in Indianapolis had come up at the last minute and, with the economy being what it was and all, he couldn't afford to turn it down. Everything he did was for her and her brother. He hoped she understood. Ernie tried to reassure her that the light media presence at the platform was probably because her group was one of the last to get back and they'd moved on to the next cycle, you know how the nets are. It didn't mean people didn't care, because they did. Then he quit apologizing and just stared at her like she wasn't real. From the back seat Gramma Rosie kept reaching up front to rub her shoulder. The car steered itself through the traffic even more smoothly than she remembered, almost as smoothly as the sensed-up transports outside of Cotabato City had dodged IEDs. Probably the same tech by now. Larry was playing a game in the back seat but she knew he was glad she was home.

When they got back to the house, Amanda went straight up to her room. Gramma Rosie had told her in the car that her room was just as she left it, which was technically accurate. Nothing had been moved, nothing was missing. But when she had been there it had never been that neat, and when she had come from work or school it had never felt that empty, so it wasn't just like she left it, not really.

For the first week or so she slept in late every day. Ernie and Gramma Rosie were fine with that, and so was Neal when he skyped in from his next job in Ft. Wayne. Gramma Rosie kept saying she knew Amanda needed to catch up on her rest. That was true enough, but soon her days had more darkness than light. At night, when everyone else was asleep, all there was to do was watch stuff onscreen and there was nothing that she wanted to watch, which meant all there really was to do was think, and she didn't want to do that. So she started setting her alarm again.

Once she got back on schedule, she still mostly stayed at home but made a point to go out during the day, not just to get out of the house but also to try to get a sense of what she had come home to. Before she had left for the war she was in the same cycle as most people she knew. Get up, go to school, go to work, go out, come home, go to sleep, get up, do it again. Where she lived was just *there* and not anything to notice. Now she walked around the town and tried to notice things. While she was deployed she had had this recurrent dream where she was walking around the town and finding all sorts of new places that hadn't been there before. In the town she returned to, there didn't seem to be anything missing, but there was certainly nothing new. It didn't feel any different than it had before, when she wasn't noticing it.

The closest thing to something new was the American Legion post. At some point while she was gone, the town had found the money to fix it up. Parts of it were shiny and parts were fake old-timey, but it was at least somewhere to go now that she was a veteran. There weren't too many people there her age, mostly older folks who had been in Iraq and Afghanistan, shooting pool, chugging beer, dancing on robotic limbs. There was one really old guy who supposedly had been in Vietnam. He had two robot legs but he mostly sat by the window and looked out at the town.

One evening she found herself talking to a woman named Sally who didn't look much older than Ernie but said she had done three tours in Afghanistan. She still had all her original limbs. Sally couldn't get over the jaunting.

"What's it like in between? Do you feel anything?"

"No. You just stand there and they throw the switch and then you're someplace else." That wasn't true. There was a split-second when you felt like you were leaving your body, like you were dying, and the first time that had happened was still the most terrifying thing she had ever experienced, way worse than anything she had encountered in the war. After a few times you got used to it. But she didn't tell Sally that. She didn't want to frighten Sally, but she didn't want to reassure her either. Sally was just someone to talk to over a couple of beers. She didn't know Sally, who shuddered and said, "Not me, sister," and gulped down the rest of her beer.

"Never say never. You know they're starting to phase it in for civilian travel."

"Like I said, not me."

"They say it'll help the economy and the climate. Less fuel. Less time."

"The climate was already fucked when I was your age. And time? Time for what?"

Amanda couldn't answer that one.

"Besides, it was bad enough being back in the world just a couple of days after you'd been out in the shit for a year. It can't help you guys any to be out in it and then back home just like that." Sally snapped her fingers. "Turnaround in seconds, not days. How can that be any kind of advantage?"

Would having a day of travel time have made the return any less jarring? Amanda decided it wouldn't have, but she didn't tell Sally that, either. Instead she ordered another round. She looked past Sally, who was already talking about something else, at two guys her own age who were at one of the tall tables that lined the wall. One of them was wearing a T-shirt that said, BOG? AIC. TMF!

Sally noticed her staring, looked over at the guys, and smiled. "Cute. You should go over and talk to them. Maybe they were out where you were."

"Nah. Drone jockeys."

"How can you tell?"

Amanda gestured towards the T-shirt, but not enough so the guy might notice. " 'Boots On Ground? Ass In Chair! Telebombing Mother Fuckers.' "

"Shit. What are they even doing here? Like they're really soldiers or something."

"They are, officially. They get medals and everything."

"Yeah, I know, but...shit." The next round arrived and Sally raised her glass. "Here's to real combat, girlfriend. Here's to actual fucking risk."

Amanda raised her glass, drank, and excused herself to hit the head. On the inside of the stall someone had scrawled, BJ4F. It seemed familiar but she couldn't quite place it. Blow Jobs for Free? How generous.

When she came back they finished their beers and Sally asked if she wanted to go to another place she knew about that was quieter. Amanda begged off and when Sally left Amanda went over and started talking to the two guys at the table, who really were cute. Turned out the guy wearing the T -shirt was the boyfriend of the other guy, who was the actual drone pilot. The T-shirt guy was an accountant or something. They were nice and it wasn't too bad talking with them about nothing in particular but when they started technobabbling about the war and the drone pilot started getting all superior about how trying to jaunt bombs to targets didn't work, how any explosive device moved with the transporter showed up at its target scrambled and useless, she lost interest and went home. The next night she came back and met a guy who had been Boots on Ground and had even been in Bravo Company just like her, although they'd been in different platoons. They went back to his place and fucked, and it was okay, but the fact that he had seen combat didn't really make any difference. Neither did the fact that he had a robot left leg. She said she'd call him but they both knew she wouldn't.

The next morning she was in the kitchen with Larry and Gramma Rosie. Ernie had already left for work and Neal hadn't skyped in yet. Gramma Rosie made morning talk as she prepared breakfast: how'd you sleep (fine), did you have a good time last night (yes, which wasn't completely a lie), did you see the news, what is Congress thinking trying to push another impeachment so soon after the last one (how should I know, and what difference does it make). But then when they were seated she started trying to talk to Amanda about what her plans were.

"I know you haven't been back all that long, dear, but your fathers and I both believe you need to start thinking about what you want to do next."

"You mean get a job? I told you I was setting aside part of my pay to help out."

"I know, and that's wonderful, it'll really help. But that's not going to last much longer, and—oh, what am I saying, it's not anything to do with money. You don't need to worry about that. Go back to school if you want."

"I'm thinking about it," Amanda lied.

"I'm sure you are, sweetheart. But don't you need to make some plans? I'm glad you've got some friends to hang out with, and God knows you deserve some time to yourself, but—we just worry, is all. We just want what's best for you."

"They're afraid you have PTS," Larry said without looking up from his eggs or his screen.

Gramma Rosie glared at him, caught herself, and said, "Larry, that's not true. Amanda is just fine. I'm sure she doesn't have post-traumatic stress disorder."

"It's not a disorder," Amanda said. "They haven't called it that in years."

"That's what I told them," Larry said. "I told them if you had PTS you'd be seeing things and shooting at them, right?"

The mandatory session before she left the islands: *During a traumatic event, your higher brain functions are subordinated to the amygdala, the part of your brain that controls emotional responses and memories. When you remember those events, the brain wants to recreate the same processes that controlled your response to the original event. That's what flashbacks are: your brain wanting your body to crank up the adrenaline and cortisol, to try to survive all over again. But even if you're not reaching for your weapon when you hear a balloon pop, you can still be at risk. Some of our scientists think the trauma can actually shrink the amygdala, which also shrinks your emotional responses. That's when we start looking at depression...*

"Right. I'm fine. Don't worry." So far she'd managed to put off the mandatory check-in at her local veterans' center.

"Of course you are, dear," her grandmother resumed. "But you fathers and I still—"

"Why do they call it jaunting?"

Larry put down his fork and looked up from his screen. It took a few seconds for Amanda to answer, she was so struck by his eyes, how deeply brown they were, almost red. Had she forgotten that? Had she never noticed?

"What?"

"The transport. Why do they call it jaunting?"

"It's from that sci-fi movie. That's what they called transport in the book."

"Did they use it for troops?"

"They used it for all kinds of things." Amanda had seen *The Stars My Destination* like everyone else and then read the novel while she was deployed. There was more down time than people realized. She had read a lot.

"How was it?"

"It was okay."

"Maybe you should watch it, Larry, and then you and your sister could talk about it."

Larry tapped his screen three times. "Got it."

Gramma Rosie smiled. A bonding moment between her grandchildren seemed to have taken her mind off her granddaughter's future. Amanda was genuinely glad, if it made her grandmother feel better. Gramma Rosie had always been there, and when Amanda was in second grade and her dads needed some time to work things out, Gramma Rosie had been pretty much the only one there. Amanda loved her grandmother and wanted her to be happy, wanted to please her, but what she wanted now more than anything else was for everyone to just stop talking. The three of them cleared the table and Amanda headed upstairs. Out of the corner of her eye she caught the news crawl on the living room screen, the words BLIND JAUNT FOR FREEDOM, and she remembered. That was what BJ4F scratched inside the stall had meant.

When she got up to her room she checked online and yes, there it was. She had heard rumors when she was deployed, but it looked like since she'd gotten back the whole thing was starting to get noticed. Some people were calling it a fad. Others were calling it an epidemic. Veterans who had gotten to the war and back by jaunting were breaking into the control booths after hours, setting random coordinates, and running onto the platforms just in time to jaunt wherever the coordinates sent them. Some wound up just down the street. Others wound up in another country. A few found themselves a hundred feet above a thousand miles of ocean, and some found themselves inside a wall. Some even found themselves back on the front lines. But the ones who survived and chose to talk about it described how they'd felt before in terms that Amanda immediately recognized, and they all said afterwards they felt better. Some of the contractor firms were starting to post guards at the control booths.

Amanda read some more and decided the whole thing was crazy. Things weren't that bad. Not for her. They just weren't. She switched the screen to a book and closed her eyes. The book's voice made her drowsy. She slept through lunch. Over dinner Ernie tried to have the same conversation with her that Gramma Rosie had tried to have over breakfast, but it didn't last very long and he wound up kissing her on the forehead and saying, "Just let us know when you're ready," without telling her what it was exactly that she was supposed to be ready for.

And then a couple of weeks later Amanda was out walking around town when she got lost. Not lost like she couldn't locate her destination, because she didn't have one. She was walking down Pickett Street towards Main, and when she turned the corner at Carter's Drug Store, she realized she didn't know where she was. She knew she had just turned onto Main Street and was walking past Carter's. She knew Gramma Rosie kept her prescriptions there even though Wal-Mart was a lot cheaper because Carter's was where she had bought her comic books when she was a kid, she knew it was where Larry had had his first summer job. But if the leader of the New People's Army himself had at that moment put a gun to her head and asked her the name of the town she was in, or even what day of the week it was, he would have had to pull the trigger. Everything outside her was like a screen with the contrast turned way too high, and everything inside her felt almost like it did just before she jaunted. She dropped to her knees and stayed there until a girl about Larry's age came by and helped her up. She said she was okay and walked away before the girl could start asking her anything. After a couple of blocks everything came back and she made her way home.

That evening down the post she told Sally what happened. She kept running into Sally and had decided she was okay.

"I told you that jaunting wasn't right," Sally said.

"It never bothered me before."

"It's a delayed reaction."

"Don't you fucking dare say I have post traumatic anything."

"I'd say dematerializing and popping up halfway around the world is pretty goddamn traumatic, wouldn't you?"

"That's not what it was."

"Then what was it? I saw a post yesterday that said jaunting actually shrinks part of your brain, flattens you out—"

"Bullshit."

"—makes anything that fucked you up in combat even worse."

The mandatory session:...*you may have heard that some preliminary studies have indicated that the jaunting process may affect the limbic system. At this point there is no conclusive evidence that this is the case...*

"There's no evidence for that."

Sally looked triumphant. "There you go. If someone says there's no evidence for it, that means someone else thinks there is."

"Look, I just got dizzy, okay? I shouldn't have skipped lunch."

Sally lost her triumphant look. Now she looked more like Gramma Rosie over breakfast. "Okay, whatever you say. But if it happens again, let someone know, all right?"

Amanda promised that she would. They had another round and Sally again brought up going someplace quieter, and this time Amanda said okay. By the end of the evening they were back at Sally's place, but when it didn't work and Sally started crying Amanda just walked out.

A week later, Amanda went with Ernie and Gramma Rosie to see Larry's summer league baseball game. Neal skyped in from South Bend. It was the closest thing to a family outing they had had since she had gotten back. She didn't tell any of them about what had happened outside of Carter's, and she certainly didn't tell them it had happened two more times since then.

The sun beat down as hot as it ever had in Mindanao, but she liked the flat perfect grass and the flawless lines of the diamond, and she liked watching the players. They weren't scattered. Orderly. They were exactly where they were supposed to be. Larry looked perfectly at ease in center field, and when he came to bat she cheered as loudly as anyone. He struck out, walked, was left on first when the next batter flied out, hit a single that drove in a run, struck out one last time. It all made perfect sense, even the fact that the other team won.

On the drive back she was unaware of anything anyone said. None of the streets seemed to have names, and when they got home she wasn't sure where she was.

That night she lay in her bed in her room that was still technically just as she had left it and still actually felt so empty. She lay in her bed and stared at the blank ceiling and tried to understand what had happened, where it had all come from. The killing field where the bodies in the mud were so rotted away they didn't look like bodies, they didn't even smell. The house call where the parents were silent and the little girl wouldn't stop screaming as they tore the place apart before Lt. Jeppson declared that it was the wrong fucking house. The guy sleeping beside her waking up screaming with a leech on his tongue—but that hadn't happened, that had been in one of the books she had read. It all should have meant something, but it didn't. Knowing the New People's Army had put those bodies in the field didn't make her want to be there. Watching the lieutenant drag the screaming girl's father outside and throw him on the ground and act like he was going to shoot him didn't make her want to leave. It didn't mean anything then, and it didn't mean anything now, and she didn't want it to. Not her dads, not the vets down the post. Not the guy from Bravo Company. Not Sally. Certainly not Sally. Gramma Rosie? Larry? She didn't want any of it to mean anything, but she wanted to feel something, she wanted to be somewhere. So she went downstairs and got in her dads' car and drove to the platform where she had popped back home and, feeling no surprise at all that it was completely unguarded, went in and set the controls just as the net instructions had said. "Here's to actual fucking risk," she declared to no one in particular and ran as fast as she could for the platform that was as perfect as the baseball diamond, as brown as her brother's eyes.

Black Butterflies

T.C. McCarthy

I HAVE THE DREAM AGAIN—the one where I guide thousands of butterflies through the clouds and into the city. Gravity is three times Earth standard. My butterflies are jet black with filmy, thin wings joined to narrow cores that hold their anti-gravity drives. The wings aren't really wings but a kind of antennae that monitors gravity waves to guide acceleration. They flutter, though. Just like a butterfly's.

The craft also carry a passenger—a robotic burrower that contains a tiny package of antimatter, one that will explode with enough force to crack through a juvenile Siph's carapace and liquefy its brain matter. This point is important: its brain case is a Siph's only weak spot, the only way to put one down. The butterflies land all over what looks like a mud dome a hundred kilometers across, and my vision switches to the burrowers' views as they start drilling through and down, eager to reach targets. When they do, the screaming will start.

"Does it still hurt?" dad asks. He's old now, his hair wispy and white across his head.

I lie. "No. Not so much. It's getting less sensitive every day." Then I reach up and touch the link ports at the back of my skull and realize again that I don't want to do what he's asking because it reinforces an already growing suspicion—that having half my grey matter replaced by silicon did something. That it changed me. But dad holds his back now, in pain, and he pants while leaning against the ag-terminal as our bots wait in a row that stretches to the horizon.

"I'm still not used to the new tech," he says. "I can't afford the damned eye implants and it's getting hard for me to see the screens. If you can just code them to cover the fields, it'll save me a lot of time. And we have about thirty that are down for maintenance; maybe you can look at them once we finish here."

"What happened to all your help?" For some reason, the question hasn't occurred to me until now. "All the guys that came in from Earth before I left."

"Dead. Conscription teams came years ago and took everyone older than eighteen and younger than forty. For all I know they could have even been with you throughout the war; I lost track of everyone. All the children left and so few of you came back after the battle at Listman."

Where the Black Butterflies lost the war—for everyone. Dad doesn't have to say it, but I know it's his next thought, maybe the reason why I have the dreams every night and why they seem so real. Before going into that mental spiral, I grab the terminal cord and slam it into the socket at the rear of my head, kicking my wetware into high gear so that sparks shoot across my field of vision—sparks that aren't real, just tiny dots of light that form as an artifact of power-up. Dad disappears. Now thousands of views of the field clamor for attention and threaten to overload my system with infrared and radar data as the bots wait to begin their sweeps. A few alarms are beeping because there are pests that dad missed the last time he combed the fields; half the crop is dying, eaten. Barely having to think, I tell the fake part of my brain what we're doing. Then my thoughts rush forward at light speed with instantaneous decisions, logic that pulls me along in a trip that makes me feel part pilot, part lightning, sliding across the fields with an army of ag bots. After a while my cells need something. The warning for hunger is distant and annoying, an intermittent nudge that feels like a low vibration accompanied by a sensation that hours have passed, but the bots have so much work to do; many of them drop offline, broken. Part of me wants to cry because it's proof that once I'm gone, dad will need help, since much of the farm is already beyond repair. So breaking for lunch would hurt him; I shut off the energy warnings and the system bends my legs to lower me to the dirt, then onto my back—to prevent damage in case I pass out.

By the time I finish, it's dark. Dad is on the ground next to me and the terminal's glow makes his face look dark gray so that he seems dead until I shake him awake and it takes him a second to blink in recognition.

"Thanks, Nick," he says. "That would have taken me days."

"I didn't know things had gotten in such bad shape."

"During the war it was hard to get repair materials and fertilizers—anything that went into building ships and weapons. There were seasons that I couldn't even spray." Then he stands and helps me up, which makes me feel guilty since he's so frail. "Come on; it's time for bed anyway—after we eat."

"I'm not hungry and don't feel much like sleeping these days, dad."

Dad holds my hand and it scares me; it's something he hasn't done since I was three years old. "Whatever happened out there, Nick, it's okay," he says, "*You're home now*," but I don't have the courage to tell him that soon they will come. For me. Siph have a shared and eternal memory and the Black Butterflies are branded into it, along with the brainwave pattern of their controllers, and Siph warriors never get tired of hunting.

My dream starts off fuzzy. The communications beam takes an eternity to connect with the factory ship, a hollow asteroid containing its own gravity drive, antimatter production, and butterfly manufacturing lines. At first my wetware can't find a local amplifier; once it does, there's intense acceleration when the satellite cracks open an aperture to another universe—where the speed of light is infinitely greater than in ours—but then I can't find a receiver signal. There should be one; there always is. The factory ship is supposed to beacon its receiver aperture location in a coded pulse, but when I query my own equipment to see if the problem is me the wetware responds with nonsense—a garbled mess that gives me a headache. Soon, though, the receiver signal arrives and the mother ship transmits a star map showing my new location, deep within Siph-controlled territory. The revelation almost pulls me from sleep. I don't remember running an operation here during the war, which means this is new, a real dream that has an ending I've never seen, and there's no choice except to settle in for the nightmare that's about to come.

The butterflies are ready. Antimatter has been loaded into their bellies and my system has to pause for a few seconds because there are millions of them crowding my mind, more than I've ever controlled at once—more than I've ever seen assembled. A last-minute query runs through my wetware, which responds in less than a second: I'm controlling enough antimatter to wipe half a planetary population.

Dad's face is white. He says goodbye and shuts off the com unit, which had woken us both up, and through the window I watch sunlight turn the sky pink. "That was Greg Simmons from downtown," he says. "He works for the local security forces, and all hell's breaking loose; a small Siph fleet is on its way here."

"Why'd he call *us*?" I ask.

"He knows you came home." Dad's voice cracks and the sound of his panic hits my stomach like a cold spike. "He said you might want to think about hiding until we figure out what they want. Just in case they're coming for you. They've been locking down human systems and looking all over the place for something—something that has to do with those antimatter drones you flew."

I can't feel my mouth. Terror makes my fingers feel as though they've inflated to the point of immobility and it muffles the words from people on the road to the point where they're impossible to understand. Everyone recognizes me. Many of them hadn't been born when I left for the war but it doesn't matter, since they see my bald head with its ports and linkages and the military tattoos over each temple to show blood type, serial number and name; it's obvious what I am. Some move to the other side of the street. Dad had warned me that it would be like this and had begged me to take his skimmer, to head in the opposite direction and into the country, so to make him happy I drove out of his sight and then turned onto a side road, looping back into town before parking.

Towns change when you leave for a long time, but everything has changed wrong. The Catholic Church is on the wrong side of the street and near it is the bakery where I worked as a teenager; it's the wrong color. This is another town and the pre-war Nick no longer exists because so much of his grey matter is gone, carbon replaced with silicon and ceramics, so much so that my heat and cold tolerances are narrower and the nerve endings more sensitive, which results in constant headaches and a never-ending supply of painkillers to beat them back. Someone yells across the street *wait*, repeating it three times before I glance and notice a girl waving at me. She looks familiar. The girl wears a black jumpsuit, its fabric covered in complex Siph codes in orange that resemble intertwined shapes and swirls that only creatures with faceted eyes can read. *Stay there!* I mean something to her. She waits for a break in traffic and I watch her jog across the street.

The girl catches her breath. "I didn't think I'd catch up. It's lucky I found you at all. We never knew that you had made it back until this morning."

"Do I know you?" I ask. She's my age, and although she has hair, bits of service tattoos still show from underneath.

"I'm Jennifer Vallaincourt; we went to school together and got conscripted at the same time." I must have been staring because she points to her temples. "The Siph want the tattoos to stay. So they can tell the difference between our ex-soldiers and civilians." Then she plucks at her uniform and her smile disappears to be replaced by a far-off look and a red face. "I'm part of the transition team. We have to be ready to help carry out any changes they want once the Siph decide to take over this place, but we haven't heard anything yet."

"Then you don't know?"

She shakes her head. "Know what?"

"A Siph fleet is on the way. Here. Now."

Jennifer grabs my wrist and pulls me along the sidewalk; the crowds that had been there minutes before are gone, but pale faces peer out from behind privacy glass, their features blurred. Buildings flash by. Doors hum shut and Jennifer pounds on several and she presses the call buttons, but none of them open for us and my mouth goes dry so that now fear trips the targeting system to show movement and distances. A data pattern outlines Jennifer. My wetware recognizes her jumpsuit markings as Siph and I have to suppress the alarms but my thoughts aren't fast enough to keep the system from stimulating my adrenal glands and everything begins to move in slow motion.

She drags me through a door before its steel lip can slide all the way shut and the motor whines when I push, forcing the slab to stay open for one second longer. Someone yells to get out. But Jennifer flashes a badge and then leads me to a booth, where she sits across from me and smiles.

"It's a bar. Not a great one but they've been open all night and we're lucky they were slow to lock up."

"Why was everyone staring at me?" I ask. "Out there."

"They're afraid—of the Black Butterfly." Jennifer whispers it and without thinking I send a signal to amplify her voice.

"What about them?"

"Not them. You. You're *the* Black Butterfly and the drone craft are *you*. After what happened at Listman, everyone knows the Siph have been looking for the one who did it and nobody wants to be close when they arrive."

"There were lots of us," I say. "My training class had about a thousand others and when we deployed there were at least a hundred in my group, more than that at Listman. I never learned their names but we all loaded into capsules at the same time; I saw them before we launched. So how can I be the only Black Butterfly?"

Jennifer shakes her head. "That's not how it happened."

"How would *you* know?"

"I was a program engineer on the team that put together the targeting systems for your wetware. Everyone who deployed with you is dead. Gone. We loaded those other capsules with troops who failed the testing phase but who volunteered to accept wetware beacons that produced an emissions pattern like yours. Only they had none of the punch. Those guys didn't even know about the butterflies."

My head goes empty, light. None of her claims seem possible but Jennifer's voice has a soft quality that makes me believe and why would she lie? "They were used as decoys—to protect me."

"Yeah. Volunteers for the cause. Do you remember me?" she asks. "I mean...at all?"

"No. I'm Nick, by the way."

Jennifer shakes her head and her expression makes me want to run because she frowns, and both shoulders square off to combine with the set of her jaw. "This would have been easier if someone had told us you were coming—to give us some time. Your name isn't Nick; as soon as you were accepted into the program we scrubbed part of your memory deck so the Siph wouldn't find any trace of Earth in the event of capture. Your father too, just in case he was a talker."

Now the fear returns, colored with an anger that makes me grab the table, my knuckles going pale. If she sees me getting angry, Jennifer doesn't show it.

"You're James McLaughlin. You and your father moved from Earth after your mom died, and I had a huge crush on you all the way through school until the war started. They took you for combat. Me for science. I thought you were gone. Then one day I heard about a promising candidate for the antigravity drone program, someone whose synapse function and test scores had blown all our neuroscientists away. You. And there were other candidates from our school on the list. Adam Hermann, Scott Tomasi..."

The names refer to piles of dust. Jennifer's voice fades as I consider the implications and the knot in my gut gets worse with each minute and tears drip from both eyes but there's no point in wiping them. Half my head is a foreign object—an invader that my own race put there; soon it will inhibit my tear ducts. While she goes on I ping the bar's network to look up the names Tomasi and Hermann and the results come back with video clips of children on Leviticus, just like she says, and in one of them I see myself. I'm taller than the others even at that age, but the boy is a stranger to me because who could be so happy in the face of what was coming and the boy must have been a fool because Jennifer is telling me that he died and was replaced by a facsimile named Nick. James McLaughlin doesn't exist now. The pictures bring back memories of a sort, echoes in my grey matter that resemble old men muttering *oh yeah, I remember Adam Hermann because he had the courage to ask Jennifer to be his girlfriend and so I had to watch him get her first kiss and first every-thing else under the pseudo-pines down on Hawthorne Drive. Her family was rich. Rich enough to have a real dog sent in from Earth, a German Shepherd that almost killed me one day when I walked into her house without knocking. Is that the Adam Hermann you wanted?* But she just keeps talking like I care, oblivious to the fact that each word is like an anti-proton that detonates inside my skull, littering it with craters and smoke along with the corpses of people I used to know but can't remember, people who are long dead from the war. Jennifer thinks she's helping; I can tell by the way she smiles that she means well but now I know my dad was right and I need to get out into the country, away from her and everything else.

"It's time to go, Jennifer. I don't feel good."

She takes my hand and leans forward. "Don't go. Stay here for a while, Jimmy, and talk. You and I are the only ones left from the old group."

"I can't. Sorry." But when I stand her face goes blank. Jennifer reaches into a pocket and pulls a black rod from it, a stun wand that she whips across the table. My wetware flicks into combat mode. The wand sparks against the wall, missing my forehead. Everything is slow now and Jennifer isn't a warrior so she can't see that she's off balance and within less than a second her arm breaks in three places when I slam it against the table, making her scream. The door is just a few meters away. But before I can do anything else it opens and military police stream through, joining a separate group of police that swarms from the back—where they must have been waiting the whole time.

Jennifer cradles her arm and backs away. "The Siph want you. I'm sorry it went this way, Jimmy, but we had no idea you'd show up when you did. Our job is to keep everything going and we've already lost contact with three human systems now that they're closing in; we're just buying time. I'll let your father know so he can come visit."

"Visit me where?"

"A holding cell. At the spaceport in Fontaine—three hours by flitter. The Siph fleet should get here tomorrow afternoon and then you're to be transferred to one of their shuttles for execution."

My dreams flicker in and out of focus and it feels good to slip into the program and let the wetware cradle me in logic. We're looking for something. There's a network of communications channels all around and its beams crisscross to surround me in a web woven by psychotic spiders. Then one pops up that's different from the rest, its communications encrypted in layers that we begin to pick apart with algorithms, one after another until I'm nestled within military communications traffic that consists of message after message regarding someone named James McLaughlin.

The name awakens a few extra synapses. But before I can dig further, the wetware's logic master drags us onto something else, a data stream that links with our planetary defense network, and the complexity washes away the name James and replaces it with a sense of hopelessness as status readouts course through. An untouched fleet is docked here at Leviticus. But most of the ships have already been mothballed and are dormant despite being ready for a war that's already lost, leaving a skeleton fleet that the Siph authorized so the local defense force can fight piracy. It's better than nothing; we dive into its comms network to begin the sequence for taking over the biggest ship, a large cruiser, to arm its weapons and target the incoming fleet. I'm about to own it when the data streams disappear.

A rifle butt slams into my skull and someone laughs in a high-pitched way that sounds as if he's insane—part laugh, part scream. The sound is piercing. My hands are up, trying to block the next blow and when this one cracks into my forearm it snaps one of the bones and I realize the laughter and screams are coming from me, and now the pain from my arm is almost unbearable and I curl into a ball and pray for the beating to end, grateful when someone yells *stop it!*

"He was trying to break into our defense network," another person says—a man who sounds out of breath and must have been the one hitting me. "Our techs couldn't handle it and he almost took over the entire fleet."

"Sedate him. I'm getting the doc."

There's minor damage to some of the wetware—gray matter linkages but already my system repairs them and the injection someone gives me will help because it's a strong sedative and provides chemicals that my system can scavenge for its maintenance. But now there's a renewed sense of terror: the man's words—that I was trying to break into the defensive network—register, and what he says can't be possible because it was a dream. But part of me is beginning to fear that I can't tell the difference between reality and fantasy anymore, and then I want to scream because just before blacking out I decide maybe the difference is negligible.

"It couldn't have been my wetware; those were all just dreams." But the words sound too much like I'm pleading, so when Jennifer shakes her head it doesn't surprise me.

Her arm is in a sling; I didn't mean to hurt her. As with mine, though, microbots have healed much of the broken bone and she doesn't show signs of pain. "I know you *really* believe that," she says, "but we had operational scans of your electromagnetic activity, specifically of your cranial area. We did it when you were awake and asleep."

"So?"

"So your wetware is only marginally active when you're awake. Storage and query processing work fine, and even lower defensive protocols, but you're not reaching any of the higher functions like comms or drone operations. At night it's a different story. We think that once you're asleep your conscious self isn't there to control things and so your wetware activates and goes back to war, using your brain for as much processing control as it needs; that's why you see it as a dream."

The thought makes my skin crawl—that my system takes over in my sleep, turning me into a kind of zombie. "That's impossible. They fried my drone and antigravity control systems when I mustered out because after Listman Command didn't want me active; they didn't want the technology captured. And I spent a year getting home just because they needed me to take a long route to scrub my exit and make sure the Siph couldn't track it. Everything went smoothly."

"Jimmy—"

"*It's Nick, goddammit!*" My shout surprises her and the guards raise their carbines, pointing them at my head.

"What is this all about?" Dad sits next to me. He seems ten years older than he did yesterday because his voice shakes and the conference room chair swallows him in synthetic fabric, which is easy because he's gotten so small and thin. I remember when he was young. There are pictures in his study of a man whose combat suit fails to hide the fact that he's huge, with muscles that almost don't fit into the ceramic carapace and that once threw me across the base pool when I was six. I move to grab his wrist—just to touch him because the guilt feels like a pressure on my chest, makes it hard to breathe—but I can't; they've hand-cuffed me to my chair.

"It's complicated, Mr. McLaughlin," says Jennifer. She sighs, and at first I think that I'll have to explain it, but then Jennifer tells him about the early program and that because of Listman I'm being handed over. The story is one that I know. Still, to hear it from her in a clinical way—detached and sterile—makes me realize that for her and others the war isn't real; it's a series of events to be discussed in boardrooms and academic think tanks, where death can be dissected using statistics and AI-modeling and where the worst consequences are the inconvenience of the occasional all-nighter or heartburn from drinking too much coffee, and for a moment I feel nauseous. But then the words stop mattering; Jennifer and the war are irrelevant. Dad stares into space and he begins to cry and it's easy to imagine what he thinks, that his son is gone and instead they've replaced him not with a monster but a machine, someone whose name isn't even Nick and whose silicon and ceramics has changed him into the new angel of death. A weapon. A criminal who needs to be chained to a chair and handed over to the Siph for all that he's done, and then dad looks at me and I almost start crying too.

"My son is a hero," he says. "They attacked us first on Aidan, and Nick did everything you asked and sacrificed himself to surgical procedures that could have killed him—all for the war. He was a kid when you people conscripted him."

She shakes her head. "Mr. McLaughlin, there are details I can't give; things that happened."

"Tell him," I say. "The Siph know and they'll be here in an hour so what difference does it make if he knows too? Tell him about my targets; tell him *why*."

Jennifer hesitates and then stutters. "I can't. I'd lose my job, Jim—Nick."

Dad looks back and forth at us. Since I'm about to be handed over, there's nothing to stop me from telling the whole truth except that I don't want him to think the worst but if I don't it means he'll be confused for the rest of his life, not understanding what made it so important for me to be handed over. I'm still thinking when Jennifer inhales with a wheeze. It's the sound she's made every time for the past hour when she's about to speak and for some reason the thought of her voice makes my decision easy.

"I killed Siph juveniles, dad. Their babies. *They* were my primary target—not their warriors—and millions of them died while they slept in their nurseries. Our antimatter bombs trigger a chain reaction with the material in a Siph juvenile's carapace and they scream in a way that makes you think millions of little girls are being burned alive." I pause but Dad doesn't react. His stare makes me ashamed and the heat of that shame is so intense that I imagine it must be visible in waves off my cheeks, and I wish there was some way to hide, so I look away. "We captured one of their bio stations early in the war—when things were still going well. We got lucky; the station had a bunch of research outlining Siph reproductive habits and someone got a brilliant idea: kill all their offspring. Destroy one generation of Siph and you annihilate the entire race."

He looks just as confused as he did a few minutes ago and shakes his head. "I don't understand. How does going after their children annihilate the race?"

"Siph reproduce once every hundred years. So their warrior cadre is a fixed number, which can't get bigger, they can't reproduce on the fly, and all the older adults die as soon as juvenile Siph become adults—*every hundred years*. It's hardwired in their genetics. So if you get rid of their kids, you win the war—assuming you can stay alive for another eighty to ninety years."

Dad's face goes white. At first I think he's going to pass out but he leans over in his chair and hugs me so I can't breathe, and then whispers into my ear *it's not your fault; you were a child and you're my son*. Jennifer motions for the guards. The three of them slip out the door and lock it shut, leaving us alone for the last hour so we can say goodbye.

Jennifer and I wait for the Siph in an airlock outside their shuttle and without warning my system activates to make my fingers tremble with adrenaline. For the first time in over a year the butterfly and antigravity controllers flick on while I'm conscious, overlaying their data patterns on both retinas. Jennifer was telling the truth: the techs never fried the drone controls like they claimed and had reprogrammed major systems so they'd stay dormant until I slept—or they'd trigger melatonin production to *make* me fall asleep. Now my fear response is so intense that it triggers full systems activation, surprising me with a feeling of exhilaration that had been missing during the dream sessions.

Targeting systems calculate escape vectors and urge me to do something—to kill Jennifer and head back through the airlock door behind us, on the other side of which is a small army of guards who would shoot me if I tried, a piece of information that slows my processors for only a second. Then we try a different tactic. The communications system sends electromagnetic beams to sweep the enclosed space, searching for anything to hack into, any way to change the calculus and give me an advantage because *it doesn't want us to die.*

"We won the war, Nick," says Jennifer. "The story that we lost is just that: a story. Another lie. You deserve to know that before...you know."

She's hard to understand, since we're both wearing respirator masks in preparation for exposure to the Siph atmosphere; I turn to face her. "What are you talking about?"

"You accomplished your mission. In ninety years we're going to take back everything we lost, and it's all because of you and what you've been doing while on the run; you wiped out over ninety percent of their juvenile population and they can't recover from it. All humanity has to do is survive. The military is taking your father to someplace safe right now, to a system that's only known to a fraction of us, and I leave tonight so I'll make sure he's safe."

I shake my head and turn back to face the far airlock door, worried that at any moment I might strangle her. "People like you don't get it, Jennifer; you weren't at Listman. As soon as I hit the first nursery they came out of nowhere and ripped open our fleet with antimatter beams—not tiny warheads. I'm talking about three-centimeter-wide, continuous beams of the shit, a kind of weaponry we had no idea they had, and I just managed to escape in a stealth pod that got picked up by one of your intel ships eight months later. I've been on the run ever since. And still they found me."

"What's your point?"

"You might make it," I say, "but you didn't hear the screams. The Siph will look for you the same way they came after me at Listman and beyond, and if they find you they won't care if neither race survives, and even if they *don't* find you your dreams will; and sometimes those are worse than butterflies."

Now I know why Jennifer told me about the planetary system where she and others hoped to hide: it's because my brain keeps secrets even from me—like the fact that it can self-destruct; the thing has a failsafe. As soon as the Siph airlock opens, my wetware has an apoplectic seizure and an intense heat sears the inside of my skull, making me scream while the airlock fills with the smell of molten plastic and burning flesh. Plastic drips onto my back. And I'm already forgetting; memories of first this day and then everything else fading into a kind of grey haze, mixing with the pool of molten material on the floor that chars my hand when I fall to my knees. But soon the pain lessens; there are colors everywhere and a sense that tall insect-like figures surround me but it's hard to get a clear view through all the butterflies, which now swarm by the thousands, forming a cloud of pink and blue and orange wings and I laugh because their fluttering tickles me and for some reason they can talk, whispering something that makes me warm and happy—that now there will be no more dreams. Ever.

Always the Stars and the Void Between

Nerine Dorman

THE LITTLE DOG STOOD ON the sill overlooking the yard. The sun had long ago bleached the cedar from which he'd been carved to the same hue as old bones. I didn't want to think about bones, but I couldn't resist picking up the figurine and running my fingertips along his spine and pointy ears.

Derik had given the dog to me so long ago: in reality, only seventeen years, but it felt like a lifetime. It might as well have been an eternity. My time serving the African Federation equalled my childhood years on the farm.

Now Derik was dead and I was back. White scars marred my skin and offered mute testament to countless brushes with death. What made it so that one of us lived and the other did not? We were both children of these mountains, who'd breathed the same air and whose bones had sprung from the same river and soil. Brave, loyal Derik, who'd followed me into the wasteland of space to fight a war for people to whom we were nameless. *Three thousand dead on Deimos Base. A troop carrier hits an interplanetary mine between Jupiter and Saturn. A gate collapses on a jump ship out from Proxima Centauri. Numbers, objects. Not people.*

Krommedrif was home. My childhood loft bedroom with its A-shaped ceiling and exposed beams where I used to dry bunches of herbs had endured, diminished somehow, but mercifully familiar. Did I dare to withdraw here like a snail into its shell? Would this house nurture me the second time 'round so that I might emerge somehow healed and ready to face the world again?

My letter of resignation in its creamy envelope with the official AF watermark was the only object I placed on the desk by the window. Though we moved between the stars—folded space, even—and warred against other nations for resources on moons and asteroid belts, some customs endured—like simple, archaic paper and ink.

"Keep it with you until the end of your leave," Magister Oroyu says.

"My mind is made up. I'm done with this. I want to go home. There is nothing for me here."

He places his dark hand over mine, and I can't break eye contact. "No, little falcon. Listen to me. Keep the letter. When you change your mind, you can always discard it and come back once your leave is over."

When. Not *if.*

I was not going to change my mind, but something in Oroyu's implacable dark stare had me obey. I'd humour him. That was all. After six weeks I'd make the trip out to Clanwilliam, where I'd mail the letter and then go enjoy a celebratory pint at the pub.

My personal effects were pitifully few once I'd unpacked them. My civvies consisted of two pairs of denim jeans, five T-shirts (white, non-labelled AF inventory), and a fitted charcoal flight jacket with the winged lion flashes that marked me as AF Special Ops, among a few other sundries. Everything about me screamed off-duty military.

The only other item that bore any stamp of my personality was the digital picture frame that I had bought at the Saldanha Space Port seventeen years ago and that had now come home with me. It was an outdated thing, made to look like a small, baroque gilt frame complete with cherubs and scrollwork. My seventeen-year-old self had thought the hideous device to be precious back then and had squandered a week's allowance purchasing it.

Over the years the gold had worn to grey, and at one point I'd dropped it; a hairline crack ran diagonally from the top left-hand corner. And still I couldn't bear to toss it away and transfer the data back down from my virtual drive onto a new frame. All my family photos were stored here: Mother, Father, my brother Johan...pictures of the farm, of the mountains. My favourite places...even old Broekgat, the pony I used to ride, though he had been dead for nine years now, according to Johan.

There were pictures from the academy days too, and those years of service that I'd seen, but I didn't want to look at those now. I'd see *his* face, and that'd hurt too much.

"I'm resigning," Michael tells me.

My heart stutters and I stare at him, unable to form the words. "Why?"

"I need to spend more time with Saskia and the kids. I'm through with active duty, and besides, what use is a cripple?"

He offers his usual self-deprecating laugh but it rings hollow. His eyes tell the truth—there's enough pain lodged there to power one of the jump ships' Gibson drives.

I followed that man into space. I could have stayed behind, perhaps even had a life on Earth and found a cushy job in admin on one of the orbital stations. Instead, I trekked after a married man I knew I could never have. Love made fools out of all of us. Oh, we'd been lovers, but Michael was never *in love* with me, and I'd been a fool to think I could convince him otherwise. I'd been doubly a fool to ignore Derik, who'd waited patiently all those years for me, for nothing.

Michael left without saying goodbye. Ten years of me playing the dutiful mistress, and all I got was an empty officer's suite and a cleaning assistant's terse explanation that Captain Michael Louw had caught the morning shuttle to the Callisto Base en route to Earth.

I tried to hand in my resignation two weeks later.

Even now I could look Michael up on the social networks. It wouldn't be difficult to find him; we both have friends in common. I don't bother making contact. Obviously. Over the years we'd been nothing but discreet. For me to go blundering into his life now like some inconvenient spectre of his infidelity would not be right. Two beautiful, blond children. An erstwhile supermodel wife who ran an NGO that supported war veterans. They were picture perfect.

Who was I to shatter these perceptions?

I was small, brown-skinned, and decidedly *native*, so far as Michael was concerned. While we'd been serving on board assorted vessels, these differences had not been so apparent—our crew consisted of a melange of other races and nationalities. Back on Earth, we were reminded of the people we'd been when we first left the planet behind us.

Like I was reminded now, in this tiny bedroom. Muted scuffling and chittering in the roof told me the resident population of serotine bats were still here. How many nights I'd watched them from this very window as they squeezed out through the gap in the eaves and hurled themselves into the star-speckled sky. How many nights I'd stared at the stars and wondered if I'd ever take wing myself.

If I'd been able to have words with my wide-eyed sixteen-year-old self who'd blithely filled in the AF application form on the sly...

Sandra was in the kitchen by the time I went downstairs, fussing with the clean dishes. Poised. Perfect. Not a bronze-tinted lock out of place.

"Hey," I said.

She paused, about half a dozen side plates grasped firmly. "Oh, hi."

"I don't think we've met, at least not properly. You weren't in this morning when Johan brought me." I'd spoken to her via a few long-distance family conference calls in the media lounge, but even a screenwall offering the illusion that folks were in the same room as you didn't quite make up for meeting someone in the flesh. Sandra was much taller than me, though for some reason she gave the impression of cowering the moment I'd entered the kitchen. My brother's white trophy wife.

Sandra shook her head. "We haven't, now that I think about it."

We stood awkwardly, saved only by Johan thumping in. "Where's the vaccine ampoules for the cows? They're not in the store room," he growled at Sandra, who looked as if she'd drop the crockery.

"How should I bloody know?" Her mouth pulled in a tight line, and she slammed the plates on the kitchen counter.

"I told you to have Essie bring them down."

"They're probably still in the deep freeze," Sandra said.

For a moment I thought an ugly argument would erupt but then a child yelled from deep within the house and Sandra darted out of the kitchen. I doubted whether my younger relative needed help but it seemed like Sandra was only too happy to abandon me to my brother's ire.

Instinctively, I pressed myself against the wall. Johan was so much bigger than me now. The past seventeen years had been bountiful, it would seem, and my brother's girth spoke of too much of a good thing. He looked like Oom Swart from Dwarsfontein over the pass.

Odd that I'd faced down enemies on a battlefield, yet when family turned the home into a warzone, I cringed like a beaten dog.

"You going to stare at me like I'm the Devil?" Johan asked, his face contorted in a ferocious scowl. He was probably embarrassed that I'd caught him bitching at Sandra.

I shook my head, hating how like a cockroach I felt in my childhood home, in the very kitchen where Ma used to bake. Try as I might I could hardly recall those warm, yeasty smells and the taste of butter melted on a crust of fresh bread.

"Well, you're going to have to sort out your life now that you're back. Can't have you lying about like the other vets. You've still got all your limbs. You gonna have to pull your weight round here."

"What the—" My anger surged hot and sudden. "My life is—" Who was he to point fingers when it seemed like his own life had visible cracks?

But he was out the door already, his back turned on me like I was no more than one of the farmworkers to be ordered around.

I stood for a few moments, just to regain my composure. I'd wanted to ask the other question that I hadn't dare voice since my arrival. *How is Ma?* Not talk about my problems light years away. I'd barely had a chance to shake the dust off my feet and we were already arguing.

Seventeen years yawned like a bottomless chasm between us, filled with accusations. *Where were you when Pa fell ill and died? Where were you when the Great Fires burnt down the plantations? Where were you when the modified anthrax killed all the livestock?*

To say that I was at war, fighting so our enemy would not lay waste to our precious farm or carry away the children, would not wash with my brother. Those who remained earthbound took it for granted that the wind always raced through the scrubby veld or that rain came in the cooler months. The sun that rose and set on their world was always tame, yellow.

If I told only a fraction of the stories I held locked away in my heart, would my family be able to sleep at night? My hands were red with blood, if only they had eyes to see, and no amount of scrubbing would ever remove the stain. I'd done it all for them.

Dare I remind them that it was my AF stipend that connected the electricity to Krommedrif or sent my nieces to a private school in Clanwilliam? It was my blood money that kept my brother's tractor pulling the plough when the crops failed.

Nowadays, the crops failed more often than not.

Ma was in a back room—one where she used to keep her sewing things and that had been set aside for guests. Now Ma lay contorted beneath a sheet. The linen was half twisted from the bed and the stench of piss hung heavy in the air. I remained on the threshold, unable to take that fateful first step that would carry me to the foot of Ma's narrow cot.

Her condition had deteriorated even before I decided to return home. I could read between the lines when they stopped letting Ma join on the family calls, which grew steadily further and further apart the longer I remained on active duty. There was always some sort of excuse—I had to train raw recruits, Johan had to bring in the crops, no secure connection...it was all too easy to reschedule our calls. After all, the farm wasn't going anywhere.

The last I'd seen of Ma she'd seemed to somehow slump in on herself, in only six months. "Where is the other one?" she'd asked over and over again, meaning Pa. Since then, within the space of three years, she'd shrivelled into this husk that made me think more of the mummified remains of those long dead in the vacuum of space rather than a living, breathing woman.

Ma climbs like one of the klipspringers, and I struggle to keep up with her. We've gone much higher than before, and below us the valley is spread out like a patchwork quilt of fields. The barley will ripen early this year. Pa's tractor is a tiny toy near the vineyard, and it raises a plume of dust behind it.

"It's here somewhere," Ma calls. "C'mon, Rachel!"

She vanishes for a moment and I scramble to follow. Then we've reached the ledge and I flop down gratefully to let my poor arms and legs rest.

Ma, however, peers at the red oxide figures painted across the rock face. They describe a graceful arc running from right to left, clutching their spears. To the far left is a big blob Ma says is an eland. When I look carefully I can still make out the white pigments the ancient artists used to denote the heads and feet of these giant antelope.

"You only ever get eland in the zoos and parks now," says Ma. "But once upon a time, in the days of your grandfather's great-great-grandfather, when Mantis still walked among the people, we hunted the eland. Your forefathers painted these pictures before the Dutch settled."

In many ways, I had become a hunter of sorts, just like my ancestors, who'd left their images on rock faces, and it was Ma who'd filled my head with all the stories about the olden times. Names, faraway places. All mixed up.

"I'm back, Ma," I whispered.

The thing in the bed that wasn't my mother anymore shifted slightly and craned its neck before it flopped down again. A broken thing, like the time I found a bird that had flown into the lounge window. I'd run to Pa with the dove and he'd taken it from me and wrung its neck. Just like that. Then given me a hiding later for crying to Ma about it.

My heart clenched painfully but my eyes remained dry. This *thing* in the bed wasn't Ma. Then the guilt for those missing years gnawed and gnawed like a mole rat. *You could have been here. All those times lost. You're a terrible daughter.*

"I want to go home," she mumbled and almost raised an arm in supplication.

"You are home," I replied.

Her only response was a garbled, ululating cry. I didn't stay to hear more.

Sandra was in the media lounge watching some stupid show about fashion makeovers. Even though I stood within range of the wall-to-wall screen, she remained so engrossed in the fashionista's efforts with a dowdy matron that she didn't bother looking up.

"Ma's nappy needs changing," I said.

Sandra glared at me. "I told Essie to do it after lunch. Should still be fine."

"It smells like it hasn't been cleaned all day."

"Essie!" Sandra shrieked, and I jerked back a step, surprised by the volume and pitch of my sister-in-law's voice. "*Where are you? Esssieee?*"

A faint response drifted toward us from somewhere within the house. "*Ja, madam?*"

Sandra stabbed at the console to silence the programme, then rose just as the hapless Essie entered the room.

Poor Essie darted her gaze from me then to Sandra and back again. I was reminded of a childhood visit to the Swarts. Old Mrs Swart had used an imperious tone similar to the one Sandra employed. Pa had always said we wouldn't order our workers around like that, and my face burnt at the sinking realisation that this was exactly how we'd become. As people had lived two hundred years ago, during the apartheid times.

Essie used to bathe me, dress me, and feed me. I grew up with her son, Derik, and we'd run all over Krommedrif together before our AF days. We were best friends forever, and it didn't matter that his dad was a farmworker and mine was the farmer.

To have Essie standing here wringing her hands in obvious distress made me want to sink into the carpeting.

"Ouma needs changing," Sandra said.

"*Ja, madam.*" Essie shuffled out.

"Happy now?" Sandra huffed at me. "Essie's very busy with the kids. She probably forgot."

"That's not an excuse. Why is Ma being kept in that room? There's not enough air, and she should be sitting up for at least part of the day. She needs to go outside a little. She'll get bedsores." I clenched and un-clenched my hands, hating the somehow supercilious expression on my sister-in-law's face.

"I've enough on my plate."

"Evidently." I glanced meaningfully at the screen.

"It's not easy, you know. You have no idea what it's like living out here, and your brother–"

"You married him," I said.

Sandra had the temerity to turn from me and unmute the programme. In fact, she dialled the volume higher. The only outward sign of her anger was the way her jaw was working, like she was grinding her teeth.

"Bitch," I muttered.

There'd be no help from this quarter, and I had little desire to fight with the woman. I might as well go find my brother and have it out with him—lay the entire figurative deck of cards on the table. If I was going to be groundside from here on in, I'd sooner sort out whichever differences existed between us before matters turned uglier.

The late-afternoon heat caught me the moment I stepped outside the house's air-conditioned confines. Behind the guest cottage, Abjater-skop gleamed like a skull in the westering sun and I had to squint across the yard. So accustomed was I to the mostly sterile atmosphere onboard space-faring vessels and stations that the air, rich as it was in the farm-yard smells of dung and livestock, was almost physically overwhelming. I'd get used to it soon enough.

The farm buildings crouched beneath the oaks, and I headed in that direction across the furrow. The old-style aluminium gate clanged shut behind me—like most of structures here, harking back to more than a hundred years ago. Here walls showed sign of intense repair—polymer composite bricks shoring up where old redbrick or even mudbrick walls had collapsed. Rusted corrugated iron warred with newer and obviously scavenged orbital-grade ceramic plating.

Out here, far away from the metropolises, farmers always had a plan.

A rooster and four hens scrubbed in the dirt and watched me warily as I passed them on my way to the kraal. I heard Johan before I saw him, and had already cringed before I rounded the corner.

"What the hell did I tell you about having that latch looked at?" Johan yelled. "Now who's going to go get the bull out from the cows?"

"Sorry, *baas*," the worker replied.

My brother moved fast and backhanded the guy, who stumbled and landed on his back in an especially mucky part of the kraal. What the hell? I quickened my pace and slipped past the gate.

"You people won't hear, then you must feel," my brother growled.

When he made to kick the fallen man—that was when I tripped into overdrive. Pa might've been a hard taskmaster, but he never beat up on the farmworkers. Where Johan had picked up those tendencies, I didn't know.

I grabbed his shoulder and, though I didn't weigh half what my brother did, I shoved hard so that his foot missed the worker and we both spun to the ground. Time congealed. My brother's motions slowed, his bellow of rage extending and deepening as my physical modifications flooded my system with stimulants. I knew exactly where to punch—short, sharp jabs—to incapacitate an enemy.

Johan didn't stand a chance, and I finished with my fingers brushing against his windpipe. Judging by his wild expression, he knew I'd had the power to crush his larynx but I'd halted. Just in time.

Scuttling sounds informed me that the downed farmworker was making himself scarce, but I did not break eye contact with my brother. Despite his skin being so much darker than my generally caramel tone, he'd paled visibly.

"When did you think it acceptable to beat your workers?" I asked him.

He twitched a little before he sucked in a breath. "What gives you the right to interfere?"

This is my farm as much as yours. I bared my teeth at him. "Father never taught us to be like this."

Straddled as I was across his girth, I was conscious of how much spare flesh he carried, and the way his heart thundered a rapid tattoo within the prison of its ribcage. Even now I could count at least half a dozen ways I could end this man's life without even a weapon at hand. And I hated myself for it.

"You disgust me," I sneered.

I disgust myself.

He lay there, watching me as I rose to my feet. Only then did I notice the liquid staining his trousers. My brother had pissed himself.

Because of me.

My shame flushed through me, sudden and hot, and I had to turn away and walk back to the house. I was like a jackal among dogs here. My teeth were sharper, but either I would eventually lash out, or they would tear me to pieces.

Little falcon, Magister Oroyu called me. *Little hunting falcon.*

There was no escaping what I truly was. That young girl whose gaze had been trained on faraway stars had turned into something feral, dangerous. For her to consider turning her back on the fast strike, the quiet death, and the pursuit—now that was madness.

I am the only one of my unit small enough to worm my way through the air ducts. I am the only one quiet enough to slip unremarked into the very heart of the enemy's holdout. The rebel doesn't see the blade I bring to his throat and, when he clutches with ineffectual fingers, his life blood spatters to the composite alloy tiles in a hot fountain. I don't need guns when I'm the weapon.

How much longer before my brother foolishly goaded me again? Then what? Would I step over that line with an unarmed civilian?

I waited in my room until the household settled for the night. No one called me for supper. I was hungry, but I'd experienced worse privations. Food could wait. My bag was already packed but there was one thing I had to do before I left. The ampoules were shiny blue gemstones in my palm, each with its own capped needle. I only needed six of the soporifics. They were synthetic opiates for the nights when my old injuries pained me more than usual. One or two were sufficient for a grown woman to sleep soundly for six to eight hours. Six would guarantee eternal slumber.

No one stirred when I made my way downstairs. I knew exactly where to step to avoid the squeaky stairs. The door to Ma's room stood ajar, and the ammonia stench was even stronger than it had been this afternoon. Essie never did get round to bathing her, and now was not the time to berate myself for not checking up on her.

My anger flexed within me but I tamped it down. Eventually Johan and Sandra's study in neglect would turn around and bite them, but I wouldn't be that dog. Ma, on the other hand...

She'd somehow rucked the linen up so that she was hunched on the plastic mattress protector. The sheet that should have covered her was piss-stained and crumpled to one side. Her eyes shone in the moonlight filtered through the gauze curtains. Her gaze was trained on me but I couldn't be sure whether she saw me.

"Ma, I've come to take you home."

She didn't stir as I encircled one birdlike wrist in my fingers. Try as I might, I couldn't find the woman who'd climbed up those mountains with me. Here lay only a withered skeleton, the skin sliding loose on fragile bones.

I could smother her, break her neck. What was a moment of pain compared to the days, weeks, or even months that awaited her otherwise? There was no telling how long a body could linger. How was it that Johan, who would no doubt shoot one of his horses if it broke its leg, couldn't do the same for Ma?

Derik has plunged twenty metres or more down a shaft in the bowels of the enemy station.

"Hold on!" I call to him, my pulse tripping as I grip the edges of the hole.

Already sounds of pursuit are not far away. We have three, maybe five critical minutes.

"Go!" he shouts back.

"I won't leave you!"

He gives a sharp cry and I shine the torch so I can see him as he contorts, trying to free himself. Derik bares his teeth at me when the light flashes in his eyes.

"I can't feel my legs! It's no use."

"I'll come down!" I shout.

"Go, woman!"

"They'll kill you."

Metal grates on metal and he cries out again. This entire subsection is unstable. Derik's slowly being crushed to death and I can do nothing to help him.

His eyes are glassy with pain as I get a bead on his forehead. Through my rifle's scope the shaft is lit up in eerie colours. Derik shines like an angel. I pull the trigger.

Ma's breathing eased by the time the third ampoule emptied. It was intramuscular so the effect would be gradual. She'd go to sleep. That was all. Gentle arms would unfold for her and whatever flicker of her that remained would ease out of existence. I could only hope someone would be my angel of mercy one day. I administered the last three measures quickly, then pocketed the evidence. No one would look for the marks on her arm—small, like mosquito bites. And even if they did find them, I'd be long gone.

Back in my room, I paused long enough to light a candle. My letter of resignation didn't burn easily, but I held the envelope to the patient, hungry flame. Libations of black smoke twisted cobwebs into darkness. The picture frame I crushed underfoot until the fragments of polymer composites squeaked across the scuffed pine floor. But I swept this up and deposited the remains in the waste basket instead of leaving it there, because Essie would be the one sent up here to clean after me and she didn't need the extra work.

The little dog stood on the sill, his muzzle pointed hopefully out the window. I almost didn't take him, but then I remembered Derik's smile, white against his burnt-sugar skin, and I tucked the little carving in my flight jacket's pocket.

Some of us were destined to nurture, to walk with the sun shining on their faces. I didn't number among them—rather, cold starlight for the hunter. Always the stars and the void between, until something stronger and faster than me came along. There would be no tears.

Enemy State

Karin Lowachee

WAR, WAR, WAR, WAR, WAR.
   I'm so sick of hearing about the war.
   It's everywhere and you're not.
   It's everywhere that you're not.

Two years into this loss, and the garage, which used to be my zen place, is now just another place. Everyone thinks asking about you might make it better because it shows concern. As if I want to talk about it. Two years waiting and I no longer want to talk about it. "How's Tuvi, Jake?" they say. "I haven't heard from him," is my refrain, while I keep my head above an engine and pray that some part of the fuel cell will spontaneously combust in my face so I don't have to answer anymore. So I don't have to think about you anymore, as if you were dead already, just a ghost. As if I can put you in a trunk with my parents' history and never look at it again. But you can't kill a memory like you can kill the enemy.

   I try anyway to kill the memory of you. I make the plans. I attempt premeditation. All this time waiting has made me a silent murderer. Is it murder when it's in war? If the enemy doesn't do it, you can count on me.

   Because they won't tell me. Because they don't know. Because you somehow can't find your way home. You're out past five solar systems and nobody knows anything. Not the media that pretends they've exposed the war, not the military that brags like they're winning it. Maybe not even you, Tuvi. Maybe you don't know where you are either. Maybe to you I'm a ghost as well, haunting all of the quiet places in your mind.

Absence is still grieving. I have nothing to throw my voice against. I go home and the walls of our apartment absorb futility as much as anger. They take the tears and don't give them back. It's not like arguing with you, there is no makeup sex. There is no mess. I've become a clinician of emotion, a recipient of symptoms. Check for signs of life. The walls and the floor and our bed hold all the memories and beat them back at me like the echo of a heart, a reminder of where you still occupy. An invasion force of your heart in mine, razing my surrendered territory.

Maybe I should've fought harder. Maybe I should've put up barricades and forced you to lay siege.

If I'd known at Anna's barbecue two years ago. A winter grilling and you walked out onto the snow like it couldn't touch you. Like this wasn't the worst cold that you'd ever felt. I noticed your boots first because they used to be white. You had that easy, unconscious swagger, parting the drifts that blew around your legs. "This is my cousin Tuvi, he's just come back from a tour." And me in my half-drunk ignorance: "A tour of what?" A tour of the islands? A world tour? A tourist? Your grin was patronizing but also a little relieved. Like you'd finally found someone who saw something else in you, before the other things.

If I'd known.

I babbled something about taking apart bikes, tricking out cars. The race I was prepping for at the end of the month. ("Yeah, we ride in any weather.") Ended by apologizing and claiming I didn't usually talk this much. "I can tell," you said. The only people who run on like that are the ones who keep all their shit stored up.

You let me trace the scar on your skull, flowing like a tributary from behind your ear to the back of your head, to meet up with another pale line. The military cut bristled beneath my fingertips but you were motionless. "There's no story to tell," you said. But don't all scars come with stories? This wasn't playtime, though. This wasn't a gathering of mats in the library before recess. The kids' swings creaked in the cold and beneath our weight, and our clothes had taken on the scent of wood smoke and ice. The party had moved inside and the gold light and faded voices could have been flickers from an aged film, echoes from a movie soundtrack. Neither of us cared to retreat into the warmth.

Inevitably I looked up at the stars. You kept pulling at your beer, two fingers around the neck, and looked instead at the shadows at our feet. You kicked the snow until ashen grass showed beneath, then buried the ground all over again.

My curiosity, but not about the stars: "I've never been up there."

Another swig of the beer. "There's nothing up there."

"There's a war out there." Rebellious company colonies that we called terrorists. "You were up there. Are you going back?"

"Yep."

It didn't have to matter then. This was only supposed to be one time.

I love a man in uniform used to be a punch line.

It was only supposed to be one time, seeing you, but the next day I let you ride one of my bikes, a vintage that you said you had experience with, yet you brought it down at the side of the road. Gravel flew like tiny meteorites. You laughed. I wanted to hit you for the scratches and the dents, for all the ways you thought my anger was funny. "I didn't do it on purpose." Sure. Anyone who liked to crash probably always did it on purpose.

It didn't occur to me until later that you'd lied about the experience. That you just wanted an excuse to do something I loved. That you dived in so readily and risked your limbs for an extra day together. "I'm not bad with machinery," you said. "Just not used to roads." We walked back to the garage, five miles pushing the bikes on snow-dusted road, with rockets from the base launching in the distance, returning your brothers and sisters to the stars. The contrails carved white across the blue sky, making wedgewood out of the Earth's canopy.

It was a clear day and maybe that had been your plan all along. This way we talked instead of the wind rushing between us. You might've even faked a limp to ease my irritation. Tough guy. Bright smile. I talked. You just listened, gathering my stories of childhood spills and sun-drenched road trips to your chest like they would keep you warm. That was exactly what you were doing, why you didn't tell me any of your own stories. Your stories, you said later, would only leave behind the cold.

Anna wore a smile the following weekend, like people do when they're in on a secret. I found it infuriating. We said it was casual. We shot pool and went for drives. The snow on the fields made you quiet and I didn't mind. You know you get along with someone when silence isn't a barrier. You know you belong with someone when breaking it opens a door.

Because you didn't tell me stories, I made up my own. Confirm or deny. The only rule was you weren't allowed to lie. It was my version of invading a foreign space, of setting up convoys and creating a supply line.

We tried to outflank each other but I don't think you tried very hard. Soldiering was all you knew. Your parents had both worked at the base. They'd shipped out early in the war and you were raised by Anna's father, your uncle. You heard about their deaths through the report of the battle. Everyone remembers the battle out by the belt. Confirmation came later, in uniforms. Some things they still do the old-fashioned way.

I changed the direction of my march when your eyes started to drift to open spaces. This was over days, picking up the conversation before and after sleep, between shared drinks and naked bodies and sheets. The truth wasn't everything, I said. Let's say we grew up together. Let's say I pelted snowballs at you and we ruined each other's forts. Let's say you broke my arm pushing me from a tree and felt sorry after.

Let's say I followed you to space.

"No."

Pretending didn't go that far. You skirted my attempts to advance.

It was stupid anyway.

So I took it back even if it was too late.

That night I knew I didn't want you to go.

But it was too late.

Pretty soon you realized my temper was a mask. "You put all of your aggression into these machines, but it can't fuel you the same way."

"Thank you, Doctor."

I wanted to rewind to the moment when I could make the decision to fortify these walls. Instead I lowered the damn bridge and beckoned you across.

It felt like a homecoming, not an invasion. That was the problem. And we had years to catch up on.

Years of when you were somewhere else, growing up, losing your parents, going off to war. And I was just here.

We spent every day together for two weeks. If only I'd forced the siege.

"Don't write to me," you said. Do you ever think about taking that back?

"I'll write to you. I just won't send it." Civilian comms didn't go that deep into the war anyway. The soldier you were didn't sit on base or on a ship somewhere waiting for the mail to light in. I watched your eyes glint in the morning sun and asked you if you'd miss it. The sun. Earth sky. Snow on the tips of your boots. I was asking something else and your gaze caught mine in the mirror.

Tough guy. Bright smile. "Of course I will."

Your uniform was black like space. I planted a kiss to the back of your shoulder and the imprint only remained for a couple seconds. Black absorbed light. It also hid blood. But it couldn't mask your heartbeat, I still felt that against my palm.

I want to joke at you, I wrote. The tenth letter and two months into your absence. I want to start this off like I started off the first one, ignoring the facts. We can be troublesome lawyers too crooked to take into consideration something as variable as the truth. You are not out there in deep space, I am not back on this planet waiting. I've never waited for anyone in my life. Nobody's ever waited for me. Remember when I told you about riding my first bike over the neighbor's yard and crashing into the fence? Of course it was on purpose. Of course my parents yelled. Of course a few more stunts like that and they kicked me out of the trailer. They didn't wait for me to come back before they left. I keep it all inside because there's nowhere to put it.

In one night, though, you heard my crash stories. I can blame you.

When you come back I want you to tell me everything.

I want to understand if this is real, or are you just good at saying the right things and listening the right way? I won't believe Anna. Your cousin isn't allowed to vouch for you. This isn't a swearing in of eyewitnesses or a pledge to a club. I won't believe the hearsay. I want you to look me in the eyes. I want you to take all of my letters. You don't have to read them, just know that I wrote them for you.

We still call them letters because they're made up of the minimal components that create language and meaning. They're not handwritten anymore, I don't have to get them stamped. Letters on a screen. Letters made of light. Letters going only as far as the transparent display over my eyes.

It's not enough just to have your feet back on Earth. You don't get off that easily. Let's just assume you'll live and you owe me something, even if we said we didn't owe each other anything. We were just ignoring the facts then too.

Apparently I have it in me to make demands. Maybe it wouldn't be this way if you just worked in another town.

But I have to know.

You might die and I have to know.

Everything you do makes my life immediate.

Six months later you showed up at the garage. I was beneath a car fiddling with the repulsor panel settings. You grabbed my ankles and yanked me out and I kicked you in the shins before I saw you. We made a scene. Crashed into one of the bikes. Fell over parts. I might've been trying to punch you. My boss said to take it elsewhere, but there was a smile on her face.

So you did. You took me elsewhere.

In bed you told me about all the parts of you that weren't human anymore. Starting with your fingers, which had been blown off three years ago, and now they're reset with mods that can arm guns and grenades with just a caress. I could've told you that, for the way they pass along my skin, detonating me.

Your eyes, at least your left one, that can see in the night or the black of space, can read radiation levels and zoom in on targets from ten thousand meters away. But to me they're green with flecks of gold, like something people used to mine, something rare and valuable that catches the light. I saw an old movie once where the cowboys bit down on coins to test their authenticity. If I set my teeth in you I would know that you are genuine.

The line of your spine doesn't show a scar, even though that was replaced, regrown, made new so you could walk. Seven years ago you'd been ripped apart, torn out like a fish, and they said you'd never walk again. Tough guy. I smiled because I didn't want to think about it. You smiled because you didn't want to say it.

This was everything. These were your stories.

The months of convalescence, physiotherapy, reprogramming, refusal. Stubbornness. Let me ask just one question, and it isn't a game, this isn't pretend.

Why did you go back?

Don't they have robots for this now? Isn't this a machine war?

But it's humans that wage war.

War is a human problem.

And the rebels have been taking our robots, reprogramming them, and sending them back. Trojan warfare.

This was more than the news said. More than the military let out.

Human beings started this war, human beings have to end it.

I touched your fingertips. Now I knew why they were so smooth. I have another question, I'm sorry.

Every time you go back to the war, they steal another part of you.

How much of you returns home? Not because these scars bother me. Not because I can almost feel the triggers when we lay our palms together.

"I don't really come back," you said. "They don't fix me for that reason."

You weren't talking about your body.

These were your stories and they left me cold.

After breakfast I gave you the letters. I wanted to leave while you read them but you gripped my hand and made me stay. Two of us on the bed with the scent of chai tea and waffle syrup, in an apartment small enough to house voices long after they died.

Thirty letters and you read every one, the light from the screen making your skin glow.

As if you weren't real.

But your thumb moved over my fingers like you didn't even know you were doing it. Moving at the same speed your eyes did as they gathered up the words. Your thumb moved over my fingers like I was a trigger.

I had the quiet and the worry, as you read.

I had my heartbeat in my ears.

Who needs romance? Reality is better.

At least in moments. At least in imprints before they fade away.

Dear Tuvi.

It's easier to write when I know you won't read it. I can be honest. More honest. I can go through all the stages of things and be imprecise about it. Things. I can say I miss you and it doesn't feel like I'm giving something away into a void. The void. Even if this is going into a void. You're not here and it's a void. You're the one in space, in a void. Write a word enough times and it begins to look funny. It becomes nothing. If I write it enough times maybe it won't exist anymore. Void.

I only have mundane things to say, but maybe that's what you want to know. About the orange cat that came by the garage and everyone wanted to keep it. About how it just took our milk then went away, never returned. I raced last weekend and came in second. I think my repulsor alignment was a little off. I'll fix it for next week. I mixed a new paint and maybe I'll add a flag to the bike. How can any of this interest you?

The truth is I'm just thinking of you.

The truth is I'm angry that I've become one of those. I never expected you, and now look.

I wonder if writing these letters makes it worse. With all my focus on the words, maybe you're more than you really are. Or maybe I made you up entirely.

I spend months missing you. It's a currency that never dries up and I get slapped with interest. Maybe at the end of this I'll be bankrupt. Maybe when you come home and decide you don't care, I'll go into foreclosure.

This is what your absence does to me. Suddenly I doubt everything. Should I wear this shirt to the bar? Do I want to talk to anyone else? I don't feel like riding this afternoon. There's no more solace in speed.

I go to sleep thinking of how long it would take for word to come back that you're dead. Sometimes I don't sleep at all.

Why can't you at least try to write?

What's so important about this war?

Why do you care when you can stay here on Earth (with me)?

I can hear you already: Tell a different story, Jake.

Tell me one about going cross country. Tell me all about getting lost in the trees. Give me your injuries one by one. The first crash and the last.

Especially the last because that one is you.

One night I met a soldier in the snow. He wore white boots and didn't seem to feel the cold.

Tell me the best thing about the seasons changing. How the trees light up like fire and warm the cool blues of the sky. Nothing is as beautiful as that. Death can be beautiful.

No, let's not take it there.

It's not death, it's transition.

It doesn't matter how many parts of you aren't homegrown from birth. Don't you see what I do for a living?

Whatever happens, I can fix you.

Yeah, I believe that shit too.

I never met anything engineered that I couldn't understand. Taking things apart and putting them back together. That's what I do.

Dear Tuvi.

Just come back.

I miss you.

Don't die.

On the last letter: Love, Jake.

And your fingers squeezed the blood from my hand.

We had two weeks the first time we met. The second time around, after six months of absence, we had another two and you said you weren't going back.

I thought you were joking and it was cruel. But the nervousness told me this wasn't a joke. You made the decision to stay. I didn't ask if it was for me. Vanity is the other side of love.

There, I said it. Doesn't matter that it's in my head. It feels loud.

You were nervous because you didn't know how to live in this world. I thought back to those first two weeks. Mostly we were alone. Even at the barbecue we were alone.

The only time we were never alone was with each other.

The secret to being in a room full of people but not noticing a thing is you.

At first we lived.

You moved in with your meager belongings.

Anna threw a homecoming and you didn't leave my side.

I saw how the laughter was a strain. I saw how you were already regretting it.

"No, no, of course not."

That was the first time you ever lied to me. I didn't call you on it because I wanted to believe. I knew it could work. It would just take time. The things beneath your skin now could be used for other things.

Vague things. A vague future but at least it's a future and you're here. Just give it time.

We all have our mantras.

I fell into the trap. The door in the floor opened up and I dropped in. It had your name on it, that was the problem. You didn't want to hear it but I would've followed you into space.

Instead I followed you into the hole, into the dark.

Same thing, maybe.

In the light that came through the window, sunlight or moonlight, I traced the curve of your spine and marveled at the technology that gave you to me.

Vanity is the other side of love. Of course it was all for me.

The hands that used to set off grenades and fire weapons now handled drinks at the bar. We met at odd hours but they worked for us. Other people didn't work for you though. Too many people. Every time the vid cycled the news you switched it to sports.

At first you tried. You came to my races. You read books while I worked on my bike, music threading between us on the driveway. You learned to cook stir fry, made me a birthday card from scratch like we were in fifth grade. Fixed the misaligned window so the rain didn't leak in.

But the other window cracked.

Little things frustrated you.

Then you didn't want to get out of bed.

Then you just kept saying, Tell me another story.

I ran out of stories.

We tried running away for your birthday, took a road trip to the mountains but the silences stretched. They became barriers. You didn't want to celebrate. You gripped my hand until I no longer had feeling in my fingers.

Please talk to me.

Don't tell me a story, just talk to me.

Or write it down if you can't say it out loud.

Just something.

It was winter again and I felt futile. The frightening part was how much you loved me without saying a word. You turned your body to the shrapnel in order to protect me. You lay down on top of me when the tanks rolled over. You gave me your last tube of oxygen and with my last breath I yelled at you, I said, I just want you to live.

Dear Tuvi.

Please don't die.

Just come back.

I miss you.

I had a dream the night before you told me. We were climbing a sloped road and it was winter. Wolves paced behind us but they just followed our tracks. At the top of the hill lay bodies in black open bags. We walked right by them and entered a bar; the Olympics were on TV and everyone looked at us with vague suspicion. I tried to order nachos and eventually you had to flag down the waitress and repeat it three times. For some reason we were lodged into a table with three other men, all older, who stared at us with the blank looks of the lobotomized. They were locals and we weren't.

We ate our nachos and left the bar. The wolves were gone. More bodies had collected on the hill. At the bottom of the hill, at the side of the road, a child was digging ditches. I asked you if you recognized any of the dead and you said no.

The dead lined up outside our door.

They wouldn't let us in.

We couldn't go home.

So I started to zip up the body bags and you churned the dirt and snow together with a shovel until it looked like cake mix.

The world was quiet and the air didn't bite. In any other dream it might have been peaceful.

The next morning you told me you were going back to space.

I yelled at you for two hours.

The things we say when we're trying not to hurt.

You have a death wish.

You're an adrenalin junkie.

You just want to kill people.

It hasn't even been a year, you can't give it a year?

You stood there with your hands open like you wanted to take all of my words, like you were inviting them.

So I threw them at you like knives.

And you bled. The red ran down your body and pooled at your feet, stained the floors, threw in spatter behind your head to be analyzed later by an evidence unit.

How many lives do you think you have?

Why don't you go to therapy?

Who's the guilty one here?

"I'm not built for anything else." While you began to pack.

I'm not built for anything else either.

I've modified myself for you. I had my organs ripped out and replaced, programmed to your genetic code. I was brought down by the side of the road. I can't scour out the scratches, can't bang out the dents. I'm running on my last fuel cell and you're just running.

"Better to get out now."

Why?

"Better to only waste a year on me."

So now it's for my own good. Unilateral decisions for my own good.

It got down to begging. I've become one of those. Because in the dream I was zipping up body bags and you're going back to war. You're going too far and I don't want to write any more letters.

I don't want your cousin to call me in the middle of the night.

The things we say when we're trying not to hurt.

I love you and I don't want you to leave.

I don't think I said that first part.

I won't wait for you.

"Good."

And you walked on out.

Do you ever want to take it back? That last word?

I lied too, you know.

I'm still waiting.

Two years waiting and Anna says no news is good news. We've been whittled to pat assurances.

You've been gone for longer than we were together. In the scale of that I wonder some days why I'm holding on.

Between the anger and the missing is some truth I have yet to grasp.

I won't call it love.

Let's say you show up at the garage again and yank me out from beneath a car.

Let's say we make a scene and it's like fighting but it's not.

Let's say neither of us apologize because we're just so happy you're alive.

Let's say it lasts.

Let's say you aren't dead already, or missing, and the war will end.

Let's say it ends and you come home for good. There are no more fronts to fight, no more rebels to put down.

Let's run through this one more time. I'll give you five scenarios, the only rule is you can't lie.

The only rule is you can't die.

Confirm or deny.

Let me tell you a story about a soldier I met in the snow.

Let me show you all the parts of him that make up the whole of me.

Dear Tuvi.

I'm sick of feeling this way.

You're a bastard.

Love, Jake.

The truth is life happens anyway. I have conversations with it too and I'm yelling at it just as much. You're not allowed to carry on. The air isn't allowed to move into my lungs. The world isn't allowed to spin. I'm not allowed to win more races. This isn't the way it's supposed to be. I don't want to drink to victory. I can't see Anna anymore. Your niece and nephew miss you. Your uncle still brings his car by. Everyone keeps asking about you.

It's worse when they stop asking.

It's worse when the news says the war is over and our boys and girls are coming home.

Everyone is lying.

If there's a way for you to stay in deep space, you will.

If I'd only known that first night how far the cold ran.

But who am I kidding?

The news shows the footage of the ships blinking in, like stars. Spontaneously birthed.

One, two, five, nine, fifteen.

Popping in like God is sticking pins into the night sky.

Almost three years you've been gone.

I can't do the math.

The theory of relativity states that the further out you are, the harder it is to forget you.

Do you know you left one of your T-shirts in my drawer? Actually two.

I'm sorry but you don't get them back.

When she told me you were at the VA hospital I nearly crashed trying to get to you.

The theory of relativity states that the second you're in my orbit again, I forget the past three years.

Time contracts right back to that moment. When you left me. Do you want to take it back?

My footsteps on the hospital floors.

Take it back, take it back, take it back.

I'll wait for you.

I'm not angry anymore.

I was selfish and scared.

I'm not brave.

I touched your spine and the scars on your skull. I was afraid with all the lives you'd lived up, there wouldn't be one left for me.

They put you to lie on a flat bed.

They're growing your insides.

They've printed out your skin.

They're giving you a new eye.

Your body seems transparent in the light of so many lasers and the glue they use to hold you together.

I imagine you turning to look at me. You see me through the doors.

You see right through me.

Here to give me a new paint job, Jake?

Let me get my hands into you. Let me meld this bone to that, drive this rivet in, attach an extra plating for heat resistance. Heart resistance. I can make you run again. I've designed you something new. You'll be stronger, faster, and happier. I'll scour out all the things you've seen, I'll burn the bad dreams until they're winter blue.

Just let me touch you.

I don't care if you're cold.

I don't care where you've been.

This is what I'm good at.

I'm good with you.

They say not to expect the same you.

I'm not the same, so we're even.

Distance and time flayed us both alive.

I promise you soba noodles done just the way you like. A little spicy, served with chopsticks. Open your eyes. It's been a long sleep. You won't remember, maybe, but that won't stop my dreams.

We don't have to leave the covers when it's a snowy Sunday morning. Later in the afternoon I'll pack your coat with ice. We'll chase each other down the block and cheat the rules. I'll teach you how to ride in bad weather and you'll dent every piece of machinery I own. The fluid in me can manufacture you. Let's pretend we grew up together. Let's be born anew. Say the scientific names of the stars because romance isn't as sweet as reality. Give me an idea of what it's like to lose gravity. I'll be the thing you fall back to.

Everyone is waiting.

We've got more places to go. I've mapped the route. We'll pass through every season and stop at the beach and all the seas. You'll get salt in your eyes and I'll allow myself to cry. We'll have a picture perfect ending that's all about horizons. There are more colors in a sunrise than there are stars in the sky. Let me show you.

I'm waiting.

Then we'll awaken and figure this out.

You don't have to know right now.

There's no more war to run back to. Just this one inside of you.

Here, that's my fingertip.

I know you can feel that. I see you move.

Even if you return to space, this time I'll follow you.

Here, tell me a story. Tell me there will be no more killing. Tell me there will be no more enemies.

Tell me a story and begin it with I love you.

War 3.01

Keith Brooke

FRIDAY NIGHT WAS GOING TO be just how Friday nights usually were. A few pints of Guinness, although it's never as good as it is back home in Donaghmede. A kebab from the Istanbul, heavy on the chili sauce. Maybe one or two JDs at the Talbot to finish. It was pretty much a sure thing he'd end up scuttered and wake up sometime Saturday with a head-splitting, sandpaper-throated hangover. That was the plan, as far as planning went. It was Friday night, after all, and he'd just been paid two days ago.

Town was more relaxed than it had been for months. People were out again, allowing themselves to get back to some kind of normal. The latest round of bioterror threats had put a damper on that for a time, but now they'd faded away without anything much new to be scared of. Time for a few drinks, some food, people's guards starting to drop at last. It was almost a party atmosphere on the streets, and it was as if Kevin could feel the weight lifting. He hadn't realised how oppressive it had all been, how much it had affected everything.

The downside was that the squaddies were out too. That always added an extra dimension for a young Irish migrant worker in a garrison town. Weedy, shorter than average, Kevin O'Farrell was easy game for skinhead soldiers pushing him about "for the craic," as they would say. That kind of shit's okay as long as everyone's having a laugh, right?

He headed up Queen Street, fists in his hoody's kangaroo-pouch pocket, sticking to the far side of the road from the squaddies' pub, The Union. The chip shop next to the pub spamyelled him, sent taste-centre endorphins kicking down to his belly, making him hungry when he was not. Special deals for our regulars, Kevin. He Xed it.

The Union burned amber on his meSphere, a threatening glow layered over the real by his enhanced-reality lenses. It was a squaddie pub and it knew from his meSphere profile that he was a Mick. There was an app for that. There always was. Fuck 'em all and back, eh?

There were three of the gobshites outside, sucking on cigarettes held in meaty-clawed hands. Pressed dark-blue jeans, heavy black boots with a mean shine, white polo shirts, tattoos of union flags and barbed wire. StreetThreat flagged the situation as level 8: squaddies, booze, a vulnerable ethnic who's fair game because he's young and male.

Kevin kept his head down.

HeadKutz spamyelled his meSphere: half-price weekday haircuts, and, for a moment before he Xed that too, his vision was overlaid with head and shoulders of how he might look with a buzz, a flick, a sweeparound, rather than the shaggy urchin mop he had now. Even as he blocked Head-Kutz, he had to smile at the real-time wizardry that had taken CCTV stills of him and realityShopped him almost beyond recognition.

Bad move, that. Walking past a squaddie pub, smiling.

Just as Kevin had layers of apps in his 'sphere feeding his enhanced perception of the world all around, so too did they. They'd be standing there with their lagers and their cigarettes and their testosterone, and they'd see Kevin: flagged up as a Mick, coming here and taking English jobs. And smiling about it.

They weren't all like that, of course, and Kevin was smart enough to know as much: he'd never make the mistake of lumping them all together the way some of them did to everyone else. But the ones that did...their realities were enhanced, their meSpheres knew what they liked and what they believed, and they filtered out the irrelevant noise. Everything was enhanced, and that included prejudices.

Kevin knew how it worked. He knew all about the fuzzy quantum mathematics that helped meSphere apps anticipate the illogical logic of human thought. Just because someone likes A and they also like B, it doesn't mean they like A and B together. The brain doesn't follow that kind of logic. Except when it does. Search engine developers had known for years that algorithms based on quantum logic could uncover meanings and patterns in data far more efficiently than classical algorithms. Quantum reasoning was a far better model for how the brain worked out those hidden meanings than any other approach. Apply these algorithms to the meSphere and you got a reality enhanced with prompts and ads and buddy-links you could almost have chosen for yourself, only better.

And so those three squaddies—with their fags and their beer and their apps that picked out Kevin and said he was the kind of scruffy gobshite that was bringing this country down—turned as one, like programmed automata. One raised a fist with a ciggie sticking out between first and second finger; another started to make some kind of gesture that involved a finger and the side of his head and lowering forward like a caveman.

Kevin kept walking.

He wanted to run, but if he did and they were serious he knew they would catch him easily.

He locced Ziggy and Emily and Matt via the meSphere. The three of them were in the Lion's Head on High Street. A couple of minutes' walk if he could just keep going and the gimps at The Union would forget about him. He pinged his friends, let them know he was on his way.

He risked a glance across and was accosted by HeadKutz again, something in his profile flagging him as a prime target for a cut-price haircut. Maybe he should. No reason why a backroom search-logic geek had to look like one.

But the three gobshites...

Two were staring at each other, and the other one of them peered up as if he could see the stars through the glare of the street lights and it was the first time he'd ever seen them.

And there was nothing.

The Union wasn't amber, flagged as no-go. StreetThreat didn't hang 8s over the three thugs. It was gone. All of it was gone.

That was when the war started. And that was when it ended.

The meSphere kicked back in with a pixelated staccato of screen-flicker. It stablised, and then a message flashed up, a semi-transparent pop-up overlaying everything.

There was a war, it read. You lost. Life will go on as normal, but with less extravagance and with the utmost respect for those who believe. We will not relent in pursuing the enemy. We control the meSphere. We won. In the name of Allah, Most Gracious, Most Merciful. We are the Brethren of the Jihad. We are your humble servants.

Kevin's head pinged with messages and alerts. Friends and family loccing him.

Ziggy: You get that bro? What the fuck? It for real ya think?

Sandeep, uber-geek on the search-illogic team: Hey Kev. Dig the profiles! They bucket-testing the shit outta this war.

Even his kid brother Eoin, back in Dublin: They shitting us or what? We just lost World War fricking Three?

"Stand down? What do they mean, stand down?" grunted one of the squaddies, the one with a ginger buzz-cut and cartoon-square features. "We's not even fucking stood up."

Kevin forgot himself and stood there staring at the three.

One of the other squaddies shrugged. "How we supposed to know?" he said. "We only got orders, init?"

They saw Kevin staring, but somehow they didn't look threatening any more. They looked confused, diminished. "You know what's happening, do you?" Kevin asked.

Ginger buzz-cut looked across at him, then let loose with a stream of violent abuse.

Kevin backed off and hurried away.

All around him, the meSphere stuttered its overlay. Restaurants spamyelled him, then fell quiet. His headspace was quiet, and then there was an abrupt flurry of pings and messages. Then quiet again.

Another pop-up appeared, empty, then vanished.

He felt dizzy, disoriented.

He had to stop, and lean against a wall. It felt like there was a war in his head, even though he knew that the war had already happened. It had started, it had finished. It was all over, lost.

But still, his head was bombarded with spamyells and visual static. Noise that meant nothing, or might have meant everything if only he could understand. His head kept reeling and he felt sick.

He concentrated on breathing. A simple thing, yet so hard.

Breathing.

He messaged Emily and Ziggy, and Ziggy sent back, Hey bro. Ya getting the news?

He blinked up a feed, but it was sporadic, frequently interrupted and washed over with random noise. What he could pick up was being doctored, realityShopped like those HeadKutz photos. The BBC stream had a new overlay in a language he didn't recognise. It used Latin characters but not in a way he was used to. Indonesian, Phillipino...he wasn't sure.

The government had resigned. Heads of the military and security services had been detained, automatically locked in their offices. Software agents of the Brethren of the Jihad had taken control of the nation's military, power, financial, and other systems, maintaining stability in this time of crisis. In his closing speech, the former Prime Minister spoke of his gratitude that at last someone had taken responsibility for tackling the moral decline of the nation and that they could all look forward to a time of spiritual maturity and respect.

It was a coup, but the powers of the land seemed almost grateful.

Jesus, but I never thought World War Three would go like this, Kevin messaged everyone in a mass reply-all. It's like the PM was waiting for it.

He reached High Street and saw that people were in the road looking dazed and confused. The Exchange flashed that it was closed until licensing laws had been reviewed. The Shackleton too.

Farther down there was a crowd outside the Lion's Head. Quick messages revealed that Ziggy, Emily, Matt and Lola were there. All turfed out.

Waiting for it? messaged Ziggy. Blown to pieces more like. I don't call that waiting for it...

Kevin found his friends, gave gang shakes and hugs. Ziggy, all dreadlocks and shell beads, said, "What you saying, they were asking for it, bro?"

Kevin didn't know what to say. He'd checked the feeds again as he worked his way along the crowded High Street. Asking for it: such a meek and humble handing over of power. "I don't know," he said. "You tell me: what's happened?"

"It's in the feeds, bro. The bombs, the snatch squads. Swift an' clinical is what they saying. A show of force so we know just how beaten we are. Didn't you check the feeds?"

Kevin shrugged, said nothing. He remembered the point, the moment when the meSphere faltered and then righted itself and then the message came through.

There was a war. You lost.

The kind of military takeover Ziggy described would never happen so swiftly. The war was in the wires. It had taken place in cyberspace, started and finished in milliseconds. A takeover of all the systems that ran the country.

Ziggy grabbed Kevin's arm, getting antsy, lairy from the drink and the adrenaline. "Hey bro," he demanded. "Don't just go ignoring me. This is big shit. What's happening?"

Kevin put a hand on his friend's wrist, calming him. "I don't know," he said. There was something nagging away in a corner of his mind. "Just give me a mo' though, would you? That'd be grand."

Sandeep! Sandeep Patel, the second-generation Indian from the East Midlands who liked to call Kevin a "bloody foreigner" and had made him more welcome at SphereIllogic than anyone else, back when he'd started there last year. His message earlier...Kevin flipped it back up: Hey Kev. Dig the profiles! They bucket-testing the shit outta this war.

Bucket-testing. A/B testing. Where a web feed showed some users a variant of a page so the owners could measure the outcomes, how many more clicked to buy; or where some passersby would get a spamyell from a shop or restaurant with a different wording, different tone. Real-time testing with subtle variations. Amazon and Google had done it all the time, way back in the when of things.

And now...Kevin looked around at all the confused, defeated faces.

How many different versions had people been fed so that the so-called Brethren of the Jihad could modify their campaign depending on user-segment responses? How many variants were there of that BBC feed, videoShopped in real-time by some semi-AI in order to model and shape and defeat a nation's head-space? How much was even true, and how much just a piece of misinformation carefully engineered to steer the collective illogical logic of the population?

Kevin grabbed Ziggy by the arms and his dreadlocked friend fell quiet, mid-rant.

"It's not over," said Kevin. "Do you see? It's not over at all. It's still happening. All around us. Everything: one big bucket test. We haven't lost, Ziggy. We only lose if we believe we've lost."

Ziggy shook himself free. "Bro, you gone mad in the head. It's all over the feeds."

Kevin turned to Emily and Matt, but they just looked dazed, lost. In their heads they'd lost and there was no getting through.

Kevin started to run. Run until his breath came ragged and his lungs burned and his legs were like jelly.

He turned back down Queen Street, heading for the Union, the squaddies. He didn't know what he was going to do, what he could find to say to them to convince them, but he had to get through. Had to try to persuade them that they were only beaten because they thought they were and that they might just still have a chance if they'd listen instead of just beating the crap out of the ranting gobshite of a Mick who was about to burst into their bar and start haranguing them.

Acknowledgments

Jaym

A few years ago, an i09.com article said I was working on military SF from the perspective of female and LGBTQ characters. At the time, it was just a half-joking idea, but a few years later, the stars aligned. There are too many people to thank, but a few in particular made this possible.

War Stories is dedicated to soldiers, and their families and loved ones. More specifically, to the wonderful community of veterans and soldiers—especially Neil, Greg, Ana, Aaron, DJ, Terry, and the guys at RangerUp—who answered all sorts of questions. Thanks for all your help, and your patience with my questions.

Thank you to the Kickstarter backers, the authors, my co-editor, our slush readers (including my wonderful mother), and everyone who spread the word and believed in us. To Jason, too, who took a chance on a potentially divisive book.

And, last but not least, to Greyson, who proved that the biggest soldier can sometimes have the greatest heart.

You all made this possible. Thank you.

Andrew

War Stories began with a conversation between myself and Jaym at the 2012 ReaderCon in Burlington, MA. It's a project that grew with each conversation, and there are an enormous number of people that need to be thanked with any sort of project such as this. I can't list everyone who deserves thanks, but know that your help, support and contributions are most appreciated.

Thanks go to John Joseph Adams, for his guidance and for passing along several stories that ended up in the book, to Jason Sizemore for giving this project a home and believing in the project over its entire lifecycle. To each of our authors, who provided us with their incredible stories, to our dedicated slush readers, Megan, Matt, Blackwell and Carey.

Thank you to everyone who pledged to the original project on Kickstarter, and for everyone who talked, tweeted and posted about this, providing encouragement and support along the way.

Thanks to Galen Dara, who makes awesome art. Thanks to Annalee Newitz, Charlie Jane Anders, and the entire crew at io9, who got me thinking about the state of Military SF (and in a roundabout way, got me started with this) and to Myke Cole and Kevin Beal for the advice and support over the last couple of years.

Finally, thank you to my parents, Alan and Ellen Liptak and to my wife, Megan Liptak (and Bram), for their unwavering support and encouragement while I spent long nights and weekends on this. This never would have happened without you.

Backers

This project never would have happened without the financial support of 357 backers. Thank you for helping to make our book a reality.

@OlliCrusoe
A. T. Greenblatt
A.C. Wise
Aaron M. Wilson
Aidan Doyle
Aidan Moher
Aimee Picchi
AJ Sikes
Alan and Ellen Liptak
Alan Smale
Alec Austin
Alec Interrante
Alex Houghton
Alex Johnson
Alex Ristea
Allen J Medlen
Allison
Amanda K. Hess
Andrew Beirne
Andrew James Fish
Andrew Maiewski
Andrew Penn Romine
Andrija Popovic
Anthony Marissen
Anthony R. Cardno
Aric Jack
Arkady Martine
Aubrey Westbourne
Bear Weiter
Ben Ireland
Benjamin Bowers
Benjamin Newell
Benjamin Read
Beth Morris Tanner
Bill Kohn
Bim

Blair Nicholson
Bob Huss
Bob Jacobsen
Bobbomb
Brandon Kanechika
Brandon St. Cyr
Brendan Sherwin
Brian J. White
Brian Oma Thomas
Brian Staveley
Brian Young
BriAnne Searles
Brittany Karns
Bryan R Brown
Caitlyn Smith
Calvin K. Li
Cara Gorman
Carey Gates
Cariad Eccleston
Carissa
Carol J. Guess
Caroline Ratajski
Carolyn Kniga
Cathie V
CD Covington
Cédric Jeanneret
Charles Nicolosi
Christina Dessi
Clay Karwan
Cliff Winnig
Clinton Bodley
D.E.S. Richard
Dan Hills
Dan Pollack
Dan Rabarts
Daniel L Hughes

Dave Chua
Dave Gross
David Annandale
David Forbes
David Francis
David Lang
David Nicklin
David Stegora
David Wohlreich
Diana Williams
D-Rock
Dustin Hawk
Ed & Dallas Nagata White
Eric Kent Edstrom
Ericka B.
Erin E. Moulton
Erik Bigglestone
Ernest Khoo
Fabio Fernandes
Fen Eatough
Francis Budden-Hinds
Frank J. Skornia
Galen Dara
Gavran
Gemma Noon
Gloria Liptak
Graeme Williams
Greg 'fritopunk' Adkins
Harry Knott
Heather Duke
Hillary Jacques
Ief Grootaers
ILICCO
Ira Lewy
Isabel Fine
Iwan Axt
J. Carl
Jakub Narębski
James Conason
James Knapp
James Turnbull
Janet L. Oblinger
Jared Shurin
Jason Andrew
Jason Daniel
Jason Sizemore

Jay Wolf
Jeff Xilon
Jen Howell
Jennifer Brozek
Jennifer Payne
Jennifer Steinhurst
Jerry Gaiser
JHG Hendriks
Jim Reader
Jim Welch
Joe DiMaio
Johannes B
John Cosgrove
John Devenny
John Holden
Jon Lasser
Jonathan D. Beer
Jonathan Warner
Jonathan Woodward
Joseph R. Boeke
Josh Vogt
JP4
Kalli J. Ritter
Kate Baker
Kate Sullivan, Candlemark & Gleam
Keith Brinkley
Kelli Neier
Kelly Stiles
Kenneth Tagher
Kevin Baijens
Kevin Henderson
Kevin Sharp
Kevin Veldman
Kyle Brooks
Landon O.
Lara Keenan & Andrew Rash
Larry Fleming
Lars Nygaard Witter
Lauren Davis
Lauren M. Roy
Lee Sims
Lisa Bucci
Logan Lamothe
Logan Z. Liskovec
Lori Ramey
Louis Luangkesorn

Lucas K. Law
Lyle Wood
Malcolm SW Wilson
Marc Jacobs
Marie-Claude Dion
Mark Jacobsen
Mark Pantoja
Mark T. Hrisho
Mark Teppo
Mark Thompson
Mark Woodson
Mary Beth Decker
Masato Naruniwa
Matt Gibbs
Matt Hurlburt
Matt Leitzen
Matt O'Connor
Matthew R. Gaglio
Matthew W. Quinn
Megan Charters
Michael A. Brunco
Michael Anton
Michael Feldhusen
Michael Hsieh
Michael Janairo
Michael Pusateri
Miha Jan
Mihir Wanchoo
Mike (Sven) Anderson
Mike Bavister
Mike Brendan
Mike E.G.
Mike Hampton
Mike Seay
Mike Strider
Morgan Ellis
N. Aucoin
Nate Herzog and Kerry Swift
Nathan Hall
Nathan O'Keefe
Nathan S. McCollum
Neal Dalton
Neil Carr
Nicole Platania
Olna Jenn Smith
Olufemi A. Oni

Parker B. Hoblin
Patti J. Exster
Paul Bulmer
Paul McMullen
Paul Weimer
Peter A Schaefer
Peter Biello
Peter Gray
Philip Harris
Polyfountain Media L.L.C.
R.S. Hunter
Rafia Mirza
Ragi Gonçalves
ran
Randy "Sherpa" Brown
Rebekah Wheadon
Revek
Rick Ahern
Rob Hobart
Robert H. Bedford
Robert Davis
Robert Farmer
Robert Rath
Ronald T. Garner
Rose Vance
Ryan Weaver
Ryland J Kayin Lee
S. Hutson Blount
Sam Fleming (ravenbait)
sam murphy
Samuel Erikson
Sandeep Sundher
Sandi Dreer
Sarah A.
Sarah Howison
Sarah Kirkpatrick
Sarah Shoker
Sareh Heidari
Scott K. Monteiro
Scott Nellé
Scott Whitmore
Sean & Jen Whaley
Sean Harrop
Seth Elgart
SGT F.P. Kiesche III
Shad Bolling

Shane Celis
Shaun Duke
Sidsel Norgaard Pedersen
Simo Muinonen
Skunkboy
Stefan Raets
Stefan Slater
Stephen Cheng
Steve Burnett
Steve Drew
Steven Mentzel
Steven Moy
Steven Saus
Svend Andersen
Tad Ottman
Taylor "The Snarky Avenger" Kent
Ted Ellis
Tehani Wessely
Terence Chua
Terrence Dorsey
Terry McGarry
Terry Somerville
TheSFReader
Todd S Maeda
Travis Heermann
Trisha Commo
TwistedSciFi.com
Vivienne Pustell
Wayne L. Budgen
Wayne L. Miller
Whitney Nellé
Wick
William Baum
Y. K. Lee
Yuri Lowenthal
Zach Rivers
Zachary McCallum
Zan Gerhardt
Zoldar
Zorba The Geek

Author Bios

MIKE BARRETTA is a retired U.S. Navy Helicopter pilot with deployments around the world. He works for a Major Defense contractor. He holds a Master's degree in Strategic Planning and International Negotiation from the Naval Post-Graduate School and is nearing a completion of a Master's Degree in English from the University of West Florida. He has been published in *Jim Baen's Universe*, *New Scientist*, *Redstone*, and various anthologies. He resides in Gulf Breeze, Florida with his wife, Mary Jane, and five children.

SUSAN JANE BIGELOW is a librarian, writer and political columnist. She's the author of the three *Extrahumans* books and *The Daughter Star*, the first in a series of epic space opera novels. Her work has appeared in the Lambda Award-winning *The Collection: Short Fiction from the Transgender Vanguard* from Topside Press, and *Queers Dig Time Lords*. She also writes a weekly Connecticut-focused political column at CTNewsJunkie.com. Susan can be found wandering around northern Connecticut and western Massachusetts with her wife, covered in cat hair.

MAURICE BROADDUS has written hundreds of short stories, essays, novellas, and articles. His dark fiction has been published in numerous magazines, anthologies, and web sites, including *Asimov's Science Fiction*, *Cemetery Dance*, *Apex Magazine*, and *Weird Tales Magazine*. He is the co-editor of *Streets of Shadows* (Alliteration Ink) and the *Dark Faith* anthology series (Apex Books) and the author of the urban fantasy trilogy, *Knights of Breton Court* (Angry Robot Books). He has been a teaching artist for over five years, teaching creative writing to students of all ages. Visit his site at www.MauriceBroaddus.com.

KEITH BROOKE's most recent novel *alt.human* (published in the US as *Harmony*) was shortlisted for the 2013 Philip K Dick Award. He is also the editor of *Strange Divisions and Alien Territories: the Sub-genres of Science Fiction*, an academic exploration of SF from the perspectives of a dozen top authors in the field. Writing as Nick Gifford, his teen fiction is published by Puffin, with one novel also optioned for the movies by Andy Serkis and

Jonathan Cavendish's Caveman Films. He writes reviews for the *Guardian*, teaches creative writing at university level, and lives with his wife Debbie in Wivenhoe, Essex.

JAMES L. CAMBIAS writes SF and designs games. Originally from New Orleans, he lives in western Massachusetts. His stories have appeared in *F&SF*, *Shimmer*, *Nature*, and several original anthologies. *A Darkling Sea*, his first novel, came out in January 2014. Mr. Cambias has written for GURPS, Hero Games, and other roleplaying systems, and is a partner in Zygote Games. He is a member of the notorious Cambridge SF Workshop. You can read his blog at www.jamescambias.com.

F. BRETT COX's fiction, poetry, essays, and reviews have appeared in numerous publications. With Andy Duncan, he co-edited the anthology *Crossroads: Tales of the Southern Literary Fantastic* (Tor, 2004). A native of North Carolina, he is Associate Professor of English at Norwich University and lives in Vermont with his wife, playwright Jeanne Beckwith.

The Central Clancy Writer for Red Storm/Ubisoft, **RICHARD DANSKY** was named one of the Top 20 video game writers by Gamasutra in 2009. His credits include Tom Clancy's *Splinter Cell: Blacklist*, *Ghost Recon: Future Soldier*, and *Rainbow Six: Raven Shield*. Richard has published six novels, most recently *Vaporware*, and is the developer for the upcoming 20th Anniversary edition of the acclaimed tabletop RPG *Wraith: The Oblivion*. He lives in North Carolina with his wife and their uncountable cats, books, and single malt whiskeys.

An editor and multi-published author, **NERINE DORMAN** currently resides in Cape Town, South Africa, with her visual artist husband, and has works published by Kensington, Dark Continents Publishing, eKhaya, Tor Books and Immanion Press. She has been involved in the media industry for more than a decade, with a background in magazine and newspaper publishing, commercial fiction, and advertising. Her book reviews, as well as travel, entertainment, and lifestyle editorial regularly appear in national newspapers. A few of her interests include music, travel, history, Egypt, art, photography, psychology, philosophy, magic, and the natural world.

THORAIYA DYER is a three-time Aurealis Award-winning, three-time Ditmar Award-winning Australian writer based in the Hunter Valley, NSW. Her short fiction has appeared in *Clarkesworld*, *Apex*, *Nature*, and *Cosmos* and is forthcoming in *Analog*. A petite collection of four original stories, *Asymmetry*, is available from Twelfth Planet Press. Find her online at Goodreads or www.thoraiyadyer.com.

The youngest writer to be named a Grand Master by the Science Fiction and Fantasy Writers of America, **JOE HALDEMAN** has earned steady awards over his 44-year career: his novels *The Forever War* and *Forever Peace* both made clean sweeps of the Hugo and Nebula Awards, and he has won four more Hugos and Nebulas for other novels and shorter works. Three times he's won the Rhysling Award for best science fiction poem of the year. In 2012 he was inducted into the Science Fiction Hall of Fame. The final novel in a trilogy, *Earthbound*, is out (after *Marsbound* in 2008 and *Starbound* in 2009), and he's working on a new novel, *Phobos Means Fear*. Ridley Scott has bought the movie rights to *The Forever War*.

Joe's latest novel is *Work Done for Hire*, out in December 2013. The collection *The Best of Joe Haldeman* came out in 2013. He just retired from a part-time appointment as a professor at M.I.T.; he taught every fall semester from 1983 until 2013. He paints and bicycles and spends as much time as he can out under the stars as an amateur astronomer. He's been married for 49 years to Mary Gay Potter Haldeman.

MARK JACOBSEN is a C-17 pilot, strategist, and Middle East Regional Affairs Specialist in the U.S. Air Force. He has flown missions to more than 25 countries, speaks Arabic, and studied Conflict Resolution in Jordan. Mark enjoys imaginative, character-driven fiction, and his own writing reflects his interests in politics and international affairs. He is the author of *The Lords of Harambee*, which has been described by reviewers as "*Blackhawk Down* in space." He is married with three children, and lives wherever the Air Force sends him. Follow Mark online at www.buildingpeace.net or @jacobsenmd.

JAKE KERR is a Nebula and Sturgeon Award nominated author whose short fiction has been translated into Chinese and French and published in science fiction magazines, anthologies, podcasts, literary journals, and has been featured in *The Year's Best Science Fiction* and on io9.com. He lives in Texas with his wife and three daughters.

RICH LARSON was born in West Africa, has studied in Rhode Island, and at 22 now lives in Edmonton, Alberta. He won the 2014 Dell Award and won the 2012 Rannu Prize for Writers of Speculative Fiction. In 2011 his cyberpunk novel *Devolution* was a finalist for the Amazon Breakthrough Novel Award. His short work appears or is forthcoming in *Lightspeed*,

DSF, Strange Horizons, Apex Magazine, Beneath Ceaseless Skies, AE, and many others. Find him at Amazon.com/author/richlarson.

YOON HA LEE lives in Louisiana with her family and has not yet been eaten by gators. Her collection *Conservation of Shadows* was published by Prime Books in 2013, and her fiction has appeared in *The Magazine of Fantasy and Science Fiction, Clarkesworld, Lightspeed,* and *Tor.com.*

KEN LIU (http://kenliu.name) is an author and translator of speculative fiction, as well as a lawyer and programmer. His fiction has appeared in *The Magazine of Fantasy & Science Fiction, Asimov's, Analog, Clarkesworld, Lightspeed,* and *Strange Horizons,* among other places. He is a winner of the Nebula, Hugo, and World Fantasy awards. He lives with his family near Boston, Massachusetts. Ken's debut novel, *The Grace of Kings,* the first in a fantasy series, will be published by Saga Press, Simon & Schuster's new genre fiction imprint, in 2015. Saga will also publish a collection of his short stories.

KARIN LOWACHEE was born in South America, grew up in Canada, and worked in the Arctic. Her first novel *Warchild* won the 2001 Warner Aspect First Novel Contest. Both *Warchild* (2002) and her third novel *Cagebird* (2005) were finalists for the Philip K. Dick Award. *Cagebird* won the Prix Aurora Award in 2006 for Best Long-Form Work in English and the Spectrum Award also in 2006. Her books have been translated into French, Hebrew, and Japanese, and her short stories have appeared in anthologies edited by Julie Czerneda, Nalo Hopkinson, and John Joseph Adams. Her fantasy novel, *The Gaslight Dogs,* was published through Orbit Books USA.

T.C. McCARTHY is an award winning and critically acclaimed southern author whose short fiction has appeared in *Per Contra: The International Journal of the Arts, Literature and Ideas,* in *Story Quarterly,* and in *Nature.* His debut novel, *Germline,* and its sequel, *Exogene* are available worldwide and the final book of the trilogy, *Chimera,* was released in August 2012. In addition to being an author, T.C. is a PhD scientist, a Fulbright Fellow, a Howard Hughes Biomedical Research Scholar, and a winner of the prestigious University of Virginia's Award for Undergraduate Research. Visit him at http://www.tcmccarthy.com.

LINDA NAGATA is the author of multiple novels and short stories including *The Red: First Light,* a near-future military thriller nominated for the

2013 Nebula award. Among her other works are *The Bohr Maker*, winner of the Locus Award for best first novel; the novella "Goddesses," the first online publication to receive a Nebula award; and the story "Nahiku West," a finalist for the Theodore Sturgeon Memorial Award. Though best known for science fiction, she also writes fantasy, exemplified by her "scoundrel lit" series *Stories of the Puzzle Lands*. Linda has spent most of her life in Hawaii, where she's been a writer, a mom, a programmer of database-driven websites, and lately an independent publisher. She lives with her husband in their long-time home on the island of Maui.

CARLOS ORSI, is a Brazilian writer and science journalist with two SF novels and three short story collections published in his native country. In the English language, his stories have appeared in *Needle—A Magazine of Noir*, *Ellery Queen Mystery Magazine*, and in the anthologies *Tales of the World Newton Universe* (Titan Books) and *Rehearsals for Oblivion* (Elder Signs Press). He lives in the city of Jundiai, Sao Paulo state, in Brazil, with his wife and a cat, and works in the University of Campinas (Unicamp).

JAY POSEY is the author of the *Legends of the Duskwalker* series of novels published by Angry Robot Books, and is a senior narrative designer at Ubisoft/Red Storm Entertainment, where he has spent many years contributing as a writer and game designer to Tom Clancy's award-winning Ghost Recon and Rainbow Six franchises. He blogs occasionally at jayposey.com and spends more time than he should hanging around Twitter as @HiJayPosey.

MIKE SIZEMORE writes a lot of stuff that ends up in development hell out in LA which is why he's so pleased that people get to read his story here. A few years ago he created something called *Slingers* which was sort of "Ocean's 11 in space" that almost became a TV show. Since then he's written a bunch of pilots and feature scripts and also adapted *Howl's Moving Castle* for the London stage with Stephen Fry. He's currently working on *Caper*, a digital series about super heroes pulling a heist without becoming super criminals that will air on YouTube in January 2014. He also has a bunch of short stories and comic book stuff in the works so hopes you'll have plenty more of his work to read soon. Warren Ellis once called him "nine kinds of wrong" after he put Peter Parker's Aunt May in a sex-suit so consider that fair warning.

JANINE K. SPENDLOVE is a KC-130 pilot in the United States Marine Corps. In the Science Fiction and Fantasy World she is primarily known for her best-selling trilogy, *War of the Seasons*. She has several short stories published in various anthologies alongside such authors as Aaron Allston, Jean Rabe, Michael A. Stackpole, Bryan Young, and Timothy Zahn. She is also the co-founder of GeekGirlsRun, a community for geek girls (and guys) who just want to run, share, have fun, and encourage each other. A graduate of Brigham Young University, Janine loves pugs, enjoys knitting, making costumes, playing Beatles tunes on her guitar, and spending time with her family. She resides with her husband and daughter in Washington, DC. She is currently at work on her next novel. Find out more at JanineSpendlove.com.

JAMES L. SUTTER is the Senior Editor and Fiction Editor for Paizo Publishing, as well as a co-creator of the Pathfinder Roleplaying Game. He's the author of the novels *Death's Heretic* and *The Redemption Engine*, the former of which was ranked #3 on Barnes & Noble's Best Fantasy Releases of 2011 and was a finalist for both an Origins Award and the Compton Crook Award for Best First Novel. In addition to numerous game books, most notably *Distant Worlds* and *City of Strangers*, James has written short stories for such publications as *Escape Pod*, *Apex Magazine*, *Beneath Ceaseless Skies*, *Geek Love*, and the #1 Amazon bestseller *Machine of Death*. His anthology *Before They Were Giants* pairs the first published short stories of speculative fiction luminaries with new interviews and advice from the authors themselves. For more information, visit jameslsutter.com or find him on Twitter at @jameslsutter.

CPSIA information can be obtained at www.ICGtesting.com
Printed in the USA
LVOW11s1706031114

411783LV00002B/668/P